HALLDÓR LAXNESS

ICELAND'S BELL

Halldór Laxness was born near Reykjavík, Iceland, in 1902. His first novel was published when he was seventeen. The undisputed master of contemporary Icelandic fiction, and one of the outstanding novelists of the century, he wrote more than sixty books, including novels, short stories, essays, poems, plays, and memoirs. In 1955 he was awarded the Nobel Prize for Literature. Laxness died in 1998.

Also by HALLDÓR LAXNESS

Independent People
Paradise Reclaimed
World Light

ICELAND'S BELL

ICELAND'S BELL

HALLDÓR LAXNESS

*Translated from the Icelandic
by Philip Roughton*

Introduction by Adam Haslett

VINTAGE INTERNATIONAL

VINTAGE BOOKS

A DIVISION OF RANDOM HOUSE, INC.

NEW YORK

A VINTAGE INTERNATIONAL ORIGINAL, OCTOBER 2003

Library of Congress Cataloging-in-Publication Data
Halldór Laxness, 1902–1998.
[Íslandsklukkan. English]
Iceland's bell / Halldór Laxness ; translated from the Icelandic by Philip Roughton ; introduction by Adam Haslett.—
1st Vintage International ed.
p. cm.
ISBN 1-4000-3425-6
I. Roughton, Philip. II. Title.
PT7511.L3I813 2003
839´.6934—dc21
2003050070

Book design by Mia Risberg

www.vintagebooks.com

Printed in the United States of America
10 9 8 7 6 5 4 3 2 1

INTRODUCTION

At first glance, *Iceland's Bell* has a few strikes against it when it comes to attracting American readers. To begin with, there is the author's name. Who is Halldór Laxness anyway? And then there is that country in the title. Am I really going to settle into a long novel about Iceland of all places? And did we mention the story takes place in the seventeenth century and revolves around forty years of intractable civil and criminal litigation? Headed for the exits yet? If so, I have some simple advice: stop. You've stumbled upon a beautiful and hilarious novel by a superb writer. This first English translation of *Iceland's Bell* confirms the author's place among the best novelists of the twentieth century. If I could get away with a one-line introduction, I would: Halldór Laxness rules.

Readers who have encountered this one and only Icelandic Nobel laureate are most likely to have read his 1934 classic, *Independent People*. Out of print for some time, it is now enjoying a revival and a widening readership thanks to a handful of devoted writers and editors who have championed his work in the last several years. I myself am the beneficiary of these efforts. A friend recommended *Independent People* to me a few years ago. I bought it with some trepidation, my gut telling me this would be one of those worthy, difficult books that ennoble through struggle. I couldn't have been more wrong. Reading my first Laxness novel is one of those experiences that I look back on with a kind of jealous fondness, loving the memory of it but wishing it hadn't ended.

Many of the same pleasures, in particular a mixture of laughter and awe unique to Laxness, can be found in *Iceland's Bell.* Written a decade after *Independent People,* the novel has a broader geographical and political scope than that book and is more expressly concerned with national identity and the role literature plays in forming it. It is also a tale of colonial exploitation and the obdurate will of a suffering people. This description might lead one to imagine an earnest and patriotic work, which *Iceland's Bell* most certainly isn't. That's because Laxness has done here what so many other writers who reach for large, historical themes fail to do: he's retained his sense of the absurd.

"There was a time, it says in books," the novel opens, "that the Icelandic people had only one national treasure: a bell."

This bell rang at the courthouse on the site of the national assembly where all the major business of government and the courts took place. As the story begins, one of the three central characters, Jón Hreggviðsson, a miserably poor farmer, has been arrested for stealing cord, or fishing line, a commodity that every poor person in Iceland seems to be after. Pressed into labor for the Danish crown, which then ruled Iceland, Jón Hreggviðsson is made to cut the bell down from where it has hung since time immemorial in order that it be melted down and its copper used in the rebuilding of Copenhagen. The Danish capital has been ravaged by the Swedes and now Iceland is being stripped of its meager wealth to finance the repairs. This insult to the pride of Iceland and the dignity of its courts heralds a descent into the misprision of justice that the characters will contend with for the rest of the book.

Within a few days' time, Hreggviðsson will be whipped for insulting the king as he cut down the bell (and a more harrowing description of that punishment I have never read). After this harsh treatment Jón gets drunk with a group of his tormentors, including the man who flayed his back. In his typically laconic style, Laxness doesn't suggest anything perverse in this; they just happen to be traveling in the same direction. Lost in a swamp, Jón passes out drunk and wakes to find the dead body of the king's hangman nearby. The judicial haggling over whether Hreggviðsson is responsibile for this death will, before the novel is over, ruin the reputations of several Icelandic aristocrats and send the man himself into an endless series of prisons and workhouses. It will also make him a pawn in a love affair between a royal advisor and the most beautiful woman in Iceland.

Readers of *Independent People* will recognize in Jón Hreggviðsson a character cut from the same cloth as Bjartur of Summerhouses, that ignorant and violent bore whom the novel's readers can't help but love. Hreggviðsson is perhaps even more violent and boorish than Bjartur. Upon returning from the workhouse in the second chapter, he finds "his sister and aunt, who were both lepers, one glabrous and palsied, the other nodous and ulcerous, [sitting] downcast in their black veils out by the dungheap, holding each other's hands and praising God." Being drunk, "he began immediately to beat his wife and his idiot son. His fourteen-year-old daughter laughed at him and his aged mother embraced him tearfully: these he did not beat to any considerable extent."

The bleakness is so total, and perhaps more importantly is delivered in prose so thoroughly nonchalant, that laughter is the only possible relief. There's no doubt Laxness intends it to be this way. Two hundred pages later, when Hreggviðsson returns to find his daughter on her bier, his retarded son laughing, and his wife cursing him, the author asks, "But what were these compared to the tragedies that had befallen the man's livestock in his absence?" And he's only half kidding. This is gallows humor to be sure, humor quite literally at the edges of death, which is what gives almost all of Hreggviðsson's scenes their beguiling combination of lightness and profundity.

If Jón Hreggviðsson were its one and only hero, *Iceland's Bell* might have ended up as a thinner version of *Independent People,* but Laxness sets the peasant farmer on a course that intersects with the daughter of Iceland's magistrate, the beautiful Snæfríður, and the man she comes to love and struggle against, the royal advisor Arnas Arnæus. The latter, based on Árni Magnússon, the great Icelandic book collector and scholar, has come to Iceland in search of ancient books and manuscripts that might contain fragments of the Icelandic sagas. The soul of Iceland lives in its poetry and its tales of brave men, but in this country, the population has been reduced to using old vellum manuscripts as shoe leather, patches for clothing, and even for food.

When visiting with local gentry, Arnæus finds pieces of the most prized manuscript of all, the *Skálda,* among the hay and garbage that makes up the bed of Hreggviðsson's mother. It's on this visit to the peasant's hovel that the young Snæfríður, afraid of Hreggviðsson's leprous family, clings to Arnæus for protection. It will be many pages before the reader understands that Snæfríður is desperately in love with Arnæus, admiring the man who works tirelessly for the honor and reputation of his country.

From these early scenes, the book opens up into a rather elaborate plot. Snæfríður helps to free Hreggviðsson the day before his execution for murder and asks him to travel to Denmark with a message for Arnæus, who has returned to Copenhagen and his books without leaving word to his young admirer. Hreggviðsson's journey through darkened jails and conscription in the Danish army is a surreal black comedy of its own. It's only toward the middle of the novel that we return to Snæfríður, years later, on a dilapidated farm, still beautiful but married to Magnús, a murderous alcoholic layabout. In one of the most pathetic and grimly funny scenes in the book, Magnús, so drunk he's weeping in a stranger's field asking for his head to be cut off, signs a contract selling his wife for a cask of booze. When she is informed of this by a priest, our heroine, in good Laxness fashion, can only laugh. When Magnús does finally come after her with an ax (too drunk to hit his mark), she goes to her sister's estate and there meets Arnæus again, this time in the role of a special crown prosecutor charged with cleaning up Iceland's supposedly crooked and overly harsh system of criminal punishment.

It is difficult to imagine another writer capable of making an ugly, wife-beating failure into an appealing character, without resort to either misogyny or machismo. But Magnús is too wrecked even to achieve an intention we might dislike him for. And here we see the unflinching generosity Laxness has toward all his characters. Like a loving and forgiving god, he details their every miserable failure but never for the purpose of castigation or judgment. The human comedy of error—and in Laxness's hands it is most definitely a comedy—is delivered up as a wry and occasionally absurd pleasure.

Regarding character, it is worth mentioning that contemporary readers are likely to find Laxness's people lacking in what you might call modern psychological depth. We get no internal description of what people think or feel but rather come to know them almost exclusively through what they say and do to each other. Together with the historical setting, this at times gives the reader the sense that the book is an Icelandic saga of its own, with the flatness of characterization we associate with folklore. This is no doubt partially true. In an interview published in 1972, Laxness admitted to making a conscious decision to mimic the style of the sagas in this book. But there is more than copying going on here. Laxness is adapting the form of the modern novel to encompass the meanings and concerns of the saga tradition.

One reaction to this hybrid, which I suspect many readers may have at first, is to dismiss the work as simplistic. If you look to fiction for news about what it's like to be alive in the world today, why read a book in which self-consciousness, the philosophical linchpin of the modern condition, is more or less ignored? The answer is, I believe, that Laxness knows precisely what he is doing and is well aware of his choices as a twentieth-century writer. *Iceland's Bell* is no act of nostalgia. Implicit in the narrative is an assertion of the role that a certain hardscrabble pragmatism and pride plays in surviving the slings and arrows of outrageous fortune—modern or ancient.

Toward the end of the book, after she has suffered through one indignity after the next, Snæfríður travels to Denmark to plead with the Danish governor to reopen the corruption case that has ruined her father the magistrate's reputation. Finally, her patience gives and she rips into the corpulent aristocrat as they stand in his splendid hall:

Excuse me for speaking up, excuse us for being a race of historians who forget nothing. But do not misunderstand me: I regret nothing that has happened, neither in words nor thoughts. It may be that the most victorious race is the one that is exterminated: I will not plead with words for mercy for Icelanders. We Icelanders are truly not too good to die. And life has meant nothing to us for a long time. But there is one thing that we can never lose while one man of this race, rich or poor, remains standing; and even in death this thing is never lost to us; that which is described in the old poem, and which we call fame: just so my father and my mother are not, though they are dust, called ignoble thieves.

Of course, this being a Laxness novel, it turns out her father *has* been a bit corrupt, but is, generally speaking, a good and respectable guy of the old school. Yet listen to the tenacity in her speech: "And life has meant nothing to us for a long time." It's a radical sentiment spoken by a woman whose people have lived through a degree of privation which it is difficult for most of us to imagine fully without the help of literature (one of the early descriptions of Hreggviðsson's mother traveling through the plague-stricken landscape is a tour de force). And it is perhaps worth noting that billions of people in the world today live in conditions not so very different from those found in this novel: failing subsistence farming, poverty, sickness, and occasional famine. I have been more earnest in the last two sentences than Laxness is throughout the entire novel. My point is simply that it would be an error to mistake the quasi-folkloric style of *Iceland's Bell* and Laxness's work more generally for a lack of psychological or spiritual insight. Like many other great modernists, Laxness uses and transforms the grand narratives of his cultural past to create a stark, comedic vision of the human predicament every bit as profound as the more psychically probing novels of Mann, Faulkner, or Woolf.

In the final third of the novel, the scene returns to Copenhagen, where the political war for control of Iceland is being waged. Laxness opens this section with a brilliant skewering of royals and aristocrats at play. After all the deprivation we've seen to this point, the description itself performs the parody with no prodding by the author required. Snæfríður and Arnas Arnæus find themselves on opposite sides of the struggle. Arnæus considers taking up the governorship of the country if it were sold to German merchants; Snæfríður wants royal edicts to reverse the verdicts that Arnæus himself handed down against her father, and for that she needs the Danish monarch. Jón Hreggviðsson remains a pawn caught in the middle, dragged, beaten, released, and jailed again, never expecting more than punishment, and never seeming to give a second thought to his orphaned children. (Children don't fare well in this book.)

The denouement brings Snæfríður and Arnæus together one last time and here Laxness indulges in what is perhaps the only real set piece in the novel, a short dialogue in which the two of them describe to each other what Iceland will be like once rid of its colonial paymasters. For one of the final improvements, "A splendid courthouse shall be raised at Þingvellir, and another bell hung there, larger and more melodious than the one that the king demanded from Iceland and that the hangman ordered Jón Hreggviðsson to cut down." Thus, the justice of the old days will be restored, trade will become fair again, and a grand library will be built to house all the collected manuscripts. At this point, the reader can take an educated guess as to whether any of this idealism will ever come to pass.

Nationalism and good literature have always been uneasy bedfellows. One seeks to enforce an ideology, the other to lay pieties bare. Laxness is aware of this and in all his characters' rantings about the doomed dignity of poor, suffering Iceland, we sense the undertow of parody. But there must have been part of him that did write out of a sense of historical grievance and a desire that his country's stories be heard beyond the shores of that cold, rocky island out there in the North Atlantic, a country whose landscape he so lovingly describes. In *Iceland's Bell* he pulls it off. He manages to have a free-flowing, open-ended conversation about the fate of his nation inside a compelling, even suspenseful novel. There are precious few writers about whom that can be said, Tolstoy being one of them.

The rise and fall (and rise again) of literary reputation is a slow, uneven, unpredictable business that, before it achieves the status of common knowledge, usually depends on the passions and devotion of other writers, editors, and translators. Thus it's a cause for optimism that a wonderful book like *Iceland's Bell* has after all these years finally made it into the English language.

ADAM HASLETT
New York City
January 2003

PRONUNCIATION GUIDE

The modern Icelandic alphabet has thirty-two letters, compared with twenty-six in modern English. There are two extra consonants (ð and þ), and an additional diphthong (æ). Readers may find a note on the pronounciations of specifically Icelandic letters helpful:

ð (Ð), known as "eth" or "crossed d," is pronounced like the (voiced) *th* in *breathe*.

þ (Þ), known as "thorn," is pronounced like the (unvoiced) *th* in *breaths*.

æ is pronounced like the *i* in *life*.

The pronunciation of the vowels is conditioned by the accents:

> á like the *ow* in *owl*
> é like the *ye* in *yet*
> í like the *ee* in *seen*
> ó like the *o* in *note*
> ö like the *eu* in French *fleur*
> ú like the *oo* in *soon*
> ý like the *ee* in *seen*
> au like the *œi* in French *œil*
> ei and ey like the *ay* in *tray*

Please note that asterisks (*) within the text indicate explanatory notes to be found on pages 407–425.

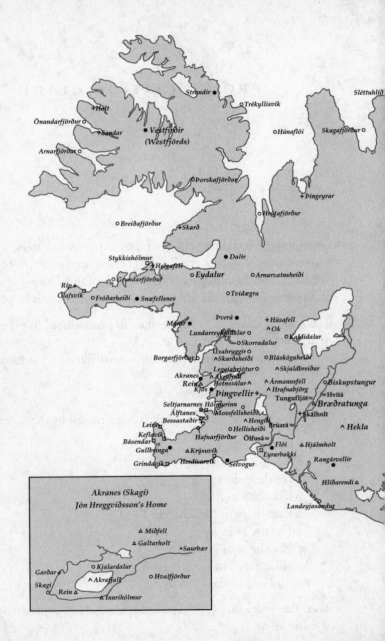

Strandir •

+Holt   Slétthulíð
Önundarfjörður ○   •Trékyllisvík
          +Sandar   •Vestfirðir
Arnarfjörður ○   (Westfjörds)   •Húnaflói   Skagafjörður ○

                    •Þorskafjörður
                                    +Þingeyrar
                          •Hrútafjörður
          ○Breiðafjörður +Skarð

Stykkishólmur   •Dalir
      ○ •Helgafell
      ○Grundarfjörður •Eydalur   ○Arnarvatnsheiði
Rip+
○Ólafsvík ○Fróðárheiði •Snæfellsnes   •Tvídægra

                          •Þverá •   +Húsafell
                Mýrar •   ^Ok
              •Lundarreykjadalur   Kaldidalur
                      ○Skorradalur
        Borgarfjörður ○ •Uxahryggir ○Bláskógaheiði
                ○Skarðsheiði ○Skjaldbreiður
              ○Leggjabrjótur
      Akranes ^ ^Akrafjall
      Rein △ •Hotnssúlur^ ^Ármannsfell ○Biskupstungur
        Kjós • •Þingvellir+ ^Hrafnabjörg
              •Hólkurinn Tungufljót≈ ≈Hvítá
      Seltjarnarnes   + △Bræðratunga
        Álftanes ◻•Mossfellsheiði +Skálholt
      Leirá • Bessastaðir • ^Hengill
      Keflavík • •Hellisheiði Þrúará≈ ^Hekla
      Básendar ◻ Hafnarfjörður • Ölfusá≈
      Gullbringa •   •Flói △Hjálmholt
        △Krýsuvík Eyrarbakki ◻
      Grindavík ◻ △Herdísarvík •Selvogur Rangárvellir

                              △Hlíðarendi △

                              •Landeyjasandur

        ┌─────────────────────────────────┐
        │   Akranes (Skagi)   │
        │   Jón Hreggviðsson's Home   │
        │   │
        │   △ Miðfell   │
        │   △ Galtarholt   │
        │   +Saurbær   │
        │   Garðar+ ○Kjalardalur   │
        │   Skagi △Akrafjall ○Hvalfjörður │
        │   Rein △   │
        │   △Innrihólmur   │
        └─────────────────────────────────┘

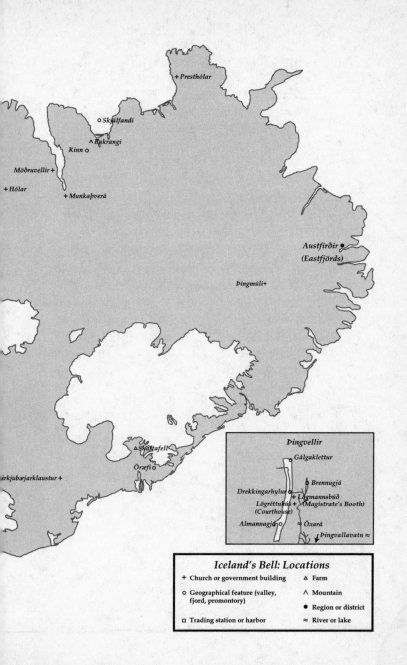

+ Presthólar

○ Skjálfandi

∧ Bakrangi
Kinn ○

Möðruvellir +

+ Hólar

+ Munkaþverá

Austfirðir ●
(Eastfjörds)

Þingmúli +

△ Skaftafell
Öræfi ○

irkjubæjarklaustur +

Þingvellir

○ Gálgaklettur

● Brennugjá
Drekkingarhylur ○
Lögmannsbúð
Lögréttuhús + (Magistrate's Booth)
(Courthouse)
Almannagjá ○   ≈ Öxará
↓ Þingvallavatn ≈

Iceland's Bell: Locations

+ Church or government building   △ Farm

○ Geographical feature (valley,   ∧ Mountain
   fjord, promontory)
                                   ● Region or district

□ Trading station or harbor   ≈ River or lake

ICELAND'S BELL

— I —

There was a time, it says in books, that the Icelandic people had only one national treasure: a bell. The bell hung fastened to the ridgepole at the gable end of the courthouse at Þingvellir by Öxará. It was rung for court hearings and before executions, and was so ancient that no one knew its true age any longer. The bell had been cracked for many years before this story begins, and the oldest folk thought they could remember it as having a clearer chime. All the same, the old folk still cherished it. On calm midsummer days at Þingvellir, when the fragrance of Bláskógar wafts in on gentle breezes from Súlur, the regent, the magistrate, and the executioner, the man to be hanged and the woman to be drowned assembled at the courthouse, and the chime of the bell could often be heard mingled with the murmur of Öxará.*

One year when the king decreed that the people of Iceland were to relinquish all of their brass and copper so that Copenhagen could be rebuilt following the war, men were sent to fetch the ancient bell at Þingvellir by Öxará.

A few days after the dissolution of the Alþingi, two men with several packhorses approach from the western side of the lake. They ride down the ravine opposite the estuary, cross over the ford, and dismount at the edge of the lava field near the courthouse. One of the men is pale, with full cheeks and small eyes, wearing a tattered aristocrat's jacket much too small for his frame and walking with his elbows extended like a child pretending to be a nobleman. The other is dark, ragged, and ugly.

3

An old man with a dog walks over through the lava rocks and steps out onto the path before the travelers.

"And who might you men be?"

The fat one answers: "I am His Majesty's emissary and hangman."

"You don't say," the old man mumbled hoarsely, in a voice that seemed to come from a great distance. "All the same, it's the Creator who rules."

"I have a letter to prove it," said the king's emissary.

"Oh, for sure," said the old man. "Everyone's got letters these days. All sorts of letters."

"Are you calling me a liar, you old devil?" asked the king's emissary.

The old man didn't want to risk coming any closer to the travelers, so he sat down on the remains of the wall encircling the courthouse and looked at them. He was no different from any other old man: he had a gray beard, red eyes, a chimney-cap, and gnarled legs, and he clenched his blue hands around his walking stick and leaned forward upon it tremblingly. His dog came over inside the wall and sniffed at the men without barking, as dogs do when concealing their savagery.

"No one had letters in the old days," murmured the old man softly.

Swarthy, the pale man's guide, exclaimed: "Right you are, pal! Gunnar of Hlíðarendi* had no letters."

"And who are you?" asked the old man.

"Oh, this is a cord-thief from Akranes; he's been lying about in the Þrælakista at Bessastaðir* since Easter," answered the king's emissary, and he kicked angrily at the dog.

The black-haired man spoke up and sneered, baring his gleaming white teeth: "That's the king's hangman from Bessastaðir. All the dogs piss on him."

The old man on the crumbling wall said nothing, and his expression remained for the most part blank. He continued to look at them and blinked a little as he sat there trembling.

"Climb up there on the house, Jón Hreggviðsson, you miserable wretch," said the king's hangman, "and cut down the bell. I find it hilarious to think that on the day when my Most Gracious Sire orders me to twist the noose around your neck, right here in this very place, no one will be ringing this bell."

"Enough with your mockery, lads," said the old man. "It's an old bell."

"If you're in league with the priest," said the king's hangman, "then tell him from me that neither quibbling nor crying is of use here. We have letters for eighteen bells plus one—this one. We've been ordered to break them apart and send the pieces to Denmark on the Hólmship.* I answer to none but the king."

He took a pinch from his snuff-horn without offering any to his companion.

"God bless the king," said the old man. "All those church bells that the pope used to own, the king owns now. But this is not a church bell. It's the bell of the land. I was born here on Bláskóga-heiði."

"Do you have any tobacco?" asked the black-haired man. "This damned hangman's too stingy to give a man some snuff."

"No," said the old man. "My people have never had any tobacco. It's been a hard year. My two grandchildren died in the spring. I'm an old man now. This bell—it has always belonged to this country."

"Who has the letters to prove it?" asked the hangman.

"My father was born here on Bláskógaheiði," said the old man.

"No one owns anything unless he has letters for it," said the king's hangman.

"I believe that it says in the old books," said the old man, "that when the Norwegians arrived in this empty land, they found this bell in a cave by the sea, along with a cross that's now lost."

"My letter is from the king, I say!" said the hangman. "And get yourself on up to the roof, Jón Hreggviðsson, you black thief!"

"The bell may not be broken," said the old man, who had stood up. "It may not be taken away in the Hólmship. It has been rung at the Alþingi by Öxará since the beginning—long before the days of the king; some say before the days of the pope."

"I could care less," said the king's hangman. "Copenhagen must be rebuilt. We've been fighting a war against the Swedes and those filthy bastard skulkers have bombarded the place."

"My grandfather lived at Fíflavellir,* some way up from here on Bláskógaheiði," said the old man, as if he were starting to narrate a long story. But he got no further.

> "Ne'er would king with arms so stout caress her
> Drape her in gems that fair bewitch
> Drape her in gems that fair bewitch . . ."

The black thief Jón Hreggviðsson was straddling the roof, his feet dangling out over the gable, singing the *Elder Ballad of Pontus.** The bell was fastened with a thick rope around the ridgepole, and he hacked at the rope with an ax until the bell fell down into the door-yard:

> "Drape her in gems that fair bewitch
> —Unless she were both young and r-i-i-i-ch . . .

. . . and now they say that my Most Gracious Hereditary Sire has gotten himself a third mistress," he shouted down from the roof, as if announcing tidings to the old man. He looked at the edge of the ax and added: "And she's supposed to be the fattest of them all. That's what separates the king from me and Siggi Snorrason."

The old man made no reply.

"Your words are going to cost you, Jón Hreggviðsson," said the hangman.

"Gunnar of Hlíðarendi would never have run away from a pale pig-belly from Álftanes," said Jón Hreggviðsson.

The pale emissary took a sledgehammer from a saddlebag, placed the ancient bell of Iceland on the doorstep before the courthouse, raised the hammer up high, and gave the bell a blow, but it only slipped a bit from under the hammer with a dull and glancing sound. Jón Hreggviðsson called down from the roof:

"'Seldom break bones on hollow ground, my man,' said Axlar-Björn."*

The king's hangman repositioned the bell against the step and struck its inner edge, and this time the bell broke in two along its crack. The old man had sat down again upon the crumbling wall. He looked tremblingly into the distance, his sinewy hands clenched around his stick.

The hangman took another pinch of snuff. The soles of Jón Hreggviðsson's feet could be seen dangling from the roof.

"Are you planning on riding the house all day?" shouted the hangman to the thief.

Up on the roof of the courthouse, Jón Hreggviðsson sang:

> "Ne'er would I with arms so stout embrace her
> Though her gleam might fair bewitch
> Though her gleam might fair bewitch
> Unless she were both fat and ri-i-ich."

They put the pieces of the broken bell in a bag, which they hung on a saddle-peg opposite the sledgehammer and the ax. Then they mounted. The dark man led the horses by the reins. The pale man rode freely alongside the packtrain, following genteel custom.

"Farewell, you old Bláskógar devil," he said. "And give God's greeting and mine to the Þingvellir priest and tell him that His Royal Majesty's emissary and hangman Sigurður Snorrason has been here."

Jón Hreggviðsson sang:

> "The kingdom's lord leads ladies and pages parading
> Throughout his lands at furious pace
> Throughout his lands at furious pace
> Throughout his lands at furious pace
> —On champing stallions they boldly ra-a-ace."

The packtrain left by the same route as it had come: over the ford at Öxará, up the slope of the ravine opposite the estuary, then southward to Mossfellsheiði, following the path to the west of the lake.

— 2 —

Actually, nothing more than usual had been proven against Jón Hreggviðsson, even though he had, as always, been charged with the crime. In general, everyone able to do so tried to steal anything they could from the drying sheds of the fishermen on Skagi* during cruel springtimes; some stole fish, some cord for fishing lines. Every spring was cruel. But the regent in Bessastaðir always needed more workers and he was delighted when bailiffs sent thieves to his workhouse, known as the Þrælakista—suspected thieves were just as welcome there as proven ones. At the beginning of the haymaking season, however, the authorities in Borgarfjörður sent word to the regent that the rogue Jón Hreggviðsson should be sent home to Rein on Akranes, because his people had no provider and were close to starvation.

The farm stood at the foot of the mountain in the place where it was most in danger from both landslides and avalanches. Christ owned the farm and its six-cow inventory.* A long time ago one of the bishops of Skálholt* had donated the farm to this particular landlord with the proviso that it be used to subsidize a widow in the parish of Akranes, particularly one who was pious, honest, and burdened with children; if no widow of this sort could be found in Akranes, one should be sought in Skorradalur. A long search was conducted but no such widow was found in either district, so Jón Hreggviðsson had been made the tenant of the farmer Jesus.

His homecoming was as might be expected considering the dwellers there were either lepers or half-wits, if not both. Jón Hreggviðsson was drunk when he came home and he began immediately to beat his wife and his idiot son. His fourteen-year-old daughter laughed at him and his aged mother embraced him tearfully: these he did not beat to any considerable extent. His sister and aunt, who were both lepers, one glabrous and palsied, the other nodous and ulcerous, sat downcast in their black veils out by the dungheap, holding each other's hands and praising God.

Next morning the farmer went out to sharpen his scythe, and

afterward began to cut the grass, loudly singing the *Ballad of Pontus.* The black veils moved reluctantly to the edge of the homefield and started pottering about with rakes. The half-wit and the dog sat on a hillock. The daughter came and stood before the door, barefoot and in a torn undershirt, to take in the smell of the newly mown grass, black and white and slender. Smoke reeked from the chimney.

Several days passed.

It then happened that a fine-looking courier riding a strong horse showed up at Rein and delivered to Jón Hreggviðsson a message that he was to appear in the bailiff's court at Skagi after a week's time. Jón saddled his jade on the appointed day and rode out to Skagi. The hangman Sigurður Snorrason was there. They were given soured whey to drink. Court was convened in the bailiff's sitting room and Jón Hreggviðsson was accused of having, at Þingvellir by Öxará, slandered our Supreme Highness and Majesty, Count in Holstein, our Most Gracious Hereditary King and Sire, with unseemly gibes to the effect that this our Sire had now adulterously acquired three mistresses. Jón Hreggviðsson denied having said any such thing about his Beloved Hereditary King and Most Gracious Sire, His Highness and Majesty and Count in Holstein, and asked for witnesses. Sigurður Snorrason swore that these were Jón Hreggviðsson's words. Jón Hreggviðsson requested that he be allowed to forswear the accusation, but counteroaths were not allowed at the same hearing. After the farmer's request was rejected, he said that it was as a matter of fact true that he'd spoken the words—everyone in the Þrælakista at Bessastaðir was talking about it—but it was out of the question that he'd intended to insult his king with these words. Quite the contrary—he'd simply wanted to say how much he admired a king who was so excellent that he was able to have three mistresses at once, in addition to a queen; at the same time he'd been poking fun at his good friend Sigurður Snorrason, who'd never made the acquaintance of a woman as far as anyone knew. But even if he had spoken these words about his Most Gracious Hereditary Sire himself, he was sure that His Highness was so benevolent that he would willingly forgive one poor, stupid man and muddleheaded beggar of such ill-advised chatter. Court was then adjourned and the sentence handed down

that Jón Hreggviðsson was to pay three rixdollars* to the king within
a month, or his skin would be taken in place of the fee. The court's
verdict was worded along these lines: that the ruling "was determined
not so much according to a large amount of testimony, but rather
according to the sufficient amount of evidence that was implicit in
the testimony." With that, Jón Hreggviðsson rode home. Little else
of interest occurred during haymaking, and the farmer gave hardly
any thought to paying his fine to the king.

In the fall an assembly was convened in Kjalardalur. Jón Hreggviðsson was summoned to the assembly and two farmers were sent by
the bailiff to escort him there. The farmer's mother mended his shoes
before he left. The Rein farmer's mare had a limp and they made the
journey slowly, arriving in Kjalardalur late in the day, toward the end
of the assembly. It turned out that Jón Hreggviðsson was to be
flogged with twenty-four lash-strokes. Sigurður Snorrason had
arrived on the scene with his leather straps and his hangman's cloak.
Many of the farmers had ridden home from the assembly, but a
number of youngsters from the nearest farms had come to watch the
flogging for fun. Floggings were carried out in a pen where the ewes
were milked during the summer; the pen had a stone crib running
through it, and the scoundrel was laid across this crib while justice
was being done. The more important men stood in the meantime in
the corners of the pen on either side of the crib, while children, dogs,
and beggars stood on the walls.

A small group of people had gathered by the time Jón Hreggviðsson was led into the pen. Sigurður Snorrason had buttoned up his
hangman's mantle and had finished reciting the Lord's Prayer; he
saved the Creed for beheadings. They had to wait for the bailiff and
the official witnesses, so the hangman took his straps out of their
sheath and stroked them respectfully and studiedly, then tested the
handles gravely and earnestly—he had fat hands, blue and scaly, and
hangnails. The two farmers held Jón Hreggviðsson between them
while Sigurður Snorrason practiced aiming the straps. It was raining.
The men looked distracted like they usually did when it rained, and
the wet youngsters stared; the dogs acted like they were in heat.
Finally Jón Hreggviðsson began to get bored, and said:

"Those mistresses are giving me and Siggi Snorrason a lot of trouble."

A few faces slipped into sluggish, joyless smiles.

"I've finished reciting the Lord's Prayer," said the hangman calmly.

"Let's hear the Creed, too, dear," said Jón Hreggviðsson.

"Not today," said Sigurður Snorrason, and he grinned. "Later." He stroked the straps very slowly, carefully, tenderly.

"You should at least knot up the poor straps, my dear Siggi," said Jón Hreggviðsson, "even if only for the queen's sake."

The hangman said nothing.

"Hardly will such an excellent king's man as Sigurður Snorrason bear taunting words from the mouth of Jón Hreggviðsson," said a tramp on the wall, in a style like that of the ancient sagas.

"My dearly beloved king," said Jón Hreggviðsson.

Sigurður Snorrason bit his lip and started knotting the straps.

Jón Hreggviðsson laughed with a gleam in his eye and his white teeth flashed in his black beard—"Just now he knotted his first mistress," he said. "He's definitely no yellow-belly. Knot it up again, dear."

The spectators began to liven up, like men standing over gamblers whose wagers are huge.

"O servant of His Royal Majesty, remember our Sire!" came an exhortative voice from the wall, the same that had previously spoken saga-style. The hangman was convinced that his audience stood firmly behind him and the king. He grinned and looked from wall to wall as he made another knot in the straps; he had small gap-teeth and swollen gums.

"Well, now he's come to the last one—and the fattest," said Jón Hreggviðsson. "Many a good man has had to give it up just before she's fully tied."

Just then the bailiff arrived, along with the two witnesses, who were wealthy farmers; they pushed the people aside and entered the pen. The bailiff saw that the hangman was knotting up the straps and ordered him to undo the knots, with the proclamation that justice would be served here, not mockery. Then he ordered the hangman to begin.

The farmer was told to loosen his clothing and wadmal* was draped over the crib. The man was stretched out prone on this bench and Sigurður Snorrason pulled down the man's breeches and slipped his shirt up over his head. The farmer's body was lean but strongly built, with convex muscles that knotted with movement. He had a small patch of black, woolly hair that reached from his rigid buttocks to just below the hams of his knees, but otherwise his body was white.

Sigurður Snorrason signed himself, spat into the palms of his hands, and began his work.

Jón Hreggviðsson made no move at the first few strokes, but at the fourth and fifth strokes his body was seized with cramps. His legs, his face, and the upper part of his chest lifted, leaving his weight resting on his tightened stomach. His fists clenched, his feet stretched away from his ankles, his joints stiffened, and his muscles hardened. His shoes were newly mended, by the look of the soles. The dogs jumped up on the wall and yelped down into the pen. After eight strokes had been delivered the bailiff said that they would stop for the moment: the criminal had the legal right to a brief respite. His back, however, had only just begun to redden. Jón Hreggviðsson could care less about a respite, and yelled through his shirt:

"Get on with it in the name of the devil, man!"

The work was continued without further delay.

After twelve strokes Jón Hreggviðsson's back had become some-what bloodied and bruised, and at the sixteenth his skin actually started to split open between the shoulder blades and at the small of the back. The dogs on the walls yelped madly, but the man lay like a solid block of wood, motionless.

At the sixteenth stroke the bailiff said that the criminal was to be allowed another respite.

Jón Hreggviðsson was heard to shout:

"In the devil's name, the devil's name, the devil's name—!"

The king's hangman spat into his palms once more and adjusted the shaft of the straps in his grip.

"Now he starts on the last—and the fattest," said the man on the wall, and he started laughing incessantly.

Sigurður Snorrason stepped forward on his left foot and with his right tried to get a grip on the slick floor of the pen, then bit his lip as he moved in for the blow. The gleam in his tightly drawn eyes testified that he gave himself with utmost concentration to the power of his craft; he became livid. The dogs kept up their yelping. At the twentieth stroke blood trickled out nearly everywhere along the length of the farmer's back, and the strap had become damp and sleek. As the work drew to a close the man's back was transformed into a bleeding and tattered sore, and splashes of blood were thrown in various directions by the hot, dripping whip, some onto people's faces. When the authority gave the signal to stop, the farmer was not so exhausted that he had to accept others' offers to help him fasten up his breeches; instead he laughed, with eyes gleaming, up toward the walls of the pen at the men, dogs, and children, his white teeth flashing in his black beard. As he girded himself he loudly sang this stanza from the *Elder Ballad of Pontus*:

"A splendid feast the pope did host, a regal banquet,
Emperor, kings, and courtiers fine
Cheerfully dined and drained their wine."

It was evening by the time various groups of lingerers rode home from the assembly, each group in its own direction. The last group to leave included the bailiff and the two witnesses, the wealthy landowners Sívert Magnússen and Bendix Jónsson, along with several farmers from Skagi, Sigurður Snorrason the hangman, and of course Jón Hreggviðsson from Rein.

Bendix Jónsson lived at Galtarholt, and because the men from Skagi still had a long way to go he invited the party home for a drink before continuing on its way. Bendix was a seigneur, very well-to-do, and he kept a barrel of brennivín* on stocks in his storehouse. He offered to loan Jón Hreggviðsson a line and sinker, which was a generous and noble gesture considering the shortage of fishing tackle and the famine that now pressed upon the tenantry of the land.

A partitioned-off platform was located at the far end of the storehouse, and it was there that Bendix led the bailiff, the king's hangman, and Monsieur Sívert Magnússen. Three lesser men and the man who'd been flogged were shown to seats on saddle-turfs and casks of flour in the storehouse's entryway. Bendix quickly poured drink into the men's glasses and the storehouse became the scene of a great communal celebration. Any distinction between dais and entryway was soon rendered irrelevant as everyone sat down in a circle in the entryway and started in on various entertainments, including storytelling, debate, and poetic recitation. The men quickly forgot about their daily toils and expressed their shared brotherhood with handshakes and embraces. The king's hangman lay down upon the floor and tearfully kissed Jón Hreggviðsson's feet, while the farmer sang and swung his cup. Seigneur Bendix was the only one in the group to remain sober, as befitted his duty as host.

It was deep in the night when the men rode away from Galtarholt. They were all completely drunk, causing them to lose their way the moment they left the homefield. They suddenly found themselves riding through a disgusting, foul-smelling mire filled with deep stagnant wells, bogs, pools, and peat-pits. The mire seemed to be endless and the travelers floundered for a good part of the night in this forecourt of Hell. Monsieur Sívert Magnússen rode into a peat-pit and invoked the name of God. It was very common for people to drown dogs in such places, and because it was so difficult for the gentleman's companions to tell the living man from the dead dogs it took them some time before they were finally able to drag him out. At last they got the man up onto the edge of the pit, due primarily to the grace of God, and he fell asleep there. The last thing Jón Hreggviðsson remembered was trying to get up on his own mare's back after helping drag Monsieur Sívert Magnússen from the pit, but his saddle was stirrupless and his horse seemed to have grown considerably, besides the fact that it wouldn't stop kicking out with its hind legs. Whether he actually made it up on horseback or whether something that prevented him from doing so occurred in the total darkness of that fall night, he could not completely remember later.

At daybreak he roused the folk at Galtarholt and asked for Seigneur Bendix. He was much the worse for his wanderings, muddy and wet and with chattering teeth. He was riding the hangman's horse and had the hangman's cap on his head. Bendix helped the man off the horse, dragged him back to the farm, undressed him, and put him to bed. The farmer was exhausted and he lay facedown because of the swelling on his back, but he slept immediately.

When he awoke around nine o'clock he asked Bendix to go with him to the mire, because he'd lost his hat and his gloves, his horsewhip, his line and sinker, and his mare.

The mare was standing in a group of horses a short distance away with its saddlecloth hanging at its belly. The mire wasn't as large as it had been during the night. They spent some time searching for the lost items near a narrow stream where Jón Hreggviðsson seemed to remember that he'd been lying. He happened to be correct—they found his belongings on the bank of the stream, the horsewhip lying in the grip of one of his gloves, the line and sinker nearby. A few steps away they found the hangman, dead. He was on his knees, propped upright between the banks of the stream, which was so narrow there that the man's body was enough to stop it up. The stream had filled in somewhat above the body, so that the water, which was otherwise not much more than knee-deep, was at that point up to the armpits. The corpse's eyes and mouth were closed. Bendix looked at it for a moment, looked next at Jón Hreggviðsson, and asked:

"Why is his cap on your head?"

"I woke up bareheaded," said Jón Hreggviðsson. "And after I'd gone a few steps I found this cover. Then I shouted, 'Ho, ho!' but no one answered, so I put it on."

"Why are his eyes and mouth closed?" asked Seigneur Bendix.

"Only the devil knows," said Jón Hreggviðsson. "I'm not his undertaker."

He moved to pick up his whip, gloves, and line and sinker, but Bendix stopped him and said:

"If I were in your shoes I would first call upon six witnesses to come and examine the evidence."

This was on a Sunday. It was decided that Jón Hreggviðsson should ride to Saurbær, where he could ask some churchgoers to come and examine the body of the hangman Sigurður Snorrason as it had been found in the stream. A large group of people rode back with him out of sheer curiosity to see the dead hangman, and six said that they would be willing to swear oaths that no wounds could be seen upon the body, nor any evidence indicating that hands had been laid upon the man, except that the eyes, nostrils, and mouth were closed.

The hangman's body was dragged back to Galtarholt, and afterward they all rode back to their own homes.

—— 3 ——

The next day's weather was bright and still and people were at their various tasks on land and sea, but Jón Hreggviðsson lay prone in bed, cursing his wife and begging the Lord with painful moans to give him tobacco and brennivín and three mistresses. The half-wit sat on the floor and laughed fervently as he pulled apart pieces of wool. The obtrusive stench of the lepers prevailed over the other stenches in the room.

Suddenly the dog starts howling from the rooftop, and a low thundering of horses' hooves rolls in from outside. Presently bridle bits rattle and men's voices murmur just beyond the door; a commanding voice orders the grooms to their work. Jón Hreggviðsson didn't move a muscle. His wife came running into the room, gasping and panting, saying:

"Lord Jesus have mercy on me, the gentry have come."

"The gentry," said Jón Hreggviðsson. "Haven't they finished flaying off my skin? What more do they want?"

But space for long-winded conversation soon vanished as the sounds of footsteps, voices, and the rustling of clothing swept in from the corridor. The visitors had invited themselves in.

First to step over Jón Hreggviðsson's threshold was a thickly set, ruddy nobleman in a wide mantle, with a hat tied under his chin, a heavy golden ring, a silver cross on a chain, and a costly riding crop. After him came a woman wearing a yellow chimney-hat, a red silk scarf, and a dark, full-length riding frock. The woman had not yet reached middle age and had rosy cheeks, though her bearing suggested a slackening of youthful tension; she was beginning to put on some weight, and an air of worldliness marked her countenance. Following her came another woman, very young. She was, with respect to her youth, a lyrical image of the first, having experienced less of the things that make a woman. She wore no hat, and her head shone with disheveled hair. Her slender body was childishly supple, her eyes as unworldly as the blue of heaven. Her comprehension was still limited to only the beauty of things, rather than to their usefulness, and thus the smile she displayed as she stepped into this house had nothing to do with human life. Her gown was high-waisted and indigo blue, with a spangle of silver at the neckline. She held up the hem with dainty fingers, revealing red ribbed stockings over her shoes.

Last in this outstanding entourage came a nobleman whose bearing was composed, attentive, and self-assured. The man was in good condition, and it was difficult to determine his age; his face was smooth and his nose straight, the appearance of his mouth both supple and sad, almost feminine, yet lacking fickleness. His measured movements testified to years of self-discipline. His glance was tranquil and determined, yet his eyes were fully sympathetic, large and lucid, giving the impression that their field of vision was wider than that of other men and that therefore less could be concealed before them. These eyes assessed everything more by nature than curiosity, faculty than effort, reminding one of the calm surface of a lake. They were the hallmark of the man. In actuality, the visitor would have more closely resembled a wise commoner rather than an aristocrat, had not his attire made the difference. Most aristocrats could be distinguished by their bearing, acting as if they ruled the world, but this one expressed himself through his careful but unpretentious taste. The aesthete in him spoke out from every seam, each pleat, every proportion in the cut of his clothing; his boots were of fine English leather. His wig, which he wore under his brimmed hat even amongst boors and beggars, was exquisitely fashioned, and was as smartly coiffured as if he were going to meet the king.

Following a few steps behind this elegant company came Jón Hreggviðsson's pastor, the parish priest at Garðar, along with his curly-tailed sheepdog, sniffing. It quickly became too crowded having so many magnates in the sitting room at once, so Jón Hreggviðsson's wife dragged the half-wit up onto the bed to allow the gentry more room.

"Well, my dear Jón Hreggviðsson from Rein, look at what fate has handed you," said the priest. "Here is the bishop of Skálholt himself, with the daughters of Magistrate Eydalín: the bishop's wife, Madam Jórunn, and her sister Lady Snæfríður, the flower of maidens. And finally, who else but Arnas Arnæus himself, the right-hand man of our Most Gracious Sire and Hereditary King, Assessor and Professor at the University of Copenhagen—all gathered here in your sitting room."

Jón Hreggviðsson gave a tiny snort, nothing more.

"Is the farmer ill?" asked the bishop, who was the only one of the visitors to extend him his hand, with its heavy golden ring.

"I would hardly call it that," said Jón Hreggviðsson. "I was flogged yesterday."

"He's lying—he was flogged the day before yesterday. Yesterday he killed someone, the poor wretch," said his wife quickly and sharply, and she slipped as swiftly as she could out the door behind the visitors.

Jón Hreggviðsson said: "I beg my venerable excellencies to pay no attention to this she-creature, for just who she is can best be seen by that little puke of hers up there on the bed—and slink yourself off, you idiot!—don't let decent folk see you. Little Gunna, Gunna! Where's my dear Gunna, who at least has my eyes?"

The girl ignored his calls, and the bishop turned to the priest and asked whether any beneficium* had reached these poor souls. He was told that they had never asked for such a thing. The bishop's wife clasped her husband's arm and leaned toward him. Snæfríður Eydalín glanced at her serene companion and her involuntary smile dwindled into a look of panic.

The bishop bade Reverend Þorsteinn announce the assessor's business and then call upon all of the house's occupants to come and receive his blessing.

Reverend Þorsteinn began his speech by reiterating what a great distinction it was for this household to receive the erudite scholar from the great capital of Copenhagen, Arnas Arnæus, friend of the king, comrade-in-arms of counts and barons, and the true pride of this our poor land amongst the nations. He desired to purchase any and all ancient tatters of writing, whether on parchment or paper: old scrolls, scraps, anything resembling a letter or a book that was decaying now in all haste in the keeping of the destitute and wretched inhabitants of this miserable land. These people, he said, no longer had any understanding of such things, due to the ill-effects of starvation and other types of divine punishment suffered by impenitent folk and those who are ungrateful to Christ. The assessor, said the priest, would find for these poor scraps of books a place of refuge in his own great mansion in the city of Copenhagen, to be stored for all eternity so that the learned men of the world could be sure that once upon a time there had lived in Iceland folk to be reckoned men, such as Gunnar of Hlíðarendi and the farmer Njáll and his sons.* Next Reverend Þorsteinn explained that it had come to his master's knowledge, through the power of prophecy possessed only by learned witnesses to divine wisdom, that the simpleton Jón Hreggviðsson from Rein had in his keeping several ancient pieces of vellum containing writings from the Catholic era, and thus had this lofty company, which was traveling to Skálholt from Eydalur in the west, detoured and made its way hither to Akranes, to discuss the matter with the wretched tenant of Christ who here napped, freshly flogged, upon his bed. The assessor was very interested in seeing these tatters if they were still in existence, in borrowing them if they were available for loan, or in buying them if they were for sale.

Jón Hreggviðsson, unfortunately, could not recall having in his possession any skin-patches, tatters, or scraps that preserved the memory of men of ancient times, and thought it sad that such a noble company should have come so far on such a hopeless quest. In this household there were no books to be found but for a shred of the *Graduale* and a copy of the half-rhymed *Kross School Hymns* written by Reverend Halldór from Presthólar.* Gunnar of Hlíðarendi, he said, would never have composed such hymns. There was no one on the farm able to read fluently except for Jón Hreggviðsson's mother:

she had attained to this art because her father had been a bookbinder for the late Reverend Guðmundur in Holt out west and had worked on old books until the day he died. Jón Hreggviðsson said that he himself never read except when he was forced to do so, though he had learned from his mother all the necessary sagas, ballads, and old genealogies, and he claimed to be descended from Haraldur Hilditönn, the Danish king, on his father's side. He said that he would never forget such excellent ancients as Gunnar of Hlíðarendi, King Pontus, and Örvar-Oddur,* who were twelve ells high and could have lived to be three hundred years old if they hadn't run into any trouble, and that if he had such a book he would send it immediately and for free to the king and his counts, to prove to them that there had indeed once been real men in Iceland. On the other hand, he reckoned, it was hardly due to impenitence that the Icelanders were now fallen into misery, because when had Gunnar of Hlíðarendi ever done penance? Never. He said that his mother had never grown tired of singing the penitential hymns of Reverend Halldór from Presthólar, but she had very little to show for it. On the contrary, he said, lack of fishing tackle had done far more harm to the Icelanders than lack of penitence, and his own misfortune had originated when he let himself be tempted by a piece of cord. But no one should think, least of all his dear lord bishop, that he was ungrateful to Christ, or that he would ever squander Christ's property; quite the opposite, he said—he thought that this landowner and heavenly farmer had always been lenient and forgiving toward his poor tenant, and that they'd always gotten along quite well.

As the householder was talking the others came in to receive the blessing of the bishop of Skálholt. The nodous aunt with exposed fingerbones and the ulcerous sister whose face had been eaten away would not be still until they had pushed themselves up into the visitors' faces, eye to eye with the finery of the world. Few disfigured folk are as quick as lepers to use any opportunity they can to display their sores, especially to those in authority, often doing so with a certain provocative pride that can disarm even the most valiant man and make the most handsome ludicrous in his own eyes: Look, this is what the Lord in his mercy has granted me, this is my deserved reward from the Lord, say these images of men, and at the same time they ask: Where's your reward, how has the Lord honored you? Or even: The Lord has stricken me with these sores for your sake.

The half-wit had always been jealous of the two lepers and took it badly that they were closer to the action now that such a great event was taking place, so he teased and harassed them as much as he could by kicking, pinching, and spitting at them, forcing Jón Hreggviðsson to yell at him several times to clear off. Reverend Þorsteinn's dog put its tail between its legs and ran out. The bishop's wife tried to smile cordially at the two lepers who lifted their black faces toward her, but the damsel Snæfríður turned herself with a cry away from this sight, raised her hands involuntarily to the shoulders of Arnæus, who stood at her side, curled herself suddenly and tremblingly up to his breast, tore herself away from him again and tried to regain her composure, and then said in a restrained, somewhat melancholy voice:

"My friend, why have you brought me into this dreadful house?"

The remainder of the occupants, the mother, the daughter, and the wife, had now arrived to receive the bishop's blessing. The old mother kneeled before the bishop and kissed his ring according to ancient custom, and His Excellency helped her to her feet. The dark, frightened eyes of the girl, convex and shining, were the house's finest ornament. The wife stood behind in the doorway, sharp-nosed and shrill-voiced, ready to disappear if something should happen.

"It would seem, as I have told my lord many times, that there is no great treasure to be found here," said Reverend Þorsteinn. "Even the mercy of the Lord is entirely more distant from this house than from the others in the parish."

There was only one man in this stately company who was not affected by anything sinister, whose aristocratic tranquillity could not be displaced, and to whom nothing came by surprise, neither here nor elsewhere. Nothing in the countenance of Arnas Arnæus indicated that he was anything other than completely satisfied in this house. He had now struck up a conversation with the old woman, slow in his speech, humble and unpretentious like a rustic who has contemplated many things in his solitude. There was a softness to his deep voice, more like velvet than eiderdown. It turned out, extraordinarily so, that he, the king's confidant, the table-companion of counts, and the pride of our people amongst the nations, this far-traveled cosmopolitan who could scarcely be considered an Icelander except according to dreams and fables, knew thoroughly the descent and origins of this paltry old woman and could name all of her relatives in the western part of the country, and he said with a gentle smile that he had more than once held in his hands small books that her father had bound for a certain Reverend Guðmundur who had died over a hundred years ago.

"It is unfortunate," he added, looking toward the bishop, "—it is unfortunate that the late Reverend Guðmundur from Holt was in the habit of having ancient manuscripts of famous sagas torn apart, when every single page, or even half-page, or even one tiny shred of these manuscripts was auro carior*—it would not have been too much to trade landed estates for some of them. Afterward he would have the parchment leaves used for covers or involucra* for the prayer books and hymnbooks that he received unbound from the printshop in Hólar, and he would give them to his parishioners in exchange for fish."

He turned back to the old woman and said:

"I thought it might be pleasurable to ask whether my dear old mother might not want to show me to the places where scraps of patched-up skin-breeches or worn-out old shoes are sometimes left and forgotten in corners: under the bed, in the kitchen, out in the storehouse, or up in the storehouse loft; or else in the wall-slats of the outer shed, where sometimes during the winters useless patches are packed into the gaps to keep the snow from drifting in. Or perhaps she might have an old bag or box of rubbish in which I might rummage around a bit, just in the hope of finding something, even if it were nothing but a miserable shred of a book cover from the days of Reverend Guðmundur from Holt."

But in this household there was no bag or box of rubbish, neither was there a storehouse loft. The assessor, however, did not look any more likely to leave because of this, and although the bishop was becoming slightly restless and wanted to finish bestowing his blessing, the friend of the king continued to smile sympathetically at the family.

"There's nothing—unless you might want to try the bottom of my mother's bed," said Jón Hreggviðsson.

"Oh yes, of course—the things our dear old ladies hoard!" said the assessor, and he took snuff from his pouch and offered some to all, including the idiot and both of the lepers.

When Jón Hreggviðsson had partaken of some of this excellent tobacco it dawned on him that something must surely have become of the old pieces of skin they'd given up on trying to use to patch his breeches a few years ago.

Dust and poison gushed up from the old and moldy hay within the woman's bed as they began their search. Mixed up in the hay was all kinds of garbage, such as bottomless shoe-tatters, shoe-patches, old stocking legs, rotten rags of wadmal, pieces of cord, fibers, fragments of horseshoes, horns, bones, gills, fishtails hard as glass, broken wooden bolts and other scraps of wood, loom-weights, shells both flat and whorled, and starfish. The bedstead was even roomy enough to accommodate several useful and extraordinary things, including girth buckles, sea beans, whipstocks, and age-old coppers.

Jón Hreggviðsson himself had crept over to help the Professor Antiquitatum* rummage in the old woman's bed. The two elegant women had gone outside but the two lepers remained behind with the bishop. The old woman stood off to one side. As they began their search a blush appeared on her shriveled cheeks and her pupils widened, and the longer they searched the more startled she became as another nerve was touched with each new item they uncovered, until finally she started to tremble. In the end she lifted her skirt up to her eyes and sobbed quietly. The bishop of Skálholt had been standing nearby, watching the assessor's methods with a skeptical eye, and when he saw the old woman begin to cry he stroked her soft, wet cheeks with Christlike mercy and tried to assure her that they would not take away anything that was of value to her.

After a long and thorough search through the old hay the noble visitor dragged out some wadded and hole-riddled parchment scraps that were so shriveled, shrunken, and hardened by age that it was impossible to smooth them out.

While he was searching through the rubbish, the quiet nobleman's eyes had reflected a modest and apologetic amusement, but this suddenly gave way to an impersonal, dutiful earnestness as he held his find up to the soft light coming through the window screen. He blew on the parchment and scrutinized it, then took a silk handkerchief from his breast pocket and dusted it.

"Membranum,"* he said finally, glancing momentarily at his friend the bishop, and they both examined it: several sheets of calf-skin gathered and threaded at the spine, the thread having long since torn or gone rotten. The surface of the parchment was black and grimy, but one could easily discern a text there, written in a Gothic script. They became eager and reverential at once, handling these shriveled rags as carefully as if they were holding a skinless embryo, and muttering Latin words such as "pretiosissima," "thesaurus," and "cimelium."*

"The script can be dated to circa 1300," said Arnas Arnæus. "It would be my guess, from the evidence, that this is a page from the *Skálda** itself."

Then he turned to the old woman, said that here were six pages from an ancient manuscript, and asked how many pages she might have had originally.

The old woman stopped crying when she saw that they didn't want to take anything more valuable from the bottom of her bed, and answered that she wouldn't have ever had more than one other page. She could dream back to having once, a long time ago, soft-ened up this tangled mess of skin and torn a page from it to use as a patch for her dear Jón's breeches, but the piece had turned out to be completely useless because it wouldn't hold a thread. When the visi-tor asked what had become of this particular page, the woman answered that she'd never been in the habit of throwing away any-thing that might be useful, least of all scraps of skin—she'd had enough trouble throughout her entire life trying to scrape together enough material to make shoes for all the feet in her house. It was a poor patch of parchment that wasn't useful for something during a hard year, when so many were forced to eat their shoes—even if it were nothing but a shoestring, it could still be stuck into the chil-dren's mouths for them to cut their teeth on. Her lords shouldn't consider it providential that she'd gotten nothing out of this scrap.

They both looked at the old woman as she stood there, drying her tears and sniffing. Then Arnas Arnæus said quietly to the bishop:

"I have been searching for seven years now, and have inquired of folk throughout the entire country whether they knew of a place where a fragment, even minutissima particula,* of the fourteen pages that I am missing from the *Skálda* might be found. The most beautiful poems in the northern hemisphere have been collected in this one single manuscript. Here we have six pages, crumpled up and nearly illegible, of course, and yet, sine exemplo."*

The bishop congratulated his friend with a handshake.

Arnas Arnæus raised his voice and turned back to the old woman. "I will take these misfortunate shreds with me," he said. "They cannot be used to patch breeches or mend shoes, anyway, and there is little chance that such a famine will come over Iceland that you would consider using them for food. But you shall have a silver coin from me for your inconvenience, good woman."

He wrapped the pieces of parchment in the silken handkerchief and thrust it under his cloak, then turned to Reverend Þorsteinn and addressed him in the kind of glad and carefree tone a man uses when he engages in lighthearted banter with a companion to whom he is bound by no other duty than the pursuit of pleasure:

"It has now come down to this, my dear Reverend Þorsteinn: these people, who have since antiqui* possessed the most distinguished litteras* in the northern part of the world, choose now to walk upon calfskin or to eat calfskin rather than to read the old words written upon calfskin."

The bishop finished granting the inhabitants his blessing.

The noblewomen who had been awaiting their cavaliers outside in the red glow of evening approached them now with smiles. More than a dozen horses on the loose, vigorous and whinnying, gnawed at the grass at the outskirts of the homefield. The grooms led four of the horses into the yard. The eminent folk mounted, and the horses galloped off along the stony path, fire flying from under their hooves.

— 4 —

A few days later Jón Hreggviðsson rode out to Skagi to collect the foxhunting fee that he received for destroying fox lairs for the inhabitants in the district. The fee was customarily paid to him in fish, but, as usual, there was a shortage of cord, so he thought he'd ride out to the bailiff's farm to borrow a small piece of cord to bind the fish. The bailiff was standing out in front of his door, along with several other farmers from Skagi, when Jón Hreggviðsson rode into the yard with his fish.

"Good day," said Jón Hreggviðsson.

The men received his greeting stolidly.

"I was thinking of asking your authority to loan me a tiny piece of cord," said Jón Hreggviðsson.

"You shall indeed have a piece of cord, Jón Hreggviðsson," said the bailiff, and turning to his men, he said: "Seize him now, in Jesus' name!"

There were three others there besides the bailiff, all close acquaintances of Jón. Two of them grabbed him, but one stood by and watched. Jón fought back immediately. He flew at the farmers alternately, punching them and jostling with them and tumbling them into the mud, giving them all they were worth, until the bailiff, who was a strong man, joined forces with them. In a short time they finally got the better of the farmer, whose fish had been trampled down into the mud beneath their feet during the encounter. The bailiff then fetched chains and shackled the farmer, telling him at the same time that he would never again rest his head beneath his own roof. The prisoner was taken to the vestibule between the servants' quarters and the main house at the bailiff's residence, where people came and went all day long, and there he was confined, fettered, and placed under guard for two weeks. He was made to tease horsehair or grind grain, and the servants were ordered to take turns guarding him. At night he had to sleep on a storage chest. The knaves and wenches made fun of him as they passed through the vestibule and one old woman ladled refuse over him from the chamber pot because he sang the *Ballad of Pontus* at night and prevented people from sleeping. A poor widow and her two children, however, took pity on him and gave him warm grease and greaves.

Finally they rode out with the farmer to Kjalardalur and an assembly was held to discuss his case. The bailiff there decreed that he had been lawfully arrested on the charge of murdering the hangman Sigurður Snorrason, and stipulated that his abjurement of the charges would require twelve compurgators, whom he himself would have to provide. The six churchgoers from Saurbær swore that when they had reached Sigurður Snorrason's corpse in the stream, they had found its eyes, nostrils, and mouth closed. Monsieur Sívert Magnússen, who had been dragged up from the peat-pit, swore that they, the hangman and Jón Hreggviðsson, had ridden away from the other men out into the darkness of the night. Not a single oath worked in Jón Hreggviðsson's favor. After a two-day trial he was sentenced to execution for the murder of Sigurður Snorrason. He would be allowed to appeal the district court's judgment before the magistrate at the Alþingi.

It was well into fall and travel was good due to the hard-frozen snow, and everyone had come on foot except for the bailiff and his secretary. On the way home to Skagi the bailiff rode out to Rein and left the prisoner standing shackled and guarded outside his own homefield wall while he went into the house.

When the inhabitants got wind of who had arrived, Jón Hreggviðsson's mother milked the cow and brought a bowl of its lukewarm milk to the farmer. When he finished drinking she stroked the hair back from his eyes. The girl, his daughter, came out to the wall and stood near the man and looked at him.

The bailiff walked straight into the sitting room at Rein without knocking upon the door.

"Your husband has been convicted of murder," said the bailiff.

"Yes, he's the worst sort of man," said the wife. "I've always said that."

"Where's his gun?" said the bailiff. "You can do without implements of death in this household."

"Yes—it's a wonder that he shouldn't have already killed us all with this gun," said the wife, and she brought him the gun.

Next she took a new, tidily folded wadmal shirt and extended it to the bailiff, saying:

"I am, as all can see, well into my pregnancy, and besides that, am a weak individual—I'm not much of a sight to behold; at any rate he certainly doesn't like to look at me much. But I'd like to ask the bailiff to bring this clothing to him; it's warm, in case he's going to be gone for a while."

The bailiff grabbed the shirt, struck the woman with it, and said as he flung it away:

"I'm not your servant, Rein-rabble."

The boy laughed uncontrollably since he always found it horribly funny when his mother was treated badly, no matter by whom. The two lepers, the one nodous, the other ulcerous, sat together upon the bed, holding tremblingly on to each other's fingerbones and praising God.

Because winter had set in and there would be no further litigation in Jón Hreggviðsson's case prior to the Alþingi, it was decided that the prisoner should be transferred to Bessastaðir, which was better equipped than other places to house prisoners for long periods of time. Some men were sent by boat south to Álftanes, with the prisoner in the stern. The weather was cold and the waves sprayed over the boat, but the men kept themselves warm by rowing and bailing. Jón Hreggviðsson sang the *Elder Ballad of Pontus*. When they looked at him he stopped for a moment, and a gleam appeared in his eyes as he laughed at them defiantly, his white teeth flashing in his black beard—then he started singing again.

At Bessastaðir the regent's steward, a secretary, and two Danish servants took charge of the prisoner. This time the farmer wasn't lodged in the Þrælakista, but instead was taken directly to the dungeon. Bolted to the top of a heap of stones shaped like a well-shed were heavy shutters, barred and set with unbreakable locks; below these was a deep and vast opening with limed brick walls. A rope ladder was run down this hole and Jón was forced to climb down to the bottom, then the regent's servants climbed down to shackle him.

There were no conveniences in this dungeon other than a narrow plank covered with a sheepskin, a chamber pot, and a chopping block. A hefty ax lay on the chopping block and next to it was an earthen jug of water. The steward's lantern momentarily illuminated the scene: chopping block, ax, and jug—and then the men turned to leave. They climbed out of the hole, dragged the ladder up behind them, closed the shutters and drove home the bars, then turned the keys in the locks. Afterward everything was quiet. It was pitch-black; not a thing could be seen. Jón Hreggviðsson sang:

> "The soldier entreated and got his way
> A maid to lie in sport and play
> Increased our love as there we lay
> Increased our love as there we lay:
> —Though at first she answered 'nay.'"

Jón Hreggviðsson sat in this prison and sang the *Elder Ballad of Pontus* throughout the whole winter and on into summer.

Time did not pass by in the usual three-hour intervals in this place, so the days could not be counted; there was in fact no way to distinguish day and night, and the prisoner had nothing to do to while away the hours. A basket of food was lowered down to him once a day, sometimes twice, but beyond this he had little contact with the outside world.

In all actuality he had almost completely forgotten what humans were when the first guests were sent to join him, so he was overjoyed to greet them. There were two of them, melancholy-looking fellows, and they received his greeting coldly. He asked them who they were and where they lived but they were reluctant to answer. When he finally managed to get them to talk he found out that one of them was called Ásbjörn Jóakimsson, from Seltjarnarnes, and the other, Hólmfastur Guðmundsson, from Hraun.

"Well now," said Jón Hreggviðsson. "The men of Hraun have always been damned criminals. But I always thought that folk from Seltjarnarnes were good-natured."

Both men had been sentenced to flogging. It was apparent, not only from their reluctance to answer and their haughty way of speaking, but also from the earnest way in which each pondered his own lot, that these were well-to-do men. Jón Hreggviðsson continued to interrogate them and to prattle. It turned out that this Ásbjörn Jóakimsson had refused to row one of the regent's messengers over Skerjafjörður. Hólmfastur Guðmundsson, for his part, had been sentenced to lose his skin for having traded four fish for some pieces of cord in Hafnarfjörður, instead of having delivered the fish to the merchant in Keflavík—his farm belonged to the Keflavík trade district according to the king's new regulations relegating control of the trade monopoly to district authorities.

"What was your excuse for not delivering the fish to the merchant in the district where my Most Gracious Sire commanded you to do business?" asked Jón Hreggviðsson.

The man said that he couldn't get any cord from the king's merchant in Keflavík—nor, for that matter, from the merchant in Hafnarfjörður, though a most considerate man at the trading booth had let him have a tiny piece. "And to think that this should have happened to me, Hólmfastur Guðmundsson," said the man in conclusion.

"You'd have done better to use the cord to hang yourself," said Jón Hreggviðsson.

Ásbjörn Jóakimsson was less of a talker than his brother-to-be-flogged.

"I'm tired," he said. "Isn't there any place here for a man to sit down?"

"No," said Jón Hreggviðsson. "This is no parlor. This plank is for me alone and I won't give it up. And don't you be roving around there by the chopping block—you might knock down my jug, which is holding my water."

There was a moment of silence, until someone sighed heavily in the darkness.

"But my name is Hólmfastur Guðmundsson."

"What about it?" said the other. "Don't I also have a name? Doesn't everyone have a name? I have the feeling that it doesn't really matter what we're named."

"When has anyone ever read in the old books that the Danes sentenced a man with my name to the whip, in his very own land, Iceland?"

"The Danes beheaded Bishop Jón Arason* himself," said Ásbjörn Jóakimsson.

"If someone here wants to start slandering my Hereditary King, just remember that I'm His hereditary servant," said Jón Hreggviðsson.

There was another long moment of silence. Finally the man from Hraun could be heard muttering his own name in the darkness.

"Hólmfastur Guðmundsson."

He repeated it, very quietly, as if it were some kind of obscure oracle: "Hólmfastur Guðmundsson."

Afterward, silence.

"Who said that the Danes beheaded Bishop Jón Arason?" asked Hólmfastur Guðmundsson.

"I did," said Ásbjörn Jóakimsson. "And since they beheaded Jón Arason do you think it matters whether the king has farmers like ourselves flogged?"

"It's an honor to be beheaded," said Hólmfastur Guðmundsson. "Even a little churl becomes a man by being beheaded. A little churl can recite a verse as he's being taken to the chopping block, like Þórir Jökull* who recited his verse and was beheaded—and his name will live on as long as the land is inhabited. On the contrary, the man who is flogged is belittled. There is no man so gallant who is not humiliated by the whip."

He added in a low voice: "Hólmfastur Guðmundsson—has anyone ever heard a more Icelandic name? And the memory of this Icelandic name will be connected with a Danish whip throughout the centuries, in the hearts of a people who write down everything in books and forget nothing."

"I wasn't belittled in the least by being flogged," said Jón Hreggviðsson. "And nobody laughed at me. I was the only one who laughed."

"It does nothing to a man, to the man himself, to be flogged," said Ásbjörn Jóakimsson. "But you can't deny that it must be slightly traumatic for the man's children to learn, when they've grown up, that their father was once flogged. Other children point at them and say, 'Your father was flogged!' I have three little girls. But after three or four generations it's forgotten—at least I don't imagine that Ásbjörn Jóakimsson is such a remarkable name that it will be written in books and read throughout the centuries; quite the contrary—I'm like every other nameless man, healthy today, dead tomorrow. On the other hand, the Icelandic people will live throughout the ages if they don't give in, no matter what happens. I refused to transport the king's man over Skerjafjörður, that's true. Neither living nor dead, said I. I'll be flogged and that's fine with me. But if I had given in, even in such an insignificant matter, and if everyone gives in always and everywhere, gives in to ghosts and fiends, gives in to the plague and the pox, gives in to the king and the hangman, then where would these folk have their home? Even Hell would be too good for such folk."

Hólmfastur did not answer, but continued to repeat his name quietly. Jón Hreggviðsson was determined not to let them up on his plank. After some time his fetters stopped rattling and the first snores came, jerky exhalations at the threshold of the senses that gradually deepened and became steadier.

As winter passed thieves were occasionally cast down to join Jón Hreggviðsson, sometimes several at once, confined there the night before they were to be branded or have their hands cut off. Jón was horribly anxious that they might try to steal the jug or even the ax. Others had to wait for their punishment for longer periods of time, mainly people from the district of Gullbringa. A cotter who rented land from the regent had refused to lend the regent his horse; he'd told him that men who were too lazy to go anywhere without the help of ninety good saddle horses, but who had none themselves, might as well get used to sitting at home—Gunnar of Hlíðarendi had never asked anyone to loan him a horse. Another, Halldór Finnbogason from Mýrar, had refused to receive communion and had been arraigned on charges of public blasphemy and desecration of holy relics. Both of these men were sentenced to have their tongues cut. The second of the two cursed and swore the entire night before his tongue was cut, and amongst those he cursed were his father and mother. Jón Hreggviðsson couldn't get any sleep and finally became so angry that he said that whoever didn't go to the altar was a fool, and he started singing the *Ballad of Jesus,* which he unfortunately didn't know very well. Apart from thieves, there were quite a few other visitors who had been sentenced for crimes against the royal trade monopoly. One had been caught with English tobacco. Another had added sand to his sacks of wool. Some had illegally purchased flour in Eyrarbakki, because the flour in Keflavík was rotten and swollen with maggots. One or two had called their merchants thieves. There were endless amounts of these petty criminals, and they were all flogged. The king's whip continued to flicker voraciously over the prone bodies of naked and emaciated Icelanders. Last but not least there were several hardened criminals of Jón Hreggviðsson's mettle who were brought to the dungeon for a night's lodging, men who were either to be executed or sent south to Denmark, to Bremerholm,* the most familiar of all places known to Icelanders in that distant country.

Jón Hreggviðsson was never allowed to see the light of day during those twenty-four weeks, except for an insignificant glimmer at Yule and Easter when he was brought to church to hear the word of God. On both of these holy days the regent's men came down into the dungeon, pulled a bag over his head, released him from his fetters, and escorted him to the church, where he was seated upon a corner bench between two brawny men and forced to listen to the customary message with the bag over his head. The rope, however, wasn't pulled too tightly around his neck, which enabled him to catch a faint glimpse of his surroundings as he sat there in the house of God. Otherwise he saw nothing that whole winter.

Around Easter another man was lowered down to the farmer, a man from the Eastfjörds who'd been sentenced to prison at Bremerholm for one of the most infamous crimes ever committed in Iceland: he'd rowed out to a Dutch dogger and bought a spool of twine. His case had been prosecuted during the fall and he was to be sent abroad that spring on a ship lying at anchor at Suðurnes.* During the winter he'd been sent from one bailiff to another throughout the land until he finally ended up here.

"No," said Guttormur Guttormsson. "They couldn't prove that I had anything but this one spool. On the other hand, the merchant's servants were spying on my trips out there. In my region everyone trades with them. A man who's never seen a Dutch gold ducat doesn't know what it means to have lived."

This was a man who spoke passionately and was moved to tears and gasped for breath every time he mentioned Dutch money.

"They're this big," he said, and he grabbed Jón Hreggviðsson's shoulder and made a ring on his forehead in the darkness.

"It would never cross my mind to betray my Hereditary King and Sire for such blood money," said Jón Hreggviðsson.

"The Dutch are made of gold," said the man. "At night when I wake up and can't fall asleep again I think about those blessed huge coins and then I feel very well indeed. Such size! Such weight! Such luster!"

"Do you have a lot of them?" asked Jón Hreggviðsson.

"A lot?" said Guttormur Guttormsson. "Whether I've got a lot or just a few—and that's not really any of your business, pal—I know what it means to have lived. I've lived many happy days. You southerners never live a single happy day."

"You're a liar," said Jón Hreggviðsson. "We love and honor our king."

"We men of the Eastfjörds have never been a mob of slaves," said Guttormur Guttormsson.

After they'd become better acquainted Jón Hreggviðsson found out from the Easterner that even if he hadn't committed any other crime than to buy a spool of twine from the Dutch—that was the only crime that had been exposed, anyway—he'd traded with them for several years and made a good profit. In the winter his wife wove woolen clothing for the fishermen, and in the summer he brought them butter and cheese, calves, lambs, and children. In return he received good quality flour, ropes and cord, pig iron, hooks, tobacco, cloth kerchiefs, red wine, and corn liquor—and gold ducats for children. "Children," said Jón Hreggviðsson.

"Yes—one ducat for a girl, two ducats for a boy," said Guttormur Guttormsson.

Sometime during the last hundred years it had become fashionable for the people of the Eastfjörds to sell children to the Dutch, with the result that the rate of infanticide was much lower in that region than elsewhere in the country. Guttormur Guttormsson had sold them two children, a seven-year-old boy and a fair-haired girl of five years.

"So all you've got is three ducats," said Jón Hreggviðsson.

"How many ducats do you have?" said Guttormur Guttormsson.

"Two," said Jón Hreggviðsson. "I've got two ducats at home in Rein on Akranes—two living ducats that look up at me."

"What did you give for them?" asked the Easterner.

"If you think that I got them with bait, then you've missed the point, pal," said Jón Hreggviðsson.

The man's papers said that he was a master craftsman, and in just a short time he was dragged up from the dungeon and sent to the Þrælakista to be put to some use while awaiting transport to Bremerholm, so Jón Hreggviðsson neither saw nor heard more of this outstanding man.

A new companion, however, joined him during the last months of winter and remained for some time. This was a sorcerer from the Westfjörds, Jón Þeófílusson by name. He was a rather lanky man in his forties who'd been living with his middle-aged sister in a little cottage in a valley. He'd had little to do with women, mostly because of his lack of sheep, so he'd tried to remedy both shortages by resorting to sorcery, which was frequently in fashion in the Westfjörds, though with disproportionate results. Another man who was a successful sheep farmer had won the heart of a priest's daughter in whom Jón Þeófílusson also had an interest, and Jón had tried to conjure up a sending* against this man. But his skills as a sorcerer were so awkward that the sending entered the priest's cow and killed it. A while later one of his rival's colts died in a waterhole that appeared out of nowhere. Jón Þeófílusson was taken into custody, and found in his possession were the signs of the Blusterer and the Corpse's Breeches. While the case was being investigated his rival's brother fell ill and died. The devil, whom the sorcerer called Pokur, appeared to this man on his deathbed and testified that Jón Þeófílusson had pledged himself in exchange for the brother's ailment as well as for the previous mishaps involving the cow and the horse. The man swore an oath to the truth of this apparition on his dying day, and thus the devil himself had become the chief witness in the case against Jón Þeófílusson, and his testimony sealed the man's fate.

Jón Þeófílusson was considerably apprehensive about being burned and spoke often about it in whispers. He said he would rather be beheaded.

"Why did they bring you here to the south? Why don't they burn you out west, you rascal?" said Jón Hreggviðsson.

"The men of Þorskafjörður refused to give them brushwood," said the man.

"That's news to me if they have enough extra firewood here in the south to use on anyone from another quarter," said Jón Hreggviðsson. "You should ask to be beheaded with me, preferably on this chopping block here, because I'm sure that there's not a better chopping block to be found in the whole country. I killed a lot of time when I was bored this winter by trying out my neck in its groove."

"All winter I've prayed to God to let me be beheaded instead of burned," said the man.

"Why don't you make your vows to the devil, man?" said Jón Hreggviðsson.

"He swindled me," said the man in whimpers. "After Þokur swindles a man, a man starts praying to God."

"It sounds to me like you're a pretty paltry fellow," said Jón Hreggviðsson. "Stop whining and try to show me one of your magic signs."

"No," whined the man.

"You could always teach me to conjure up the devil," said Jón Hreggviðsson.

"I never had much luck with that myself," said the man. "Þokur insisted that I had, and because of that got me convicted in court, but it's a lie. On the other hand I got hold of a Blusterer and fiddled around with it on account of a girl. I also had the Corpse's Breeches."

"What?" said Jón Hreggviðsson. "A Blusterer? On account of a girl?"

"Yes," said the man. "But something went wrong."

"Do you have one of these Blusterers here?" asked Jón Hreggviðsson. "Better late than never. Who knows, maybe we can conjure up a few hussies of our own. What was once an urge is now a necessity."

But the authorities had already confiscated the man's Blusterer.

"Can't we make a Blusterer ourselves?" asked Jón Hreggviðsson. "Can't we scratch that damned sign with the ax-point onto the chopping block and get a beautiful, chubby woman in here tonight, right now—or preferably three?"

It was no easy matter to create such a sign, because in order to do so the two men required much greater access to the animal kingdom and the forces of nature than conditions in the dungeon permitted. The sign of the Blusterer is inscribed with raven's gall on the rust-brown inner side of a bitch's skin, and afterward blood is sprinkled over the sign—blood from a black tomcat whose neck has been cut under a full moon by an unspoiled maiden.

"Where'd you find an unspoiled maiden to cut a black tomcat's neck?" asked Jón Hreggviðsson.

"My sister did it," said the man. "It took us three years to get the raven's gall. But on the first night that I tried it, when I climbed onto the roof over the priest's daughter's bedroom and held up the Blusterer and rattled off the spell, it was all over for me, since the cow was dead."

"What about the girl?" asked Jón Hreggviðsson.

"There was a man sleeping with her," said Jón Þeófílusson, in tears.

Jón Hreggviðsson shook his head.

"By the way, didn't you say something about the Corpse's Breeches? I can't really see how you could've gotten into such a scrape if you had the Corpse's Breeches, because I've heard that there's always money in those things if one looks closely."

"I'd gotten hold of the sign of the Corpse's Breeches, and had even stolen money from the widow to put in them. But I never actually owned the Breeches themselves. I paid a man to let me cut off his skin after he died, but he's still going strong even though he's almost ninety. Anyway it was too late because the cow was dead and the foal had fallen into the waterhole. And a short time later Þokur appeared to the departed Sigurður on his deathbed and testified against me."

It was silent in the hole, except for the sound of the sorcerer sobbing in the darkness. After a few moments Jón Hreggviðsson said quietly:

"You'll definitely be burned."

The sorcerer kept on sobbing.

— 5 —

An old woman wants to make a journey.

During the mornings as the seamen shove off from land she loiters on the beach, accosting one man after another, claiming that she needs to go south. On this day they all refuse her passage, but she is there again the next. She is wearing new shoes, and her blue nose pokes out from a brown shawl wound around her head. She is accoutered like a female pilgrim, carrying a walking stick and a pouch made of curried hide, her skirt tucked up and tied.

"It scarcely bodes much ill luck to allow one poor wretch to float along with you and to put her ashore somewhere at the tip of the cape."

"There's enough of a crowd of beggars at Suðurnes," they say.

Time passes, and the moving days have ended.* Yet still the woman totters down to the beach every morning, wanting to make a journey. Finally some steersman gives up and takes her on board with a curse, puts her ashore by Grótta,* and rows away. She creeps over kelp-grown rocks and sea-beaten stones until she reaches a grassy bank. Well then, she'd crossed over the sea. The mountains of her home, Akrafjall and Skarðsheiði, appeared hazy blue in the distance.

She set out, following the promontory toward the mainland. The spring day was bright and calm, and she walked up the slope at the center of the cape to have a look about. Cottages cowered amidst the tangle down below the flood-line. On the far side of the fjord south of the cape the sun gleamed off the residence at Bessastaðir, where the king's men held sway; on the cape's northern side were oblong buildings on low, flat skerries out in the sea and a merchantman at anchor: the trading station of Hólmur.* Distant blue peaks on the mainland flanked smaller mountains whose darkish slopes were patched with strips of green. She walked along the coastline for most of the day, crossing over stony hills and soggy marshland until she came to a river that fell in two brisk branches into a bight, the stream gleaming white and blue in the sun. She knew there wasn't much chance that she could cross over by her own strength. A foot-steady individual in the prime of his life might have taken off his socks and waded over, but she was an old woman. She decided to sit down and recite a penitential hymn composed by Reverend Halldór from Presthólar. She took a fishtail from her pouch and gnawed on it as she recited the hymn, and drank the river's blue water from the palms of her hands as she tried to remember what verse came next, because the Lord stipulated that prayers would be granted only when they were said correctly. She took care, moreover, to recite the hymn in the right tone, drawling at every other line and easing off at the end of every verse, sadly, like a finger slipping over a sounding string.

As she finished reciting the hymn a number of men leading a packtrain crossed over from the east, and she begged them tearfully, in Jesus' name, to take a miserable wretch eastward over the branches, but they answered that there were already enough vagrant old women on the other side. After they were gone she stopped weeping and carried on with her penitential hymn. Then another packtrain arrived from the west, transporting stockfish. She begged them tearfully to help a poor old creature, but they were drunk from brennivín and said that they would beat her senseless with their whips if she didn't turn around and go back to wherever it was she'd come from. Water splashed over the woman as the packtrain crossed. She stopped weeping and recited more of the hymn.

Early in the evening a shepherd girl from one of the farms west of the river came riding out to tend her sheep on the islet between the branches. The old woman promised to ask God to bless the girl if she would help her cross over. The girl said nothing, but stopped her horse at a convenient knoll. The old woman climbed up behind the girl and they crossed over both branches, then the girl stopped the horse at another knoll and waited while the woman clambered off the horse's back. The woman kissed the girl farewell and bade God bless her and all her offspring.

Day had passed into night.

On the farms to the west of the heath there were crowds of people everywhere, especially men leading packtrains to the south coast to procure stockfish; some of them had traveled long distances from the east. There were also solitary travelers, wealthy landowners who had business at Bessastaðir or with the merchants in Hólmur, and these took priority with regard to lodging. All sorts of other folk had congregated here as well, especially those who were forced to spend their lives endlessly roving in search of sustenance, which ill luck guaranteed to be always on the other side of the mountain. This group included paralytics and other invalids, poets, branded thieves, eccentrics, half-wits, girls, preachers, hunchbacks, fiddlers, and lunatics. One family came from out east in Rangárvellir, a man and his wife and five children; they'd squandered their livelihood and were on their way to their kinfolk south in Leira in the hope of fish. One of the children was at death's door. They reported that the carcasses of itinerant vagrants lay scattered before men's doors throughout the entire countryside to the east. Nineteen thieves had been branded at Rangárvellir in the winter and one hanged.

The men from the packtrains had to stand guard over their loads of stockfish wherever they took lodging for the night. Tramps hung about on the footpaths and walls and provided various types of entertainment for anyone who wanted to listen, while the lepers reached out with their bare fingerbones and praised God. One particular fool stood up on a gablehead and performed a dismal routine that he called "The Ballad of Breaking Wind," and he even charged small change for it. A preacher put on a woman's riding frock and intoned for his in-laws, in the voice of the bishop of Skálholt and through a hardened cod-gill, the so-called *Gospel of Mark in the Midhouses,* about two daughters and two casks of whale suet: ". . . whoever dishonors my daughters at Yule will not get to see their glory at East-e-er." Then he switched to the voice of the bishop of Hólar and sang: "The mouse jumped up to the altar and bit the candle with his long gray tail and his dark red sho-o-oes." And in his very own voice he chanted:

"Drat it, confound it, and fie,
What a piteous creature am I,
The loon waddles off in retreat,
Flapping on fumbly fe-e-ee-e-eet."

No one wanted to see or hear the fiddler, so they cut his fiddle strings.

Finally the old woman asked the way eastward over Hellisheiði and said that she was thinking of continuing on that night.

"Where're you going?" somebody asked.

She said she had a trifle of an errand with the bishop's wife in Skálholt.

The men stared at her vacantly. One said:

"Didn't two vagrant old crones die out on Hellisheiði on Easter night earlier this spring?"

Another said: "The bailiffs have forbidden any further transport of beggars eastward over the great rivers."

A third, who seemed to be a beggar himself, said: "The tightwads to the east are in the mood for murder, my dear lady."

As evening wore on clouds gathered and it started to drizzle. The woman's feet were sore. The birds twittered gladly and vigorously in the luminous night and the warm moss covering the lava was so lushly green that it illuminated the mist. The woman walked for so long that in the end her feet were no longer sore, but benumbed. She crept into a small hollow near the path and tried to rub some life back into them, then ate a bit of hardfish and recited a penitential hymn.

"Oh, well then, so what if they did get caught out here on Easter night, the two old dears," she murmured to herself between verses. "Oh, well no, so that's the way it was, you poor old creatures."

In a moment she was fast asleep, her chin resting on her knees.

Toward evening of the next day, when she'd come as far east as the Ölfus River, she found that everything she'd heard south of the heath was true: travel permits were being demanded of dubious individuals at the ferry landing. Waiting in a swarm of terns on a sandbank at the edge of the river were six vagrants, amongst them one corpse. The ferryman said no. One of the vagrants said that he'd tried to beg for milk at the nearest farm, but was told that the salmon were sucking the cows. He said he'd offered to tell a story in exchange, since he was a poet and knew more than a thousand stories, but at this time of year no one was willing to part with even one bowl of skimmed milk, no matter what was being offered in return.

"What would Gunnar of Hlíðarendi have said if he'd seen other such folk?" said the poet. "Or Egill Skallagrímsson?"*

"There was a time when I worked as a silversmith for the gentry," said a blind old man who was holding the hand of a blue-eyed boy. "Now I have to beg for a fin."

This comment was somewhat out of place, like most of the things that blind men say, and the entire thread of conversation, if there ever had been one, snapped. The beggars stared long and silently at the glacier-colored streamwater passing by.

The corpse was of a young girl, and it had been placed neatly on the sandbank, but no one claimed responsibility for it. Someone said that she'd been insane in the life of the living. If one lifted the hair from her forehead one could see that she'd been branded.

"Two ravens have been croaking for a long time east of the river," said the blue-eyed boy who was leading the blind man.

"The raven is the bird of all the gods," said the poet. "It was the bird of Óðinn and the bird of Jesus Christ. It will also be the bird of the god Skandilán, who has yet to be born. Whomever the raven rends attains salvation."

"And the tern?" said the boy.

"The Lord gave all the earth and all the sky to some birds," said the poet. "Lie down flat on your back like me, young man, and study the flight of the birds for yourself, but do not speak."

The glacier stream continued to pass by.

A distended-looking beggar, his liver most likely swollen, had been sitting there on the sandbank with his legs stretched out, looking down between his feet. Now he lifted up his sluggish eyes and said:

"Why silver? Why not gold?"

The blind man answered: "I've also worked gold."

"Why didn't you say gold then?" asked the distended one.

"I'm more fond of silver than gold," said the blind one.

"I'm more fond of gold," said the distended one.

"I've noticed that very few people are fond of gold for itself," said the blind one. "I'm fond of silver for itself."

The distended man turned to the poet and asked:

"When's silver ever mentioned in poetry?"

"If you were an unbetrothed maiden," said the poet, "which would you prefer to marry, one man or thirty whales?"

"Is this supposed to be a riddle, or what?" asked the thicker beggar.

"My girl married thirty whales," said the poet.

"From evil company, parce nobis domine,"* said an old, ancient-mannered woman, and she turned her back on the men and wandered off.

"She didn't want me," said the poet. "And at that time I was at my best. There was a famine then, like now. That same spring thirty whales were washed up on the beaches of a seventy-year-old widower in the countryside."

"Gold isn't precious because it's a better metal than silver," said the blind man. "Gold is precious because it resembles the sun. Silver has the light of the moon."

Two important-looking men who crossed over from the east took charge of the blind man and his boy and they were ferried over. One man took charge of the popish old woman and even the distended man turned out to have a leprous brother in Kaldaðarnes. But no one would claim responsibility for the poet, nor for the corpse, nor for the woman come lately from Skagi. She wept for a while and beseeched the farmers in the name of Jesus, but it was useless; they boarded the ferry and the oarsman locked in the oars. Three remained behind, two living, one dead.

The poet said: "You're new to begging, good woman, if you think that God's mercy still exists. God's mercy is the first thing to die in an evil year. What can be done to reduce the tears in Iceland? Not only let beggars be borne across the rivers by oar, but let them glide over the seas on wings."

The old woman said nothing. She set off up the riverbank, carrying her walking stick and her pouch, thinking that there must be someplace where the bellowing streamwater would be only a little rippling brook, where a child might step over without wetting its feet.

The poet and the corpse were left behind.

— 6 —

The old woman's destination, Skálholt, the episcopal seat and site of the learned school, offers with its throng of turf-covered dwellings an inhospitable welcome to unfamiliar travelers. It was so long into the spring that the mires had dried up. Folk there paid no heed to strangers and did not return the greetings of petty visitors, but passed by without asking the news, like shadows or speechless wraiths in dreams. All the same, it was invigorating to breathe in the vapor that emanated from the place, a blend of smoke from cooking-fires, the odor of fish, and the stenches of manure and refuse. The turf huts numbered, without doubt, in the hundreds, some lopsided and battered, their roofs nearly bare, others burly-looking, with smoking chimneys and grass-grown roofs, practically new. The cathedral towered up and over these scraps of earth and turf, a tarred wooden building with a belfry and tall wedge-shaped windows.

She guessed her way to the bishop's residence. This was a large, garreted house, also built with turf except for one lime-washed wooden wall facing the church. In this wall was a row of four-paned windows midway up from a comely paved footpath. One could see into the residence from the footpath. Glinting within were tankards and pots made of silver, tin, and copper, elegantly painted chests, and magnificently carved woodwork, but no one was to be seen inside. Double doors closed off the entry—the outer door was weatherworn and ajar, but the inner door was made of select wood and carved with dragons, and had a copper ring at the lock. The windows above the entry were within her arm's reach, with only two panes in each and brightly colored curtains that came together in the middle of the windows at the top and were drawn out to the sides at the bottom.

Now when the traveler had finally reached her destination and stood on the footpath before the bishop's residence in Skálholt, with nothing left to do but knock upon the door, something like irresolution came over her; she sat down on the path before the bishop's windows, her knotty feet stretched forward off the flagstones, her chin sunk down to her chest. She was tired. She sat there unmoving for some time before a woman walked up and asked what she wanted. The old woman lifted her head slowly and extended her hand in a gesture of greeting.

"Vagabonds are not welcome here," said the other.

The old woman dragged herself up and asked after the bishop's wife.

"Beggars must report to the steward," said the churchwoman, a vigorous widow, authoritative and contented, in the prime of her life.

"The bishop's wife knows me," said the old woman.

"How could the bishop's wife know you?" said the churchwoman. "The bishop's wife does not associate with beggars."

"God is with me," said the woman. "And that's why I can speak to the bishop's wife in Skálholt."

"All vagabonds say that," said the churchwoman. "But I am certain that God is with the rich, not with the poor. And the bishop's wife knows that if she spoke to wretches then she would have time for nothing else, and the parish of Skálholt would fall to ruin."

"All the same, she came to my hovel last year and spoke to me," said the old woman. "And since you think that I'm poor, good madam, whoever you are and whatever you're called, then let me show you something here."

She reached into her blouse and drew forth her silver coin, which was wrapped tightly in a kerchief, and showed it to the churchwoman.

"The bishop's wife is not at home," said the churchwoman. "She rode west with the bishop, home to her mother to refresh herself after this dreadful spring. They found corpses lying here on the pavements sometimes in the mornings after folk had gotten up for work. She's not coming back before the middle of the summer, after the bishop has completed his visitation out west."

The hand holding the coin sank slowly back down and the visitor looked tremblingly at the parishioner. It had been a long journey, and her tongue had gone dry from reciting Reverend Halldór of Presthólar's penitential hymns.

"They've probably finished beheading men at the Alþingi by now," she said finally.

"Beheading? What men?" asked the churchwoman.

"Poor men," said the visitor.

"How should I know when miscreants are beheaded at the Alþingi?" said the churchwoman. "Who are you, woman? What do you want? And where did you get that coin?"

"Where might the aristocrat from Copenhagen be now, the one who came with the bishop to Akranes last year?"

"I suppose you mean Arnas Arnæus, my dear? Where else would he be but with his books at home in Copenhagen? Or maybe you're one of those women who expects her comforter to arrive on the Bakkaship,* haha!"

"And where is the slender maiden whom he brought last year into our hovel at Rein?"

The churchwoman pointed to the windows over the door and lowered her voice, though this particular subject always worked to loosen her tongue. "If you're asking about Lady Snæfríður, the magistrate's daughter, my dear woman, you'll find her sitting here in Skálholt. Some say she's betrothed, and even more, that she's going to have to learn how to mingle with countesses. One thing is certain—they're teaching her Latin, history, astrology, and other arts far beyond the reach of any other woman who's lived in Iceland. She herself made it clear this spring that she was expecting a little something to arrive on the Bakkaship, and that there was no way she was going to go west with her sister despite her protests. But the Bakkaship arrived over a week ago and no one has heard anything new. On the contrary—those who were prowling around here late on winter evenings are now riding up and down the pavements here in the bright light of day. And the schoolmaster's hardly ever sent for anymore. Climb high and fall far. That's the way the world goes, my dear. I was taught that everything's best in moderation."

She led the old woman to the upper floor of the bishop's residence, to the bower of Snæfríður the magistrate's daughter, who was sitting there embroidering a girdle, clad in flowery silk. She was extraordinarily slender, with almost no bosom, her golden appearance of the previous autumn having long ago given way to a delicate paleness, though the azure of her eyes was even more vivid than before. Her countenance was joyless, her glance distracted, her lips closed so that her natural smile was denied; indeed, it appeared as if the expressive quality of her mouth had been wiped away by unnatural effort. She looked out from a kind of incredible distance at the grimy, decrepit image of a person who stood in her doorway with an empty pouch and bruised and bloody feet.

"What does the old woman want?" she asked finally.

"Does my lady not recognize this old woman?" asked the visitor.

"Who can tell one old woman in Iceland from another?" asked the damsel. "Who are you?"

"Do you not recall, my lady, a little hovel beneath a mountain by the sea?"

"A hundred," said the damsel. "A thousand. Who can tell them apart?"

"A renowned and noble maiden stands in a little house one day in the autumn and leans up against the greatest man in the country and the best friend of the king. 'My friend,' she says, 'why have you brought me into this dreadful house?' That was the house of my son Jón Hreggviðsson."

The damsel laid aside her handwork and leaned back in her armchair to rest, her long, nearly transparent fingers drooping over the ends of the chair's carved arms, higher than the life of the land. She was wearing a large golden ring. The air within was heavy with the scents of musk and nard.

"What do you want from me, woman?" she asked lazily, after a long silence.

"It isn't often that a woman from the south travels such a long way east," said the woman. "I've come this whole way to beg my lady to free my son."

"Me? Your son? From what?"

"The ax," said the woman.

"What ax?" asked the damsel.

"I know that my lady wouldn't mock an old woman, even if she were a fool."

"I don't understand what you're talking about, good woman."

"I heard that your father was going to have my son beheaded at Þingvellir by Öxará."

"That's of no concern to me," said the damsel. "He has a lot of men beheaded."

"My lady may yet give birth to a son who will be the fairest of all Icelanders," said the woman.

"Have you come here to frighten me with evil prophecies?"

"May God protect me from prophesying evil against my lady," said the old woman. "I never once thought that I would even see my lady. I came all this way to meet the bishop's wife, because no woman is so powerful that she doesn't understand other women. I had hoped that she who is the magistrate's daughter and the wife of the bishop would recall the time when she stepped into my house and take pity on me, now that my son is to be beheaded. But now, since she's gone, there is no one who can help me but my lady."

"How could it possibly cross anyone's mind that we sisters, two muddleheaded women, could have any influence over laws and judgments?" asked the young girl. "Your son will hardly be beheaded for no reason at all. My son would not be spared from guilt even if he were the fairest of all Icelanders. Nor would I, for that matter. Wasn't the queen of the Scots also beheaded?"*

"My lady can influence the laws of the land, and she can influence the judgments," said the old woman. "The friends of the king are the friends of my lady."

"I have no place in the events of the day," said the girl. "These things are ruled by strong men—some with weapons, others with books," said the girl. "They call me the fair maiden and say that the night is my domain."

"The night is said to rule over the day," said the old woman. "In the morning the maiden shall be praised."

"I'm the kind of woman who'll be praised when I'm burned," said the girl. "Go back home, blessed mother."

At that moment someone came riding into the yard, and a groom was ordered gruffly to his work. The lady gave a start and raised a fist to her cheek.

"So he has come," she whispered. "And I am alone."

Then, in an instant, booted footsteps and the rattling of spurs resounded upon the steps. The door was heaved open before the girl had a chance to smooth out the creases in her skirt, comb her hair, or tidy up her face.

He was tall, broad-shouldered, and well-built, but stooped slightly as if he considered it too openhanded to stand up straight. He had a surly, sideways glance, not unlike a bull's, and he moved with an awkward sulkiness.

"Greetings," he said, weakly and sullenly. He looked away from the girl with a fastidious grimace, just like a dandy who pretends to be worthless even though he might be the most noble match for a woman in the land. Emanating from him was a mild odor of brennivín. He was wearing high, double-soled boots, a soiled Spanish collar, a blue cloak with wide, ruffled sleeves, and a long, full peruke like the ones worn by ostentatious Danes, so high that he had to hold on to his feathered hat with one hand. Instead of bowing to the damsel and kissing her hand he pointed in the direction of the visitor and asked, in the same tone of voice as he had made his greeting:

"What old woman is this?"

The damsel stared into the distance with a look so cold that it seemed the light of day would never be able to penetrate and reveal the secrets of her heart. The cavalier went straight up to the shabby woman, shook the stock of his whip at her breast as she stood there leaning on her walking stick, and asked:

"Who are you, granny?"

"Do her no harm," said the magistrate's daughter. "She is speaking with me. I am speaking with her. As I said, old woman—even the queen of the Scots was beheaded. Powerful kings have been beheaded, along with their best friends. No man can save another from the ax. Every man must save himself from the ax, or else be beheaded. Magnús from Bræðratunga, give this woman a coin and show her out."

The cavalier said nothing, but took a coin from his purse and gave it to the woman, showed her out, and shut the door.

— 7 —

It was overcast in the morning on the day that Jón Hreggviðsson and the sorcerer were fished up from the pit at Bessastaðir, placed upon horseback, and transported to the assembly at Öxará. Later it started to rain. They arrived at their destination late in the evening, soaking wet. Special orders had been given concerning Jón Hreggviðsson, who had murdered the king's hangman and was therefore less to be trusted than other criminals. He was to be placed under personal guard and housed alone in a tent behind the regent's booth, whence he would be fed. He was shackled as soon as he arrived. Sitting upon a stone before the tent-flaps was a huge giant, with a clay pipe in his mouth and a brazier at his side. The brazier contained a few glowing embers that the giant tended carefully, making sure they did not burn out. He gave Jón Hreggviðsson a sideways glance, silently, then lit his pipe and smoked.

"Give me something to smoke," said Jón Hreggviðsson.

"No one gives me anything to smoke—I pay for my tobacco," said the guard.

"Sell it to me then."

"Where's your money?"

"You'll have a lamb after the roundup."

"Not likely—the only way I'd stick a pipe in your mouth would be for payment in cash," said the guard. "But I won't take back-payment from a beheaded man, as I am called Jón Jónsson."

Jón Hreggviðsson looked keenly at the man for some time, and laughed with a gleam in his eyes as his white teeth flashed and his chains rattled. Then he started singing.

On the next day the magistrate sits with the members of the court and the king's proxies at a rotting table in the decaying, leaky, and cold courthouse whence the bell had been taken the year before. Only two of these dignitaries were wearing good cloaks, the magistrate Eydalín and the regent from Bessastaðir, and the regent was the only man wearing a ruff. The rest were wearing scarves, and were clad in poorly tailored capotes or frayed doublets. One or two of the

bailiffs were pale and had soft hands, but most there had been colored dark red by hard weather; their hands were callused and scabby,
their knuckles blunt, their limbs crooked. All of their faces were ugly,
each in its own particular way. Some of them were tall and others
short; some had broad faces, others long; some were fair-haired, others dark-haired. It was a gathering of the most dissimilar of peoples,
yet they all shared the single distinguishing feature of their race: their
shoes were in terrible condition. Even Magistrate Eydalín himself, in
his new foreign cloak, was wearing old boots that were cracked,
stretched, and shrunken from neglect, badly soled and crusted with
dirt. Only the Danish regent was wearing lustrous topboots made
from soft, deep brown, newly tanned leather, the tops turned down
at the knees and the heels fitted with polished silver spurs. Standing
facing the country's grandees was a ragged man wearing a tattered
smock girded with a horsehair rope, his feet bare and black, with
small hands, chafed, swollen wrists, coal-dark hair and beard and an
ashen complexion, brown eyes, and a sharp, coarse manner.

The documents concerning his case that had been prepared in
Kjalardalur the previous autumn were now read to the court. In the
judgment rendered by the bailiff of the Þverá district, which Jón
Hreggviðsson wished now to appeal before the magistrate at the
Alþingi, the defendant had been sentenced to death; the judgment
was based upon the testimony of six men, the churchgoers from
Saurbær, who had examined the deceased, Sigurður Snorrason, in
the stream on the first Sunday of the winter. These men had sworn
oaths to the truth of their story: that the body of the hangman was
stiff when they came to it in the stream that runs eastward from the
farm Miðfell in the parish of Strönd in the Þverá district; that the
eyes, nostrils, and mouth were closed, but that the head was erect
and peculiarly rigid. Furthermore, it was attested that on the previous day, a short time before the deceased had flogged Jón Hreggviðsson at Kjalardalur, the latter had taunted and threatened the hangman,
though in somewhat vague terms, and had cursed him in the devil's
name and said that he would definitely get his due before he'd tied a
knot good enough for his last and fattest whore. Also described was
Monsieur Sívert Magnússen's sworn testimony that on the evening of

the murder, Jón Hreggviðsson and Sigurður Snorrason had gone a different direction than their companions as they rode away from Galtarholt into the darkness. Finally it was attested that Jón Hreggviðsson had roused the folk at Galtarholt just before daylight, riding Sigurður Snorrason's horse and wearing the hangman's hat upon his head. Twelve men had been summoned to the Kjalardalur assembly to give their opinions, under oath, as to whether Jón Hregg-viðsson was guilty or innocent of the death of Sigurður Snorrason, and the oath that they swore contained the following allegation: the oath-sayers considered the fact that Sigurður Snorrason's sense organs were closed as definitive proof of the work of a man, and that Jón Hregg-viðsson more than anyone else was the man responsible.

The magistrate sat there in his hat and peruke, bloodshot-eyed and slightly bleary, suppressing a yawn as he asked the accused whether he had anything to add to the statements that he had pre-viously made at Kjalardalur. Jón Hreggviðsson reiterated that he couldn't recollect any of the deeds sworn against him, neither the threats and taunts made against Sigurður Snorrason before the flog-ging nor their riding off together away from the other men out into the darkness. The only thing he remembered about the night ride was that the travelers had wound up in a wide bog in the dark-ness, and that he, Jón Hreggviðsson, had played a substantial part in dragging Monsieur Sívert Magnússen up from a peat-pit, into which this honorable personage and pillar of the district had fallen, down amongst the rotten dogs—the defendant proclaimed this rescue oper-ation a verifiable success. After he, Jón Hreggviðsson, had finished rescuing this precious man's life, he had intended to try to mount his nag, and the last thing he remembered was that the mare had started kicking, besides the fact that she'd grown unreasonably larger in the still of the night and looked well-nigh unclimbable, so he was not entirely sure whether he'd ever actually mounted her. He remembered nothing more about his traveling companions either: they'd all dis-appeared by the time the story reached this point. In all faith, he thought that he'd then simply dropped down and fallen asleep. When he awoke the first glimmer of dawn shone faintly in the sky. He stood up and saw some rag or other lying in the grass and picked it up; it was Sigurður Snorrason's cap, and he placed it on his head because he'd lost his own. A short distance away a four-footed beast loomed into view; he walked over and discovered it was the hangman's horse, so he rode it to Galtarholt. Jón Hreggviðsson concluded by proclaiming this to be the long and short of what he could recollect concerning the events of that night: anything else that supposedly occurred that night was above and beyond his reckoning. "I call as witness," said he, "the Lord who created my soul and my body and who pressed these two things together into one—"

"No, no, no, Jón Hreggviðsson!" interrupted Magistrate Eydalín. "You have no right to call upon the Lord here."

Then he ordered that the prisoner be removed.

After the guard had refettered Jón Hreggviðsson, he sat down upon the stone before the tent-flaps, stoked the embers in the brazier, and lit his pipe.

"Stick that pipe just once in my trap, you devil, and you'll have a sheep," said Jón Hreggviðsson.

"Where's this sheep?" asked the man.

"It's up on a mountain," said Jón Hreggviðsson. "I'll give you a deed."

"Where's the scribe?"

"Bring me a piece of paper and I'll scribble it out," said Jón Hreggviðsson.

"Am I supposed to chase the creature up around the mountains with the deed?"

"What is it you want?" asked Jón Hreggviðsson.

"I make no deals for anything but cash," said the guard—"least of all with dead men. As I am called Jón Jónsson. And you shut up."

"We should speak more politely to each other," said Jón Hreggviðsson.

"I'm finished speaking," said the guard.

"You should be called Dog Dogsson," said Jón Hreggviðsson.

This was on the last day of the Alþingi.

In the evening judgments were handed down and around midnight Jón Hreggviðsson was dragged back into court to hear the verdict in his case.

The verdict stated that after the most thorough examination and attestation, and witnessing the fact that credible men had publicized the various villainous affairs of Jón Hreggviðsson, it was the unanimous decision of the magistrate and the members of the court, invoking the mercy of the Holy Spirit, that Jón Hreggviðsson was ascertainably a killer and the murderer of the late Sigurður Snorrason. The court confirmed the bailiff's judgment in all items; the sentence was to be implemented duly and immediately.

But because it was late and the men were worn-out after the day's activity, the magistrate bade that the beheading be postponed until morning, and suggested that the executioner and his assistants use the night to bring their instruments into peak condition. Jón Hreggviðsson was led back to his tent behind the regent's booth and placed in chains for his final night. The guard Jón Jónsson sat down in the entrance, with his extremely broad backside inside the tent, and lit his pipe.

The whites of Jón Hreggviðsson's eyes were uncharacteristically red and he uttered a few expletives through his beard, but the guard paid no attention.

Finally the farmer could no longer keep his thoughts to himself and said annoyedly:

"What sort of manners are they to tell a man you're going to behead him and then to give him no tobacco?"

"Say your prayers and go to sleep," said the guard. "The priest'll be here at daybreak."

The dead man did not answer and there was a long silence, broken only by the sound of an ax falling rhythmically upon a block of wood; the strokes echoed with a metallic hollowness off the ravine wall in the still of the night.

"What's that hammering?" said Jón Hreggviðsson.

"A sorcerer from the west is to be burned tomorrow morning," said the guard. "They're chopping up the brushwood."

There was silence again for a short time.

"You'll have my early-bearing cow for tobacco," said Jón Hreggviðsson.

"Aw, what buzzing is this?" said Jón Jónsson. "Then what—what do you, a man as good as dead, plan to do with tobacco?"

"You'll have everything I own, man," said Jón Hreggviðsson. "Go get some paper and I'll scribble out my will."

"Everyone says you're maladjusted," said Jón Jónsson. "And underhanded."

"I've got a daughter," said Jón Hreggviðsson. "I've got a young daughter."

"It's all the same to me even if you're as shrewd as they say—you won't be able to trick me," said Jón Jónsson.

"She's got sparkling eyes," said Jón Hreggviðsson. "Bowl-shaped. And a high bosom. Jón Hreggviðsson of Rein swears by his landlord Christ as his final wish and commandment that she'll marry you, Jón Jónsson."

"What sort of tobacco is it you're asking for?" said the guard reluctantly, turning around in his seat and peering with one eye into the tent. "Huh?"

"I ask, to be sure, for the one kind of tobacco that suits a man condemned to death," said Jón Hreggviðsson. "That tobacco you alone can deliver me the way things stand now."

"Then it's I who'll be beheaded," said the guard. "And what are the chances that the girl will say yes even if I do get away?"

"If she sees a letter from me she'll say yes no matter what I ask for," said Jón Hreggviðsson. "She loves and respects her father above everything else."

"You think my wretch of a wife out in Kjós isn't already enough for me?" said the guard.

"I'll deal fully with her this very night," said Jón Hreggviðsson. "Don't you worry about her."

"Are you threatening to kill my wife, you bastard?" said the guard. "And to put me on the chopping block! Your offers are mirages like everything else that comes from the devil. It's true mercy that a crook like you won't be allowed to grow old!"

— 8 —

A small, sturdy man wearing a priest's outfit stands in the doorway. He is dark-skinned, with black eyebrows and red lips, and he is accustomed to moving slowly. He is somewhat afraid of the light.

"Good day, mademoiselle"—he is also accustomed to speaking slowly and determinedly.

Her dense locks fall about her cheeks and shoulders. In the early morning the tranquil azure of her eyes reminds one of being far from home.

"The archpriest! And I've only just woken and haven't had the least chance to put on my wig."

"I apologize, mademoiselle. Put it on. I shall look away. Mademoiselle must not be frightened."

She made no rush to put on her wig.

"Am I usually frightened of the archpriest?"

"Mademoiselle's eyes look unacquaintedly and aloofly at things that occur in time. It is true—the things that occur in time are coarse. And mademoiselle's eyes have no home in time."

"Then am I dead, my dear Reverend Sigurður?"

"Some have received the gift of eternal life here on earth, mademoiselle."

"Monsieur on the other hand has his home in his cathedral, a man through and through—but for his eyes, perhaps; he forgives! The first time I came here to Skálholt and heard monsieur preach, when I was a child, it seemed to me as if one of the carved and painted apostles on the pulpit had come to life and was speaking. Your dear departed wife gave me a box of honey. Is it true that you sing the *Ave Maria* in secret, Reverend Sigurður?"

"Credo in unum Deum, mademoiselle."*

"Oh, do you really want to squander your Latin on a little girl? And yet, Reverend Sigurður—I can conjugate 'amo' in most modi and tempora."*

"I have often praised God for the sanctity and beauty of the blossoms in this land," said the archpriest. "When men cease to rise from the dust, the blossoms give us the promise of eternal life."

"What are you talking about?"

"Let us take the forget-me-not. The forget-me-not is slender, but it has received the natural gift of charity, and because of this its eyes are beautiful. When you came to Skálholt for the first time—"

"I don't like slender blossoms—I want huge flowers thick with perfume," interrupted the girl, but he paid no attention and continued.

"When you and your sister, that great woman who was to take charge of the keys to the bishopric, came here for the first time, you were only a little maiden—and it was as if the forget-me-not had come here itself, clad in the likeness of a human."

"Yes, you are a famous poet, Reverend Sigurður," said the girl. "But you seem to have forgotten that the forget-me-not has another name—cat's eyes."

"I come to you in the brightness of dawn and greet you in the name of Jesus and say: Forget-me-not! Other guests come to you at other times with other thoughts and whisper in your ears other words."

After saying this he finally looked up at the girl. His eyes were dark and fervent, and his mouth trembled slightly.

She looked him in the eye and asked coldly: "What do you mean?"

He said: "I am your suitor, awaiting your answer. You have permitted me to be called as such."

"Indeed," she said. "In Jesus' name? Yes, perhaps. Yes, hm."

"You are a young girl, Snæfríður, only seventeen years old. The audacity of youth is the most incredible thing on earth—next to the meekness of youth. I am a thirty-eight-year-old man."

"Yes, Reverend Sigurður, I know that you are an experienced man, a gifted man, a learned man, and a widower. I also respect you very much. But whoever comes and whenever they come and whatever they say, you must know that I love only one man."

"Your suitor is not making enquiries. He also knows most assuredly that there is only one man hewn from Icelandic stone who befits you. The one who loves you best cannot wish for you anyone better than him. When he comes I cease to exist. I vanish. But while he is away, heed me well, mademoiselle Snæfríður—I listen, I wait, I watch. I might perhaps hear hoofbeats in the night—"

"I cannot bear innuendo. What do you mean?"

"In as few words as possible, mademoiselle, I am a man in love."

"Indeed—I have never been able to imagine anything so ridiculous as an archpriest in love; no—do me no ill though I do the same to you. And promise me that you won't mention this again until all of the ships have come, Reverend Sigurður."

"All of the ships have come."

"No no no, Reverend Sigurður, you can't say that. The Bakkaship has come, but there may still be ships in the east, or the west, that haven't come. And no one knows yet who might be on those ships."

"This man's presence could never be concealed, no matter where he steps onto land. And if you truly believed that he has come then you would not have received another guest."

She stood up, stamped her feet on the floor before him, and said:

"If I'm a whore then I demand that you have me drowned in Öxará!"

"God forgive mademoiselle for giving voice to a word so vile that by pronouncing it just once she stains the same veil by which heavenly grace covers her virginity."

"What have my guests to do with this? You sneak here in the morning in Jesus' name. Others come riding at evening in the devil's name. I'm human. Testify against me and have me drowned, if you dare!"—and she stamped again before him.

"Beloved child," he said, extending his hand. "I know that you are not angry with me. You are speaking to your own conscience."

"I love one man," she said, "and you know it; I love him while awake; while sleeping; living; dead; love him. And if I can't have him then God doesn't exist, Reverend Sigurður; and you, the archpriest, don't exist, nor does the bishop, nor my father, nor Jesus Christ; nothing—except for evil. Dear God almighty, help me."

She cast herself down onto her divan and pressed her face into her hands, icy in her despair. She looked up again with dry eyes at the archpriest and said in a low voice, "Forgive me."

He raised his closed eyes to heaven and prayed tearfully to God, stroking her hair at the same time; she leaned up against him, her mind elsewhere, then she stood up and walked away from him, picked up her wig, and put it on. He continued to pray for her, piously and consolingly.

"By the way," she said coldly, from somewhere within her sleep-lessness, as a certain trifle crossed her mind. "Does a man named Jón Hreggviðsson exist?"

"Jón Hreggviðsson," repeated the archpriest, opening his eyes. "Does mademoiselle speak the name of such a man?"

"Oh, then he exists," said the damsel. "I thought I'd dreamed him. What has he done?"

"Why does mademoiselle want me to speak with her concerning that miserable scoundrel? I know nothing more than that he was sentenced to execution out west in Borgarfjörður in the fall, for having murdered the hangman from Bessastaðir one night, and that the verdict will soon be confirmed at the Alþingi."

She burst out laughing and the archpriest looked at her in surprise, but when he questioned her she answered only that she found it ridiculous that His Royal Majesty's hangman should be murdered by an out-and-out scoundrel—"It seems to me as if I, a vulgar sinner, am to preach to the archpriest! Or perhaps it's no trouble to kill a man?" she asked.

The archpriest did not join in her laughter, not because her suggestion offended him, but rather because a poor cleric raised strongly in the theological doctrines concerning the freedom of the human will in choosing between good and evil could not understand the frivolous viewpoint of a young maiden, sprung of the seed of blossoms, to whom mortal deeds appeared to operate independent of law, and who considered not only sins, but also deadly crimes, as ridiculous, and even asked whether it was difficult to commit them.

She stopped listening to him and went back to work tidying up her bower, with a look of earnestness. Finally she said, distractedly:

"I've changed my mind. There's nothing left to wait for here. Ask the steward to find me a good horse. I'm bored. I'm going west to Dalir, home."

— 9 —

"Child," says the magistrate Eydalín. He and his drinking companions look up in amazement as the damsel Snæfríður, wearing a riding frock, steps quickly in through the doorway of the magistrate's booth at the Alþingi on a bright night at the close of the assembly. They all wait silently. "Welcome, child—and what brings you here? What has happened?"

He stands up and walks toward her, somewhat hesitant in his stride, and greets her with a kiss.

"What has happened, good child?"

"Where's my sister Jórunn?"

"The bishop and his wife have ridden west to your mother's. They delivered your greeting, and said that you would remain at Skálholt this summer. They said that they had left you under the care of the schoolmaster and his wife. What has happened?"

"Happened? Why do you ask me this thrice in one breath, father? If something had happened then I wouldn't be here. But nothing has happened and that's why I'm here. Why can't I ride to the assembly? Hallgerður Langbrók* rode to the assembly."

"Hallgerður Langbrók? I do not understand you, child."

"Aren't I human, father?"

"You know that your mother does not care much for independent-minded girls."

"Who knows?—maybe I've changed my mind. Who knows but that certain things are afoot?"

"What things are afoot?"

"—or, phrased more correctly, are not afoot. Who knows—maybe I suddenly wanted to go home—to my father. I'm just a child. Or maybe I'm not a child?"

"Child, where am I to find a place for you? There is no lodging here for women. The assembly is at an end, and these gentlemen and I will sit here tonight and keep watch until dawn, when we must stand witness to the execution of several criminals. Immediately afterward I will ride south to Bessastaðir. What do you think your mother would say—"

A cavalier in topboots with spurs, a long goatee and a peruke that hung down to his ruff, girded with a sword, rose to his feet with the festive and self-contented air of an adequately drunken man, stepped forward, struck his heels together German-style, bowed deeply to the damsel, gripped her hand and raised it to his lips, then addressed her in German. Since he would be sitting here, he said, at the invitation of his Lordship the father of his gracious lady, until the time came for them to attend to their business in the morning, his gracious lady was heartily welcome to make his pavilion and everything she might find therein her own, and he would immediately wake his cook and his page to serve her. He himself, he said, the king's regent at Bessastaðir, was, to be sure, the most humble of all the servants of his lady. She watched him with a smile, and he proclaimed that the night did honor to her eyes and, bowing before her, kissed her hand again.

"I want to see Drekkingarhylur,"* said the girl as she and her father stepped out to go to the regent's booth. Her father said that it was too much trouble to go out of their way, but she pleaded urgently and when he asked why, she answered that she'd long been pining to see the place where condemned women were customarily drowned. In the end she got her way. They could hear a hammering sound from somewhere within the ravine and the cliffs lent a musical murmur to the noise. When they reached the pool the girl said:

"No, look, there's gold at the bottom. Look at how it shines."

"That is the moon," said her father.

She said: "Would I be drowned here if I were a condemned woman?"

"Do not speak vainly of justice, child," he said.

"Is God not merciful?" she asked.

"Yes, good child: in the same way as the moon in Drekkingarhylur," said the magistrate. "Now let us leave this place."

"Show me the gallows, father," she said.

"Such things are not for young maidens," he said. "And I must not be away from my guests for too long."

"Oh, papa," she said whiningly, as she took him by the arm and leaned up against him. "I do so want to see men killed."

"Ah, then you have never left your room in Skálholt, my poor child?" he said.

"Oh, please say that you'll let me see men killed, papa dear," whined the girl. "Or maybe you don't love me?"

He consented to take her to see the gallows on the condition that she go straight to bed afterward. They walked through Almannagjá in the still of night, stopping at an open space as green as a homefield and encircled by overhanging rock walls. A spar had been placed over a cleft in one wall, with a removable platform beneath. Two nooses of newly spun wool were coiled around the spar.

"Goodness, these are beautiful cords," said the girl. "One hears so often that Iceland is in need of cord. Who's going to be hung?"

"Ah—two outlaws," said the magistrate.

"Did you sentence them?" she asked.

"They were sentenced in district court. The Alþingi confirmed the sentences."

"And what is that log for, lying there on the grass?"

"Log?" said the magistrate. "That is no log. That is a chopping block, my child."

"Who's going to be beheaded?"

"Ah—a knave from Skagi."

"Not the one who killed the hangman?" asked the girl. "I've always thought that's such a funny story."

"What did you learn in Skálholt this winter, child?" asked the magistrate.

"Amo, amas, amat," she said. "Amamus, amatis, amant.* And what strokes are these, so regular and so heavy, echoing so strangely in the silence?"

"Are you still unable to fix your mind on any one thing, child?" he said. "Learned men carry on serious discussions, and the same goes for well-bred women. They're cutting up brushwood."

"Now, what were we talking about?" she said. "Weren't we talking about murder?"

"What nonsense is this?" he said. "We were discussing what you learned in Skálholt."

"Would you have ordered my execution, papa, if I had killed the hangman?" asked the girl.

"The magistrate's daughter is not a killer," said he.

"No, but she might commit adultery."

The magistrate stopped in his tracks and stared at his daughter. The effects of the brennivín had worn off him in the presence of this unfamiliar young woman. He looked her over: she was much too thin, with the eyes of a seven-year-old child and glimmering locks. He started to say something, but stopped.

"Why don't you answer me?" she said.

"There exist young girls who cause everything around them to become unstable—air, earth, and water," he said, and he tried to smile.

"That's because they have the fire, papa," she said immediately. "The fire alone."

"Quiet," said her father. "No more nonsense!"

"I won't keep quiet until you answer me, father," she said.

They walked together silently for a few steps and he cleared his throat.

"A naive act of adultery, my child," he said, in a staid, bureaucratic tone of voice, "is a matter which people must take up first and foremost with their consciences. On the other hand, such an act is often the precursor and cause of other crimes. But magistrate's daughters do not commit such crimes."

"But if they did, then the magistrates, their fathers, would work quickly to exculpate them."

"Justice exculpates no one."

"Then you wouldn't exculpate me, father?"

"I do not understand what you are getting at, child. I am not in the business of exculpation."

"Would you demand that I perjure myself, like Bishop Brynjólfur* did of his daughter?"

"Bishop Brynjólfur's mistake was that he did not estimate his daughter any higher than a common girl. Such things do not occur amongst people of our standing—"

"—even though they occur," added the girl.

"Yes, my child," he said. "Even though they occur. Your lineage is the finest in the country. You and your sister are the only individuals in Iceland who have a better lineage than I."

"Bishop Brynjólfur misunderstood justice then," said the girl. "He thought it applied to everyone."

"Beware of the poet's tongue that you inherit from your mother's side of the family," said the magistrate.

"Father," she said. "I can't walk alone—let me lean against you."

They headed toward the regent's booth, he broad-shouldered and ruddy in his flowing cloak, his small white aristocrat's hands sticking out from the sleeves, she short-stepped and slender, in her riding frock with its soft hood, holding on to his arm and stooping forward; at their sides rose the precipitous cliff walls.

"The copse you see there," he said, "is named Bláskógar or Bláskóga-heiði. The mountain just beyond the copse is called Hrafnabjörg and is said to have a beautiful shadow. Then come other peaks. Farthest away you see a low heap, like a shadowy image. That is Skjaldbreiður, which is actually the highest of all the peaks—much higher than Botnssúlur, towering there to the west of Ármannsfell. The reason for its—"

"Oh, father," said the girl.

"What is wrong, good child?"

"These cliffs frighten me."

"Oh, yes, I forgot to tell you that the place where we are standing is called Almannagjá."

"Why is there such an awful silence?"

"Silence? Do you not hear me speaking to you, child?"

"No."

"I was saying, child, that when a man regards the mountain Botnssúlur, it appears to be frightfully high only because it is close by. But if he then looks toward Skjaldbreiður—"

"Father, haven't you received any letters?"

"Letters? I have received hundreds of letters."

"And none with greetings for me?"

"Hm, yes, you are absolutely right. The assessor Arnæus sent his regards to your mother and to you two sisters."

"But nothing for me?"

"He asked me to make enquiries concerning whether a page from any of Helgafell cloister's old books, which had been torn apart and thrown away, might not have been saved by some chance."

"And he said nothing else?"

"He said that the books were worth more than all of the most fertile farmland in Breiðafjörður."

"Didn't he say anything about himself? Why did he decide not to come on the Bakkaship, like he said he would in the fall?"

"He mentioned unfavorable prospects and various other curae."*

"Curae? Him?"

"I have been informed by a reliable source that his collection of handwritten as well as printed books concerning the ancient history of Norway and Iceland is in danger. On the one hand, the books are in danger of damage from poor storage conditions, and on the other, the assessor has accumulated so much debt that it seems imminent that he will lose them."

She gave her father's arm an impatient tug and said: "Yes, but he's a friend of the king."

"As far as that goes, we have occasionally witnessed examples of kings' friends being stripped of their rank and thrown into debtor's prison. No one has as many enemies as a friend of a king."

She released her father's arm and stood erect and unsupported on the path, facing her father, and lifted her eyes to meet his.

"Father," she said. "Can't we help him?"

"Come, good child," he said. "It is time that I returned to my guests."

"I own farms," she said.

"Yes, you and your sister were given several small farms as tooth-money," he said, and he took her by the arm again and continued on.

"Can't I sell them?" she asked.

"Although an Icelander might think it an achievement to gain possession of a mediocre farm, a few hundreds of land* is of little worth in foreign countries, good child," said the magistrate. "The gemstone upon the ring of a rich count in Copenhagen is worth more than an entire district in Iceland. I could collect rent for many years and still not have enough to pay for this new cloak. We Icelanders are prohibited from trading or sailing and because of this we have nothing. We are not just oppressed—we are a folk in danger of our lives."

"Arnas has given up everything he owns collecting old books so that the name of Iceland might be saved even if we perish. Are we then supposed to stand by and watch as he's locked away in debtor's prison in a foreign country for the name of Iceland?"

"Love for one's neighbors is a beautiful doctrine, good child. And a true one. But when one's life is in danger, the general rule is that each man helps himself."

"Then we can do nothing?"

"What matters most to us, my child, is that the king is my friend," said the magistrate. "There are many people who envy me, who importune the counts and slander me in the hope of preventing me from obtaining the king's rescript for the office of magistrate, which is, as we know, called the most important office in Iceland, though it is nothing but a trifle compared to the office of floor sweeper in the Chancery, especially if that man can claim to be descended from German pirates or coxcombs."

"What good is a rescript, father?"

"Having the king's rescript for such an office provides numerous privileges. We can own more and larger farms. You become an even better match for a man. Good men will be asking for your hand."

"No, father. Trolls will take me; monsters in the shape of beautiful animals that I would like to hold and pet will lure me into the forest and tear me apart in a cave. Have you forgotten all of the fairy tales you told me?"

"That is not a fairy tale, it is a wicked dream," he said. "By the way, your sister told me something about you, something that I am sure will sadden your mother."

"Really."

"She said that a distinguished man had asked for your hand this winter and that you had shown little interest in his offer."

"The archpriest," said the girl, and she laughed coldly.

"He is descended from some of the finest men in Iceland. He is an exceptionally learned man and a poet, and he is wealthy and virtuous. I have no idea what sort of a match you have in mind if you cannot consider him good enough for you."

"Arnas Arnæus is the most splendid of all Icelanders," said the damsel Snæfríður. "Everyone is agreed on that. A woman who has met a splendid man finds a good man ludicrous."

"What do you know about a woman's feelings, child?" said the magistrate.

"Rather the worst than the next-best," said the girl.

— **10** —

The regent's booth had an inner lining of brightly colored cloth, a clean wooden floor, a bedcloset, a table, benches, and two armchairs. A statuette of our Most Gracious Majesty on horseback stood upon a shelf. Near the ravine walls behind the booth were two tents. One was large and elaborate, and two Danish-speaking servants emerged from this tent. The other was closer beneath the rocks, small and soiled, made of brown wadmal; sitting outside it was a ruffian who wore hide socks and smoked a pipe.

The regent had sent orders to his servants to prepare lodging for the magistrate's daughter, and they brought her roasted meat and wine, but the magistrate bade his daughter good night and left for his own booth to attend to his guests. The damsel's complexion was pale as she stood in the doorway of the booth while the servants set the table, and she looked to the east, at the clouds that shone gold with the light of the unrisen sun. She regarded in turn the black walls of the ravine and the murmuring river, the mountains, the copse, and the lake.

"Why is this huge man sitting outside this little tent?" she asked.

They said, "That's the guard."

"What guard?" she said.

"Housed in the tent is a shackled evildoer we brought with us from Bessastaðir—he's going to be beheaded in the morning, praise God."

"Oh, I would like to see him," said the damsel, and her face brightened. "I would really like to see a man who is going to be beheaded in the morning."

"Our lady is joking," they said. "Our lady would be frightened. This is that black devil Joen Regvidsen, who stole some cord, cursed His Majesty, and killed the king's hangman."

"Go to the regent," she said to one of the servants, "and tell him that I'm frightened. Tell him from me that I want a guard posted here at the entrance while I sleep."

She nibbled at the meat like a little bird and ate a few bites of porridge and drank three sips of wine, then spent some time cleaning her fingers and cooling off her forehead with water from a silver bowl. She adjusted her hair and dabbed on perfume that she kept in a small box. The servant came back with the message that Joen Joensen would protect the gracious lady while she slept.

"I want him to sit at my doorstep," she said.

They called to the guard and told him to stand watch over the gracious lady, who intended to go to sleep.

"But the murderer," he said.

"Which is more important, one black murderer or the honor of our gracious lady?" they said.

The man stood up ponderously and moved the brazier to the damsel's doorway, sat down on the stone step, and continued to smoke. He ordered the servants to go to bed.

"Are you Icelandic?" she asked the guard.

"Huh?" he said. "I'm from Kjós."

"Kjós," said the girl. "What's that?"

"A place called Kjós," he said.

"Are you armed?" she said.

"Huh?" he said. "Puh."

"What are you going to do if someone attacks me?" she said.

He showed her his pawlike hands, first the backs and then the palms, then he clenched his fists and shook them at her, spat through his teeth, and continued to smoke.

She went in and closed the door behind her. Everything was silent but for the murmur of Öxará coalescent with the calm and rhythmic ax-strokes of the placid and faithful man who was chopping up the brushwood.

In a short time, however, when everything was as still as could be, the magistrate's daughter winds her way out of the regent's bed, lifts the door from its posts, and peeks out. The guard was still sitting on her doorstep, smoking.

"I was making sure that you hadn't double-crossed me," she said quietly.

"Huh?" he said. "Who?"

"You're my man," she said.

"Go to sleep," he said.

"Why are you so impolite to me?" she said. "Don't you know who I am?"

"Puh," he said. "All flesh is dust."

He gave a long yawn.

"Listen, Strong Jón," she said. "What's on your mind?"

"I'm not called Strong Jón," he said.

"Wouldn't you like to come in and sit down at my bedside?" said the damsel.

"Who? Me?"

He twisted his head around very slowly and, with one eye half-closed, stared at her through the tobacco smoke, then spat in a long arc. "Aw, damn it," he added, and he stuck his pipe back in his mouth.

"Don't you need tobacco?" she asked.

"Tobacco? Me? No."

"What do you need?" she asked.

"Pipes," he said.

"What kind of pipes?"

"Clay pipes," he said.

"I don't have any clay," she said.

He said nothing.

"On the other hand, I do have silver," she said.

"Aha," he said.

"You're not much of a talker, are you?" she said.

"Go to sleep now, good madam."

"I'm not a madam," she said. "I'm a damsel. I have gold."

"Oh, yes?" he said. "You don't say. Huh?"

He turned his head stiffly and looked at her again.

"You're my man," she said. "Do you want gold?"

"No," he said.

"Why not?"

"I'd be hanged," he said.

"But silver?"

"If it were minted, maybe. No one would know the difference."

She took a silver coin from her purse and gave it to him. "Go to the tent at the foot of the cliff," she said, "and release the man sitting there in chains."

"Huh?" he said. "The man? What man? Jón Hreggviðsson? No."

"Do you want more silver?" she asked.

He spat.

"We're letting him go," she said, and she handed him more silver, then grabbed him by the armpits and forced him to stand up.

"I'll be beheaded," he said.

"If you're found guilty," she said, "then remember that I'm the magistrate's daughter."

"Puh," he said, and he looked down into his pipe: it had gone out.

She half-dragged the man behind her, untied the tent-flaps, and peeked in. Jón Hreggviðsson was lying there asleep in tattered clothing, grimy from head to toe, his face upon the bare ground. His hands were behind his back, in chains bolted to the fetters around his ankles. His shoulders trembled slightly with each breath. At his side was a small bucket containing leftover scraps of food. The girl came all the way into the tent and she looked the foul man over, at how calmly he slept with his swollen wrists and his scraped and fettered ankles, his thick hair and beard tangled into a shabby shock.

"So he's sleeping," whispered the girl.

It took the guard a few moments to squeeze his way through the tent's opening.

"Well now," he said, after finally dragging himself in. He had to kneel in order to avoid bumping his head against the top of the tent.

Jón Hreggviðsson didn't stir.

"I thought they stayed awake," said the girl.

"He has no soul," said Strong Jón.

"Wake him up," said the girl.

Strong Jón stood halfway up and kicked at the man's back so briskly that it was impossible that he wouldn't wake up. Jón Hreggviðsson's eyes shot open bewilderedly and he sprang up like a hook flying off a steel spring, but the iron ball chained to his feet jerked him back and he fell in a heap to the floor.

"Have you come to take me to the chopping block, you devil?" said Jón Hreggviðsson. "What does this woman want?"

"Quiet," said the girl, putting a finger to her lips. She ordered the guard to release the farmer, and he took his keys from his purse and unlocked the irons. The man was free, but he remained crouched there on his knees, cursing, with his hands behind his back.

"Stand up, man," said the girl to the prisoner. And to the guard: "Get out of here."

When she was alone with the dead man she pulled the golden ring from her finger and gave it to him. It was shaped like a snake biting its own tail.

"Get aboard a dogger to Holland," she said. "Then go to Copenhagen, find Arnas Arnæus the friend of the king and ask him to rectify your situation for my sake. If he should think that you have stolen this ring, than give him the greetings of the fair maiden; of the slender elf-body;—these words have not traveled widely. Tell him this, that if my lord can save the honor of Iceland, even if I am disgraced, his face shall still shine for this maiden."

She took a coin from her purse, gave it to the man, and left the tent.

Afterward all was quiet at Þingvellir by Öxará but for the murmur of the stream and the echo of ax-strokes from Brennugjá.*

— **11** —

Jón Hreggviðsson got to his feet and licked his wrists. He peered out through the tent-flaps but saw no one and heard nothing suspicious, so he went out. There was dew upon the grass. He kept glancing around—it was the time of year when night is inconvenient for criminals. A whimbrel sat upon a rock. The man climbed out of Almannagjá in a place where a landslide had fallen from the cliff walls, and he concealed himself for a moment in a crevice as he thought about what to do next. Then he started running.

He headed for the uninhabited land east of Súlur and afterward north to Uxahryggir, threading watercourses and gullies and keeping himself as far away as he could from the common routes. The man was good on his feet and didn't mind being cut by the stones and brushwood, because the dirt here was clean, unlike the offal on the floor of the black pit. He let his feet choose his course and allowed himself no other break than to throw himself down on his stomach at a spring and drink. Curious moorhens pursued him. The sun came up and shone on the man and the mountains.

He arrived around midmorning at a farm on the heath above Lundarreykjadalur and claimed that he was traveling with a pack-train from Skagafjörður. He said he was searching for two horses from the stock south in Kjalarnes that they'd lost up near Hall-bjarnarvörður. He was given a bowl of skyr* and sheep's milk. The old woman gave him tattered shoes. After he ate he set out again, first toward the inhabited areas, but as soon as he was out of sight of the farm he turned up the valley near Ok and climbed onto the glacier to cool off and take his bearings. From the crest of the glacier he could see all of the land to the north.

Midway between nones and midevening he found himself look-ing down at the parsonage of Húsafell, which sits nestled at the head of a valley just below the highlands, on the main route taken by trav-elers journeying through the uninhabited areas separating the coun-try's quarters.

The skyr at Vörðufell hadn't been enough for the farmer, and he was starting to feel hungry again. The traveler had reached the point where the lowlands gave way to the tremendous heaths that divide the southern half of the country from the north, Arnarvatnsheiði and Tvídægra, and he was without provision. He had no desire to show himself on the road to the parsonage, where he knew that tough, experienced men could be lying in wait for fugitives. He met a shep-herd boy and asked if any travelers had passed by on their way north from Kaldidalur, but the boy said that he hadn't seen anyone riding northward that day, and that they didn't expect any visitors from Kaldidalur until around midevening. The farmer calculated that since he'd set out so early and had taken the straightest line possible north-ward he still had quite a jump on the men from the assembly.

Housemaids were making a pile of brushwood and sheep dung behind a house, and Jón Hreggviðsson carried on with his story about the packtrain from Skagafjörður and losing the two horses

from Kjalarnes near Hallbjarnarvörður, even though he knew nothing about the latter except for its name. They ran to the farm and
told the priest that an outlaw had arrived. The priest, a giant of a
man for his age, was sitting in the loft composing a ballad about
Illugi Gríðarfóstri,* and now he laid aside his chalk, hitched up his
breeches, came singing down the hallway, and stepped out the door
of the farm.

"If you're from Skagafjörður then give us a poem that tells how
beer is quaffed and women seduced, and food shall be given you."

Jón Hreggviðsson sang:

> "Daylight is waning. Soon we shall raise
> Mead cups brightly glowing.
> Hail to you maiden, I sing your praise.
> Red blood's briskly flowing."

"Neither the tune nor the mood is Skagafirthian; in fact it sounds
to me like this is an introductory verse from the *Elder Ballad of Pontus*. It would probably have been better for you if its composer had
fallen into a peat-pit—but because you have met my challenge, you
shall have food no matter who you are."

Jón Hreggviðsson was invited into the sitting room, though he
made sure not to sit too far from the doorway. He was served moss-
mash, soured tripe, hardened codheads, moldy butter, and brown
shark meat. The priest sat in the loft and sang his ballad for his guest
in a frightful voice; it was all about troll-women with poetic names
like Pig-Headed Wrinkleskin, Saggy Socks, and Craggy Hussy, and
he sang the entire time that his guest was eating.

When the farmer was finished listening to the ballad and eating
the food he kissed the priest in thanks and said that he had to be
going.

"I'm going to take you out to the corner of the sheepfold, my
boy," said the priest, "to show you the rock where seven criminals
were forced to bow down before my grandfather and where I myself
quashed seventy-one devils."

He brought his guest out through the yard, locking the man's emaciated upper arm in his bullyish steel grip and pushing him forward. Two women were stretching out wool to dry upon the churchyard walls, one old, the other young, and a pantry-bitch slept on the path. The priest called out for the women to follow them eastward over the homefield wall.

"My mother is eighty-five and my daughter is fourteen," said the priest. "They're used to stirring the blood."

Both women looked vigorous but not in any overblown way.

East of the homefield stood a sheepfold of stone, shaped like a heart, divided in two with gates to the north and south. The surrounding landscape of high glaciers, brush-covered hillsides, and perennial gullies seemed to bow in repose to this place—it was as if the land had its home here. The fold extended northward from a huge turf-grown rock set in a southern gateway; this rock had, according to the priest, proven to be outstanding as both a chopping block for criminals and a tombstone for devils. Jón Hreggviðsson was relieved that there was no ax to be seen in the vicinity of the rock. On the other hand, there was another stone block lying in the field near the southern gate. The cleric called this boulder a slab and invited his guest to lift it up onto the end of the wall to show his gratitude for the hospitality that he had enjoyed on his travels.

Jón Hreggviðsson bent down to take hold of the rock, but since it was sea-beaten basalt and therefore difficult to grasp, he was unable to lift it off the ground, although he did manage to set it on edge and roll it forward a few paces. The female line of Húsafell stood stockstill a short distance away, their faces like stone as they watched the man. Finally the guest said that he really had to be going.

"Good mother," said the priest. "Will you carry this speck around the sheepfold, to show this boy, before he goes, that there are still women in Iceland?"

The old woman was broad-shouldered and extrusive, strong-looking with hair on her forehead and beneath her chin, her skin as gray and rough-complexioned as a bird's. She moved in to grab the rock, bowed down and bent her knees slightly, then heaved it first to her thighs and next to her chest. She set off around the fold with the rock in her outstretched arms, her pace steady and ever more measured as she walked. She put the boulder down calmly at the end of the wall. The guest swelled with so much anger at this sight that he forgot he was in a hurry, and he gripped the rock again and pushed harder, but as little happened as before. The daughter watched him with clear eyes and blue cheeks and a face an ell broad, just as the ancient sagas describe young troll-women. Then suddenly her stony expression broke and she laughed. The old woman, her grandmother, gave a tiny monotone bleat from somewhere deep inside. Jón Hreggviðsson stood up cursing.

"Little daughter," said the priest. "Show this man that there are still young maidens in Iceland, but don't run more than two or three times with this knucklebone around our little pen."

The girl bent to her task, and although she was lacking in height she was so well-grown down below that no stronger pillars of support could be found under another adolescent girl in all of Borgarfjörður. She grasped the rock and stood straight up, then laughed and leaped around the fold three times as if she were carrying nothing but a sack of wool, and finally set it down again at the end of the wall.

The priest said: "Go now under God's care, in that gray belt you wear, Jón Hreggviðsson from Rein. You've been fully punished in Húsafell."

When Jón Hreggviðsson was an old man, he said that he'd never in his life felt greater humiliation before God and men than at that moment. He ran off as fast as he could. The yapping pantry-bitch chased him as far north as the river.

—— 12 ——

He ran the whole day and all the next night and drank plenty of water, since Tvídægra contains the most lakes in all of Iceland. He continued to avoid the common routes, but tried to take the shortest path he could from Ok to the northern coast. The weather was calm, though the silence was broken at times by the loud screeching of swans; these vile creatures were all over the heath, sometimes in flocks larger than several flocks of sheep. The sun emerged late in the evening, and he ran and ran until his feet gave way. He hadn't noticed that he was tired but now he fell exhausted onto a lukewarm patch of reddish loam. He slept deeply and evenly the whole day, first facedown, though later rolling over to face the sky, as the sun continued to shine and the ground grew warm. He awoke when the sun was high in the sky. A flock of ravens had gathered around him and the birds were obviously preparing to peck out his eyes since they thought he was helpless or even dead. He was slightly fatigued but not thirsty; on the other hand he regretted not having eaten more shark meat in Húsafell. The heath hadn't grown any smaller while he slept.

He felt no more light-footed now than he had before he slept. Yesterday he'd looked over the entire heath, but now it seemed endless. The northern part of the country constantly moved farther away the farther he walked.

Suddenly three bearded men with creels full of trout rode up before him. The lead rider was a wealthy farmer from Borgarfjörður on his way back from a fishing trip on Arnarvatnsheiði. They dismounted and the man from Borgarfjörður asked Jón Hreggviðsson who he was and whether he had supernatural powers. At first his two servants didn't dare come any closer, but Jón Hreggviðsson wept and kissed all three of them. He said that he was a beggar from the north and was supposed to have been branded for thievery south in Biskupstungur, but had managed to escape. Tears streamed down his face as he wept and prayed aloud to God and begged the men to pity him in the name of the Holy Trinity. They gave him a bite to eat. After slaking his hunger he started reciting prayers of thanksgiving, but the farmer said:

"Aw, shut up, Jón Hreggviðsson."

Jón Hreggviðsson immediately stopped both crying and reciting prayers, looked up at the men, and asked "What?" in amazement.

"Do you think we Borgarfirthians don't recognize the people we whip?" asked the man. "Stop going on like that—others could hardly have borne themselves better."

The two servants had risen instinctively to their feet at this newest disclosure. Jón Hreggviðsson followed suit.

"It looks to me that you'd like to try him out, boys, is that right?" asked the farmer.

"Is that the one who killed the hangman from Bessastaðir?" they asked.

"It is," said the farmer. "He killed the king's hangman. Now you've got the chance to take revenge, boys."

They looked at each other. Finally one of them said:

"It wouldn't hurt the king to get himself a new hangman."

The other added: "And I'm not looking for the job."

The third one, the farmer himself, settled the matter formally like this: Because their meeting had taken place in the wilderness, where law and justice, in particular God's Ten Commandments, have no validity, it would be best if they all sat down and had a sip of brennivín. The men sat back down. Jón Hreggviðsson did the same. He was through crying and praying. Instead he looked down at his bare feet—the tattered shoes the woman had given him had worn away—and started to cleanse his cuts with spittle.

Rain clouds gathered to the north shortly after the men from Borgarfjörður left, but the day had been warm. In no time at all the wind whipped around him and a fog rolled in quickly from the north, like a pugnacious army on the march, glowing red throughout like smoke from burning coals, and then darkening until the sun was consumed and the man enclosed. The cloud was dense and so dark that he could hardly see anything. At first he continued on in the direction he thought the fog had come from, but he soon realized that it was standing still. When he ran for the third time into the same waymark, piled up on top of a low, flat rock, he got a good idea of the extent of his plight. He sat beneath the waymark to think the situation over.

He sat for a long time and twilight came over the heath. When he was thoroughly drenched he recited a verse from the *Elder Ballad of Pontus* and added an extra line: "The Bessastaðir lice on Hreggviðsson will freeze to death tonight," then he laughed, cursed, stood up and punched himself, sat back down, and pressed his back up against the waymark. He sat there again for a good long time before he thought he saw a rather large mound-shaped object moving slowly toward him over the heath, like a man riding upon a black horse. After watching it for a moment he stood up and stepped off the rock onto the peat, but only halfheartedly, since he wasn't feeling entirely too pleased with his journey. The closer the shapeless mass came, the larger it grew. Jón Hreggviðsson stood stock-still and thought about calling out to the approaching man, but as soon as he opened his mouth, foreboding gripped him and he said nothing—he stood silently upon the peat, openmouthed, peering through the fog. The heap continued to draw nearer and to grow larger, until it was close enough for him to make out its form through the fog: it was a troll-woman, coming for him. He couldn't tell whether this was the mother or the daughter of the cleric from Húsafell, but he was certain that she was from the same family. Her face was an ell broad and her teeth were about the same size. She was wearing short breeches, with huge pillars beneath them and loins like a horse that's been allowed to rest and eat well all summer in preparation for its work in the mountains in the fall. Her fists were clenched at her hips and her elbows stuck out, and the look she gave him could hardly be called cheerful. He was pretty sure that if he tried to run away from this woman, she would promptly drag him back, shove him down and break his back on a rock, tear off his limbs, and gnaw the flesh from his bones. And thus the saga of Jón Hreggviðsson would come to a close.

But as he stood there more strength and daring welled up inside him than he'd ever felt before. It was most like being overcome by a berserk frenzy, and he heard himself say these words:

"Because there are indeed women in Iceland," he said, "it will now be proven to you, you ugly wench, that there are also men in Iceland!"

In a flash he jumped at the monster and the fight began. The struggle was fierce and lengthy and both of them fought with everything they had. He discovered that although she completely overpowered him, she was neither as supple in her limbs nor as quick in her reactions. They drove each other around the heath, and the earth was torn up beneath their feet. The fight went on for most of the night, with hard shoves and heavy punches, scratching and clawing, until Jón Hreggviðsson got a good grip around Drilla's waist. He bent back, lifted her into the air, and threw her down onto the heath with a loud thump. He fell and landed on top of her, and the ogress wailed terribly in his ear and cursed him with these words:

"Now exploit the fallen, Jón Hreggviðsson, if you are a man!"

When he finally came to, a wind was blowing from the south, forcing the fog down off the heath. He could see Hrútafjörður, its long and narrow mouth opening into Húnaflói, and the mountains of Strandir looming blue against the horizon. He had a vague feeling that things would turn out better than they'd looked just a short time ago.

He didn't slacken his pace until he'd come as far north as Strandir; he raced equally over heaths and mountain tracks and lied about his name and business. No one said anything about Dutchmen until he reached Trékyllisvík.

No crime was more severely punished than the crime of trading with Dutch fishermen, which made it incredibly difficult to gain the trust of strangers engaged in such business. When Jón Hreggviðsson asked about the Dutch, people would naturally point at the tanned sails of the banned doggers lying off the coast, and when he explained what he was doing here in the north they said that his case looked pretty much hopeless; the Dutch, they said, never took on men as cargo, apart from the odd child that they bought from the natives for fosterage, as they called it—especially red-haired boys. It wasn't until the folk in Trékyllisvík knew for certain all the details of Jón Hreggviðsson's circumstances and had found out exactly what sort of hardened criminal he was that they thought about lending him any sort of assistance. Then one night when the doggers were close to shore one of the farmers rowed the dead man out in his boat to them. The skipper looked disapprovingly at this black-haired beggar who'd been reduced to such poor shape during his stay at Bessastaðir that he wouldn't even do for shark bait. When the man from Trékyllisvík made the skipper aware that Jón Hreggviðsson had murdered the Danish king's hangman it didn't take long for the news to spread over the entire ship. The sailors shouted happily and hugged Jón Hreggviðsson and kissed him and bade him welcome: the Danish king was in the habit of sending his warships up the coast to sink their ships at every opportunity, or else to seize them under suspicion of trade for profit, and because of this the doggermen hated this king most of all men.

They brought the man on board, gave him a line, and let him fish, though the stocky little ship was already well laden. Jón Hreggviðsson didn't understand a word of their language but when they handed him a tin full to the brim with food he bent over it eagerly and wasted no time emptying it. In the evening they came with a pailful of seawater and set it down in front of him, but since he thought they were making fun of him he took offense and kicked it over. They rushed at him, tied his hands and feet and tore off his clothes, cut off his hair and beard and rubbed something similar to tar onto his head, then poured seawater again and again over the naked man while they laughed and shouted, and two boys in sabots danced a ring around him while another blew on a flute. Jón Hreggviðsson admitted later that right about then he was convinced that it was all over for him. But after working him over like this for a while they untied him and handed him a cloth to dry himself off. Next they handed him underclothes, wadmal breeches, a sweater, and sabots, but no socks, and they stuck a wooden pipe in his mouth and let him smoke. He started singing the *Ballad of Pontus*.

On the next day Jón Hreggviðsson awoke to find the ocean's rim grazing the high summits of the mountains of home—they'd put out to sea. He cursed his country and bade the devil sink it.

Then he continued singing the *Ballad of Pontus*.

—— 13 ——

Rotterdam, on the Maas River, is a great market town, etched with canals that the Dutch call grachten. The canals are used as anchorage by huge numbers of fishermen and tradesmen, who enjoy the fact that commerce in Rotterdam is unregulated. The Dutch are free to travel in their ships across the seas and throughout the whole world, each as he pleases, some to buy wares, others to fish, and the whole country is ruled by a single magnificent duke. The harbor was full of ships being fitted out for sea; some were tarred and others stained, and there was scarcely a cockle that wasn't in what could be called the best of shape—it was obvious what sort of clever and thrifty men inhabited the place.

The skipper asked Jón Hreggviðsson what he was planning to do now that they'd arrived. He mentioned Copenhagen. They tried to make it clear to him with miming gestures that he'd be beheaded if he went there. He fell to his knees and wept and invoked the name of the Danish king and tried in this way to communicate to them that he wanted to gain an audience with His Most Gracious Majesty and plead for mercy. This they could not understand. They'd gotten along extremely well with him on board and wanted to take him with them on their next fishing trip to Iceland, and had hoped that he would quickly learn their language so that he could translate for them when they did business with the Icelanders. He, however, wouldn't budge.

They asked: "You killed the Danish king's hangman, didn't you?"
He said: "I didn't."

Then they felt that he'd cheated them: he'd come to them as the enemy of their enemy, the Danish king, and now he pretended to want to go meet with this sourpuss of a king. Some of them said that he should be dragged behind the ship's keel as ballast or else be forced to run the gamut, but they finally let the matter stand by threatening to kill him if he didn't leave immediately. He scurried onto land. He was relieved that they hadn't driven him right out of his pants, sabots, and sweater.

The streets of the town were laid out in peculiar curves not unlike the gaps in worm-chewed timber, and people's houses were packed closely together, the gables like belts of stone on mountain slopes and the gableheads like peaks. The streets most resembled maggot-infested cesspools, full of people, horses, and carriages, and at first it looked to him like everyone was on the run, as if the town were on fire. He was mesmerized by the horses: they were, next to whales, the largest creatures he had ever seen.

In Holland everyone was either a great aristocrat or at least arrogant, and one could go a long way without seeing anyone beneath the rank of bailiff, if one could reckon them by their clothing: in every direction he looked there were perukes and feathered hats, Spanish collars and Danish shoes, and cloaks so wide that he could have cut from one of them enough clothing for nearly all the destitute children in the parish of Akranes. Some were so stately that they drove in carved and glistening carriages of the most elegant craftsmanship, with windows and damask curtains. Throughout the streets drifted women of high degree, audaciously dressed, and slender ladies bedecked with all sorts of haughty ornamentation: ruffs hanging out over their shoulders and brimmed hats just as broad, wide pleated skirts and high-heeled shoes with golden clasps over the instep; they held their skirts up coyly, showing off their feet.

Jón Hreggviðsson had one silver coin in his purse when he arrived in Holland. Since day was drawing to a close he started to search for lodging. The lanterns that hung over every door cast a gleam onto the half-darkened, twilight streets, and in a narrow lane surrounded by antique houses that seemed to bend toward him he saw a woman standing in a doorway; she had a cheery complexion and a strong voice, and she asked the farmer the news. They started chatting and she invited him in. The way to her abode led through the house, along confined and florid corridors, then through a courtyard where silent cats sat arching their backs and pretending not to notice the others, each on its own doorstep. When they arrived at her room she invited the guest to sit beside her on the bed. She spoke to him excitedly, then took hold of his purse and felt about in it until she found the coin. At this she grew even more excited. She reached in again and again to feel the coin and told him how beautiful it was. Jón Hreggviðsson found the woman's mannerisms to be comparable to those of the women in Iceland who are considered best in most aspects, but at the same time she was extremely friendly, fleshly and flippant, and a bit musky in the bosom; he was convinced that she was the wife of a priest or a provost here in Rotterdam. Since she was sitting so close to him he thought she might be hard of hearing, so he raised his voice and tried to let her know that he was famished, but she placed a finger on his lips to indicate that he didn't need to speak so loudly. Then she went to her pantry and brought out cold roasted veal, bread and cheese, and some peculiar, bittersweet red fruits, along with a tankard of wine; he was sure that he'd never enjoyed a better meal. The woman ate with him, and then they had sex. The fishermen at sea had made sure that he did more than his share of the work, allowing him little time for rest, so now after all this luxury he grew incredibly drowsy and fell into a deep sleep alongside the woman in her bed. During the night two ruffians came in and started beating him, and when he jumped up they grabbed him and carried him out and threw him like carrion into the street; and thus disappeared Jón Hreggviðsson's coin.

He couldn't make heads or tails of Rotterdam by night. When it grew light he found a road leading out of the place and headed north, hoping that he would find the realm of the Danish king. The countryside reminded him of a potful of porridge: there wasn't a hill or even a hillock in sight—there were only church steeples and wind-mills afloat here and there. The fields were pasturable, however, and the farmers seemed to be doing well. He saw herds of grazing cows everywhere, hefty livestock, and noticed that the natives didn't seem to be too inclined toward sheep farming. Most of the farmhouses and barns were in excellent condition, with high timbered walls like the buildings at Bessastaðir, though there were quite a few crofters' cot-tages, either clustered together or scattered about, with dirt walls, straw roofs, and hens pecking around outside—this bird clucks like a swan and is unable to fly. Other monstrously sized birds gaggled before men's doors; they looked like swans but had shorter necks, and they were vicious, ruffling their feathers and attacking strangers with a great screech. He guessed that these were the birds the ancient poems and ballads called geese. The dogs here looked fairly danger-ous as well, but luckily most of them were chained. Haymaking and harvesting were in full swing, and the farmer thought it a great sight to see folk transporting their loads home on cattle-drawn wagons, though he did see a few people here and there carrying the hay on their backs. Seawater was diverged into deep lakes and canals throughout the whole land, causing it to resemble a large lung. The canals were filled with flat-bottomed cargo boats drawn by oxen or horses walking along the banks. Some of the boats had roofed houses with windows containing curtains and flowers, and chimneys poking up from the roofs, and smoke wafting up from the chimneys as the womenfolk cooked inside. The men sat out on deck and smoked tobacco while they urged on the beasts and steered the boat, and the children played, and sometimes fat, bare-legged girls could be seen, sunburned and radiant, as well as picturesque women plucking fowl. It looked to Jón Hreggviðsson like a very agreeable way of life.

The roads here were unlike those in Iceland; here they were made by men's hands, not horses' hooves, and the wagons drove easily along. He encountered wheeled contraptions of all different shapes and sizes, and great aristocrats riding comfortably in fluttering cloaks, and troops of soldiers with muskets and swords. Whenever he encountered a crossroads Jón Hreggviðsson automatically chose the road that seemed to go farthest north, but the day passed by here differently than in Iceland and in the end he lost track of time—and thereby lost his bearings.

They'd forgotten to throw his sabots out the door after him at the priest's wife's, but actually it didn't matter—he'd run barefoot over Iceland's hard ground, so why couldn't he do the same over Holland's soft ground? On the other hand, he'd been traveling for so long in the calm, dry air that he was starting to feel thirsty, but the muddy canals contained only saltwater. A man who was branding livestock in his farmyard gave him water, and a little later a woman at a well did the same, but both of them gave him fearful looks. He'd passed through so many crossroads by now that he no longer had any clue as to which road led to the realm of the Danish king. He sat down flat on the ground, brushed himself off, and looked questioningly at his feet. One scoundrel who came down the road shouted at him, and another cracked his whip over his head. Two middle-aged farmers drove by in a wagon full of cabbage-stalks, roots, and bundles of hay. Jón Hreggviðsson stood up, walked out in front of them, and asked:

"Where's Denmark?"

The men stopped and looked at him in surprise, but they obviously weren't familiar with the country he named.

"Denmark," he said, and he pointed at the road. "Denmark. Copenhagen."

The men looked at each other and shook their heads, having heard neither of the country nor the city.

"King Kristján," said Jón Hreggviðsson. "King Kristján."

The men looked at each other.

It suddenly occurred to Jón Hreggviðsson that he might have mis-remembered the name of His Most Gracious Majesty, so he corrected himself and said:

"King Friðrik. King Friðrik."

But the men hadn't heard of King Kristján or King Friðrik.

He availed himself of more wayfarers but very few of them answered him; most of them started walking faster or spurred on their horses when they saw this black-haired savage approaching. The few who did stop were entirely ignorant of Jón Hreggviðsson's king. Finally an impressive-looking gentleman came driving up, wearing an ample cassock, a ruff, a peruke, and a tall hat, his blue jowls hanging down around his collar and a prayer book resting upon his potbelly. If this man wasn't the bishop of Holland himself, then he was at least the provost of the district of Rotterdam, and Jón Hreggviðsson walked out in front of him and started weeping bitterly.

The wayfarer ordered his driver to halt and said a few reproachful but inobstinate words to Jón Hreggviðsson, and the stray traveler got the impression that he wanted to know who he was and why he was walking upon the roads of Holland.

"Iceland," said Jón Hreggviðsson, drying his tears and pointing at himself: "Iceland."

The man scratched himself delicately behind one ear, obviously having a difficult time making sense of this, but Jón Hreggviðsson continued.

"Iceland; Gunnar of Hlíðarendi," he said.

Suddenly the bishop's eyes widened and his face displayed more than a little panic. He gave Jón Hreggviðsson a consternated look and asked:

"Hekkenfeld?"

Jón Hreggviðsson didn't know what Hekkenfeld was and tried again with the name of the Danish king, Kristján.

"Christianus," repeated the honorable gentleman, and his manner relaxed considerably. He understood the matter thusly: although this miscreant had indeed come from Hekkenfeld, he was a Christian. "Jesus Christus," he added cheerfully, and he nodded his head toward the beggar.

Jón Hreggviðsson was for his own part so pleased with the fact that they'd hit on a name they both knew that he forgot everything he'd been planning to ask and resorted to repeating that name: the name of his landlord, Jesus Christ. Then he signed himself in the name of the Holy Trinity to show that he was a true farmer of Christ, and the gentleman took his purse from his belt, took out a little silver coin and gave it to Jón Hreggviðsson, then ordered his driver to continue.

Near sunset he strolled into a great farmyard that looked to him to be owned by hospitable folk, since it was teeming with wagons, horses, and drivers. Fat, well-dressed travelers walked out onto the flagstones and stroked their potbellies after their meal. Some smoked tobacco from long pipes. One member of a packtrain noticed Jón Hreggviðsson and started gaping at him, and then the others did the same. Jón Hreggviðsson said that he was an Icelander but no one understood. Little by little a mob of people gathered around him and chattered at him in different languages. Finally he decided to try out the words that had done so well for him with the nobleman on the road:

"Hekkenfeld. Jesus Christus."

Some of them thought he was a heretic and a blasphemer from Welschland* and one invoked Mary and Joseph and shook his fist at him.

Jón Hreggviðsson continued to repeat the words "Jesus Christus Hekkenfeld" and to make the sign of the cross.

More and more people kept joining the group: large-loined housemaids in short skirts and hoods, chefs with leather aprons, stout aristocrats with huge codpieces, ruffs, and ruffled sleeves, wearing feathered hats on top of their perukes—they pushed their way into the innermost ring to see what was happening but found nothing but a foreign beggar committing blasphemy. The meeting was concluded when a certain cavalier wearing a feathered hat, topboots, and a sword pushed his way through the throng, raised his whip, and started thrashing Jón Hreggviðsson, each lash smarter than the next. First he struck the man right across the face and then over the neck and shoulders, until he sunk to his knees and fell forward with his hands covering his face. The massive cavalier ordered the people to get back to work, and only a small portion of them kicked at the fallen man as they walked away. Jón Hreggviðsson came to his senses after the crowd dispersed, and he felt around to see if he was bleeding anywhere, but luckily he was just a bit bruised. Afterward he continued on his way.

In the evening a man and woman who owned a small field gave him something to eat. He gave their child the silver coin since the farmer refused to take it in payment. After eating his fill he went out to the hedge and lay down to go to sleep, since the weather was warm and looked as if it would stay that way. The Dutchman pointed him toward the loft of the cowshed, and the traveler took this as an admonition and slept in the straw during the night. Next morning he was woken by the screeching of a strange bird that flew back and forth before the window, letting its feet hang down as it flew—it had a nest up under a crossbeam. The Dutchman came down and Jón Hreggviðsson went out to the field with him and they harvested grain the whole day. Neither of them spared himself and the Dutchman let him know that he thought him a good man. Jón Hreggviðsson took it sorely that he couldn't tell the man the story of Gunnar of Hlíðarendi. He harvested grain for two days and on the third learned to use a flail on the threshing floor. He was given enough to eat but when he let them know that he needed money it turned out that the Dutchman was too poor to be able to keep a hired hand, so Jón Hreggviðsson decided to leave. The whole family cried at the thought of losing this two-footed beast of burden. Jón Hreggviðsson cried a bit in return for courtesy's sake, then kissed the people in farewell. The man gave him sabots, the woman gave him socks, and the child gave him a blue bead, as if it were a pearl.

Jón Hreggviðsson continued on in the same direction as before, but the gifts of these respectable people didn't really help to get him anywhere. Within two days he had to hire himself out again. This

time he worked for a powerful count who owned several districts in
the region, and who had in his service a thousand crofters, slaves and
half-slaves, servants, overseers, and viscounts, but who himself was
not to be seen—everyone said he lived in Spain. Jón Hreggviðsson
worked here for what was left of the summer at various jobs that
required a great deal of physical strength and persistence, and he
learned enough Dutch to be able to tell people how he'd come to be
traveling in this corner of the world. Everyone in Holland was familiar with Hekkenfeld in Iceland, under which burn the fires of Hell,
and they were very eager to hear tales of this mountain. They called
the man van Hekkenfeld.

Naturally, the invisible count in Spain cheated him of his pay. The
viscounts said he ought to praise God that they didn't hang him, but
several poor God-fearing men in Holland collected some small silver
and copper coins for van Hekkenfeld so that he could journey
onward to meet his king. When he left he stored his coins in one of
his socks, and he twisted the other one around his neck like a shepherd, so that he wouldn't lose his way. He tied the sabots together
and carried them over his shoulder, one in front and one in back, but
he had already lost the pearl.

—— 14 ——

AN ADVENTURE WITH THE GERMANS

It was well into winter by the time Jón Hreggviðsson reached Germany. He'd worked time and time again as a drudge for the Dutch in
order to support himself, but still had only barely managed to scrape
by. Although the Dutch were wealthy enough they were also misers,
like almost all well-to-do farmers and other such reluctant wage-payers.
On the other hand, a lucky man could occasionally get his hands on
something decent without too much trouble—because of their prosperity the Dutch weren't as afraid of thieves as the Icelanders. Jón
Hreggviðsson himself was able to steal a pair of sturdy boots from a
duke who had control of three rural districts. He'd been working as
an errand-boy for this man, who was invisible like all the other

important men in Holland, but he ran away because he was starving. The rich men in Holland were as stingy with food as those in Iceland. He found the boots in a pile of garbage and hid them in a thornbush for half a month before he left. He didn't dare to put them on before he'd gone about forty miles, but instead carried them in a sack upon his back. But when the weather worsened and the going got rough the boots came in handy, because although Holland is naturally more supple, its mud is cold, especially in the fall.

The weather was drizzly and the sun was beginning to set. The traveler was soaked and the duke's boots were waterlogged, which made the going even worse. In the cold fog and darkness ahead loomed Germany, home to the most warlike men in the world. Jón Hreggviðsson wasn't even carrying a staff. He ached for food. The border-post consisted of a few rows of houses, a church, and an inn with provisions for long-distance travelers. Huge carriages hung with lanterns left the inn in the evening on their way to the empire, drawn by teams of eight snorting horses and full of brawny, well-dressed travelers with genteel wives and loads of cash. The womenfolk settled comfortably in their seats in nests of pillows and blankets, and the men, all of them highborn, hung their belts and swords and feathered hats on hooks over the seats and drove away. Jón Hreggviðsson had a few coins on him and was thinking of buying himself a small cup of tea, an excellent drink from Asia, but he was not allowed inside the inn.

He was standing in front of the church, cursing, when he suddenly caught a whiff of warm bread. He started looking around and followed his nose to a bakery where a man and a woman were taking loaves of bread from an oven. He bought a loaf, then knocked on the door of a poor-looking house and scrounged warm beer to wash down the bread. He ate and drank sitting upon the threshold, since the folk there could see that he was a thief and murderer and refused to let him in. The whelp yapped furiously at him from the kitchen and woke up the hens, and the cock, the hens' husband, started crowing.

He stuck what was left of the bread under his shirt, bade the people there good night, and walked out into the rain refreshed, in

the trail of the postal carriages. They drove out through a gate where
two Dutch soldiers were standing with pistols and muskets, letting
folk pass through unimpeded. There was a small wooded area on the
other side of the gate, and beyond this stood a castle on a barren
patch of ground encircled by a moat. There was a bridge over the
moat, and the road ran right through the middle of the castle. Coni-
cal black lanterns hanging on either side of the castle's huge stone
portal gave off faint gleams of light, which appeared through the
drizzle like golden-colored, blue-tinged wisps of wool. The road
through the portal was cobbled, causing the iron-reinforced carriage
wheels to clatter and spark as they rolled over the stones. The castle's
roof was flat and edged with breastwork, with gaps for the catapults
and cannons. This was the gateway to Germany.

A number of men brandishing weapons stood at the portal.
Behind them were several others in colored clothing, with registers,
scrolls, and feathered pens, taking down people's names and occupa-
tions. The postal carriages had gone through. The German soldiers
were huge and wore enormous helmets topped with spikes shaped
like spear-blades, and their twisted beards looked similar to rams'
horns. Jón Hreggviðsson stood before these men and looked through
the gate, intending to continue on his way, but they immediately
pointed two spears at his chest and interrogated him in German.
Whatever he answered did him no good. They grabbed him and
frisked him, but found nothing on him except for a few Dutch coins
that they promptly divided amongst themselves. Then they blew
their trumpets. Soon another man joined them: a fat, blue giant. The
others wanted to hand Jón Hreggviðsson over to this man but he
obviously wasn't interested, if one could tell by the harsh tone of his
reply. A heated argument followed, in which the only word that Jón
Hreggviðsson understood was "hen-gen": "Let's hang him." The others finally prevailed and the newcomer was compelled to take Jón
Hreggviðsson into custody. He pressed the point of his sword up
against the farmer's back and drove him into the castle and up a long,
dimly lit flight of steps, then along platforms and passageways out
into some distant wing of the castle, until they came to a large chamber with a number of windows that let in both wind and rain. The

ruffian pushed Jón Hreggviðsson through the doorway. It was dark but for the dim light of the ruffian's lantern. When he moved to shut the door Jón Hreggviðsson thrust his foot into the doorway and demanded an explanation in Dutch. As is frequently the case amongst border-folk, this man could understand both languages when he felt like it, and he answered that Jón Hreggviðsson wouldn't walk through this doorway a second time. Unfortunately, he said, the man whose job it was to hang people wasn't available; he and his assistant had already hung so many people today that they were worn-out and had gone home to bed. This being said, the big lout pressed the point of his sword against Jón Hreggviðsson's stomach to make him move out of the doorway, then bade him good night.

"Hey," shouted Jón Hreggviðsson, in order to stretch out the conversation. "You should do yourself a favor, pal, and hang me yourself. I could probably help you."

The other man, however, was only a sentinel, in German Wachtmeister, without the rank and privileges of hangman, and he said that no mortal power, nor our Lord God, could compel him to take another man's duties upon his own shoulders, nor to neglect the duties allotted to the Wachtmeister by the Kaiser. "But what's that you've got there in your shirt?"

"Leave it alone," said Jón Hreggviðsson. "That's my bread."

"What the Hell are you planning to do with bread?" said the Wachtmeister. "They're going to hang you in the morning. I now confiscate this bread in the name of the Kaiser."

He pointed his sword at Jón Hreggviðsson's chest while he reached in after the bread, which he started tearing into handfuls after sheathing his sword.

"Damn, this is good bread," he said. "Where'd you get this bread?"

Jón Hreggviðsson said, "In Holland."

"Ja, you Dutchmen are wimps," said the Wachtmeister. "All you think about is bread. We Germans don't bother with bread. Cannons are worth more than bread. Listen here, you don't happen to have any cheese in there, do you?"

He frisked Jón Hreggviðsson again but couldn't find any cheese.

"Someday," he said with his mouth full, "someday we Germans'll show bread eaters like you Dutchmen what it costs to think about bread. We'll crush you. We'll level you. We'll wipe you out. You don't happen to have any money, do you?"

Jón Hreggviðsson told it as it was, that the men in colored clothing had robbed him of his last few coins.

"Ja, don't I know it," said the Wachtmeister. "Those toll-bastards probably aren't leaving much behind for poor children."

Someone outside shouted:

"Fritz von Blitz, shouldn't we be getting back to the game?"

The Wachtmeister shouted back: "Coming!"

"Now stay put and keep quiet until the hangman gets here," he said to Jón Hreggviðsson. "And trust me, if you try to jump out the window you'll be killed. But now I've got to go. My gambling partner is starting to get bored."

Having said this, the oaf squeezed through the doorway and locked the heavy oaken door behind him. Jón Hreggviðsson swore both loudly and quietly for several moments, then tried to feel his way around in this drafty, dismally cold abode. He kept bumping into what felt like wooden logs hanging from the ceiling, similar to the carcasses that hang in the kitchen loft. Every time he ran into one it started swinging to and fro. Luckily, the moon happened to peek for a moment through the rainy haze, casting a pale gleam upon the faces of a number of men who'd been strung up here. They hung from the rafters, tilt-headed, slack-mouthed, with swollen faces and white eyes, their hands tied behind their backs, their toes pointing straight down, in a sort of dim-witted helplessness that wakened in a man more the desire to give them a good shove and watch them swing rather than the motivation to climb up and cut them down. Jón Hreggviðsson went from one to the next and groped their feet to see if any of them might be wearing useful shoes—actually more from an old farmer's habit than from any expectation that he'd have need of whatever shoe leather he managed to find. As it turned out, the condition of these men's shoes was not in the least enviable.

The farmer had few ideas at all as to how he, a one-night guest, might keep himself entertained in such a dreary house. Even the *Bal-*

lad of Pontus seemed out of place here. Still, he remembered having heard that it was profitable for a man to sit under what the Icelanders called a hangi: a gallows-pole with a dead man hanging from it. This was the custom of the evil king Óðinn and other famous elders and adepts in the old days—they'd received all sorts of revelations by doing this. Jón Hreggviðsson decided to follow the same course. He chose the ghoul that was hanging farthest away so he could lean up against the wall while having his revelation. But the farmer was so exhausted that he'd hardly sat down upon the floor before lethargy and boredom sank in upon him. In a moment he was dozing beneath the hanged man, with his chin on his chest and his shoulders against the wall. The moon had disappeared behind the gloom again and it was pitch-black in the hall. Jón Hreggviðsson had been sleeping for just a short time when suddenly he was wakened by a creaking in the rafters above him—in the next instant the hanged man frees himself from his snare and jumps down. He wastes no time at all, but goes straight for Jón Hreggviðsson. He started trampling the farmer as hard as he could, using the incredible strength that only dead men possess, and the longer he trampled, the more his strength increased. In the meantime he sang the following verse:

> "Merry is the man hung once
> In the hall of ghosts.
> Never has a man hung twice
> Known the light of day.
> We're well-hung, let's trample
> The heart in need of hanging
> The acorn of the spirit
> In the unhanged's breast.
> Let's trample Hreggviður's son,
> Whose heart's grown far too hard."

"You've trampled enough!" shouted Jón Hreggviðsson, who was on the verge of suffocation from such harsh treatment. He managed somehow to break out from under the ghoul and to throw him down, but a fierce scuffle ensued and the stone floor was torn up beneath them. The other hanged men descended from their snares and started dancing clumsily around them and reciting intolerable, poorly worded poetry built on dubious assertions. This went on for a very long time, and all Jón Hreggviðsson could think was that he'd never joined in such a close dance. In the end the devil got such a tight grip on the farmer that he knew he couldn't hold out much longer against his opponent. It was a contest of life versus death, as mentioned in the hanged man's verse: "The hanged can't be killed twice, no matter how much or how hard one tries." Jón Hreggviðsson's only chance was to try to wriggle out of the fiend's grasp and make a break for it. And because dead men aren't nearly as lithe as their pinches are hard, he was finally able to free himself, and he ran to the window, clambered up to the window ledge, and threw himself out headlong without caring in the slightest what would happen next. Water flew from the moat up onto the castle walls and the man sank for some distance without hitting the bottom, then he shot to the surface and started splashing about. It was just like falling into a peat-pit, except that floating here were the putrefied limbs of men instead of dogs. Jón Hreggviðsson dog-paddled his way across the moat, scrambled onto the bank on the other side, and coughed up water. His teeth started rattling. He took his bearings and decided to head back to Holland for new adventures there, rather than risk any further adventures with the Germans.

15

He made his way to the city of Amsterdam, a great trading center situated near a huge stretch of water that cuts through the northern part of Holland, called by the Dutch Zuiderzee. From Amsterdam men sailed to Asia. He had started to get a grip on the language, and thus was able to find work as a porter for a trading company that owned a warehouse alongside a canal. He was given a place to sleep at night with the man who looked after the warehouse dog. The nights were often filled with a loud howling, sometimes until dawn.

Jón Hreggviðsson said: "Your dog howls loudest of all the dogs in the warehouse yard."

The man said, "That's because he's the wisest."

Jón Hreggviðsson said: "Dogs aren't praised for their wisdom. And only bitches howl. In the ancient sagas it says that in the old days the man was rightly chosen king who had the most vicious dog; not the one whose dog howled loudest."

"What good's the Danish king's dog?" said the man.

"Your duke owns a bitch," said Jón Hreggviðsson.

"My bitch can slice up your dog," said the man.

"My dog may be a fleabag," said Jón Hreggviðsson, "but the Germans, who are war heroes and real men, wouldn't deliberate for long over what they'd do to yours."

Jón Hreggviðsson was always mentioning the Germans, who ate men's bread and then hanged them—at least as long as the hangman was available. He bore a shuddering veneration for this fantastic race and felt quite proud of the fact that he'd become acquainted with it firsthand. The dog kept howling. One night just before dawn, Jón Hreggviðsson went out and found a length of cord, then hanged the dog and threw it into the canal.

He wandered for a long time along the canals and over the bridges. No one was awake but fishermen and ferrymen. Steam rose from one boat where the men were heating their tea water. He shouted to them and asked them to give him some tea. They asked who he was and he said that he was from Iceland, where Hell is. They invited him out to the boat and gave him something to drink and questioned him about Mount Hekla. He said that he was born and raised at the foot of the mountain and for that reason was called van Hekkenfeld. They asked whether a man could see down into Hell from the summit of Hekla, through the swarm of noxious birds that hovers eternally, shrieking and quarreling, over the crater. He said no, but added that he'd once caught one of these birds with a hooked pole that he'd brought with him up onto the mountain; they were similar to ravens, he said, except for their claws and beaks, which were iron. They asked whether such birds could be eaten and he laughed at their foolishness, but said on the other hand that one could use the claws for hooks and the beak for a pick. "Pick?" they said. "Why not pincers, man?" "Yes, why not pincers?" he said. They offered him more tea. One of them asked whether he was planning to go back to Iceland that evening. He answered no, and said that he was planning to go to Denmark to try to meet with His Most Gracious Majesty. They said they prayed that the Danish king would never thrive and that the duke of Holland would declare war on him as soon as possible. "Watch what you say," said Jón Hreggviðsson. They said that they would gladly fight for their duke until the bitter end and never retreat. There was a ship from Denmark anchored here in the canal, they said, and it would be true justice if they bored a hole in it. Jón Hreggviðsson thanked them and bade them farewell.

He found the Danish cutter lying at anchor in the harbor and shouted his greetings to the crew. They said that they were from Glückstadt in Holstein, fetching malt and hops, and they gave him a decent welcome. He asked to be allowed to see the captain, and told them that he was an Icelander looking for passage to Denmark. When they heard this they started insulting him, since Danes find Icelanders the most contemptible of all men. Jón Hreggviðsson fell to his knees before the captain and tearfully kissed his hand. The captain said that he didn't need any more men, least of all an Icelander, but that he could come back in the morning. Then they gave him something to eat, explaining that the Icelanders would perish if it weren't for the charity of foreign nations. Jón Hreggviðsson thanked them sincerely and courteously. He hung around the ship that whole day, feeling like a criminal in Holland ever since he hanged the dog, and at night the crew allowed him to sleep under a sail on deck. Then the farmer's luck changed just as it always did, because on that very same night two of the sailors went into town to have some fun, and one of them was killed and the other maimed. The captain let himself be persuaded to put Jón Hreggviðsson to work in place of the man who'd been killed, and he was allowed to sleep below deck the next night. One day later they set sail from the harbor.

Jón Hreggviðsson was forced to pay for his nationality so exorbitantly aboard ship that when they got caught in bad weather near the coast of Friesland and were driven out to sea, they blamed him for it, and would have tied him up and cast him overboard in the hope that the sea would subside, had not the ship's boy, who would probably have been next, crept to see the captain and begged him to see to it that this wretched devil be allowed to live.

When the weather calmed down Jón Hreggviðsson tried to make himself somewhat bigger in their eyes. In his situation it was of course useless to mention the fact that Hell burns under Hekla in Iceland, because the Danes would consider even Hell insignificant if it were located in Iceland. Instead he decided to describe for the crew his forefather Gunnar of Hlíðarendi, who was twelve ells high and lived to be three hundred years old and was such a great warrior that he could leap his own height backward as well as forward. Jón Hreggviðsson asked them if such a man had ever existed in Denmark.

"In days of yore," they said, "we also had champions in Denmark."

"Yes," said Jón Hreggviðsson, "maybe Haraldur Hilditönn. But he's also one of my forefathers."

Jón Hreggviðsson finally achieved his goal at Glückstadt on the Elbe Estuary in Holstein, inasmuch as he had now arrived in the domain of His Most Gracious King and Hereditary Lord. The farmer stepped lightly onto land one evening, and he would have doubtlessly repaid the ship's boy for saving his life had the captain not driven him from his sight with threats of a beating in place of payment.

Glückstadt was certainly not any great sight to see in the eyes of this well-traveled man from Holland. Even worse was the fact that he no longer understood, if it could be called that, any language, except Dutch when he got angry. Until now he had thought he could tell Danish apart from other languages, but the dialect there made it completely impossible for him to even guess at what people were saying. There was a chilling fog. He had a Dutch silver coin the size of a fingertip. He searched for lodging for the night and showed the coin, but everywhere he went he was cursed and driven out and told that his coin was counterfeit. Some people were even on the verge of dragging the farmer before a court of law because of the coin. He was hungry and the streets were slippery and the townspeople had closed the shutters on their windows and gone in to eat steaks. When anyone with a lantern approached the man, the light looked at first like a gray wad of wool, then like a blue halo, and finally like an egg yolk. The aroma of endless amounts of roasted meat continued to issue from the houses, and from the inns came the fragrance of spices, tobacco smoke, and alcohol. He realized that his best chance for lodging would be in a stable or in the loft of a cowshed behind a house somewhere.

No sooner had he started searching for such lodging, however, than he suddenly and unexpectedly bumped into a man holding a lantern. The man was energetic-looking, with a moustache, a goatee, and a feathered hat, wearing topboots and a cloak. Emanating from him was the outstanding smell of brennivín. The man greeted Jón Hreggviðsson companionably. Neither could understand the other's language, but Jón Hreggviðsson got the feeling that the townsman had come to bring him some sort of good news, or might even offer him a tankard of beer, and he started to think that he would soon find what he'd been hoping for in this the land of his lord, which had for a time been only the land of his dreams.

They walked together to a good-sized tavern where a number of men, mostly in uniform, sat around thick oaken tables, drinking heavily. The place was very lively but only moderately comfortable. The townsman showed Jón Hreggviðsson to a seat at the end of a table in the corner and sat down by him, and the landlord, a fat blue-black oaf, brought them each an unordered tankard of beer. The townsman's tankard was slightly smaller and had embossed illustrations and a silver lid, while the farmer was handed a plain but very large stone pitcher. Immediately afterward they were presented with brennivín—Jón Hreggviðsson's goblet was twice normal size and made of tin, while the squire's was dainty and made of silver.

When it became obvious to them that Jón Hreggviðsson was unable to converse in perfectly comprehensible languages, the landlord and the townsman contemplated their guest for a short time and spoke quietly together as if they were in doubt as to whether they'd found and brought the right man to this place. Nonetheless they filled the farmer's tankard and goblet again as soon as he finished off his drink, and he, for his part, could have cared less even if they had mistaken him for someone else—he was going to drink and enjoy himself whether they called him Jón Hreggviðsson from Rein or something entirely different. Whatever the cost, they continued to fill his tankard and goblet. And whoever he was, he started singing the *Ballad of Pontus* over the crowd:

"We level our lances to pierce the hearts
Of lords arrayed for the fight—"

The squire took a piece of paper from his wallet and wrote something on it, then placed it before the farmer for him to make his mark, and the landlord came with ink and a freshly cut pen. Jón Hreggviðsson thought that the aristocrats would be disappointed if they were inviting him to set his name to something beautiful, so he resolved to continue drinking and singing while there was still a drop left in his tankard and goblet, and answered them only with the word "hen-gen," dragging his index finger around his windpipe at the same time. By this he meant that they were welcome to hang him whether he signed or not, but if there was still anything to expect besides the gallows or any other implement of that sort, he was just as eager now as before to experience whatever it might be without signing his name.

The squire gave a signal to the uniformed men who had been sitting minding their own business at the other end of the table. They rose immediately to their feet and rushed toward Jón Hreggviðsson. The farmer wrestled a bit out of old habit, but he didn't stop singing, and his white teeth gleamed in his black beard during the scuffle:

"We level our lances to pierce the hearts
Of lords arrayed for the fight,
Whether their mantles withstand our darts
Whether their mantles withstand our darts
Shall soon be proven ari-i-ight."

He gave two of the men strong clouts and a third a good kick before they were finally able to subdue him, and then they gagged and bound him. Just as they were completing their work he was overcome by a pleasant numbness, causing him to remember little of what happened next.

Next morning he awoke to the sound of trumpets. He was lying on the floor of a storehouse that was dimly lit by lanterns hanging in the rafters. He watched as other men in the same boat as he was

awoke from their sleep in patchy piles of haulm, and then as a supervisor moved amongst them with a cudgel and drove them to their
feet. Another supervisor came and looked over the new arrival and
swore by Jesus and Mary like a Frenchman at the farmer's filthy
appearance, then he dragged him out to a church where they stored
their weapons and made him put on a doublet, leggings, and boots,
placed a hat on his head, and girded him with a belt. This sergeant-
at-arms asked him his name and nationality and first wrote this
information in a book, then upon a patch of cloth that he fastened
inside the farmer's doublet. The patch read as follows: "Johann Reckwitz. Aus Ijsland buertig."*

They were given bread, beer, muskets, and swords. Next they were
made to march out onto a field in the faint gleam of morning. It was
windy and rainy, just like the night before. Jón Hreggviðsson managed the march to the field, though there was a certain amount of
gruff urgency on the part of the supervisor, but when they started
doing various exercises appurtenant to the art of war his comprehension broke down entirely and he did everything backward. The gruff
orders changed quickly into vicious threats in that difficult language,
and finally into cuffs on his ears. It didn't seem too hopeful to Jón
Hreggviðsson to repay like with like in such a place, and he didn't
understand the orders any better no matter how much he was
beaten. Finally the supervisor gave up and looked agitatedly at the
patch inside the man's doublet and discovered that he was an Icelander. At this everyone started laughing. After a long and exhausting
day of training they were marched back to their barracks and given
warm broth.

Jón Hreggviðsson was beaten and shouted at for three days before
he was transferred to the mess hall and made to fetch water, chop
firewood, carry out ash and garbage, and do any of the other least
important jobs there. The stewards and cooks were German and
could care less whether there was a country called Iceland or not, but
the scullions were Danish, as was the man who turned the officers'
roast, and they smugly explained to Regvidsen time and time again
that Iceland was not a country and Icelanders were not people. They
insisted furthermore that the lice-infested pack of slaves that lived on

that funnel of Hell scrabbled along only on whale oil, rotten shark meat, and alms from the king. Regvidsen said that in Iceland there was, as a matter of fact, one hole leading down to Hell, and that one could often hear Danish coming out of it. It was also a fact, he said, that Iceland outrivaled the rest of world, because all the men in Iceland were noble heroes and skalds. The Danes called Regvidsen a black hound. Every day the mess hall was the scene of bickering and cruel pranks.

Luckily the thoughts of these people turned occasionally to other topics, especially concerning how long it took for the soldiers' wages to be paid. The army's ranks included not only Danes but also mercenaries of various nationalities and social classes: Saxons, Estonians, Wends, Poles, Bohemians, robbers, farmers, and vagrants. Many of them wondered whether the regulations concerning the payment of wages became valid only if the army defeated the enemy and won territory. Little by little Jón Hreggviðsson came to understand that the army assembled here would soon be sent south, to a certain mountain range called the Carpathians, to fight there for the German emperor. Another Danish army had been sent there before them and had seen a lot of action, but was now in need of additional troops so that it could turn the tide of the fight, and the Danish king had promised that two thousand troops would be sent from Glückstadt to join them as soon as possible. The Danish king and the German emperor were excellent friends.

The man who turned the officers' roast insisted that the army was sure to achieve fame and fortune when it reached the Carpathians. The man who stoked the fire reminded them how it had gone one year not so long ago, when the Danish army had fought for the German emperor to win Spain and the emperor had promised to pay the Danish king a hundred thousand louis d'or for an old debt, in addition to a hundred thousand guilders as a reward if he should be victorious. "But let me ask you this," he said, "when did the emperor ever conquer Spain?"

"Never," said the assistant cooks.

"And when were the louis d'or paid?"

"Never," said the assistant cooks.

"And when the guilders?"

"Never," said the assistant cooks.

"And where are the troops who were supposed to be paid?"

"Dead," said the assistant cooks.

"That was like every other unlucky military expedition," said the man who turned the roast. "Both good and bad fortune are encountered in war. The Danish army that was sent last year to Lombardy achieved great fame. Its name lives on in the stars. They fought at the fortress of Cremona, which was being held by the French, and now they're called the Danish Falcons of Cremona."

"Not quite," said the man who stoked the fire. "An Italian monk lured them into a sewer running from the fortress into the river Po. True, some sort of battle was apparently fought in the sewer and some of them made it out alive. But let me ask you this, what happened to those Danish Falcons of Cremona who made it out of the sewer? I heard it from a German who was there that when the survivors went to collect their wages, it turned out that Count Schlieben, their commander, had wasted all their pay shooting dice in Venice, so they weren't allowed to return home and instead were driven like lambs east to the Carpathians and told to fight there against the Magyars, who are a race of wildmen. Now they've supposedly been promised their wages, and the king a hundred thousand louis d'or, if they can take over those mountains. That's just what those dead men need to take over those mountains—two thousand more dead."

"I've always wanted to see mountains," said the roaster. "It must be exciting fighting in the mountains. I might even think that it'd be better to be defeated in the mountains than to be victorious in a sewer."

The man who kindled the fire asked, "What do you say, Regvidsen—you who've fought with demons and devils on top of Hekla?"

Jón Hreggviðsson said nothing more than that it was pretty obvious as to who got the shillings around here.

"One spoonful for that," said the roaster, and he went over to where Jón Hreggviðsson was sitting on the butcher's block and slapped him in the face with his ladle, toppling him to the floor.

On the next day the roughhousing in the mess hall started anew. Jón Hreggviðsson pinned down his overseer, the roaster who wanted to fight in the mountains, pulled down his pants, and whipped him. Trumpets were blown and the regimental guards seized the farmer and hauled him off to headquarters. But the officers, all German, were busy preparing to set off with the army south to the Carpathians, which meant that most of them were drunk, and they couldn't reach an agreement as to what should be done with the rascal. Some of them wanted to quarter him immediately, instead of wasting time by first cutting out his heart and slapping his face with it and then quartering him afterward, which was the punishment specified in the regulations for discipline-breakers in the king's army. Others wanted to follow the regulations down to the last detail, because justice eternally protects mankind's affairs. The matter was finally referred to the judgment of the colonel, who had hired out this and more armies for the Danish king and acted as absolute authority over his soldiers' lives and limbs, and thus it turned out that this incident caused the man from Skagi to lose his place in his division and his chance to travel with the army to the south to fight for His Most Gracious Majesty.

The colonel was an outstanding, well-educated gentleman, a count and baron and peer from the land of Pommern. He resided in a stately mansion close by, and Jón Hreggviðsson was taken there. Several soldiers with drawn swords guarded the door. In a hall whose large windows overlooked apple trees in the garden below sat a gaunt cavalier in a golden sash, a goatee, and a peruke, with a sword at his belt and snow-white ruffles at the ends of his sleeves. He was wearing golden, tight-fitting silk trousers and red topboots that hung down in double folds just below his knees, and a blue velvet cloak with an extensive train. He sat with one elbow upon a table and a long index finger upon his pale cheek, reading from huge books. This was the colonel. Sitting like a statue to one side of him was his adjutant, staring out into the blue; to the other side sat his secretary, stooped over his feather pen. Jón Hreggviðsson's guards informed the doormen that this was Johann Reckwitz aus Ijsland, who had whipped his superior. The head doorman reported this to the adjutant. The colonel continued to read his books, one hand upon his sword and the other beneath his chin, until the adjutant reported to him that the Icelander had arrived. The colonel then ordered that Reckwitz was not to stand more than one span over the threshold, that all of the doors were to be opened behind him, and that all of the windows in the house were to be opened all the way. A draft blew through the hall. The colonel stared at Jón Hreggviðsson for a moment and ground his teeth. Suddenly he swept up the train of his cloak, sprang to his feet, took several lightning-quick steps forward, and sniffed in the farmer's direction with a look of predetermined loathing. Then he returned to his seat, picked up a silver box, took a long and careful pinch of snuff, and told all the others to do the same. When they were finished he said something in German that only the adjutant heard, and he continued to stare at Jón Hreggviðsson. The adjutant addressed Jón Hreggviðsson in coarse Danish, without moving an inch.

"My lord has read in reputable books that Icelanders emit such a foul stench that men have to position themselves upwind when speaking to them."

Jón Hreggviðsson said nothing.

The adjutant said: "My lord has read in reputable books that the abode of the damned and of devils is in Iceland, within the mountain named Hekkenfeld. Is this correct?"

Jón Hreggviðsson said that he couldn't deny it.

Next: "My lord has read in reputable books, primo, that in Iceland there are more specters, monsters, and devils than there are men; secundo, that Icelanders bury shark meat in the dungheaps by their cowsheds and afterward eat it; tertio, that starving Icelanders remove their shoes and cut pieces of them into their mouths like pancakes; quarto, that Icelanders live in mounds of earth; quinto, that Icelanders do not know how to work; sexto, that Icelanders loan foreigners their daughters for purposes of procreation; septimo, that an Icelandic girl is considered to be an unspoiled virgin until she has had her seventh illegitimate child. Is this correct?"

Jón Hreggviðsson gaped slightly.

"My lord has read in reputable books that Icelanders are primo, thievish; secundo, liars; tertio, arrogant; quarto, lice-ridden; quinto, drunkards; sexto, debauchers; septimo, cowards, unfit for war—" the adjutant said all of this without moving and the colonel continued to grind his teeth and stare at Jón Hreggviðsson. "Is this correct?"

Jón Hreggviðsson swallowed to try to wet his throat. The adjutant raised his voice and repeated:

"Is this correct?"

Jón Hreggviðsson straightened up and said:

"My forefather Gunnar of Hlíðarendi was twelve ells high."

The colonel said something to the adjutant and the adjutant said loudly:

"My lord says that whoever commits perjury beneath the standard shall suffer the wheel and the rack."

"Twelve ells," repeated Jón Hreggviðsson. "I won't take it back. And he lived to be three hundred years old. And he wore a golden band around his forehead. His halberd sang the sweetest song that has ever been heard in the North. And the girls are young and slender and come during the night to free men, and are called fair maidens and are said to have the bodies of elves—"

— 16 —

Before the doorway of a noble mansion in Copenhagen stands a soldier, wearing a black hat, high rubber boots, and a new coat. He is girded with a belt but carries no weapons. He shuffles for some time before the house, creeps up the doorsteps, and stands a while longer at the top, stooping a bit at the knees, staring up at the sheer gable with his fists clenched around his thumbs. Affixed to the door is a brass clasp with a hammerhead that is used to strike a tiny anvil beneath and thus send a clapping sound into the house, but the new arrival can't figure out how to work such a machine and instead announces his presence by rapping three times upon the door. He waits for a moment or two but no one comes. On his next attempt he doubles the strength of his knock, again with no result. The soldier grows restless and starts pounding the oak with his fists over and over, heavily and hard.

Finally the door is opened, and a dwarfish woman steps into the doorway. She is hunchbacked, with a ledge-shaped mouth and a chin that hangs down to the middle of her chest, arms too long and too thin, and drooping hands. She fixed the soldier with an evil stare. He greeted her in Dutch. She gave a shrill bark and ordered the black devil to clear off immediately.

"Is Arnas home?" he asked.

At first the woman was so utterly sickened to hear a common soldier mention the name of such a man on his own doorstep that she could say nothing. When she stemmed her gorge she spoke to him in Low German, and the soldier got the distinct impression that she was calling him a black devil in that language as well. Next she tried to close the door but he stuck his foot between it and the doorpost. She pushed against the door for a few moments, but she quickly realized that strength had precedence over principle here and disappeared into the house. He withdrew his foot but didn't have the courage to follow the woman in. Several moments passed.

Both the house and the surrounding neighborhood were completely quiet, and the soldier continued to dawdle on the doorstep, becoming ever more distressed. Finally he heard a rustling sound at the door. A pair of eyes peeped out, and then a thin nose emerged, snorting.

"What's the matter?" snorted an Icelandic voice. But since the soldier wasn't able to think straight in that language, he bade good day in Danish.

"What's the matter?" came the snort again.

"Nothing's the matter," answered the soldier in Icelandic.

Then the door opened.

Standing there was an Icelander, with a reddish complexion, a long face, thin, flat hair, slightly twitchy wether's eyes, colorless eyelashes, and nearly hairless eyebrows; he was wearing a dress coat with patches on the elbows. The man did not possess the self-confidence necessary to be the servant of a nobleman, but his quirky mannerisms certainly distinguished him from other commoners: he snorted and blinked incessantly, jerked his head as if he were trying to avoid being bitten by midges, and rubbed his nose with an index finger; he would also distractedly scratch one of his calves with the instep of the other foot. It was difficult to tell if he was old or young.

"Who are you?" asked the Icelander.

"My name is Jón Hreggviðsson, from Rein on Akranes," said the soldier.

"Welcome, Jón," said the Icelander, extending his hand. "Good. And he's gone and enlisted as a soldier."

"I'd traveled a long way and they nabbed me in Glückstadt out in Holstein," said Jón Hreggviðsson.

"Yes, they're cruel men for taking roving knaves," said the Icelander. "It's better to stay put in Akranes. Good. By the way, I don't suppose you're keeping company with Jón Marteinsson?"

Jón Hreggviðsson answered no to that—he wasn't familiar with the man he named; on the other hand he did have urgent business with Arnas Arnæus—"or am I mistaken in thinking that he's the master of this house?"

"Doesn't know Jón Marteinsson, good, good," said the Icelander. "And comes from Skagi. What's the news from Akranes?"

"Oh, they're doing alright," said Jón Hreggviðsson.

"No one's dreamed any significant dream?"

"Not that I can recall—except sometimes children dream about the future. And old women feel pain in their thighs before the wind shifts to a northeaster," said Jón Hreggviðsson. "Who're you?"

"My name is Jón Guðmundsson from Grindavík—I am called Grindvicensis," said the man. "I do as a matter of fact hold the title Doctus in Veteri Lingua Septentrionali; but my favorite indulgence nowadays is scientia mirabilium rerum.* As I was saying: good. I don't expect you have anything to report? Haven't heard anything new? Haven't heard tell of any peculiar creatures or suchlike on the shores of Hvalfjörður?"

"Well, no, damn it," said Jón Hreggviðsson. "On the other hand we do get bites from sea monsters out on Akranes, and some of them are darned ugly, but such a thing is hardly considered news, even if someone lands in a tussle with one of them. But since we're talking about freaks of nature, some kind of satyr came here to the door—a blend of troll and dwarf, though in the shape of a woman, and I've never had it worse in seeing such a creature because she called me a black devil in German when I asked about the householder."

At this report the Icelander Grindvicensis snorted and gaped, then rubbed his right instep against his left calf and vice versa. When he could finally speak again he said:

"May I point out to my good compatriot that when he says that he wants to speak with my master, my master is not the kind of householding farmer one finds out in Iceland, though he is indeed an Icelander—he is a refined and venerable lord, Assessor Consistorii, Professor Philosophiae et Antiquitatum Danicarum,* and His Royal Majesty's Erudite Archivist. And consequently, his wedded wife and affectionate darling, the mistress of this house, is also of noble standing and is therefore to be accorded praise, not derision and mockery.* And who is it who has sent you, a rank-and-file soldier, to meet with my master?"

"That's my story," said Jón Hreggviðsson.

"Oh, good. But what sort of testimonial, written or otherwise, do you have from a high-ranking individual allowing you to speak with my master?"

"I have the kind of testimonial that he understands."

"Indeed. I wonder if this might be merely some sort of scheme contrived by that coxcomb and gallows bird Jón Marteinsson to finagle books and money," said the Icelander Grindvicensis. "Or might I, my master's famulus in antiquitatibus,* be permitted to have a look at this testimonial?"

Jón Hreggviðsson said: "I'll give my token to no one but him. I sewed it into my rags up north in Trékyllisvík. And when I was made a soldier I put it into one of my shoes. Thieves looked down on me as scum of the earth and therefore it never crossed any of their minds that I might be carrying such a treasure. You can tell that to your master. I could have bought my own life with this treasure many times over, but I chose instead to suffer starvation and beatings in Holland, the gallows in Germany, and the Spanish Jacket* out in Glückstadt."

The learned Icelander now stepped out of the house and locked the door behind him, then told Jón Hreggviðsson to follow him around the corner. They entered an orchard behind the house, where the black bare boughs of tall trees drooped with silver frost. Grindvicensis invited the visitor to take a seat upon an icy bench. He himself went and peered around the corner and behind the trees and bushes as if to make sure that the enemy was nowhere near, then finally returned and sat down upon the bench.

"As I was saying: good," he said, in the same schoolroom tone as before, filled with enthusiasm for his own wisdom. He said it was unfortunate that he hadn't ever really had the opportunity to examine the world with his own eyes, except as a schoolboy on his trips from Grindavík to Skálholt, when he had tried as far as he was able to observe and record everything astounding, incredible, and incomprehensible, especially in Krýsuvík, Herdísarvík, and Selvogur. On the other hand he had always willingly collected material from well-informed persons of high as well as low standing, with the result that he had a number of books in the making concerning these subjects. Now as he understood Jón Hreggviðsson to be a man well acquainted with Germany, he was eager to hear whether it was true that there still lived in the depths of Germany's forests those creatures, called elgfróðar in Icelandic, that are half-man and half-horse?

Jón Hreggviðsson replied that he'd never run into such a creature in Germany, but he'd once wrestled a hanged man there. At this the learned Icelander interrupted and said that he was overly vexed by such phenomena, because anyone who mentioned specters was usually reproached for being superstitious and repudiated by the learned popinjays here in Copenhagen, not least among them Jón Marteinsson, since the doings of dead men in this world were not to be ascribed to natural science and hardly to mirabilia* either; it was up to the theologians to forswear such things. He then asked Jón Hreggviðsson whether he'd had any dealings with giants, because he had a tiny Latin text in the works concerning that subject. Did the farmer know whether a troll-bone might have been found in the earth in his highland pasture or on the heaths above Borgarfjörður?—foreigners pay a great deal of heed to documentary evidence written up in books, he said. Jón Hreggviðsson said no to this, because he thought it likely that such a large bone would be quite soft and would disintegrate rather quickly. On the other hand, said the farmer, about a year ago he'd come to grips with a living troll-woman on Tvídægra, and, after having thought about his dealings with the monster as thoroughly as possible, he'd come to the conclusion that she'd been questioning his masculinity. The learned Icelander found this hugely interesting and his opinion of the soldier increased to no small extent at this revelation; he said that he would copy down this information exactly as he'd heard it in his book *De Gigantibus Islandiae.**

"By the way," he said, "I don't expect that you've heard mention of a child, if it could be called a child, having, as it did, a mouth upon its chest, which in the year before last beheld the light of day at Ærlækjarsel in Flói?"

Jón Hreggviðsson wasn't sure about this; on the other hand, he was familiar with a lamb with a bird's nose that had been born in Belgsholt in the parish of Melar three years ago. The learned Icelander declared this excellent news and said that he would record it in his book *Physica Islandica*—he said that Jón Hreggviðsson was a wise and discerning fellow for a man of the mob, and was most likely an entirely decent chap; ". . . but," he added, "I don't think that the lord of this house, my master, would have any interest in conversing with such a lowly man. However, I will attempt to make enquiry on your behalf, if you haven't already lost interest in the matter."

Since this was definitely not the case, the learned Icelander took it upon himself to report the visitor's business, going into the house by the main door, stooping and snorting, puffed up with responsibility. He had not so much as disappeared into the house when Jón Hreggviðsson heard a yawning beside him upon the bench, and when he turned around he was surprised to see a man sitting there. The man must have congealed there like the rime, because he hadn't been seen coming in through the front gate nor from out of the house nor from over the wall—besides the fact that the learned Grindvicensis had taken a look to make sure that nothing was hiding in the bushes or behind the trees.

They examined each other for a moment. The man was blue from the cold and had his hands pulled up within his sleeves.

"What a crap of a country—now there's rain as well as frost," said this surprise visitor, and he sucked at his upper lip with his lower one.

"Who're you?" asked Jón Hreggviðsson.

"There's no need to get to that right away," answered the stranger, and he started poking at the farmer's boots. "Let's make a deal for the boots instead. I'll trade you my knife."

"These are His Majesty's boots," said Jón Hreggviðsson.

"Screw His Majesty," said the stranger apathetically, almost emptily.

"Screw your own appetite, pal," said Jón Hreggviðsson.

"Alright then, let's trade knives, instead of doing nothing at all," said the other man. "Straight up, sight unseen!"

"I never buy anything without seeing it first," said Jón Hreggviðsson.

"I'll show you the hilt," said the man.

They traded knives. The man's knife was a fine piece of work, but Jón Hreggviðsson's had a rusty blade.

"I always lose," said the stranger. "No one trades fairly with me. But it doesn't matter. Now let's get up and go to Doctor Kirsten's and pay for a tankard of beer with the knife."

"Which knife?" said Jón Hreggviðsson.

"My knife," said the man.

"Which happens to be my knife," said Jón Hreggviðsson. "I won't drink away my knife. On the other hand, you can drink all the beer you want for the rusty one."

"Nothing gets past you, Jón Hreggviðsson from Rein. You're not only a murderer and a thief, you're also the worst of men. May I ask what you're doing hanging around outside this miserable house?"

"It doesn't look to me like you're much better than a beggar yourself," said Jón Hreggviðsson. "What're those on your feet, may I ask? You call those shoes? And why're you squeezing your hands like that up into your sleeves? And where's your house?"

"My house is a massive palace compared to this one," said the man, full of passionless obstinacy, like a hackney.

"In my opinion," said Jón Hreggviðsson in response, "there's never been an Icelander, since Iceland was settled, who has owned such a magnificent house as this one—and there were a lot of people who had good houses in the old days."

The stranger could not be convinced. He seemed to need to say something, then spoke quickly and tenderly and somewhat grumblingly, with a slight drawl, as if he were reading from an old book: "Many a king lost all that he owned in his quest for a pearl. And many a man's son was prepared to lose the breath of life for a princess and to undergo trials to take possession of the kingdom. Let them be sea-kings and men of Hrafnista, lying with witches after landing in perilous storms up north in Gästrikland, or in Jötunheim—such things happened to heroes as famous as Hálfdán Brönufóstri, Illugi Gríðarfóstri, and Örvar-Oddur himself, and they weren't considered lesser men because of it.* But to sell the pearl and the princess at once, and the kingdom besides, for one witch—such a story is not to be found in all the realm of antiquitatates."

At that moment the learned Icelander Grindvicensis reemerged from the house. When he cast his eyes upon the latter visitor seated next to the former, he raised his hands halfway in a gesture of despair, then let them fall powerlessly back down as if he no longer knew what to do.

"Oh, as if I couldn't have seen it coming," he said. "Jón Marteinsson, I order you to give me back the *Historia Literaria** that you stole from me on Sunday. Jón Hreggviðsson, good, you may see my master in his bibliothèque*—but tell me first what sort of tricks this foul knave has been up to."

"We traded knives," said Jón Hreggviðsson, showing his knife.

"I should have expected it: the knife my master lost this morning"—and he snatched the knife away from Jón Hreggviðsson.

Jón Marteinsson yawned discourteously, as if this did not concern him. As he entered the house, Jón Hreggviðsson heard him ask the learned Grindvicensis to loan him some money for a tankard of beer.

— 17 —

"Greetings, Jón Hreggviðsson, you are welcome here after your long journey," said Arnas Arnæus, slowly, deeply, and calmly, his voice like that of an omniscient being speaking from somewhere within a black crag on a bright summer day, telling the wanderer the story of his adventures from the beginning. It was not quite clear to the farmer whether ridicule or friendship dwelled in the depths of this voice.

This was a huge chamber, with vaulted ceilings and stone walls set with bookshelves from the floor to the rafters so that one had to climb a ladder to reach the highest shelves, just as one did to get to the highest bales in the hayshed. Set high in the walls were windows with small leaden panes, which did not let in enough light to allow one to work there without the aid of a desk lamp. In one shadowy corner tall armchairs were arrayed around a thick oaken table, upon which stood a pitcher and several stone tankards. A statue of a man or a god stood in another corner and a lit stove in a third.

The master of the house showed his guest to a chair, then he screwed open a small barrel resting upon a trunk in one alcove. He poured foaming Rostocker beer into a tankard and placed it before the farmer:

"Have a drink, Jón Hreggviðsson."

Jón Hreggviðsson thanked him and drank. He was desperately thirsty. After emptying the tankard he heaved an extremely contented sigh of relief at the taste of the beer in his mouth, and he sucked at his beard. Arnas Arnæus watched him. Finally, after waiting for some time for his guest to begin explaining his business, he asked:

"What do you want from me, Jón Hreggviðsson?"

Jón Hreggviðsson bent forward and started to take off one of his boots.

"Are your feet wet?" asked Arnæus.

"No," said Jón Hreggviðsson.

As he pulled off the boot he revealed his foot wrapped in rags, and when he finished unwinding the rags it came to light that he had a golden ring on one of his toes. He slipped the ring off, rubbed it on his trouser leg, and gave it to Arnæus.

Arnæus looked coolly at the ring, and when he asked his guest where he had gotten this object his voice knitted to a small extent, as if he were suddenly far removed.

"The fair maiden," said Jón Hreggviðsson, "the fair maiden asked me to say—"

"That's enough," said Arnas Arnæus, and he placed the ring on the table in front of his guest.

"The fair maiden asked me to say—" repeated the guest, but the master of the house interrupted him again:

"No more."

Jón Hreggviðsson looked at Arnas Arnæus and for perhaps the first time in his life felt a twinge of fear. One thing is certain: although he had finally reached his destination, he didn't dare to deliver the message that he'd stored in his heart the entire long way, the words that he'd been entrusted to say.

He said nothing.

"I hear that you've killed a man, Jón Hreggviðsson," said Arnas Arnæus. "Is this correct?"

Jón Hreggviðsson raised himself in his seat and answered:

"Have I killed a man or haven't I killed a man? Who has killed a man and who hasn't killed a man? When does a man kill a man and when doesn't a man kill a man? To Hell with it if I killed a man. And yet . . ."

"There now, that was a strange jingle," said Arnas Arnæus, but he did not smile. Neither did he look at the ring again, but instead continued watching Jón Hreggviðsson.

"Do you think that you're a killer?" he asked finally.

Jón Hreggviðsson answered: "No—but things go worse for me when I say that, sometimes."

"I don't understand," said Arnas Arnæus. "I read in the documents from Iceland that you were accused of murder and convicted last year at the Öxará Assembly, but that you escaped from your detention by some unknown means. Now I ask you what the truth is in your case—and I'm not trying to trap you."

Jón Hreggviðsson started telling him the entire story of his dealings with God and the king, beginning with the time that he stole the cord to use as fishing line during the famine three years ago, and how he'd gone to the Þrælakista; then how he had, the year before last, helped to demolish Iceland's bell for our Most Gracious Majesty; then how his jaws had worked against him in his conversation with the king's hangman and how he'd reaped a flogging, as his lord already knew, since he'd paid him a visit in his ramshackle cottage at Rein the day after the punishment was carried out; then about the untimely death of Sigurður Snorrason and his, Jón Hreggviðsson's, waking in the suspicious vicinity of the deceased flesh; next about his life at Bessastaðir in endless deathly darkness, without having seen the light of God except for a peek at Yule and Easter; about his sentencing at Þingvellir by Öxará, the place where poor men in Iceland have had to endure untold amounts of pain and disgrace; and about the night before his beheading when his chains were unlocked and he was given gold and told to go to his lord and beg him to redeem his head; and about his travels, how he'd left Iceland sinking under the swell of the sea and how he'd cursed it, and how finally, after all sorts of adventures out in the wide world, he'd arrived at this chamber, an ignorant, insignificant individual from Skagi, wishing and pleading that he might make peace with His Most Gracious Majesty, just so that he might go on looking after his own little house—

Arnas Arnæus listened to the story. When it was finished he walked down the length of his hall, cleared his throat, and walked back.

"Quite correct," he began somewhat dreamily, looking past his guest as if he had already started to think about something else. "In the fall I took a look, out of curiosity, at a copy of the court documents in your case that I found lying here in the Chancery. It was difficult for me to see how they could have convicted you according to the testimony that was used as the basis for the verdict. I could see no clear link between the verdict and the investigations that had been made into the matter. It seemed, in other words, to be one of those outstanding verdicts that our wise fathers and pillars of the land there at home feel themselves compelled to hand down for some more valid reason than the satisfaction of the demands of justice."

Jón Hreggviðsson asked whether the king's friend and table-companion of counts couldn't somehow arrange to have his case retried and concluded with a new and better verdict here in Copenhagen.

Arnas Arnæus walked through the hall, just as before.

"Unfortunately," he said, "you are in the wrong house, Jón Hreggviðsson. I am not the keeper of law and justice in this kingdom, neither by calling nor office. I am a poor bookman."

He gestured with an open hand at the book-covered walls of his hall and, looking at the farmer with a peculiar gleam in his eyes, added:

"I have bought all of these books."

Jón Hreggviðsson stared openmouthed at the books.

"When a man has bought so many precious books it shouldn't be such a great matter for him to speak the words that can buy Jón Hreggviðsson mercy," he said finally.

"In your case, Jón Hreggviðsson may not matter," said Arnas Arnæus, and he smiled.

"What?" said Jón Hreggviðsson.

"Your case is not so important as far as you are concerned, Jón Hreggviðsson. It is a much more serious matter. What good will it do anyone even if the head of one beggar is saved? A nation does not survive by mercy."

"The fire's hottest for the one who burns himself," said Jón Hreggviðsson. "I know that it wasn't considered manly in the old days to beg for mercy, but what power does one desolate beggar have to fight for his life against the entire world?"

Arnas Arnæus took a few moments and carefully considered this man who had been flogged in Kjalardalur, placed in chains at Bessastaðir, sentenced at Öxará, beaten on the highways of Holland, sent to the gallows by the Germans, put in a Spanish Jacket in Glückstadt, and who now sat here as his guest with one of his boots at his side, one of the king's boots—and who wanted to live.

"If your case has taken a wrong turn," said Arnas Arnæus, "then it would be easiest if you yourself went to the king and brought to him in your own words your supplication concerning an appeal, a reopening of the case. The king is not opposed to looking into the faces of his servants, and he will solve their problems eagerly and benevolently if he can find good reason to do so. But do not entangle me in this case, because nothing would be saved even if I were to save you. And it would only make matters worse if I were to intercede for you in such a small matter in this place."

"So that's it," said Jón Hreggviðsson, drably. "All of this must have been for something. Otherwise it was only bad luck that sat me down beneath the hanged man. And here's the token lying in front of me. I hope it's not too much if I ask you to fill up my tankard."

Arnas Arnæus filled the man's tankard and let him drink.

"I mean you no harm, Jón Hreggviðsson," he said. "I might be better inclined toward your old mother, who preserved six pages from the *Skálda,* but because of that, I'd like you to benefit as well, if only in a small way. The treasure lying there before you once graced the hand of a noblewoman from the south. And I had the good fortune, one summer's night in Breiðafjörður, to be able to place it upon the hand of another queen. Now she has sent it back to me. I give it to you. This thing, which the queens called their good gold, the dragon that bites its own tail, I give now to you, Jón Hreggviðsson—use it to buy yourself a tankard of beer."

"What does this soldier want here—or maybe I hadn't already ordered him away from this house?!"

The hunchbacked witch stood before them, her face outstretched, her hair rising in pillars above it and her long chin like a cliff-ledge hanging downward and outward, set in such a way that her mouth looked like it was in the middle of her belly. Her shrill voice tore through the library's calm.

"My delight!" said Arnas, and he went over to her and stroked her long cheeks tenderly. "I'm so glad that she has come!"

"Why has the soldier taken off his boot inside my house?" said the woman.

"Perhaps his shoes were chafing him, my darling," said her husband as he continued to stroke her tenderly. "This is an Icelander who has come to speak with me."

"It's obvious that this is an Icelander, because he's stinking up the whole house!" said the woman. "And naturally he's begging for alms like all Icelanders do whether they're at home or abroad, whether they're wearing sweaters, overcoats, or soldiers' jackets! Wasn't it enough, dearest, that you dragged back here that insane Johan Grindevigen and that evil devil Martinsen, who stole two fine hens from me yesterday and who was lurking about here in the garden this very morning?—and you said you wouldn't be scraping together any more of this disgusting race. This entire half-year since I became your wife I've been forced to buy more perfume than I ever had to do in my previous long and blessed marriage!"

"Oh, darling, these are simply my impoverished people," said the Erudite Archive-Secretary, Assessor Consistorii and Professor Antiquitatum Danicarum, and he continued to fondle his dejected wife.

— 18 —

Jón Hreggviðsson strolled down the street without knowing for sure what he ought to do next, though he'd been granted leave for the entire day. He wanted to go to a tavern and cool himself down with a drink, but he had only a few coins. He stood irresolutely on the street corner as others passed by. He became so lost in thought that he didn't notice it when someone started speaking to him.

"Huh?" said Jón Hreggviðsson.

"I told you it wouldn't do much good," said the man cheerlessly.

Jón Hreggviðsson said nothing.

"Ah, I do pity the boy."

"Who?" said Jón Hreggviðsson.

"Ah, who else but poor Árni," said the man.

"You stole the woman's hens," said Jón Hreggviðsson.

"Who cares? She inherited a large farmstead in Sjaelland from her previous husband," said Jón Marteinsson. "Besides the gardens, the ships, and the barrels of gold. Listen, pal, what sense is there in standing here? Don't you think we ought to go to Doctor Kirsten's and buy ourselves a mug of beer?"

"I was thinking of that," said Jón Hreggviðsson, "but I don't know if I have enough to pay for it."

"That doesn't matter," said Jón Marteinsson. "At Doctor Kirsten's beer is always brought to the table, as long as men are wearing decent boots."

They walked down to Doctor Kirsten's Tavern and ordered Lübeck beer.

It turned out that the Icelanders in Copenhagen were very familiar with Jón Hreggviðsson's case and his escape from Þingvellir at Öxará during the past spring. Concerning his fate, on the other hand, they had heard nothing, until he appeared here as a soldier registered in the king's book, newly transferred to Copenhagen from Glückstadt. Now the adventurer himself got the chance to tell the story of his journeys between toasts. He took care not to reveal how he'd actually gotten out of his fetters so as not to betray anyone, but said only that a woman of distinguished lineage had given him the good gold to bring to the man who was now considered the best of Icelanders, with the request that he be granted reprieve and pardon. Jón Hreggviðsson then told this new friend of his, much too willingly, how his business with this renowned man had ended. He let Jón Marteinsson see the ring and Marteinsson weighed it in his hand.

"Aw, Hell, I've known women of distinguished lineage, even bishops' daughters," he said. "Every girl's the same as the next. Now let's have some brennivín."

When they finished their brennivín Jón Marteinsson said:

"Now let's have some cognac and—soup. Iceland is sunk, no matter what."

They ordered cognac and soup.

"I think it might be sunk many times over because of me," said Jón Hreggviðsson.

"It's sunk," said Jón Marteinsson.

They sang in harmony, "O Jón, O Jón, drunk today, drunk yesterday, drunk the day before that." Someone in the tavern said that it was easy to hear that the Icelanders had arrived. "And easy to smell," added another.

"It'd be something to celebrate if it were sunk," said Jón Hreggviðsson.

"It's sunk," said Jón Marteinsson. "I didn't say it might be sunk."

They drank more cognac. "O Jón, O Jón, drunk today, drunk yesterday, drunk the day before that—drunk indeed!"

After a short time Jón Hreggviðsson asked Jón Marteinsson to act as his intercessor before the king and the counts.

"Then we have to have some roast venison and French red wine."

Jón Hreggviðsson ate for a while, then drove his knife into the table and said:

"There, I finally got something good to eat. Now the land is slowly starting to rise again."

Jón Marteinsson crouched greedily over the food.

"It's sunk," he said. "It started sinking when they put the period at the end of *Brennu-Njál's saga*. Never has any land sunk so deeply. Never can such a land rise again."

Jón Hreggviðsson said:

"Once a man from Rein was flogged. And Snæfríður Iceland's sun comes and leans up against the most noble knight in the land, against the one who knows the stories of the ancient kings, but behind him in the shadows stand countless leprous faces and all the faces are mine. Once there was a man condemned to death at Þingvellir by Öxará. In the morning you'll be beheaded. I open my eyes and she stands over me, white, dressed in gold, not more than a span's length around her waist, with those blue eyes—and I, all black. She rules over the night and sets you free. She is and will be the true queen of the entire northern world and the fair maiden with the body of an elf even if she is betrayed; and I, black."

"Aw, is there no end to vanity?" said Jón Marteinsson. "Leave me in peace while I eat this beast and drink this wine."

They continued eating. When they finished the beast and the wine the old woman brought them punch in mugs and Jón Marteinsson said:

"Now I'll tell you how to lay a bishop's daughter."

He moved right up to Jón Hreggviðsson, hung over him, and openly described all the details of this work to the farmer, then straightened up again in his seat, struck the palms of his hands together, and said:

"That's the long and short of it."

Jón Hreggviðsson seemed unimpressed.

"Before, when he gave me back the ring, I said to myself, which one of us is poorer, him, or Jón Hreggviðsson from Rein? I wouldn't be surprised if a great misfortune has yet to visit such a man."

Jón Marteinsson sprang up in his seat as if he'd been poked with a needle, then he clenched his thin fists and thrust his head threateningly forward toward Jón Hreggviðsson; suddenly he wasn't of the same mind.

"What're you cursing now, you bastard?!" he said. "If you dare to pronounce the name that you have in mind you'll fall down dead with that name upon your lips."

Jón Hreggviðsson gaped:

"I seem to remember you yourself calling him a boy and a wretch just a short time ago, and his house a miserable one."

"Try saying his name!" hissed Jón Marteinsson.

"Get your face away from me so I can spit," said Jón Hreggviðsson. But since he said nothing else, Jón Marteinsson leaned away from him again.

"Never pay any attention to a sober Icelander," he said. "God in his mercy sent the Icelanders only one truth, and its name is brennivín."

They sang "O Jón, O Jón," and the other guests stared at them in horror and disgust.

Jón Marteinsson leaned up against Jón Hreggviðsson again and whispered: "I'm going to let you in on a secret."

"Aw, I'm tired of hearing about this goddamn bishop's daughter," said Jón Hreggviðsson.

"No more bishop's daughter," said Jón Marteinsson. "Upon my honor."

He leaned toward Jón Hreggviðsson's ear and whispered:

"We have only one man."

"We have a man—who?" said Jón Hreggviðsson.

"This one man. Besides him, no one. Nothing more."

"I don't understand you," said Jón Hreggviðsson.

"He's gotten them all," said Jón Marteinsson, "all the ones that matter. The ones that he didn't get in church lofts and in kitchen-nooks or in moldy bedsteads he bought from great aristocrats and wealthy landowners for farms or chattel until all of his folk ended up penniless—and his family was well-off to start with. And the ones that'd been shipped out of the country he pursued from kingdom to kingdom until he found them, one in Sweden, another in Norway, now in Saxony, then in Bohemia, Holland, England, Scotland, and France, yes, all the way south to Rome. He bought gold off of usurers to pay for them. Bags of gold, casks of gold, and never once did anyone hear him haggle over the price. He bought some from bishops and abbots, others from counts, dukes, princes, and emperors, several from the pope himself—it even looked likely that he'd lose whatever he had left and be thrown into prison. And never throughout eternity will there be any Iceland except for the Iceland that Arnas Arnæus has bought with his life."

The tears streamed down Jón Marteinsson's cheeks.

And the day wore on.

"Now I'm going to show you Copenhagen, the city that the Danes got from the Icelanders," said the farmer's new guardian and guide late in the evening, after they'd paid their bill with the good gold in Doctor Kirsten's Tavern—they even had enough left over to visit a whorehouse. "This city was not only built with Icelanders' money, it's also lit with Icelandic whale oil."

Jón Hreggviðsson sang from the *Elder Ballad of Pontus*:

> "Whenever you're able to buy a cask
> Throw all you've got into it,
> Stave off sleep till you've done your task
> Stave off sleep till you've done your task—
> Till you and the boys drink through it."

"And there's the King's Pleasure-Garden," said Jón Marteinsson, "where noblemen in sables rendezvous with aristocratic girls wearing low-cut dresses and gold on their shoes while other folk plead tearfully for pig iron and rope."

"Alright already, don't you think I know there's a shortage of hooks and line?" said Jón Hreggviðsson. "Now I want to go to a whorehouse."

Their path led from the harbor through the center of town. The sky had lightened considerably with the calm frost and the moon added to the glow of Icelandic whale oil illuminating the place. The households of the noblemen towered over each other, each one more splendid than the next, with the cold and unimpressive appearance that is a true witness to the world of wealth. In the doorways of these massive houses were heavy doors made of choice wood, locked tightly. Jón Marteinsson continued to brief the out-of-towner:

"In this house sits my blessed Maria von Hambs, who at this moment owns the single largest financial share in the Iceland trade. A short time ago she donated a large sum of money to be used to buy soup for the poor once a day, so that she wouldn't go to Hell. So you can see it's not only the one-third of the townspeople who are worth anything that makes its living off the Iceland trade; now it's also the earth-lice, the sons of Grímur Kögur,* who get their meals from it—the ones who were previously roaming the streets with empty paunches and rolling those who starved to death into the canals. The Treasurer Hinrik Müller, who controls the harbors in the Eastfjörds, owns that brightly lit house there encircled by fruit trees—do you hear those sounds of music and dancing?—it's not just you and I who're feasting tonight, pal. And the house with the angel at the gate is owned by the most handsome cavalier in town, Peder Pedersen, who controls the harbors at Básendar and Keflavík—he supposedly doesn't have to do anything more than pull out his handkerchief for the king during their next drinking party in order to be made a true nobleman, with his name ending in 'von' and some other long German word."

Finally they came to a great orchard surrounded by high stone walls. They peered in through chinks in the wall. Glazed frost coated the trees and the lawn was covered with rime. Moonlight reflected scatteredly off the glaze and gleamed golden upon the orchard's quiet ponds. Two shimmering swans glided over the water and stretched their necks majestically in the tranquillity of the night.

A lofty palace dominated the center of the orchard, shining under the shelter of the expansive crowns of oak trees. It was newly raised, with steep roofs and florid gables, oriels of red sandstone, and niches containing statues perched on columns. The palace had four towers with stacks of balconies, each tower topped with a tapering spire; the finishing touches were being put on the final spire. The moon shone on the burnished copper of the roofs and towers.

Jón Marteinsson continued:

"This palace has been built as splendidly as possible in order to overawe foreign ambassadors and dignitaries; they searched for the materials far and wide before it was raised and nothing was spared in its expense. A Dutch master built it; an Italian sculptor did the exterior ornamentation; the chambers within were decorated by French painters and engravers."

Jón Hreggviðsson felt like he would never be able to tear his eyes away from this vision: the forest of white porcelain, the polished copper roofs of the palace in the moonlight, the lake and the swans that continued to glide over the water and stretch their necks as if in a dream.

"This palace," rattled off Jón Marteinsson, with a cosmopolitan's straightforwardness—"this palace is owned by Christian Gyldenløve, the king's kinsman, Lord of the County Palatine of Samsøe, Baron of the City of Marselisborg, Knight, General-Admiral, Lieutenant-General and Postmaster-General for Norway, Governor and Chief Tax-Collector for Iceland—an exceptionally honest and excellent lord."*

Jón Hreggviðsson awoke suddenly from his reverie, stopped peering in through the openings in the wall, gripped handfuls of the shaggy hair hanging out below his hat, and scratched himself.

"Huh?" he said distractedly: "Did I kill him? Or didn't I kill him?"

"You're drunk," said Jón Marteinsson.

"By my Creator, I hope I killed him," said Jón Hreggviðsson.

— 19 —

Occupying the territory on the opposite side of the Øresund were the Swedes, a race that had waged a continual war against the Danes for more than a hundred years.* They repeatedly sent armies to Denmark, besieged the Danes with occupational troops, bribed the farmers, blackmailed the king, raped the womenfolk, and shot cannonballs over Copenhagen; they had even bullied the Danes into relinquishing the excellent territory of Skåne. The former frequently enlisted the help of a wide variety of foreign nations in their struggle against the latter, though the latter were occasionally able, with God's help, to convince distant heads of state, such as the Great Czar in Moscow, to send troops to fight against the former.

Now conflict was raging once again and both combatants had sought assistance in distant lands. Jón Hreggviðsson arrived back at his barracks late after having drunk away the golden ring with Jón Marteinsson, and he was in a suitable mood for telling off the scoundrels who never got tired of harassing a lice-ridden Icelander. Unfortunately no appropriate opportunity for fighting presented itself. Extra guards had been posted and everyone was under strict orders to maintain discipline, since the Swedish infantry was thought to be right around the corner. Jón Hreggviðsson gave one or two men an earful but they didn't pay any attention; no one even wanted to kick him. Everyone was thinking about the war. One man said that the Swedes certainly wouldn't stop at Skåne—Sjaelland would be next, then it would be Fyn and Jylland.

Someone asked, "Where's the navy—isn't the navy going to defend the channel?"

Another said, "The English and Dutch have brought their warships into the channel and have supposedly sent legates to Moscow to talk with the Czar. And our Admiral Gyldenløve's come ashore and he's holed up in his palace squeezing Amalie Rose."

Jón Hreggviðsson sang an introductory verse from the *Elder Ballad of Pontus:*

> "Dawnlight is breaking. Now we shall raise
> Battle-cries once again.
> Fare you well, maiden, whose beauty I praise.
> Blood pours from murdered men."

On the next day the men repaired their boots and reinforced the straps on their parkas. Early in the morning on the day after, drums were beaten and pipes, bugles, and krumhorns were blown as the army set off to fight the enemy. Each man had to carry close to fifty pounds upon his back. The weather was damp. The road was an unbroken stretch of mud and many had difficulty keeping the pace, amongst them Jón Hreggviðsson. Inebriated German officers rode alongside the company, bellowing and brandishing whips and pistols in the air. The marching music soon stopped because the pipers' hands were numb with cold, though it was replaced by the sound of someone whining.

They received news that Swedish warships lay offshore and that the Danish advance guard had already engaged a Swedish scouting party. Jón Hreggviðsson was ravenous; the same went for the Wendish man marching next to him. It kept on raining. Cackling crows flocked in the fog suspended over the bare black treetops. They marched past farms comprised of one-stalled longhouses, the custom in Denmark being that men and sheep lodge together under one roof, each at the opposite end of the building. Horses and sheep grazed in the green hayfields. The houses' straw-thatched roofs hung down so low that a man walking by would brush his shoulders on the eaves, and the rooms had tiny glass windows covered with curtains. Young girls peeped out from behind the curtains, watching the soldiers who were on their way to thrash the Swedes for their king in this soaking weather, but who were so wet and weary that they gave not even the slightest thought to the girls in return.

In one such village three dragoons came riding up the road toward the division, spurring on their horses with cracks of their whips. They exchanged words with the officers, and the company was ordered to halt. The officers rode alongside the ranks and scrutinized the men. They stopped opposite Jón Hreggviðsson and pointed their whips. One of them called to the farmer, using one of the German names they'd invented for him during the days of war:

"Joen Rekkvertsen!"

He misunderstood the name at first, but when it was shouted a second time his companion gave him a shot with his elbow to let him know that they meant him, and Jón Hreggviðsson saluted in soldierly fashion. He was ordered to break rank.

When the officers had verified the man's identity two drivers were selected from the ranks, and Jón Hreggviðsson was chained, shoved onto a wagon, and driven back to Copenhagen accompanied by the dragoons.

When they arrived in Copenhagen he was taken to an unfamiliar house, dragged before some German officers, and interrogated. The officers wore colorful uniforms, were girded with swords, and had twisted beards and feather-tassels. They asked whether this man was Johann Reckwitz aus Ijsland buertig. The farmer was sullen and black, muddy and wet, and was being held fast by two armed soldiers. He answered:

"I'm Jón Hreggviðsson from Iceland."

"You are a murderer," said the officers.

"Oh," said Jón Hreggviðsson. "Who says that?"

"Does he presume to question us?" said one of the officers in surprise, and the other ordered one of the soldiers to fetch a whip and beat the man. The soldier returned with the whip and beat Jón Hreggviðsson several times, both back and front, then on the nape of the neck and a bit in the face. After a short time the second officer ordered the soldier to stop and asked whether he was a murderer.

"It's useless to beat an Icelander," said Jón Hreggviðsson. "We notice it about as much as we notice lice."

"So you are not a murderer," said one of the officers.

"No," said Jón Hreggviðsson.

The officers ordered the soldier to fetch the Paternoster, which turned out to be a wreath of knotted cords that they shoved onto the man's head and twisted with sticks until the knots drove into his skull and his eyeballs bulged. Jón Hreggviðsson realized that this was going nowhere and said that he was a murderer. They ordered that the Paternoster be taken off him.

After this adventure Jón Hreggviðsson was taken to Blue Tower and shoved into a cell shared by murderers of children and hen-thieves; his clothes were removed and he was placed in a foul burlap sack and shackled to the wall. Affixed to the wall was a huge chain ending in three steel cinches. These were squeezed around the man: one around his thigh, another around his midsection, the third around his neck, and a nail was driven in to secure the collarpiece. This was called the King's Ironwork.

It was past suppertime and Jón Hreggviðsson was given nothing to eat after such a busy day, so as soon as the men who shackled him took their lanterns and left he decided to sing several choice introductory verses from the *Elder Ballad of Pontus* as he sat with his back against the wall.

> "For vigor the belly's our strongest bower,
> In the gut our sense does dwell,
> For a meal alone has almighty power
> For a meal alone has almighty power
> Eternal it is as we-e-ell."

The other prisoners woke up and cursed him. The cell soon resounded with argumentation and agitation, weeping and grumbling, but Jón Hreggviðsson said that he was an Icelander and that he could care less no matter how much they complained, and he carried on with his verses.

After this everyone there realized that it was useless to hope for better, and they gave themselves in silent terror over to the power of their fate.

— 20 —

Seldom before had Jón Hreggviðsson encountered another such collection of men with no homes, no families, and almost no knowledge as he did now in this tower. They were tied up like cattle and forced to tease hemp as long as there was any glimmer of daylight. The only sounds they uttered were obscenities or curses. Jón Hreggviðsson demanded that as a soldier of the king he be transferred to the Stokhus, the army's prison, along with decent folk. The wardens asked in return whether this wasn't entirely respectable company for an Icelander.

He wanted to know by what laws he'd been sent hither and asked to see a copy of the verdict, and they answered that the king was just. Several inmates who heard this cursed the king and said that he'd get caught in a pinch with Boot-Katrin.*

There seemed to be no path lying from this tower toward life, neither by way of law nor lawlessness. Stout iron staves barred the windows, which were set so high in the wall that it seemed impossible that anyone had ever taken a look out of them. The only entertainment they had in this place was when the fleeting shadow of a broadwinged bird flying past a window passed momentarily over the wall. The oldest of the inmates, a criminal who'd done nearly an entire life sentence here, claimed that twenty years ago he'd once been allowed to look out one of the windows, and he insisted that the tower was either built upon an island far away from land or else was so high that one couldn't see the ground beneath it; he'd seen nothing outside but an endless expanse of sea.

One day a newly arrived convict brought news that the war was over, at least for the time being. The Swedes had landed at Humlebaek and defeated the Danes. But since the battle hadn't been a bloody one, loss of life wasn't a factor in the defeat; nor, for that matter, was loss of land. Our Most Gracious Majesty, on the other hand, had been forced to submit to hard terms of peace: Destroy all major fortifications and pledge to build no new ones. And to top it all off he'd been coerced into paying the Swedish king a hundred thousand special-dollars* in cash.

One of the criminals wanted to know how the king, who was in such bottomless debt that he couldn't even afford tobacco, had been able to scrape together such a fortune in these difficult times.

"It was Count von Rosenfalk who took care of it," said the new inmate. "When the enemy started scowling and saying, 'Out with the money,' the king sent messengers to this lovely young man and he went straight to his cellar and ordered his servants to bring out the gold."

The first convict: "Who's this Count von Rosenfalk?"

The second convict: "Peder Pedersen."

The first convict: "Which Peder Pedersen?"

The second convict: "The son of Peder Pedersen."

The other convicts: "Now which goddamn Peder Pedersen?!"

Jón Hreggviðsson: "He leases the harbors in Básendar and Keflavík. I once knew a man named Hólmfastur Guðmundsson who did business with him and his father."

Jón Hreggviðsson pleaded with the guards day after day, week after week, if not in a rage then with friendly cajolements, sometimes even in tears, that they deliver his request to have his case retried to the castle's commandant, but it was all in vain: no court would have anything to do with it. The farmer never received any explanation as to how he'd come to be here nor why he'd been sent hither.

One morning when the warden came with rye-meal porridge he went straight over to Jón Hreggviðsson, kicked him as hard as he could, and said:

"Here, take that, goddamn Icelanders."

"My darling!" said Jón Hreggviðsson, smiling. "I'm so glad you've come!"

"I was drinking with one of your countrymen at Doctor Kirsten's last night," said the warden. "And he drank my boots off me. I had to walk home barefoot. You can all go together to Hell."

And now it so happened, because Jón Marteinsson had been drinking with the warden from Blue Tower, that not more than a few days passed before a German officer and two guards strode into the prisoners' cell. The officer ordered the guards to release Jón Hregg-viðsson, and they escorted him out of the cell.

"Are they finally going to behead me now?" he asked happily.

They did not answer.

First Jón Hreggviðsson was taken to the commandant. Several books were leafed through and the name Johann Reckwitz aus Ijs-land buertig was found in its place. The officer and the commandant looked at the man and spoke together in German and nodded their heads to each other. Next he was taken to a deep cellar where two old washerwomen stood in a thick cloud of steam over kettles and tubs of water, and these old hags were ordered to scrub Jón Hreggviðsson from top to bottom and to rub lye into his scalp, causing the farmer to feel like he hadn't landed in a worse spot since the Dutchmen had shined him up in their dogger off the coast of Iceland. Then he was given his uniform, cleaned and mended, and the same boots, newly polished, that he'd managed to keep out of Jón Marteinsson's hands. Finally a barber's apprentice was brought in from town to give his hair and beard a close trim, and in the end the farmer looked like a churchwarden on a Sunday. He reckoned that the upcoming beheading would be an elaborate and elegant affair in the eyes of the proud noblemen and their guests.

"Will the ladies be coming as well?" asked Jón Hreggviðsson, but no one understood his question.

A two-horse wagon was waiting outside. The German stepped in and sat down in the backseat. Jón Hreggviðsson sat opposite him, with a guard on each side. Nothing of human life stirred in the German officer after he was seated except when he burped now and then. The guards were silent.

After a long drive into the city they pulled up at a huge house. Before the house was a broad winding staircase and two pillars topped with imperious, dreadful-looking lions, and over the doorway was a grisly stone mask with the face of a beast, a man, and a devil. On the staircase stood troll-sized, heavily armed soldiers, stiff as blocks of wood, their brows furrowed.

Jón Hreggviðsson was led up the staircase, level after level, then through a high and shadowy foyer where candles burned in brackets on the wall. He stumbled on the cold flooring slabs, but they kept going, up more stone steps steeper than the others, where he lost his footing again. They then passed through a great labyrinth of alternating corridors and chambers, where black-clad aristocrats sat in judgment-seats, or where despondent, cowled men, gray-haired and shriveled, bent over their desks and wrote out grave sentences. The farmer was convinced that he'd arrived at the Great Courthouse, to which all the others answered.

They finally entered a medium-sized chamber brighter than the others. The window reached the floor and was heavily curtained, causing dusky shadows to engulf the scene partway, lending the place a miragelike air. Hanging on one wall was a colorful portrait of His Royal Majesty and Grace in his youth, wearing a peruke that hung down to the middle of his upper arm and a fur-lined cloak so long that it trailed for three ells along the floor behind him; there were also portraits of his blessed father of praiseworthy memory and of both of Their Highnesses the queens.

Around an oaken table in the center of the hall sat three peers in wide cloaks, silver-tinted perukes, and imposing ruffs, and one general bedecked with golden braids, golden spangles, and golden spurs, with diamonds on his sword hilt, a blue face, and a beard so twisted that its points reached to the red bags under his eyes.

Out near the window, half-illuminated, half-fused with the curtain's heavy shadows, stood two notable aristocrats who conversed quietly and paid no heed to the four sitting at the table. It was as if these two bystanders had their home here, and yet not. They did not look at the visitor when he arrived, and the silhouettes of their profiles continued to play against whatever warm light came in through the window. Jón Hreggviðsson thought that if one of these men wasn't Arnas Arnæus then he wasn't able to tell people apart.

A secretary came with a book and the process of verifying whether the man was Jón Hreggviðsson began once again. When the verification was completed The Grandees began to browse through their documents and one lifted his chin majestically from his chest and spoke several solemn words to the farmer. When he was finished the blue-faced man with the diamonds on his hilt said several words to the farmer in much the same way, but more brusquely. Jón Hreggviðsson couldn't understand them.

One of the notable aristocrats walked away from the window and came over to Jón Hreggviðsson. He was a tired and sad-looking man, but unpretentious, with gentle eyes, and he addressed the farmer in Icelandic.

He explained to Jón Hreggviðsson, slowly and quietly, that in the winter word had gotten about that there was an Icelander serving under the king's standard, an escapee from prison who had during the previous spring been sentenced to death at the Öxará Assembly. No sooner had this been confirmed than the authorities had ordered that the man be arrested and tried without delay. These orders had been a hair's breadth from being implemented, but at the last minute a noble Icelander had pointed out to the king several faults in the verdicts handed down against Jón Hreggviðsson by both the district and general courts in Iceland. Next the Icelander asked the Three Grandees for the king's letter. They handed it over and he read several items to the farmer: "Whereas it is in certainty difficult to see by what reasoning judgment in his case has been delivered, We have now according to Jón Hreggviðsson's most humble wish, most mercifully granted and extended to him, under Our protection, full freedom to travel to Our land Iceland, to present himself in person to his rightful judge at the Öxará Assembly, and, if he so pleases, to appeal his case before Our Supreme Court here in Our city of Copenhagen. He is with this letter equally promised Our most merciful protection to travel a free man from this Our land Iceland and to return to this Our city of Copenhagen to await judgment of conviction or acquittal, according to the just estimation of Our laws and Our Supreme Court."

The Icelander received a second letter from the general's hand. He called this second letter by its Latin name, salvum conductum,* and read from it that Johann Reckwitz aus Ijsland buertig, infantryman under the command of Lord Captain Trohe, was hereby granted by Colonel-General Schønfeldt a four-month leave of absence to travel to Iceland to pursue justice in a certain lawsuit, and to return afterward hither to the kingly residence of Copenhagen to continue his service under the standard.

At that the Icelandic official handed the two letters over to Jón Hreggviðsson, the king's letter of safe-conduct containing the Supreme Court appeal, and the salvum conductum of the Danish army.

Arnas Arnæus stood motionless at the window, light upon one of his cheeks and shadow upon the other, staring absentmindedly out at the street. It seemed as if he had played no part in this meeting, and he did not look in the direction of Jón Hreggviðsson from Rein.

The farmer was never able to remember how he came out of the huge house, but he suddenly found himself standing upon the square outside, the two lions and the hideous head of the man, beast, and devil at his back. The guards who had sat beside him in the wagon followed him out and were gone. The German officer had also disappeared like dew before the sun. The sky was cloudless. The farmer noticed that summer had arrived: the trees stood topped with verdant crowns, a fragrance of copsewood filled the air, and one small sparrow chirped ceaselessly in the dry calm.

THE FAIR MAIDEN

— I —

The Tunga River flows on, placidly and broadly, its current heaviest in branches pouring into Hvítá, the glacier river, east of the see of Skálholt. On the headland between the rivers is a wide marsh of sedge, then the land rises and a great settlement begins, lorded over by a landed estate, surrounded by tenant farms. The place is called Bræðratunga. Seated there in her bower is a blue-eyed woman, her complexion golden-cast, embroidering upon a cloth the ancient wonder of how Sigurður the Völsung destroyed the worm Fáfnir and carried its treasure away.*

Polished glass gleams in the window of her loft. Through it can be seen folk traveling through the district, their paths lying across the open plains and down along the riverbanks to ferries that cross in various directions. Skálholt itself remains hidden from view, lost behind Langholt. She is seated in a carved chair, a stool at her feet, encircled by flossy pillows. Drawn before her bedcloset is a curtain woven with ancient images. Against the wainscoting opposite, close beneath the slope of the ceiling, are her clothes-chest, painted green, and a stout birchwood bureau. On a frame near the door sits her saddle, the greatest of treasures, a high-bowed side-saddle bedecked in repoussé, bow and boards clad in brass and embellished with diverse designs, dragons, men, and angels between the bosses, maker's name and year engraved on the endboard, embossed leatherwork fastened down with studs, and lying over the seat a beautifully crafted blanket, folded neatly, the bridle hanging from the bow: it seems the woman is ready to leave. A fragrance hangs over her still, foreign, somewhat thick.

Several men approach from the direction of the Hvítárholt ferry, which one takes to go down to Bakki.* Three are on horseback, two on either side of the third, holding him up on his horse; a fourth walks before them, leading the center horse by the reins. The man upon this horse is apparently the pivot-point of this expedition, yet his head hangs down to his chest, and his hat hangs over his face. The man's peruke sticks out from a pocket in his cloak. He had evidently been rolled up out of a clay pit, if not something worse. These men head toward Bræðratunga.

When one looks toward the farmstead from the thoroughfares its features magnify: fifteen gabled houses, some garreted, facing south-west, a timbered houseroom farthest out with two wood-paneled end-walls, the manor house towering beautifully over the green, level land on a bright spring day like today, when sunshine glows off the planking and the roofs.

But if the traveler breaks the spell of distance a different view meets his eyes. Proximity is the true enemy of these houses. Here desolation has its home. All the buildings are on the verge of collapse, the walls sunken or fallen like swathes of grass ripped from their roots by the elements, the turf dug away by water and stones rolled off their stacks, gaps under the wall plates, the roofs warped or tumbled down, giving shelter to fungus, not men or beasts, the planking, the bargeboards, the door-frames and other timberwork either rotten or broken into pieces, snippets of turf stuffed into the worst of the chinks, in all the houses only a single windowpane whole, the others everywhere cracked, broken open, and stuffed with saddlecloths or hairsacks filled with hay, the flagstones either sunken, set askew, or standing on their edges. For such a large residence incredibly little man-life was on the move. Two fat workmen sleep in the midday calm beneath the homefield wall, their caps over their faces, around them twittering birds, while an old woman in a short skirt, her legs like sticks of wood, rakes rubbish off the grounds; she is, however, too late—the grass is already too high.

The housekeeper knocks on the door, then thrusts her head through the housewife's doorway:

"Oh, my dear Snæfríður, the squire has come; three farmers are here with him from the south, from Flói."

The housewife continued her needlework without looking up, so insignificant did she consider the news, and answered as disinterestedly as if she were talking about the calf:

"Tell them to carry him to his bed in his houseroom, then put a bowl of whey beside him and lock the door from the outside."

"And if he leaves through the window?" said the woman.

"Then our whey is still not strong enough for him," said the housewife.

"Shouldn't we do something for the others?"

"Give them a sip of blanda* from the pitcher if they're thirsty," said the housewife. "I've had more than enough of regaling folk who drag him home."

After a short time the expedition members turned back, this time spitting in contempt. The third member, who had been leading the horse by the reins, was now on horseback—the fourth, the man riding in the middle, had been left behind. Upon leaving they took the trouble of skirting the footpath and riding furiously through the homefield, tearing up the sward beneath the horses' hooves. The workmen continued sleeping beneath the homefield wall. A shout was heard from the farmhouse.

In a moment the loft stairs shook and the door was shoved off its post. The housewife bent a bit more deeply over her work, and from her cloth plucked burls that perhaps were not there. The man stood laughing in the open doorway. She let him laugh for a moment before she looked up. Then she looked up. His beard was more than a week old and he had a black eye, in addition to a slanting, scabby, blackened gash across his cheek and nose. He was missing two front teeth. His hands were scratched. He laughed, scowling furiously, and stumbled and pitched backward and fore, making it hard to tell which direction he would fall, into the loft or out of it.

She said: "There is much I could have forgiven you, Magnús mine, if you had not let those two front teeth be beaten out of you last year."

She looked back down at her work.

"How dare you address the squire of Bræðratunga directly?" he said. "What hussy are you?"

"Your wife," she said, and continued her needlework.

He twisted and pushed his way into the room, threw himself down upon her clothes-chest, kneeled against it in a lifeless heap for a time, then finally made an effort and raised his head; his eyes were white specks amidst black swelling, every human feature upon him obliterated.

"Am I not perhaps the most noble and well-bred man in the entire country? Am I not the son of the legislator in Bræðratunga, the richest of men in three districts? Did my mother not weigh over two hundred pounds?"

She said nothing.

"It may be that you're higher-born than me," he said. "But you're a soulless woman; and what's more—you've got nothing for a body."

She said nothing.

"The matrons here in Bræðratunga have always been fat," he said. "And my mother had a soul besides. She taught me to read in the *Book of Seven Words*.* But what are you? An elf-woman; a color; a mirage. What am I, knight, squire, and cavalier, supposed to do with this slender waist; with these long thighs? And you came here spoiled from your father's house, sixteen years old. A girl who falls in childhood never ripens. Damn it! I want a woman. Get out of here! Come here."

"Try going down to your room to sleep it off, Magnús mine," she said.

"Next time I need brennivín I swear I'll sell you," he said.

"Do it," she said.

"Why don't you ever ask me what's new?" he said.

"When you wake up I'll ask you—if you don't cry about it too much."

"Don't you even want to know who's come?" he said.

"I know that you've come," she said.

"You lie," he said. "I'm gone. Someone else has come."

Then he shouted, "He's come!" and sank back into a heap as if he had expended his last bit of strength in expelling this cry. He paused, then began muttering to himself: "He has finally come to land—on the Bakkaship."

She looked up sharply and asked: "Who has come to land?"

He continued muttering to himself for a while, then started shouting again:

"Who else but the man who shall annul all the verdicts! Who else—but the one man whom the magistrate's daughter loves! He whom this soulless woman lets cuckold me! He whom this girl slept with in her father's house before she could bear children! He whom this slut—the man she will never have, he has come!"

She looked up and smiled:

"It should comfort you some to know, my dear Magnús, that I wasn't forced to accept you. Many excellent men were making offers for me," she said.

"Whore," he said. "You haven't lived a single day with me without loving another man"—he staggered to his feet, tore the cloth from her hands, and struck her in the face, but was far too drunk to beat her in any way that would make a difference. She gave him a timid shove and said, "Stop beating me now, dear Magnús—you'll regret it more when you wake," and he fell backwards onto the chest, his coarse words slowly dying out on his lips as he sat there cowering beneath the ceiling-slope, his chin hanging low, his mouth slack. In a moment he had begun to snore. She watched him sleep, and not a single quiver on her lips betrayed her thoughts. Finally she laid aside her work and rose from her seat. She fetched a tin cup of water and lye, then moved the man around until he was lying with his feet hanging over the end of the chest. She pulled off his boots and slipped off his clothes by lifting him here and there, then cleaned him carefully and finished by washing his feet.

When this task was finished she pushed the man-covered chest slowly up to her bedcloset, pulled the curtain aside, took the quilt off the bed and raised the duvet, then rolled the man off the chest and onto her bed and spread the sheet, white as driven snow, over him. She pushed the chest back to its place, drew the curtain, sat back down in her chair, and continued to embroider her ancient scene.

— 2 —

The squire spent the next day in bed; he was still lying there when visitors showed up at the farm. There were four of them altogether: Vigfús "the Wealthy" Þórarinsson, bailiff in Hjálmholt; his son-in-law Jón from Vatn, smuggler, the only man in the Árnes district who had brennivín to trade for men's money or property when the trade manager in Eyrarbakki had run out himself; and finally two other farmers of the more privileged class, besides some grooms. The behavior of these visitors was striking. They made themselves at home, dismounting at the edge of the homefield and telling their servants to allow the horses to graze inside the wall, a short distance from the place where the workmen had lain down to sleep in the clement noonday weather, just like yesterday and the day before; they then proceeded to poke about in the hovels. They tested the rotten wood with their knuckles, tilted their heads left and right before numerous doorless doorways, and finally headed to the farmhouse to undertake the same investigation there; in no time at all they were walking down the main passageway, without having once thought to knock on the door. The housewife had been standing at the window, and now she called over to her husband, who lay sick in her bed, and asked: "What does the bailiff want here?"

"For sure I've done something wrong," mumbled the squire, without moving.

"He's not here looking for me," she said.

The squire pulled himself forward off her bright bed, looking like a man who has begun to rot in his grave, and she draped a piece of clothing over him; then he went down to greet the visitors.

It turned out that the squire had sold his homestead and patrimony, Bræðratunga, in all its fixed and liquid assets, to Jón from Vatn, the bailiff's son-in-law, and the new owner, along with the bailiff and the assessors, had stopped in on their way to an assembly in order to fix the value of the livestock and buildings, as this had not been completely agreed upon on the day of the sale. On that day a portion of the price had been duly paid and the farmer from Vatn had Magnús Sigurðsson's acknowledgment for it; today he had brought with him the amount that was to be paid out according to their agreement. They entered the squire's timbered houseroom at a spot where the planking had burst, where debris from the walls— earth, rocks, water—had tumbled through. They took their seats, one or two on a chest, the others on a worn-out old bed, then drew forth the contract and presented it to him. It was all as they said; the document was in all respects legal and valid, written in Eyrarbakki, signed and authenticated by witnesses. He had sold his estate, eighty hundreds of land, for a hundred and sixty rixdollars, forty paid, forty to be paid at the transfer of the land, which was to take place today, the remainder to be paid over the next ten years. The farmer from Vatn had the right to purchase the buildings and livestock at the price he set, and they began now to question the squire concerning the value of these goods. The squire, for his part, answered little, saying that he hadn't been in the habit of counting livestock. If it was cattle, they should ask the old maid who worked in the cowshed; as for the sheep, they could go and take a look in the fields if they wanted. They asked whether he would like some brennivín, but he refused.

The estate at Bræðratunga had from time immemorial been the allodial tenure of the same aristocratic family, comprised of chieftains, bailiffs, and other royal officials, some of them ennobled—and hence the title "squire," which usually became bragging material when the men of that family had drinks in their hands. When Magnús Sigurðsson inherited the land from his deceased father, the legislator, the property was still worth something. The family line, however, had suffered a decline. The siblings of the young squire Magnús had died young, of consumption. He himself grew up coddled and undisciplined in his father's house, and when he was later sent to Skálholt for schooling he wasn't able to accept the constraints of discipline nor consign himself to the exertions that grammatica* demands of Minerva's sons. Instead all his vital motions inclined themselves downward, toward sloth and torpor, and retreated before any form of trial. The man was well-off, there was no doubt about that—his easy life had made him sleek, handsome, and svelte, but he was bashful even from an early age, with a moping expression as if it were too much of a burden for him to look up at people. He was standoffish toward others and spoke with a slight whine; women said he had the fairest eyes of all men. He was an aristocrat. But there in the land where emaciation is the most common cause of death during the spring, the aristocrat was never born who, though his own pantry-shelf might bend under the weight of butter and cheese, was not himself touched by communal infirmity.

Now the legislator in Tunga* was informed by the schoolmaster that there was very little chance that his son would ever distinguish himself through book learning, but since the boy had seemed not to be ill-tempered toward certain types of artifice it was decided that he should be sent to the city of Copenhagen, there to study, if possible, some sort of craft befitting an Icelandic nobleman. Members of this family had always been good craftsmen, though they were usually sent for book learning to satisfy the demands of their age, but the young Icelandic aristocrat, keeping company with the dandies out in Copenhagen, ascertained quickly that in foreign countries craftsmanship was no longer considered to be as suitable for magnates as it had once beseemed Skallagrímur,* while apprentices to the trade were not regarded as anything better than tramps, and were perhaps lower still, since they were in many ways simply slaves of their masters, receiving only one glass of brennivín on Sundays and forced to rise at dawn to tend the pigs or run the housemaids' errands; they were late to bed, and were beaten by their masters and scorned by the servants.

For half a year Magnús from Bræðratunga contented himself with learning to make saddles, and for the other half with silversmithing, but for the next two years either drank or was sick; after three years he went home. He did, however, make the most of the superficial knowledge he had gained in his two crafts ever afterward, and in the first years of his marriage he would occasionally, during periods of calm between binges, occupy himself by constructing a saddle or embossing latten. He engaged in these tasks with a peculiar precision and the type of meticulousness that mediocre hobbyists often employ in greater measure than trained craftsmen, besides following his own innate good taste, which approached the level of artistry; the fruit of his between-bout penitential labor was the emergence of a reputation for genius in craftsmanship, and his fame traveled more widely than that of true smiths. Later the length of time between his drinking bouts decreased so much that he gave himself no opportunity to cultivate his skill other than to refurbish the buildings and farm implements, but even this amounted to little.

At home he was always sober. Every bout began with his disappearance from home, which most commonly occurred when a so-called vital errand compelled him to go south to Eyrarbakki. He would start off every expedition in the company of Danes, casual tradesmen who were gradually attaching themselves to the place, the trade manager on the first day, the clerk on the next. By the third day he would usually have landed in the company of the agent or even the warehouseman. But as the bouts wore on his companions dwindled; presently he would find himself plunged into the company of drunken priests from Flói or Hreppir, but these also disappeared before he knew it. Then he would fall in with the cotters in Bakki and other common louts, and after them beggars, and sometimes the game took place in other districts by mysterious means, since one of the particular marks of these bouts was that they were accompanied by an unclear but eternal movement, a journey in which there was little apparent connection between the places where he eventually ended up. On occasion the squire would come to his senses out in the middle of nowhere, on some unlikely gravel bank or under a wall in another district, or else on an unknown mountain track whence it took him more than an entire day and night to wander back to the settlements; sometimes he ended up athwart some dirt road, jumping up from sleep with a vagrant dog pissing in his nose and mouth. He would wake at times half-sunk in a stream or waterhole, or on an island out in a river. Sometimes he was lucky and awoke in a tenant farmer's hovel, now in his own vomit and other men's spit out on a bare earthen floor, now in the bed of a pauper, who was more than likely leprous, or else alongside some mysterious hussy, though every now and then, by the grace of God, in an unfamiliar marriage bed. After such toilsome periods of captivity he would finally make it home, sometimes carried on or tied to a horse-drawn litter by people who took pity on him, since his own horses would either be lost or sold for brennivín, sometimes crawling along on his hands and knees by night, wet to the bone, usually sick, quite often beaten to a pulp, bloody and bruised, sometimes broken-boned, always lice-ridden. His wife would usually bring him in and clean him off like something dead, pick the lice from him and lock him in his houseroom where he slept. If he were in particularly poor condition she would let him lie in her own bed in the loft for a time. When he regained consciousness he could scarcely bear himself up for long, and she would give him strong moss-tea or other medication to stop his weeping. After several days he would rise from the dead, pale, comely, and transfigured, sorrowful and slightly bearded, his eyes lustrous, having in truth caught a glimpse behind death's curtain, not unlike some of the saints as they are painted on altarpieces. He had always been taciturn, of course, except at those times when he worked his way down the long row and came to the glass called Hilarius,* and on most days not a sound came from him but a murmur and a mumble; he was never more silent, however, than at the end of an expedition. This spring was cruel like every other spring, the sheep spring-meager as usual; the cows were skin and bones and could barely stand, much less give milk throughout the summer, the horses weren't strong enough to transport hardfish, and what was there to trade anyway? The squire answered his workers one by one as they came to report the situation on the farmstead: You're the shepherd, aren't you? Don't you work in the cowshed? If you want hardfish, ask the housekeeper, I don't dish out the meals.

The housekeeper Guðríður Jónsdóttir had been sent directly to Bræðratunga by the wife of Magistrate Eydalín at the start of the first year of Snæfríður's married life to make sure the young matron would not be reduced to begging for her sustenance; this woman acted as if she had no other obligations to God or men. In spite of the fact that Guðríður Jónsdóttir prided herself on being in the service of Madam Eydalín, or, closer to the truth, on being her legate to another quarter of the land, and a poor one at that, almost all the household management of this foreign home was relegated to her, since her mistress Snæfríður paid heed to no work other than her embroidery—she had never once attempted to manage the domestic affairs, nor had she ever shown the slightest concern for the household finances. Thus it happened that this daleswoman, a domestic from a different quarter, was obliged to become, completely counter to her own will, governor and chancellor of a reputable southern estate—anything less and she might not have been able to fulfill the duties entrusted to her by the madam, to see to it that her daughter be provided with the necessary sustenance and service at table and bed, and that her bedroom remained weatherproof and heated during cold spells by a small stove.

When the squire regained his health after a drinking expedition he would usually see to his wife's loft—he would climb up to the roof to inspect whether the turf was in place, or to add a beam or plank if the wood appeared rotten anywhere, because he loved his wife passionately and feared only the single threat that Gudda would leave and take his wife with her. Sometimes before the next breaker crashed over him there was sufficient time for the squire to commence repairs elsewhere on the buildings, but unfortunately the times were so tough that he scarcely ever owned a serviceable piece of wood. Seldom was the squire domiciled for many days after an expedition before he was visited by all sorts of authorities: the bailiff, the parish administrator, priests, and summoners, whose job it was to inform him of his liability for various misdeeds committed during his most recent expedition, or to induce him either to close on various deals he had made or to fulfill various obligations he had accepted, as spelled out in the legal documents produced during the same expedition. It would then emerge that he had perhaps sold a portion of his lands, with the result that he had forfeited most of them by now, and during the previous winter he started cutting into the estate itself by selling off tenancies. Sometimes he would sell a horse or livestock. Usually whatever profit he made would have mysteriously disappeared by the time he found out about the sales from the contracts he himself had signed. He frequently sold his own hat and boots on these expeditions and once he arrived home without any breeches. Sometimes during an expedition he would buy horses, livestock, or land, and men would show up at his door, valid contracts in hand, demanding payment. More often than not compensation would be claimed from him for various types of damage he inflicted on others during an expedition—he would frequently destroy other men's hats or tear their clothing. Sometimes redress was demanded of him for having lodged with cotters in Bakki and having had intercourse with their wives. Others had been forced to endure his slander, having been called thieves or dogs or even thief-dogs and threatened with murder in the presence of witnesses. In the end the man became enwrapped in a ceaseless series of lawsuits and fines.

As a matter of fact, when he was sober Magnús Sigurðsson was a reticent man, averse to quarreling with others, and timid, most resembling an animal that longs only to cower in its hole undisturbed. He desired more than anything to be able to buy himself peace soberly, and he was eager to pay back everyone with something for his drinking transgressions, especially if it could be accomplished without too much discussion. If he had any money he would hand it over to his claimants; otherwise he paid with livestock living or dead, or even with farm implements taken from his workers' hands if the demands were not too lavish. He gladly yielded several lengths of rope to the man whose wedded wife he had regaled contrary to the Ten Commandments, and even plucked off his own rags of clothing to make up for having called someone from Bakki a thief or someone from Flói a dog, all without looking up, and with no desire whatsoever to prolong discussion of the matter. Some said they would be completely satisfied if he were to beg their forgiveness openly, and he considered this the gravest obligation. When the claimants finally left him he would often wind his way silently up to his wife's bower and weep there without saying a word, sometimes entire nights, until daylight rose.

"He's sold the land," said the housekeeper Guðríður, who had been eavesdropping and now rushed excitedly up to her mistress's loft. "I know for certain my mistress the madam in Eydalur will never forgive me for this."

"My husband has always been a man who can get things done," said the housewife.

"He hasn't left you a single cow bone," said the daleswoman. "That devil of a bailiff has come here in person to take the property and we're to vacate today. They're sending you out with the beggars. How can I look in the blessed madam's face?"

"I've wanted to be a beggar-girl for a long time," said the housewife. "It must be exciting sleeping up in the heather with the ewes and the lambs."

"Most right would it be indeed if I drowned myself," said the daleswoman, "and God knows this was the only duty she entrusted to me, to see to it you wouldn't have to go begging; and now, at this very hour, you're out with the beggars, and here I stand and have to answer to my mistress."

"Maybe she'll be the next one to have to go begging," said Snæfríður, but the daleswoman made it a point not to respond to useless chatter.

"How many times," she continued, "haven't I had to take a little pinch of food, your portion of good butter, fish-strips, pickled eggs, and lamb, and stash it away like I'd stolen it, so he wouldn't use it to pay for his rubbish about some fool from Flói or for sleeping with some tart out in Ölfus; and it wasn't any longer ago than last winter that the coffers were ripped open and emptied out right in front of me one night, and if I hadn't gone secretly that night over to Skálholt to talk to your sister I wouldn't have had any breakfast for you next morning, and this is just one tiny example of the war I've had to wage against that tyrant whom the Lord has stricken with boils. And now it's come down to this—you don't own a single piece of land to stand on here in the south. I can't see any way around it—we've got no choice but to ride west with you, home."

"Anything but that," said Snæfríður in a melancholy, temperate tone, without looking up. "Anything but that."

"Oh how I wish my God might grant that these dreadful southern waters would take me out to sea so I wouldn't have to enter into the sight of the blessed madam laden with shame," said this big, strong woman, and she was about to start wailing, but at that moment the magistrate's daughter stood up and kissed her on the forehead.

"There, there, Gudda mine," she said. "Let's keep ourselves dry.

Now go down to the bailiff and give him my greetings and tell him that the housewife wishes to welcome her old friend."

This was one of those old, honorable gentlemen who could be seen every spring amongst three dozen or so of his kind in the law-court at the Alþingi. His face was grooved and weatherbeaten, the expression of his eyes feeble and slightly drowsy, though his brows were uplifted like those of a man who has had long experience trying to fend off sleep while listening to the arguments of wearisome opponents; it was one of those faces that looked as if it could stand secure against most types of reasoning, but especially against the type built on reference to human frailty. The distaff side of the family of Snæfríður the magistrate's daughter had been accustomed to the frigid protection of such men since time immemorial—she understood the nature of such men all the way down to their shriveled boots.

She received him with a smile at the doorway of her loft and bade her father's colleague and honored guest welcome, saying it had always been a great cause of sorrow to her if distinguished gentlemen who had business on the estate did not condescend to exchange pleasantries with one slender chit—and she had hoped that she would benefit from her mother's, Madam Eydalín's, renown for generosity.

He entered her room and she bade him sit, then she opened her bureau, took out a bottle of voluptuous claret, and poured glasses for them both.

He stroked his long gray jawbone, rocking slowly in his seat and breathing audibly—it was difficult to tell whether he was humming or groaning.

"Goodness me," he said, "m-m-m-I remember my darling great-grandmother. She was born during the papacy. She was slim and fair and remained that way for many years, and finally, as a fifty-year-old widow of two bailiffs, married our departed Reverend Magnús from Rip. There have always been beautiful women in Iceland; sometimes very few, goodness me, especially these last several years—since when everything dies what is beautiful dies first. But one or two were always hidden here and there. Quod felix.* Goodness me. Here's to her."

"And how unfortunate it is also," said the housewife, "that fewer true knights are made now than when you were young, my dear Monsieur Vigfús Þórarinsson."

"My darling grandmother was no less a great woman," said he. "M-m-m-. She was one of those esteemed women who have always lived in Breiðafjörður, one of those true island-women, who besides being able to understand Latin and versificaturam* inherited a hundred hundreds of land, twelve-reckoned,* and found herself a man all the way out east in Þingmúli, then sailed with him to Holland, where he learned the barber's art and later became the governor's proxy and the greatest Latin poet in the Nordic lands. And what's more, she had such blue eyes and such airy shining hair—which was not, I might add, golden. When I was a boy, no one ever spoke of her otherwise than as the image that dominated the West. Goodness me. There have always been women in Iceland. Here's to her."

"Here's to," she said—"those old and wizened cavaliers who displayed to beautiful women true chivalry, eager to wade through fire and sea to do their utmost to uphold our honor."

"My darling mother, Guðrún from Eydalur, was and is a true noblewoman though her hue does not match that of her foremothers. She is the one woman in my family who I believed would have been most suited for king's halls in the lands where Icelanders were considered men in ancient times; she was at the same time the sort of woman of virtue, adorned with honor, who is most highly loved by the lowly. She possessed the charitable kindness of a true Christian aristocrat, but still reserved her heart for her children, as beseems only one woman: the woman who reckons as proper to her own nature nothing less than the sort of female pride that existed nowhere more than in the Nordic lands in olden times—and who possesses, on behalf of her husband, ambition, for she never would have given him any peace, even if he had been less of a man than dear old Eydalín, unless he had first made himself the greatest of the men with the name of authority here in Iceland. Proud women have upheld this land, but now it will sink. Here's to her."

"I have considered myself fortunate to have no daughter," said Snæfríður. "For what shall become hereafter of Icelandic women

who are born with the great misfortune to love one of those magnificent men who use their power to destroy dragons, like Sigurður
Fáfnir's-bane upon my cloth?"

"I have always known, my darling, that you are one of those great
women who exist in Iceland. And the last time I stayed at your
mother's it looked to me like she was probably not sleeping too
soundly at night, since she was forced to consider the possibility that
maybe not all of the women in her family were born during the century—m-m-m—when Brynhildur slept on the mountain.* But now
I must leave, my darling, the day is passing. And may peace be with
those who provided for me. I thank my friend's daughter for inviting
me to speak with her. I am an old man and was never counted along
with kindhearted folk. Goodness me. But since I see that her grace,
my darling, is in possession of a most outstanding saddle, might she
permit this old admirer of her mothers and foremothers to leave his
most able workhorse here before her door, if she would have it? I
bought it out west in Dalir last year; it knows the way back."

Vigfús Þórarinsson lifted his glass in farewell, stood up ponderously, and stroked her in thanks with a blue paw, bidding God have
mercy on them all.

Shortly afterward she heard them leave. They rode eastward, up
through Tungur.* Magnús slouched up to his wife's loft; he spoke not
a word, but cast himself facedown onto her bed.

She asked: "Are we to leave today?"

"No," said the squire. "After he came down he said we could
remain here for ten days."

"I didn't ask for reprieve," she said.

"Nor did I," he said.

"Why didn't you promise to leave immediately?" she said.

"You've never asked me about anything, so don't ask me about
anything," he said.

"Forgive me," she said.

Then she went down.

The door to the houseroom was standing ajar and she saw two
columns of beautiful special-dollars standing side by side on the
table, the contract close by. She walked out of the farmhouse, onto

the footpath, the sun gleaming off the Tunga River, the smell of grass in the wind. A rust-colored horse stood tied to a horseblock, restless to have been left alone in this unfamiliar place. When it became aware of the woman's presence it jerked at its reins, glanced sideways at her with its young, extraordinarily keen, glassy black eyes, and whinnied shyly; it had completely shed its winter coat, its body was sleek, its muzzle silky-soft, its neck taut, its croup stately and slender.

The two workmen were still napping beneath the homefield wall with their caps over their faces, and the spear-legged woman was still raking the field.

The housewife walked out to the men in the homefield and woke them up.

"Do this for me," she said. "Fetch a knife from the farm and slaughter the horse standing there tied to the stone. Put its head on a pole and turn it south toward Hjálmholt."

The men sprang up with a start and rubbed their eyes. Never before during their stay on the farm had the housewife ordered them to work.

— 3 —

On the next day Snæfríður rode to Skálholt to speak to her sister Jórunn, the wife of the bishop. Madam Jórunn was accustomed to traveling west to Eydalur every year at the start of the Alþingi, to take her leisure with her mother for ten days, and this year was no different.

"Perhaps you should ride west as well, sister," said the bishop's wife. "Mother would be much happier to see you for one spring than to see me for ten."

"Mother and I were much the same in many ways, but there was never any love lost between us," said Snæfríður. "And I doubt very much that the story about the prodigal son will be twisted onto the female line of our family as long as there is a woman who resembles her mother in that family, sister Jórunn. There's a certain small matter that I would like to discuss with my father this spring, but I'm afraid it's not enough to justify my riding to meet him at Þingvellir. By the way, sister, will you be passing by the Alþingi?"

She said that this was so, that she would ride as usual to Þingvellir with her husband the bishop and remain there for one night, then continue westward with her attendants.

"I really would prefer to ask my father to ride east to meet me," said Snæfríður, "but since the magistrate is supposedly tottering from old age and isn't up for running odd errands, and since we in Bræðratunga have very little means to entertain great men, I would like to ask you, sister, for both these reasons, to bring him a message from me."

She then willingly told her sister what had happened: her husband Magnús had sold his estate to the wealthy Vigfús Þórarinsson the bailiff and his son-in-law Jón the brennivín-dealer at Vatn, and the new owners had given them notice to quit without further delay. At these tidings the bishop's wife went over to her sister and kissed her tearfully, but Snæfríður bade her be still and continued her narrative: she said that what she wanted to discuss with her father was whether he would talk over the matter with Vigfús Þórarinsson and buy the land back from him; she herself, she said, did not have enough of a grip on the bailiff to be able to get him to resell the land, but the authorities in Iceland, she said, knew each other well and had always been able to persuade the others to agree to all sorts of deals.

"Beloved sister, I know you could not possibly be referring to our father," said the bishop's wife. "When has anyone ever heard that another authority in this land was able to persuade him to agree to something he knew in his heart to be unjust?"

Snæfríður said that it would be best if they kept their opinions on such matters to themselves for the moment. She did, however, insist that their father had the power of several authorities in his own hands, more than anyone else, and was far more successful at convincing the others of his will—as much now as ever before. She was certain he could buy the land back from wealthy Fúsi if he wanted to, she said, and for any price he set. After their father retook control of the estate, she herself would buy it from him with the farms she owned in the west and the north; farms that had not been paid out as part of her dowry when she had married without the consent of her kinsfolk before she reached the age of twenty.

The bishop's wife looked over her sister for a moment, with a slight expression of pity for the fact that a certain agreeable slackness of body and soul, obtainable through long acquaintance with affluence, was not also to be found in her—instead this thirty-two-year-old woman was still fair and slender, with a hidden savageness in her blood and a tautness to her body, like a maiden.

"Why, sister, why?" asked the bishop's wife finally.

"Why what?"

"Oh, I don't know, good sister. But in any case, if I were in your shoes—I would thank my Redeemer if Magnús in Bræðratunga left me a beggar, so that I could not be blamed for leaving him."

"To go where?"

"Anywhere. Our mother—"

"Yes, and next you're going to tell me that she would slaughter the calf. Thanks indeed. Go home to your mother, Jórunn, after the bishop sells Skálholt out from under you."

"Forgive me, sister, if I speak wrongly to you—I know you are more like our foremothers than I. And that is precisely the reason why, Snæfríður, that is why it is such a grave sin, that is why it is too grievous for tears, that is why it cries out to heaven."

"What are you talking about?"

"I did not think I would have to spell out for you that which everyone in this country has been talking about for a long time now. You know that our mother's health is failing—the proud woman."

"Oh, hush now, she'll outlive all of us," said Snæfríður. "The diocese of Skálholt is a good daughter—it keeps her in good health, even if the cottage at Bræðratunga gives her a touch of rheumatism now and then."

"This I do know, my dear Snæfríður: the Lord always combines mercy with trial," said the bishop's wife. "To those who meet with misfortune he gives strength of spirit. But more than anything else, we must defend ourselves against dangers of this sort: hardening of the soul in place of the Lord's mercy, and contempt for God and men, even for one's own parents, in place of a humble heart."

"I don't take instructions for happiness from prayer books, good sister. And I doubt that there are many women in Iceland more fortunate than I," said Snæfríður. "Least of all would I trade shoes with you, madam."

"You are scarcely in your right mind, dear Snæfríður—we should end this conversation at once," said the bishop's wife.

"The widow in Lækur," said Snæfríður, "killed her seventh child at Mary-mass last year.* It was her third illegitimate child. Now she's to be drowned at the Alþingi at Öxará in just a few days. Last summer her children survived on horsemeat and chickweed porridge. But one Sunday in the spring, three of them, skinny and swollen, were standing in the rain on the pavements at Bræðratunga along with their ancient grandmother, staring at me as I stood there at my window. The other three were dead. I am a fortunate woman, good sister."

"It is true, we humans cannot comprehend the Lord, my dear Snæfríður," said the bishop's wife. "And there is no doubt that folk in this country have lived in carelessness throughout the centuries and are now paying the penalty for it, as we hear our blessed clerics say so often. Nevertheless, God is not served when those whom he has willed to be born into a higher class subject themselves freely to his punishing rod."

"It was in springtime—since everything here in Iceland happens in springtime—in a grassy hollow here, not far from Hvítá—they found two little girls and a pillow of cotton grass. Their household had been broken up, the estate divided, and this pillow was allotted to these twins. They had both leaned their little heads on their pillow and died. The vermin got to them. No one wanted to do anything with their bones—it was I who stepped in to have them buried. They could have been my girls. No, good sister, I am a very fortunate woman."

"Why do you trouble yourself with tales of woe, dearest sister?" said the bishop's wife, and by now a blush of impatience had replaced her normally cheerful-looking demeanor.

"Recently, at Cross-mass,* they finally decided to hang the sheep-thief in Krókur. He'd been sentenced many times before and had once had a hand cut off, but of course that solved nothing—he simply stole as many more sheep as he had fewer hands. The men up in Biskupstungur rode him home from the gallows to his wife and children—they threw his body across a saddle and shoved it down before his door as they rode by. No, good sister, if there is a fortunate woman in Iceland, it is I, for I weave ancient images into my fabric and sew altar cloths and priests' copes for the churches and collect silver in my little coffer, and what's more, God has made me barren, which is perhaps the greatest fortune that can fall to the lot of an Icelandic woman."

"We are not going to quarrel about that, sister; though it seems to me that it is the Creator's will that every good woman should desire to bear a healthy son. I myself took such great delight in my two sons when they were small. But if a woman is childless in her marriage, then she is not to be blamed, since God has ordained it. But if she is a high-class woman, then she does wrong, and in fact blasphemes God, if she reduces her life to the same level as beggar-folk and criminals. And you are much changed, sister, from what you once were, if even the worst suits you now."

"I've always been the kind of woman who is never satisfied," said Snæfríður. "That's why I've chosen my lot—and have learned to live with it."

"Those who live in strange fantasies never know whose playthings they are until it is too late," said the older sister. "You married without your kinsmen's consent, against the laws of God and the land, and the only reason that our father did not formally annul the marriage was to save you from even more disgrace. Now I do not think it unlikely that he would think twice before buying out Magnús Sigurðsson's estate for you in exchange for the farms he had no desire to entrust you with as part of your dowry. I do know of one man, however, our devoted though reserved friend who never tires of discussing your welfare and who commends you to the Lord's guidance night and day. The bailiff Vigfús and his brother-in-law owe this man no less a debt than they do our father. He is the man who administers to you your pastoral care, the great Latin poet and doctor, the righteous man of God, Reverend Sigurður Sveinsson, the single most wealthy man in the diocese."

"I had been thinking of something else, that is, if my father were to fail me in this matter," said Snæfríður.

The bishop's wife wanted to know what her sister's proposed alternative might be.

"I have heard rumor," she said, "that a friend who has been away for a long time has returned."

The elder sister's gracious and enduring smile disappeared in an instant, involuntarily. She turned blood red. A violent look appeared in her eyes. She became another woman. She tried to speak, then stopped. She was silent for several moments, and then asked, in a musicless voice:

"How do you know he has returned?"

"You and I are both women, good sister," said Snæfríður. "And we women have the gift of divination in certain matters. We learn things though we don't hear them with our ears."

"And you have thought about going south to Bessastaðir to meet him, or, if it were possible, to meet him here in Skálholt, to ask him to buy back Bræðratunga on behalf of you and Magnús Sigurðsson? Are you such a child? Is the world and everything worldly just a closed book before you? Or are you mocking me, beloved sister?"

"No, I'm not going to ask him to buy the estate for me," said Snæfríður. "But I've heard rumors that he is here to investigate the conduct of the authorities. The contract that those two kinsmen, the bailiff and the brennivín-dealer, made with my husband might not be such a worthless piece of paper in the hands of a man who collects documents about Icelanders."

"Do you know what kind of a man Arnas Arnæus is, sister?" asked the bishop's wife, gravely.

"I know," said Snæfríður, "that I despise the next-best, which you and my other kinfolk desired for me, more than the worst. That is my nature."

"I shall make no attempt to decipher your mysterious expressions, sister. And I find it hard to believe that a woman of your stock here in Iceland would choose to plead the cause of criminals in direct opposition to her irreproachable old father, to defend the condemned rather than to stand with their true judge, to support those who wish to incite the commoners to confrontation with His Lordship and to tear apart the public, Christian, and proper order of the people of this land."

"Who is doing all this?"

"Arnas Arnæus and those who support him."

"It was my understanding that Arnæus has returned only because he carries a higher mandate than any other authority who has ever lived in Iceland."

"Of course he is said to be riding to the Alþingi with a letter supposedly signed by the king," said the bishop's wife. "And that he claims to have been appointed as judge over the merchants, and is investigating them at their trading stations in the south and either casting their wares into the sea or placing them under the king's seal, so that poor folk are forced to come running in tears to him to get a fistful of flour or a plug of tobacco in their dire need. He proclaims himself the advocate of rogues and the prosecutor of the authorities. But those who know better truly believe him to be an operative of those in Copenhagen who have driven out the aldermen and the illustrious noblemen from the king's council, to replace them with apprentice craftsmen, beer-brewers, and vagabonds. And report of his arrival here is hardly out and about before you express yourself more than ready to place yourself in his service, in opposition to our good father. May I remind you, dear sister, that Didrik of Münden,* who also claimed to have letters from the king, is lying under a pile of stones in Söðulholt just there on the other side of the stream."

Snæfríður was unmoved. She stared at her sister and noticed that the madam's cheeks were covered with seemingly permanent red flecks.

"Say nothing more to me about Arnæus, good sister," said Snæfríður. "And nothing about Magistrate Eydalín either. And forgive me, madam, if I find in your words little love for our father, to measure his irreproachability against the pranks of a brennivín-dealer, and to call the man who impugns the deeds of wealthy Fúsi the enemy of Magistrate Eydalín."

"I never said that the authorities can do no wrong," said the bishop's wife. "We know that all men are sinners. But I do say, as do all good folk, that if the Icelandic authorities are to be subjugated and castigated at Bremerholm, and the better men of this destitute land laid low, then Iceland will no longer be able to stand. The man who comes to disrupt and destroy the standards of decency and order that have up until now kept our wretched folk from being lumped all together into a single mob of vagrant thieves and arsonists, and who imprints the commoners' flour and tobacco with the king's seal and calls into question our good merchants' scales and balances, when they put themselves to so much trouble to sail over the wild sea— what should such a man be called? Do not disdain me if I find myself at a loss for words when you presume to put your trust in such a man. And when you make intimations that you know him as well as you know your own father, then forgive me for asking: how can it be that you know this man so well? Granted, he did spend part of a summer with our parents out west, while he made arrangements to have the books he found, containing stories of our renowned forefathers, gathered together and transported abroad, and I recall the autumn when he accompanied us, myself, the bishop, and you, to Skálholt on his way to his ship. Can he have confounded you so completely? I rebuffed anyone who perpetrated any rumors about it—you were really nothing more than a child, with no more knowledge of men than a cat has of the Seven Sisters—he, of course, had married a rich hunchback in Denmark before the year was through. But I am eager to hear, sister, how things really went for you, since you now, after sixteen years, place your trust in this traitor rather than accept the certain support of your true and devoted friends."

"If my father, one of the pillars of this land, has no desire to attend to the matter that I ask you now to entrust to him," said Snæfríður, "and if, on the other hand, the man whom you call a traitor frustrates my hopes and shrinks from undoing what wealthy Fúsi has done, then I promise you, good sister, that I will declare myself divorced from Squire Magnús and assent to my suitor and faithful friend the archpriest Sigurður, your protégé; but not until then."

A short time later they finished their conversation, one burning hot, the other skin cold. The bishop's wife promised to bring up the matter with their father at the Alþingi, and Snæfríður rode home to Bræðratunga.

— 4 —

At the start of haymaking the squire was overcome once again with the feeling of restlessness that always led to the very same thing. His haughtiness increased, and he grew more rigid in his dealings with others. He rose early each morning but accomplished nothing, leaving the farm implements he'd been repairing untouched alongside his tools in the woodchips strewn across the floor of his workshed. One day around daybreak he was standing out on a low hill, staring into the distance; in no time at all he was up by the river, hindering travelers. A little while later he was heard singing a few stanzas of a ballad in the farm's main passageway. He ordered his riding horses brought in, inspected them carefully, went to his smithy and repaired a horseshoe, scratched the horses for a long time, brushed off the crusted dirt and spoke to them gently, let them loose for a while but kept an eye on them, went out to the tenant farms and bristled a bit at the cotters, wandered to and fro. The daleswoman Guðríður brought food to the farmer in his houseroom, since he never ate with his servants; it was skyr, hardfish, and butter. He scowled and asked:

"Isn't there any tripe?"

"I don't recall my housemother, Madam Eydalín, saying anything about tripe," said the woman.

"What about pickled testicles?"

"No," said the woman. "The sheep that fell here in the spring gave neither testicles nor tripe."

"Have our tenants up north stopped paying their rents?"

"I don't know about that," said the woman, "but there's whey dripping from the squire's estate."

"Bring me soured whey," he said, "well-soured, and cold."

"By the way," said the woman. "Will my housemother's daughter be thrown out or is she supposed to leave of her own accord, and when?"

"Ask Magistrate Eydalín about that, good woman," said the squire. "He's withheld his daughter's dowry from me for fifteen years."

When the daleswoman came with the whey, the squire was gone. He disappeared like birds die—no one knew where he went. He didn't ride out along the walled path that led from the farmhouse to the thoroughfare, but instead meandered off along a rutted track while the workers took their midday naps. No one saw him leave for certain, but he was gone. His ax and hammer were lying on the windowsill where he had planned to install a screen, where he had even begun to repair the trimmings. Woodchips lay in the grass.

This time he brought silver with him, and even though the king's seal was affixed to the doors of the merchant's warehouse, brennivín could be procured easily for such a reward, along with company befitting a squire: the merchant, the ship captain, other Danes.

When such men gathered they found no shortage of things to discuss, and the newest topic was the royal envoy Arnæus. Apparently, after having arrived on the Hólmship, he had ridden to most of the trading stations in the south, lastly to Eyrarbakki, and had adjudged the merchants' wares fraudulent: he had ordered more than a thousand casks of flour discarded, claiming the flour to be nothing more than maggots and grubs; he had proclaimed the wood fit only for the fire, the iron cinders, the ropes rotten, and the tobacco coarse. The weights and scales were also under suspicion. The starving cotters watched tearfully as the flour was carted down to the sea—they feared that the merchants would never again sail to such a thankless land.

"This business'll go straight to the Supreme Court," said the merchant. "The crown'll be forced to pay. That is, if the king isn't too good to bleed for his men in Iceland, when all he gets back from them is filth and disgrace. And not a single foreign king, emperor, or tradesman has jumped at the offer though he's put the country up for sale plenty of times before."

A look of fury came over the squire's face when he heard his country slandered, since he suddenly recalled that he was one of its chieftains, and in order to prove that Icelanders were heroes and champions he drew one handful after another of shining, newly minted special-dollars from his purse and flung them around the room. He called out for steak, demanded to sleep with the serving-girl, slammed the door as he left, and went and bought a plot of land in Selvogur. He acted the same way for the next two or three days, but since Iceland grew no greater in the Danes' eyes despite the squire's grandiose efforts, and since his pocket money was at an end, it came to the point where he had nothing left to use but his fists to prove that Icelanders were champions and heroes. He didn't have long to wait before the Danes grew tired of his company. Before he knew it he found himself stretched out in the cesspool on the grounds outside the Company's buildings.

This happened at night. When he came to he tried to break back into the merchant's, but the doors were shut and securely bolted. He called out for the girl, but she would have nothing to do with such a man. He threatened to set fire to the house, but since there was either no fire to be found in Bakki or the squire knew nothing of the art of arson, the house remained standing. The squire shouted from midnight until matins without giving any indication that he would ever stop, until finally the clerk appeared in the window in his nightclothes.

"Brennivín," said the squire.

"Where's your money?" said the clerk, but the squire had nothing at hand but a sketchy deed for a plot of land in Selvogur.

"I'll shoot you," said the squire.

The clerk shut the windows and went back to sleep; the squire had no gun.

Toward morning the squire finally woke the boothkeeper.

"Where's your money?" said the boothkeeper.

"Shut your trap," said the squire.

The conversation went no further.

The squire shouted and cursed and beat on the house for almost the entire night until the drink started to wear off him, then he went and fetched his horses.

Around midmorning he arrived at Jón Jónsson's in Vatn, and by then was fully sober but quite hungover. The farmer and some farmhands were mowing in the homefield.

The squire rode up through the field, but the farmer was surly and told the recreant to clear off his unmown grass.

"Do you have any brennivín?" asked the squire.

"Yes I do," said Jón from Vatn. "What's it to you?"

The squire asked the farmer to sell him some brennivín, saying that he would absolutely pay him, but that he had no silver handy at the moment.

"Even if all the lakes in the land were to turn into one great sea of brennivín under my name," said Jón from Vatn, "and all the dry land were to turn to silver marked Magnús Sigurðsson from Bræðratunga, I'd more than likely be lying out dead somewhere before I'd see as much as half an ounce of your silver for a glass of my brennivín."

The squire said that even if he hadn't ever ridden a fat horse away from one of their business meetings, his most recent memory was of drinking himself into beggardom on the brennivín of the farmer from Vatn, and that his wife was most certainly being evicted from the cottages at Bræðratunga at that very moment.

Then the reason why the farmer from Vatn was so sullen toward the squire was revealed: two days ago the farmer's father-in-law Vigfús Þórarinsson had sent word for him to come to the Alþingi, where Magistrate Eydalín had pressured father- and son-in-law, under threat, to resell Bræðratunga to him for a disgraceful price, and had then awarded the land to his daughter Snæfríður by special decree. It made no difference even when the squire held up the title deed for the plot of land in Selvogur—the farmer from Vatn would not place his reputation in any further jeopardy by doing business with the magistrate's son-in-law. The squire sat down in the new-mown hay and wept. Jón from Vatn continued to mow. When he came near to where the squire was sitting he ordered him once again to clear off, but the squire pleaded: "In Jesus' name, take your scythe to my neck."

The brennivín-dealer took pity on the man and out of the goodness of his heart invited him to a storehouse, where he poured him a measure of brennivín and cut a slice of brown shark meat for him with his clasp knife. The squire began to revive slowly. After he'd slopped a sip from the measure and gulped down the shark meat he remembered that his father had been a notary, legislator, cloister steward, and much more, and his great-grandfathers on both sides of the family grandees, some of them ennobled; he said he wasn't accustomed to pulling off fistfuls of shark meat in an outhouse like a rustic, and that he'd feel much better being escorted to the sitting room in the farmhouse, where he could be served at table and in bed by the housewife or the farmer's daughters, as befitted his social class. The farmer from Vatn said that it hadn't been that long since the squire was sitting weeping in the field, begging to have his head cut off. The opinions of guest and host now began to diverge sharply, and the former looked as if he were likely at any moment to lay hands upon the latter due to what he considered the latter's inadequate hospitality. The host was a weak man and knew nothing about brawling, so he yelled for his farmhands and told them to tie up his guest and put him in a sack. They put the squire into a hairsack and bound it tightly, then took him out onto the field with them. The squire spent the rest of the day in the bag, either screaming or kicking, but in the end he fell asleep. At day's end they untied the ropes and dumped out the bag, put the man upon a horse, and sicked four horrendously ferocious dogs after it.

By evening he was back in Eyrarbakki. He knocked at the merchant's and the clerk's, then tried to get himself rowed out to the merchantman to meet with the captain, but the Danes refused to have anything more to do with him. Even the boothkeeper wouldn't answer him. He was very hungry, but famine had hit Eyrarbakki and the neighboring farmlands. A poor widow, however, gave him a bowlful of whipped milk and a handful of dulse, along with a hardened codhead, which she had to tear into pieces for him because he suddenly recalled that he was too great an aristocrat to tear up hardened codhead.

The trading booth was still closed, and the men who had traveled in packtrains from distant places, some from Skaftafell in the east, had found it necessary to pile their wool and other wares in stacks along the wall, while the merchant sat alone inside eating steak and wine, having given orders that he was not to be disturbed. Peculiar countryfolk stood outside the warehouse doors, examining the king's seal. Others started in on making a ruckus, especially boys and casual workers. Still others were in tears as they talked about writing up a petition, several were capping verses or trying their strength at picking up huge stones on the seashore. Some farmers from Öræfi in the east, a journey of thirteen days away, decided to try their luck at pressing their packtrains southward over the heaths before nightfall, hoping they'd still be able to trade in Básendar. Eyrarbakki was dry; not a drop trickled out of the storehouse, but a single prosperous man who had brennivín left over from the previous year's stores gave the squire a sip, which only made him mad with hunger for more. By midnight the place was deserted; they'd all dragged themselves off somewhere to their own grief, some beneath the walls along with their starving dogs. The squire was the only one who remained, besides the white and crescent moon over the sea, and there was no more brennivín.

Suddenly Þórður Narfason—otherwise known as Túre Narvesen—arrives; his movements are jerky, his face tarred. He has white teeth, red eyes, a lopsided nose, and large fists. When he saw the squire he took off his tattered and ugly knitted cap and fell to his knees before him. In his youth he'd been an attendant to the bishop in Skálholt, but was expelled from the post due to certain affairs he'd had with the girls. Even so, he could recall several Latin words ever afterward. He'd murdered his best beloved—some said two—though it was apparently through no fault of his own. One thing was certain, he hadn't been executed, but rather sentenced to hard labor—he was well acquainted with Bremerholm. He was a great artist, a poet and a writer, a good drinker, and an excellent ladies' man, and he spoke Danish so well that he got along with the Danes as if he were one of them. He was a knave and worked as an errand-boy for the trading company and was allowed to sleep in the pigsty; since he was an artist he often assisted the cooper during the autumn, and he called himself a cooper when he was in the company of Icelanders, though he was considered only a half-cooper by the Danes. Around this time Túre Narvesen was some sort of Royal Majesty's Master of the Watch over the place, it being his duty to stand guard at night to hinder the work of anyone who showed any desire to set fire to the buildings or to violate the king's seal.

The squire drove his foot into this courtly man's chest as he knelt there on the ground, the grimiest of the charmers whom a girl in Iceland has at some point called her angel before the very same man put her to death.

"Give me brennivín, you devil," said the squire.

"My honored lord. Brennivín—at this pernicious hour?" said Narvesen, shrilly.

"Do you want me to kill you?" said the squire.

"Aye, your grace, it makes no difference: the world is perishing, no matter what."

"I'll give you a horse," said the squire.

"My dear squire would give a horse," said Túre Narvesen, and he stood up and embraced the squire. "Salutem.* Long live my lord."

He started to walk away.

"You'll own land in Selvogur," said the squire, and he grabbed a handful of Túre Narvesen's rags and held on to him with a convulsive, locking grip. When the man realized that there was little possibility for escape he embraced the squire again and kissed him.

"Haven't I always said a gentle heart wins the world?" said Narvesen. "And since such great things are happening I don't think we could do any better than to go to meet the swineherd."

The squire followed Túre Narvesen to the pigsty. Housed there were the animals that alone of all creatures lived in comfort and decency in Iceland, not least since the king's specially appointed representative had tyrannically banned two-footed creatures from eating maggots and grubs. Farmers were sometimes graciously allowed to take a look at these wondrous creatures through the grating, and they would generally become nauseated at the sight, particularly since the beasts were the color of naked folk, the folds of their flesh the same as in rich men, looking out over these folds with the wise eyes of poor men; many a man spewed gall at such a vision.

The sty was made of wood and tarred like the houserooms of noblemen, and at one end lay the man who tended the animals, Jes Ló by name, an occasional warehouseman, Túre Narvesen's friend and companion from Bremerholm. The general public distrusted the man who raised such animals in the land where humans and their children gave up and died of emaciation by the hundreds and thousands in the spring. Túre Narvesen knocked on the door using a special code his friend recognized and was let in, but the squire had to wait outside. They chatted together in the sty for a considerable amount of time and the squire started to get restless, but the shutters

were well-drawn, so he had no choice but to start shouting and cursing again, and to threaten them with murder and fire. Túre Narvesen
finally came out. He was incredibly downcast and said that the
deputy clerk Jes Ló had turned a deaf ear to his case; everything here
was shut and sealed according to the king's command and there was
no brennivín to be had for gold—Jes Ló's message to him was that it
would be best for the Icelanders to go to their countryman Arnesen
and get from him whatever brennivín they felt they needed. The
squire asked Túre to tell the swineherd he would receive land in
Selvogur. Túre said that the swineherd could care less about owning
land. The squire said that the swineherd should name his price. Túre
Narvesen reluctantly agreed to try to pit himself once more against
the swineherd, and the squire seized his opportunity and pushed his
way into the pigsty after him.

The condition of Jes Ló's flesh was not unlike that of the animals
he tended and he smelled about the same as they did. He lay on a
bunk in a corner of a platform, the creatures behind a grate close by:
the boar in one corner, the sow in another with twelve piglets, several
young swine in the third. The thriving livestock were awake and
grunting. No Icelander could stand their stench, but since the squire
could smell nothing he grabbed the swineherd and kissed him. The
door stood open; outside were sea and moon. The swineherd said
that even the most cunning thief couldn't get into the warehouse,
since that devil's Iceland-dog Arnesen had put the king's seal, doubtless falsified, on all the doors except for the secret door from the
booth-cellar, and no one had the key to that except for the merchant,
and he slept with it. Squire Magnús Sigurðsson continued to offer
property and privileges, but this had no effect: no one put any stock
in his possessions and no one knew exactly who owned his property,
he himself, or brennivín-dealers in various parts of the land, or
maybe even the magistrate his father-in-law. The squire said it would
be most appropriate if he were to kill them both. Túre Narvesen gave
Jes Ló a collusive look and said shrilly, with false, fricative humility:

"My brother has heard that his benevolent lord has one possession
that is still said to be in his custody, unsold and unpledged, and that
this would be, namely, his praiseworthy and virtue-bedecked wedded
wife—"

At the mention of this woman things changed—without any further discussion, the squire jammed his fist into Túre Narvesen's nose. Túre Narvesen abandoned courtesy and struck back. Then they started to fight. Magnús Sigurðsson took no precautions and tried his best to mutilate the man. Jes Ló crawled out of his bunk, hitched up his breeches, and joined in punching the squire. They flew at it for quite some time, and in the end they managed to bring down the squire, but he was so enraged that it was out of the question to try to talk sense into him without tying him down. They uncoiled a rope and after some effort were able to bind the man's hands and feet, then they pushed him through the grating to join the pigs. The cavalier shouted and rolled over several times in the dung-trough, but couldn't get himself loose. The swineherd handed the murderer Túre Narvesen a butcher's knife and ordered him to guard the ruffian while he stepped out. Túre stood at the railing and engaged in pulling hair from the scoundrel, drawing the hair along the edge of the blade, or whetting the knife blade carefully on the palm of his hand. Once again he became his old courteous self, singing the praises of the squire and his wife for their probity and virtue and excellent lineage, but the captive squire continued shouting in the dung-trough; the pigs were stricken with terror and flocked together and entangled themselves one on top of the other in the corner of the sty. Finally the swinekeeper returned. He had returned with an eight-pot cask of brennivín, along with a flask. He set the cask down on the platform next to the grating, and he and Túre took turns drinking from the flask. The squire received nothing.

When the two companions had finished amusing themselves to their hearts' content, Túre said to the squire:

"Our friend Jes Ló is eager to sell his venerable lord this cask, but regarding this matter papers must first be written, for brennivín is at the present time dearer than gold and whoever trades in it does so under the threat of losing his skin or being sentenced to prison at Bremerholm."

"Give me a drink," said the squire softly, when he finished shouting—"and after that you can cut off my head."

"Oh, we would never stoop to such a trade, even if the times were tough. And we would certainly never venture to cut a nobleman's head from him, unless we were forced. What a stroke!" said Túre Narvesen. "On the other hand, I shall here scratch out a little contract upon paper which we shall afterward validate with our signatures."

Jes Ló brought forth the writing implements that he had fetched along with the brennivín, and Túre Narvesen sat writing for a long time with a plank upon his knees for a desk. Jes Ló sat by in the meantime and sipped on brennivín. After prolonged exertion the document was completed and Túre Narvesen stood up and started to read, while behind him the incredibly fat swineherd stood grinning sarcastically.

The letter began with the words "In nomine domini amen salutem et officia,"* witnessing to the fact that its writer had at one time served the bishop, and continued afterward in the solemn, refined, and devout style characteristic of this particular murderer. It stated, as follows, after having specified the exact number of years that had passed since the birth of God, that there had, out in the country named Iceland, in the merchant's pigsty at the trading station Ørebakke, come together three worthies, the honorable Monsieur Magnes Sívertsen, cavalier and squire at Brødretunge, the august and cultivated gentlemen Jens Loy, tradesman, clerk, and supervisor of the station's especial Danish stock, and the widely traveled artisan and erudite poet Túre Narvesen, former subdeacon to Schalholt, now royal cooper and polity-master for the Handel company, who had arranged to execute the following authoritative and authorized missive and charter, which they, postulating the grace of the Holy Spirit as guarantor, have sworn to adhere to in all points and articles and which by no man shall be violated excepting His Most Gracious Sire the King, with the full consent of his kingdom, and containing the matter given as follows: The cask of brennivín that stands on the platform between the parties shall be the lawful and inviolate possession of the aforementioned cavalier and squire M. Sívertsen, in exchange for which the same respectfully mentioned shall immediately upon the signing of this deed fulfill for the aforementioned gentlemen the following articulated proviso, being as such: that he readily and graciously lend and relinquish to the repeatedly and respectfully mentioned upright and cultivated gentlemen Jens Loy and Túre Narvesen, for complete and matrimonial coition for three nights item* three days his, Squire Sívertsen's, in virtue of her beauty, artistry, and pedigree, and renowned as the finest match throughout the land, most dearly beloved, his own probity-loving and virtue-bedecked wedded wife, spouse, and housemistress, Snæfríður Björnsdóttir Eydalín, and shall the cavalier Monsieur M. Sívertsen simultaneous to this deed issue therewith his own missive and attestation styled according to this his own afore- and respectfully mentioned etcetera—

When the recitation reached this point the cavalier was heard to say:

"In those eyes heaven itself has descended. I know I lie bound in filth."

—maintaining the understanding, the missive continued, that just as the brennivín in the heretofore named cask is hereby proclaimed to be a singularly genuine and pure brennivín, at precisely the correct degree of strength though not watered down in the least, so also shall Squire M. Sívertsen's wife exhibit to the missive's deliverers, perfectly and completely, a generous and Christian reception, refraining from riot and unquiet, extending to them absolute tractability, benevolence, and determined optimism, and therewith granting to them all that belongs to the household, especially soured tripe, ram's testicles, and butter from the churns, no less than if they were each in his own right, and both at once, her probity-loving honor's true and affectionate wedded husbands—

"The stars shine wreathlike about her brow," said the cavalier. "I know that I am leprous, lice-ridden Iceland."

The two gentlemen paid no heed to the squire's interjection, and Túre continued reading until the missive stated, in conclusion, that this contract should be as confidential as it was clear according to the agreements of great men, so that neither the common mob nor begging-creatures could get hold of the three partners between their teeth, and on the other hand so that none of them would find himself molested or demoralized by having his reputation come under the attack of indefensible prosecutors, and that this single copy of the missive should by its writer be housed, stored, and protected. Affixing here below our signatures as testimonial and thorough attestation to all the aforewritten—

The captive was no longer crying, shouting, or tossing about. Instead he lay calmly and silently on the floor of the sty, the cask no more than an arm's length away beyond the bars. Finally he rose halfway, still bound, and looked straight up at the ceiling of the sty. His face was twisted in a grimace and the nape of his neck arched over onto his back as he addressed the one who dwells above:

"God, even if I were to spit in your face in the doorway of your church on Good Friday, still I know: it is you."

Then he fell back down to the floor and said, low-voiced, to the men:

"Give me the cask."

They said that the one and only condition was that his name be affixed to the bottom of the contract. He said it should be so. Then they released him. He signed his name to the missive in several quick strokes as the pen spurted ink. Túre Narvesen signed his own name next, in a staid hand quite unsuited to his large fists, but the swineherd Jes Ló made a cross, since he was illiterate, like most Danes; afterward Túre attested his name beneath the cross. In the end they handed the cask to the cavalier, and he immediately set it to his lips.

He drank for some time, then looked around and discovered that his business partners were gone. He had now become perchance like many others who finally acquire their most desired treasure of treasures: he was disappointed. He stood up stiffly. He sauntered dizzily from the swinehouse out into the trading station, cask in hand. There was a smell of kelp and a white light from the moon. He called out for the others, but they were nowhere near. He tried to run, without knowing which way to go, but his legs were sluggish and the earth stood on end; in the next instant he found himself lying horizontal, his cheek in the dirt, without having felt himself fall. Then the earth tilted away from him again. He tried to walk steadily, but the earth continued to surge. Finally he sat down beneath a housegable, leaned his back against the wall, and waited until the earth settled back in its place. He drooped his head and mumbled about the chief courtiers, knights, bailiffs, poets, pilgrims to Jerusalem, and notaries who were his verifiable forefathers. He did not resemble a man, even less a beast. He called himself the lowest thing a mortal creature could be and the greatest aristocrat in Iceland. In the end all he could do was start to sing the sad passion-hymns and death-prayers his mother had taught him in his youth.

Now the story turns to the other party, the two lucky men who had bought the man's wife. They ran off with the papers in their hands. The night was completely still. A thousand little turf-roofed farms cowered down upon the earth—not, however, out of irreconciliation with the sky. One by one the dogs howled. The swineherd had concealed the flask of brennivín under his jacket, in case the men needed to lift their spirits now that there was such important work at hand. They had determined to rush to Bræðratunga straightaway that night with the contract, since the Dane said that women were hottest in the morning. They were both in the grips of that blessed condition of the soul when the realization of a plan seems as simple as its formulation. Horses were the only things they lacked, but luckily there were enough of them in the pastures and they set off to choose their mounts. Here there were both hobbled cargo-nags from faraway places and studhorses grazing alongside the creek, but the horses didn't take well to the men, especially the Dane, and sauntered away, refusing to acquiesce. Finally Narvesen was able to catch two horses and get ropes around them, but since there was no riding gear handy they had no other choice but to ride bareback. Of course the Icelander, like most others, had mastered this art, but the Dane had never once been on a horse, neither bareback nor in a saddle, and since he was a corpulent man and past his best years, and quite drunk besides, it was difficult for him to climb up onto the animal's back, but he finally succeeded by stepping up off a high hillock. When he found himself up so high, however, he began to swoon, and subsequently became almost completely sober. He was sure the horse would either fall sideways or head-over-heels, and then he, its rider, would vault off at a horrific speed and thus lose his life. Every movement the horse made put the man in mortal danger. He implored his companion to go slowly, stretched himself forward along the horse's back, and grabbed its neck with a death-grip. Túre Narvesen said they had a long way to go and had to ride hard, and that they would also have to wade the horses across great rivers to shorten their journey if they expected to reach Bræðratunga by morning, when their wedded wife, whom they jointly owned, would still be warm in bed.

"I'll fall off this creature," said the Dane.

"Maybe you'd rather stay behind, friend, and walk there tomorrow," said Túre Narvesen.

"It'd be just like you to swindle me, and I was the one who got hold of the brennivín," said the Dane. "You know I'm weak-footed, and that there's no way I can walk over Iceland."

"Dear brother," said Túre Narvesen, "I didn't say anything but that if you wanted, I could dawdle there before you and give her your regards until you arrive around noon."

"How am I supposed to find the way there if you ride off without me?" said Jes Ló. "I'm sure I'll never make it to Brødretunge. I have absolutely no idea which way I should ride. I'll probably get lost and plunge off the horse and die, and you'll be there already, having already gotten the girl and swindled your friend; and I was the one who stole the brennivín."

"Now, you mustn't forget, dear brother and friend, that I wrote the contract," said Túre Narvesen. "Danes are big men in their own country, but here they've got no chance, whether or not they can write, walk, or ride. Here in Iceland we don't wait around for anyone. The one who gets there first gets the girl."

Jes Ló was by now starting to tilt to the side, so Túre Narvesen shoved him in the chest, and since the Dane's horse was more inclined toward standing still he felt it best to ride close behind it to spur it on. But as it turned out, the Dane's mount was a mare and consequently somewhat touchy concerning its virginity, and it started to kick out with its hind legs and squeal at the too-close pursuit. At this kicking the Dane dropped quite beautifully forward off the mare's neck, and the soles of his feet turned up toward heaven.

"There you go, a Dane in his best light," said Þórður Narfason, and he dismounted and kicked at the man.

"You bastard, you kick me while I lie here wounded and dazed!" said the Dane.

Þórður Narfason pulled the man up and poked at him and discovered that he was soaked with brennivín, since the flask had been smashed to bits; apart from this he was uninjured.

"Since you've pulverized the flask I am no longer duty-bound to you," said Þórður Narfason. "Our partnership is finished. I proclaim myself divorced from you. Now each of us goes his own way. The one who gets there first gets the girl."

The swineherd grabbed Túre Narvesen's legs and said:

"I'm an upright Danish man, in the service of my merchant and my company and my king, and it is I who stole the brennivín and I who own the woman."

"You Danes really are a sorry lot," said Þórður Narfason, as he continued kicking his friend, "if you think that the day will dawn when you'll get hold of Snæfríður, Iceland's sun."

Finally the Dane's patience came to an end and he tried to sweep the feet out from under his friend the murderer, who by now had become his outright competitor for the woman's hand. With that the battle had begun. It soon became evident that this fat, upright Dane was really quite a strong man and knew a few dirty tricks that took the Icelander completely by surprise. The Icelander wanted to fight standing up and use wrestling throws but the Dane preferred to attack from a prone position and use the strength of his frame. They fought for a very long time and shredded each other's clothing until they were both nearly naked; they scratched and squeezed each other and blood poured from both of their noses and mouths, but neither had been so provident as to bring weapons along. Finally Þórður Narfason managed to land a decent blow upon his friend and knocked him senseless: the swineherd's head fell back and to the side, powerless, his tongue stuck out at the bloodied corner of his mouth, and his eyes closed. Þórður Narfason sat down some distance away, exhausted from the battle. The sun was coming up. There was no brennivín. He saw the contract lying in the turf and picked it up. He had twisted his ankle and could hardly walk; the berserk frenzy had run off him somewhat and he started to feel more and more pain in his body. The gulf remained quiet but for the murmur of water; the egg-laying was for the most part finished. He spied his horse a short distance away and dragged himself over to it, mounted, and rode away. The horse was exceptionally lazy and budged along only when its rider drove his legs into it with all the powers of his life and soul. Finally it stopped inching forward and stood completely still. The man dismounted and kicked at the horse, then lay down with his back against a hillock and looked up at the sky. The moon hadn't vanished yet despite the sunshine. He drew the deed out from under his brazen belt, likewise the letter concerning the woman, read both of them carefully, and found in neither of them any gaping errors.

"Praise God I'm a learned man and a poet," he said.

One of his eyes started aching a bit as he read, and he found that he was unable to keep it open; it was starting to swell furiously. He tried to stand up but his head spun. He hadn't accomplished every-thing even though he'd succeeded in dispensing with the Dane. He still had a long way to go to Bræðratunga and to the lukewarm woman. He wanted brennivín, but lacked the energy to stand.

"It's likely best to catch some sleep," he said, and he stretched himself out on the road, contract in hand, and fell asleep.

— 5 —

Around nones on the day after these events took place, Snæfríður Björnsdóttir Eydalín and another woman are strolling through the homefield at Bræðratunga. The herbs that they have gathered hang from a string tossed over Snæfríður's shoulder. She has inherited her foremothers' skill in identifying medicinal herbs—from some she prepares elixirs, from some dyes, others she picks for their perfumes. She is clothed in an old blue shift, bare-necked and bareheaded in the sun, her hair hanging loosely about her shoulders, sunburnt from her daily excursions in search of herbs. The woman and the home-field share the same golden hue.

Not far from her she spied a fat black horse, tied to a horseblock at the farmhouse, and a short, lean man, darkly clad, walking back and forth along the flagstones, stooping and holding his hands clasped, palms downward. It was the archpriest in Skálholt. When he saw the housewife he removed his high-crowned hat and held it in his hands as he walked out to join her in the homefield.

"An unexpected honor," she said, and she smiled and curtsied and walked directly up to him, extending her sunburned and slightly dirty hand in greeting; wafting from her was a warm, strong scent of thyme, reed, dirt, and heather. He took care not to look directly at her, but greeted her and praised God for having met her in good health, then put his hat back over his ceremonial peruke and clasped his hands as before. He looked down at the backs of his hands, which were blue and swollen with age.

"The day is so fair that I could not refrain from taking my dear Brúnn out for a ride," he said, as if in apology for his presence.

"The giant's ox* always takes to flight during the dog days," she said. "I always want to run off into the wilderness somewhere at this time of year."

"In this destitute land where everything dies, such days reflect the very nature of eternal life," he said. "They are apex perfectionis."*

"How delightful it is to meet monsieur in heaven—in this home-field," she said. "You are welcome."

"Nay, nay," he said, "it was not my intention to preach delusion, and madame must not think that I have begun to embrace heathen-dom, praising created things before their Creator. I only meant this, that they are perfect days indeed when one's prayers transform, as if of themselves, into thanksgiving: a man starts to pray, but before he knows it he finds himself giving thanks."

"Next time you come to me, my dear Reverend Sigurður, I am certain you will tell me that you have met a lovelier girl, that you have experienced eternal life and summum bonum,"* she said. "And I hear that you have found a grotesque crucifix in some old ruins, and that you invoke it in secret."

"Credo in unum Deum, madame," he said.

"You must by no means think that I suspect you of being a heretic—even if you do possess an idol, my dear Reverend Sigurður," she said.

"What matters are a man's thoughts concerning idols," he said, "not the idols themselves. What is most important is to believe in the truth that may be concealed even in an imperfect image, and to live for it."

"Indeed," she said. "The other day I had to leave out the right horn on Abraham's ram, because I needed room for my monogram and the date in that corner of the tapestry. Do you think this will cause someone to believe that the ram broke its horn in the thicket? Of course not; everyone knows that Abraham's ram was sent from God and had two picture-perfect horns."

"Since the conversation turns to images," he said, "I shall explain to you my view. There is only one image of images—our image of life, the one we ourselves make. Other images are beneficial if they show us where we are deficient and how we can improve our way of life. This is why I saved that old effigy of Christ, a relic from the days of the papacy, found in a digging."

"You are a wise and sensible man, Reverend Sigurður, but I do not know whether I would weave into my tapestry all those useful images you mention."

"And yet, what we read in the doctores,"* he said, "remains firm: the truth displayed in a good life is the fairest of images."

"Might I invite the Doctor angelicus* reborn in Flói to enter my poor house and accept a simple, homemade drink?" said the housewife.

"My dearest thanks," he said. "Blessed is the man who is ridiculed by madame. But just as a giant's ox creeps along the ground for eleven months, then flies in the sunlight in the twelfth, so it may be that one ex-priest shall also have his day: might I not rather walk side by side with madame out onto the homefield, for just a moment, to discuss with her a certain matter that has preoccupied me?"

They walked out onto the homefield.

He still had not looked up, but walked cautiously and conscientiously, lingering in every step as if to find its correct working both upon the ground and in himself. He was slightly shorter than she.

"Just now we were discussing images," he continued lecturing, his hands in the same position as before, "true and false images, the images a man makes correctly and those he makes incorrectly though God has provided the raw material for them: I know that you wonder why I have come to you with such idle chatter. But I am, after all, your pastor. I believe it is God's will that I speak. And I have prayed for Him to enlighten me. I believe it is His will that I speak to you these words: Snæfríður, the Heavenly Father has given you more than you have ever wanted to receive."

"Is this meant to be an accusation?" she asked.

"I am not the one who accuses you," he said.

"Then who?" she asked. "Have I done someone wrong?"

"You have done yourself wrong," he said. "God says it and the whole land knows it, though no one as well as you yourself. The life you have lived all these years does not beseem such a splendid woman."

Finally he looked at her, though with only a swift glance. His mouth quivered, and his black eyes were repulsed by her golden complexion.

She smiled somewhat absentmindedly and answered nonchalantly, dully, as if he had caused her to notice a slight stain on her sleeve: "Oh, does the bride of Christ now take an interest in such a pitiably innocent glimmer as my life?"

"I did not expect," he said, "that I would once again have to undergo such a trial as to parley with a noblewoman, especially a woman so bewildered as madame as to have at one time performed a deed which, whether in civilibus or in ecclesiasticis,* would be called a crime, and to have to admonish her concerning her way of life."

"You frighten me, Reverend Sigurður," she said. "It sounds as if you were reading over either *Merlin's Prophecies* or *Tungdal's Vision** before you set out today. I would give a great deal to understand exactly what you mean."

"Blessed would I be if I knew the way to your heart, but it is not in the power of a simple cleric to find his way through such a labyrinth, least of all if you yourself have no desire to comprehend what you are told," he said. "And though your heart may be a wall in which a poor poet can find no door, I am, all the same, compelled to speak."

"Speak then, my dear Reverend Sigurður," she said.

"When it comes to conversing with madame, she should realize that I am not totally ignorant concerning the one with whom I speak: you are as noble a woman as has ever lived in the Nordic lands, wise like the women in Iceland who were once called cultivated, trained in grammatica since your youth and so skilled an artist that your tapestries are celebrated in foreign cathedrals; apart from this, you of all women have been graced physically with such a life-giving fragrance by the mother of the Lord that your sojourn here, besides that of our own tiny blossoms, gives promise of the fact that the protective hand of our Lord Jesus shall always uphold this desti-tute land despite our Father's rightful wrath. Those few inhabitants of this land who are still able to maintain some semblance of virility are burdened by grave obligations during these troubled times, and a woman like the one I described just now has no right, before God, to squander her life in company with an individual who is antipathetic to the honor of her fatherland. It may cause you consternation to hear from the mouth of a priest words spoken in opposition to that which the Lord has joined. But I have watched and waited. I have implored the Holy Spirit. And I am certain that your problem will be solved in casu.* I am convinced that even the pope himself, who pro-claims matrimony to be an unshakable sacramentum,* would annul your marriage, considering the fact that it is more scandalous than adultery."

"Oh, I had almost forgotten one thing, Reverend Sigurður: you were once my suitor," she said. "In your view I should divorce Mag-nús and wed the archpriest. But listen to me, my dear: were I to do this then you would cease to be my suitor, and suitors are the most blissful of all people—apart from the objects of their affection. And besides, what would your Christus, the one you dug up in a rubbish heap, have to say about it?"

He said: "I have always known that the poet's tongue that you inherited from your forefathers and foremothers sprang from a hea-then root. How can I, a tenderhearted cleric, who is allowed to think so little and say even less, withstand her? One thing I have known only too well for a long time, despite the old joke that is now forgot-ten, is that the magistrate's daughter's heart was not inclined toward me. This was most readily apparent in the choice she made when that great cosmopolitan, her lover, deserted her. And how much less would this pitiable cleric, soon an old man, consider his chances with such a woman, even if she were free, now that the man has returned whom he would never have thought to compete against in his younger years?"

She became just slightly agitated and said: "Oh, stop reproaching me for the bugbears that supposedly confounded an ignorant little girl in her father's house. Few things inspire one to more heartfelt or innocent laughter than adolescence."

"Whether in jest or in earnest, madame, your conscience shall decide," he said. "This I remember clearly—a fully grown woman told me, to my ear, that she would love him awake or asleep, living or dead. And it would not surprise me if by your acquaintance with him the warp-lines that support your life's web become tangled. I do not suppose it was this great cosmopolitan, half-foreign, who first led your weak feet up the slippery slope to the precipice where you stand now? He was the comrade of princes and counts across the wide sea, wearing English boots and changing his Spanish collar weekly, thoroughly versed in all the apostatical heresy, heathen dialectic, and contemporary French learning that plagues the scoffers of God's kingdom. The Lord sometimes occupies men with peculiarly reflecting illusions. He has allowed the Tempter to roam the earth clad in the dress of the light. As is always described in the exempla, action perpetrated by blind desire confounded you, and you awoke alongside a monster, as all cosmopolitans appear in the sight of God: of course this one owned no palatinate on the other side of any stretch of water broader than the Tunga River, and he had only one ruff, bent quite out of shape; nonetheless, he was no less versed than the former in the mockery of holy relics, following the prognostications of the spiritus mali,* which in the eyes of God is viewed in the same light as French learning and heathen dialectic, though here it is known as brennivín."

"At first I thought that you had come here to try to destroy my relationship with Magnús," she said, "but now I can see that it is actually someone completely different whom you have in mind: the man whom you claimed to be the best my devoted friend could wish for me. If he is the Tempter in the image of a man, as you say, then you wished me no well when you spoke those words."

"When I was a twenty-year-old roving youth, I stood over the grave of the good and beloved woman who had been my sister, my mother, and my bride all at once, my guiding star and refuge. She was twenty-five years older than I. I stood at a crossroads. An over-arrogant lust for the world overcame me and I, entranced, watched the sparks flying out from under the fine saddle horses of the men who held the mandates; I made so much of the world's frills that Christ vanished before my sinful Adam. And I was the suitor of the young magistrate's daughter—she had said that I would be next. The worldly lord had come and gone, the only man I envied, the first man to have gained your affection. I was certain that you would never have him. I was certain that he would never return."

"And now that you know he has returned to this country, you feel that the time has come to speak your mind concerning him."

He answered: "You are no longer speaking to an infatuated suitor, madame, but rather to an experienced eremite who has dug his Christ out of a rubbish heap, just as you said—and who no longer pales before the lords of the world. And though I am an aged eremite, you are still a young woman, with a long life ahead of you and duties to your land and to Christendom. And it suits me to attend to the lot of your dear soul—for the glory of God."

"And what lot has monsieur now chosen for me in God's glory, if you please?"

"I am certain that your sister, Madam Eydalín, would rejoice if you were to abide with her in Skálholt for a year or so while your divorce from Magnús is being settled, and while you take some time to examine your conscience."

"And then?"

"As I said, you are a young woman," he said.

"It's all clear now," she said. "Leaving you out, dear Reverend Sigurður, what sort of lout or low-grade priest do you have in mind for me, for the glory of God, after the year is up?"

"You would be able to choose from wealthy landowners and great aristocrats," said the archpriest.

"I know whom I would take," she said. "I would take old Vigfús Þórarinsson, if he would condescend to have me. He is not only rich in lands, he also has bags of silver; besides that he is one of the few men in Iceland who know how to speak to ladies."

"Perhaps another man with even higher authority might find his way to Skálholt this year, madame."

"Now I really don't understand," she said—"hopefully the arch-priest doesn't have in mind for my dear soul the devil himself—for the glory of God?"

"A wise woman, if she devotes herself to virtue and bears concern for the honor of her people together with the same love of justice that made her father an elder in this land, will wield agency and authority higher than any king's missive. It may be that God has determined that madame shall, like Judith, genially vanquish her father's enemy."

"It's easy to be openhanded with that which a man doesn't have, dear Reverend Sigurður," she said, "and excuse me when I say that this conversation reminds me overmuch of the children's rhyme that starts out, 'My ship has come to land.' I shall make no attempt to understand your insinuations about my father's name and will concern myself even less with your arrangements regarding the king's envoys. But when you and Madam Jórunn try to relocate me like some kind of blend of loose tramp and dependent pauper, then I will remind you that I am the matron in Bræðratunga, and that I love my husband no less than my sister Jórunn loves her husband the bishop, and therefore neither of us need act as provider to the other—and I thought she would have known that before she sent you on this mission."

By this time the archpriest had unclasped his hands, which were visibly trembling. He cleared his throat to temper his voice.

"Though I have known you since you were a child, Snæfríður," he said, "an unskilled poet can never learn how to travel the narrow path of words that leads to the doors of your heart—therefore this conversation shall now cease. But since my words are powerless, the only alternative left to me is to inform you of certain miraculous occurrences that I would rather have chosen to conceal from you."

He reached into his cloak and took out a torn and crumpled document, unfolded it with a shudder, and handed it to her. It was the contract that had been made in the pigsty in Eyrarbakki the night before, when her husband the squire had sold her, for a cask of brennivín, into a complete and matrimonial conjugation for three nights with a Danish swineherd and an Icelandic murderer. She took the document from him and read, and as she did, his eyes were prepared to swallow any movement on her face. Her face, however, was still; her mouth was closed, her expression perfectly empty, having returned to the state it always preferred, ever since her childhood, whenever her smile disappeared. She read the contract carefully twice, then started laughing.

"You laugh," he said.

"Yes," she said, and continued reading and laughing.

"It may well be," he said, "that I am an ignoramus, and deserve from you only scorn and ridicule in place of honest and friendly conversation. One thing I do know is that a proud woman would never laugh, nor pretend to do so, at such an unthinkable disgrace as is found written here."

"There's just one thing I'm not sure of," she said. "What part do you play in this affair, Reverend Sigurður? Where, by chance, is the contract you've made on your own behalf with the swineherd and the murderer?"

"You know full well that I have not forged this grotesque text," he said.

"I never would have thought that either," she said. "Therefore it's yours to prove that you played a part in the deal. Otherwise the maiden will just have to wait until the real gentlemen show themselves."

— 6 —

A few days later Magnús from Bræðratunga came home. He sat at midmorning outside her door, soaked to the skin from the rain. He was tattered, bloodied, filthy, foul-smelling, bearded, disheveled, emaciated, and livid. He neither looked up nor moved when she walked by; he just sat there like a deranged mendicant who has crept into an unfamiliar house to take shelter for the night. She led him in to her room and nursed him, and he cried for three days as usual. Then he arose. He stayed put for the time being, going out to the hayfields around midday to cut grass, usually the only one on any given strip of land. He kept himself well away from his folk and had no contact with them. He did not take his meals outside, but went home when there was no longer enough light to work and ate his evening meal in his houseroom before retiring. He went frequently to his smithy and did odd jobs making things ready for his workers, tempered the scythe, tinkered with the tools, but spoke very little or not at all.

Even after haymaking was finished there was still no sign that the squire was likely to disappear. Instead he continued to make himself useful around the household, either by patching up the buildings or, more often, by remaining in his smithy for days on end, repairing various broken household implements: bowls, troughs, churns and buckets, distaffs, wool-boxes, and storage chests. His pale golden complexion and soft skin returned; he shaved his beard and wore clothing that his wife had cleaned and pressed, assuring that not a blemish or a wrinkle was to be seen upon him.

Around the time of the roundup the autumn rains let up. The weather was calm and clear and the night frosts mild, giving the puddles an icy sheen and the grass a glaze of hoarfrost.

Guðríður from Dalir went up to Snæfríður's loft and told her that an aged man was standing outside, asking to speak with the housewife; he said he'd come from the Þverá district out west.

"Oh, what's that to me, dear Guðríður?" she said. "It's not my job to look after tramps. If you want to give him a pinch of butter or a bit of cheese, then do it yourself, but leave me in peace."

It turned out that the man was not there looking for handouts, but was traveling to Skálholt and had stopped at Bræðratunga to discuss some urgent business with the housewife, who, he said, would certainly recognize him if he were allowed to see her. He was escorted to her bower.

He was middle-aged and greeted the housewife companionably, removing his knitted cap as he walked through the door. His eyebrows were still black but his hair was wolf-gray. She looked at him, answered his greeting coolly, and asked what he wanted.

"You don't recognize me—that's unexpected," he said.

"No," she said. "Have you had dealings with my father, or what?"

"A little," he said. "I had a scrape with him one spring, unfortunately."

"What's your name?" she said.

"Jón Hreggviðsson," he said.

She couldn't recall the name.

He continued looking at her, smirkingly. His eyes were black, but shone red when they caught the light.

"I'm the one who went to Holland," he said.

"To Holland?" she said.

"I've owed you a rixdollar for a long time," he said.

He reached into his jacket and withdrew several shining silver coins from a pouch of tanned hide wrapped in wadmal.

"Oh," she said. "Is it you, Jón Hreggviðsson? I remember you as having black hair."

"I've grown old," he said.

"Stick those coins back in your pouch, dear Jón, and sit down there upon the chest and tell me the news. Where did you say you live?"

"I'm still one of old Christ's tenants," he said. "The farm is called Rein. I've always gotten along well with the old man. And that's because neither of us owes the other anything. But once more, I've been too long in paying you back your rixdollar."

"Would you like soured whey or milk?" she asked.

"Oh, I'll drink anything," said Jón Hreggviðsson. "Anything that runs. But I want to pay you back this rixdollar. If I should have to travel again somewhere, whatever God decides, then I want to be free of debt to your good grace, in case I need to come to you again."

"You never came to me, Jón Hreggviðsson, I came to you. I was a little girl. I wanted to see a man who was going to be beheaded. Your mother walked east to Skálholt. You were black-haired then. Now you're gray."

"Everything changes but my lady," said he.

"I've been married for fifteen years," said she. "Keep your tricks to yourself."

"My lady endures," said he.

"I endure," said she.

"Yes," said he. "My lady endures—my lady."

She looked out the window.

"Did you ever deliver my message?" she asked.

"I returned the ring," he said.

"Why didn't you bring me his reply?"

"I was told to keep silent. And there was no reply. Except that I wasn't beheaded—at least not then. The woman's mouth was in the middle of her belly. He gave me back the ring."

She looked at her guest aloofly—"What do you want from me?" she said.

"Oh, I hardly know," he said. "Forgive this poor, hopeless man."

"Would you like something to drink now?"

"I drink when someone puts drink in front of me. Anything that runs is a gift from God. When I was in Bessastaðir I had a jug of water—and an ax. A well-sharpened ax is a fine tool. On the other hand I've never been fond of the gallows, and never less than when I wrestled a hanged man."

She continued to look at the man from the incredible distance that the azure gave her eyes; her mouth was closed. Then she stood up, called to her servants, and ordered them to bring the man something to drink.

"Well now, it's always good to get something to wet one's whistle," he said—"though those fellows in Copenhagen, my old friends, would have thought such drink a bit thin."

"Are these your thanks?" she said.

"It'll be a long time before this farmer from Skagi forgets the beer his honor poured for him from his pitcher when he came out from Glückstadt wearing the king's boots."

"Whom are you talking about?"

"The one you sent me to meet—the one I'm going to meet now."

"Where are you going?" she said.

He reached back down into his pouch and took out a tattered letter with a broken seal and handed it to the housewife.

The letter was written in an elegant hand. She read first the artless words of formal address, simplified for a commoner: "Greetings, Jón Hreggviðsson," then the signature, "Arnas Arnæus," in his own hand, hastily signed, though adequately legible, made with the broad strokes of a pliant pen, scripted in such wondrous accord with his own voice that one could hear its echo in his written words. She paled.

It took much longer than she expected to read through such a short letter: it was as if a mist veiled her eyes, but in the end she managed to accomplish the task. The letter had been written at Hólar, around midsummer, and contained the following information: Arnas Arnæus had summoned the Rein farmer to meet with him on an appointed day toward the end of September, by which time he would have arrived in the south from the eastern part of the country. He wanted to discuss the farmer's old case, since it seemed that it still had not been lawfully concluded in full accord with the explicit instructions contained in the letters that His Most Gracious Royal Highness had formerly issued in connection with the case. The letter's author informed Jón Hreggviðsson that he had been appointed by the king to investigate those court cases here in Iceland that, for the last several years, the country's jurists had not prosecuted according to the letter of the law, and to attempt to secure justice in these cases in the hope that the security of the general public might subsequently thrive in future generations.

She looked out the window. Her gaze stretched across the meadow pale with the hues of autumn and came to rest upon the glistening reflection of the sun on the river.

"Then he is here in Skálholt, across the river?" she said.

"He's summoned me there," said Jón Hreggviðsson. "That's why I've come to you."

"To me?"

"When you freed me at Þingvellir I was still young and it wasn't any trouble for me to run across the country," he said. "Now I'm old and weak-footed and wouldn't trust myself any longer to run alone over Holland's soft ground—much less over Iceland's hard ground."

"What are you afraid of?" she said. "Weren't you acquitted by the king many years ago?"

"Well, that's that, you see," he said. "A commoner never knows whether he actually owns the head he's got on his shoulders. Now the day I've been dreading for a long time has come—the day they start digging around in this again."

"And what is it you want from me?"

"I hardly know," he said. "Maybe someone somewhere listens to what you have to say."

"No one listens to me anywhere—and so I say nothing."

"Well, it's like this, you see, that whoever it is who owns this ugly wolf-gray head you see here has you to thank for it. I was sleeping. Tomorrow you'll be beheaded. I was awake and you'd set me free. It's really a frightful story, and now they're going to hash it all up one more time in front of the judges."

"According to this country's laws I am of course a criminal for having set you free," she said. "What else have you done, from the beginning? Are you a robber? Or a murderer?"

"I stole a piece of cord, good lady," said Jón Hreggviðsson.

"I see," she said, "I was like every other stupid little girl. It would have been far better if you'd been beheaded."

"Then they said that I'd slandered the king and murdered the hangman," he said. "And now I've supposedly murdered my son, but such a thing makes little difference—the authorities don't bother about it when a man kills his children during a famine if a man does it well. There're enough beggars left anyway. The only thing that's been weighing me down all these years are the letters."

"Letters?" she asked distractedly.

He explained to her how he'd returned to Iceland with two letters from the king many years ago, and how he'd traveled from a remote corner of the country back home to his farm on Akranes, only to discover his household in ruins: his sixteen-year-old daughter with shining eyes lay upon her bier and his half-wit son was laughing; his two leprous kinswomen, one nodous, the other ulcerous, were praising God, and his decrepit mother was singing the half-rhymed *Kross School Hymns* written by Reverend Halldór from Presthólar, while his pitiable she-creature of a wife sat with their two-year-old child in her lap, cursing her husband. But what were these compared to the tragedies that had befallen the man's livestock in his absence? The sheep and cattle the farmer had birthed himself had been confiscated and handed over to the king as payment for the crimes he'd already answered for, and the chattel that had come with the farm and were owned by Christ had dropped dead like beggar-folk, because his miserable family had been so busy praising God that it had forgotten to cut and store hay to give to the creatures while the man was fighting for his king in a foreign land.

Next he told her how he'd had to start from scratch on a new life, after he'd nearly turned fifty, and what's more, how he'd had to get accustomed to new children after the old ones were dead. He said he'd asked himself: "Maybe I'm not really descended from Gunnar of Hlíðarendi?" Many years had passed now since Jesus Christ had taken back his chattel. And he, Jón Hreggviðsson, had built himself a fisherman's hut at Innrihólmur, and named it Hretbyggja,* and there outfitted an eight-oared fishing boat.

"Nothing's cast shadows but the letters," he said finally. But since she knew very little, if anything at all, about his case, and was unenlightened concerning the letters that had cast their shadow over the joy of this farmer from Skagi, he explained everything to her in detail regarding his Supreme Court appeal, which was supposed to have been published in court, and the travel passes that granted him protection and a four-month leave of absence from the king's army while he tried to resolve his case in Iceland.

"Indeed," she said.

"The letters were never published in court," he said.

"So what was?" she said.

"Nothing at all," he said.

"Why didn't they behead you, since the letters were never published?"

"That's where my lord magistrate's story picks up again," said Jón Hreggviðsson.

"My father never stabs anyone under the table," she said.

"I'd always hoped," he said, "that the blessed magistrate would be the last man Jón Hreggviðsson could ever criticize, except, in the very least, for his overkindness toward me and others. And if I'd been in his shoes I wouldn't have let Jón Hreggviðsson off a second time with his head raised."

Now he explained how, after his return home all those years ago, he'd gotten himself a horse and taken the letters to the Alþingi at Öxará to meet with Magistrate Eydalín. As could be expected, the magistrate did not return the greeting of the man whom he'd condemned to death, but he did read the letters carefully, then gave them back to him and said that he should bring them with him to court, where they would not be ignored. So for three days in a row Jón

Hreggviðsson took the letters to court. He sat waiting on a bench with others tangled up in lawsuits, staring up at the judges who'd condemned him to death two years ago, but his name wasn't called. On the third day he received a message from the magistrate that he should come again to his booth, and when he did so the magistrate spoke these words: "Jón Hreggviðsson, I advise you not to wave these papers around in public; instead, leave this place as quietly as you can. Know this—it is in my power to have you beheaded right now, here at this assembly. And know this as well, that if your case comes before a higher court out in Copenhagen, you will not lift your head a third time before me. Although you have now succeeded in getting those rogues out in Copenhagen to help you procure these documents, which they have obviously done more from their habitual desire to swindle us than out of any concern for a beggar and murderer, we will make sure that you never have another chance to raise a troop of cacklers and meddlers against the authorities in this country."

"My father does not threaten people. He condemns them if they are found guilty," said the magistrate's daughter.

"I started thinking about Copenhagen," he said, "and I remembered an Icelandic aristocrat, a really straightforward man in that huge house where they hold high court, who explained these letters to me on the same day that I thought they'd finally cleaned me up for my execution, and I caught a glimpse of my friend Árni Árnason standing near their great curtained glass window. He didn't look at me and he didn't greet me, but he knew what was happening, since it was all his own work. And I said to my lady's father, my judge: 'You are the most powerful man in Iceland,' said I, 'and you can most certainly have me beheaded right here and now. But these letters are signed by my Supreme Highness and Grace Himself, my Hereditary King and Lord.' When my honorable lord magistrate saw that I wasn't afraid and that I really only wanted to make a friend, he wasn't angry with me any longer."

"My father lets nothing threaten him," she said.

"No," said Jón Hreggviðsson, "I know that very well. But my friend, the friend of my lady, is also a man no less than my judge, my lady's father."

Snæfríður looked aloofly at Jón Hreggviðsson for a moment, then suddenly gave a sharp laugh as if the man had touched a nerve.

"Magistrate Eydalín said, 'For these letters I return to you your property and belongings, adding interest from the time when your livestock was taken away; everything shall be as it was.' And he said plenty of other things useless to mention, since there were no witnesses. I asked, 'What will my king say if his letters aren't published?' 'I will take care of that,' he said. 'Just turn them in tomorrow in court when your name is called.'"

She asked what had happened next and he answered that he might have done worse under the circumstances, because when his sheep were driven back home to him at Rein there were two heads on every beast.

"My father bribes no one," she said. "And the letters?"

He said that on the next day, when his name was finally called in court and he was questioned about his business there, he answered that he'd come with letters from our Most Gracious Highness and requested that they be given a reading. Then Guðmundur Jónsson, his bailiff from Skagi, had stepped forward, grabbed the letters from him, looked them over for a moment along with the king's regent from Bessastaðir, and handed them to the magistrate. The magistrate asked the bailiff to read the second letter, his travel pass, aloud, and when this reading was completed the magistrate said that they had read enough, Jón Hreggviðsson had been shown great mercy, and he should now return to his home and quarrel with men no longer.

The farmer was silent and when she asked if there was anything more to the story he said that there was only this letter, written fourteen years later, signed by Arnas Arnæus.

"What do you want from me?" she asked.

"I'm an old man," said Jón Hreggviðsson. "And I've got a fifteen-year-old daughter at home."

"Even so," she said.

"I've come to ask you to tell him that Jón Hreggviðsson was once young and black-haired and didn't know what it meant to be afraid; but that time is now past. I want to ask you to tell him that a tearful old man with white hair has come to see you."

"I don't see any tears," she said. "And your hair isn't white, it's gray. And I can't see how you, an innocent man, would have anything to fear even if your case were opened again. If the court proceedings were in error the first time, then it will only be to your benefit, even if it is somewhat after the fact, if your innocence is confirmed."

"It's all the same to me whether I'm innocent or guilty as long as I'm left in peace with my sheep and my boat," he said.

"Is that so?" she said. "Then why did you run across those soft and hard lands? Wasn't it in the hope of justice?"

"I'm a simple commoner," he said, "and I understand nothing but what I can touch. An ax I understand. And water in a jug. A poor man considers himself lucky if he can get by on his own."

"Has it never occurred to you that life and justice are close cousins, and that justice can be used to save poor men's lives?"

"I've never known justice to be used for anything other than the taking of poor men's lives," said Jón Hreggviðsson. "That's why I'm begging you, since you know how to speak to great men, to protect Jón Hreggviðsson from justice."

"You've lost your mind, Jón Hreggviðsson. I don't know how to speak to great men. And no one these days puts any stock in a woman's idle chatter. In my opinion your case is in good hands. Is anything left in the pitcher? If you are no longer thirsty, then I think you had better be going."

Jón Hreggviðsson stood up, extended a small, dirty hand to her, and expressed his deepest gratitude for the drink.

He stood there and two-stepped for a short time but made no effort to leave.

"I know," he said, "that in the ancient sagas no one was thought more contemptible than a coward who begged for mercy. King Óðinn never forgives a man who pleads for mercy. This ugly gray head here might as well blow away. But what would my lady say if the ax were to slip off course, toward higher-born necks?"

"Oh, now I finally understand your business here," she said, and she smiled. "You've come to warn me that my head will blow away at the same time as yours, as punishment for having redeemed yours here many years ago. As you please, my friend. You are a most charming old man."

At the housewife's words Jón Hreggviðsson knelt down upon the floor and started crying into the palms of his hands—of all the hardships that he'd been forced to endure in his days nothing hit closer to his heart than these words, he said with a whimper.

She stood up and walked over to him—"Allow me to wipe your eyes," she said, but he refused; his eyes were dry. He stood up.

"It doesn't really matter whether Jón Hreggviðsson kills the hangman or the hangman kills Jón Hreggviðsson," he said. "But if my judge Eydalín did hand down a true verdict sixteen years ago, then my helper Arnæus, the king's envoy, might find himself in the dungeon, and our king's reputation might suffer serious damage. On the other hand, if Jón Hreggviðsson is declared innocent, then the magistrate over Iceland is in danger of losing what a man of power values more highly than his own head: his honor."

The smirk on his face was cold and impudent, his white teeth in his hoary beard reminding one of a dog that bares its teeth after a beating. She noticed that he was girded with a new piece of cord.

— 7 —

A few days later the squire was gone. He must have ridden away during the night, because one morning the hammer ceased to sound from the smithy. The ax lay in the woodchips. It started raining again. Ferocious winds drove the rain on, day and night. The lakes and rivers flooded their banks. The earthen walls and turf roofs of the buildings at Bræðratunga continued to sop up the flood until they turned into mounds of mire. Emanating from these mounds was a foul, house-penetrating damp, colder than frost. Cesspools formed in the farmhouse's passageways and entryways, making it nearly impossible for anyone to get anywhere. The housewife wrapped herself in her duvet and refused to rise, as if succumbing to eternal dusk. One night so much water leaked into her loft that she was forced to spread a horsehide over the bed. The drops kept falling, and every hollow in the hide became a pool. Then the rain stopped. One day at twilight cloudless skies returned, and the moon and stars reappeared.

Later that night Magnús came home. Iron bits rattled outside—at least he hadn't sold his horse. After a considerable amount of time he came up the stairs steadily, without reeling. He knocked upon her door and waited until she told him to step in. She sat holding her needlework beneath her pilastered lamp. She looked up and he greeted her with a kiss; there was not much of a stench upon him. All his movements, however, had a certain quality of airy emollience, different from those he made when sober, and there was a kind of alien barbarism frosted over his eyes, the type of frozen, placid crapulousness sometimes seen in sleepwalkers and others who are aware of their deeds the moment they are done but are oblivious to them afterward.

"I had to run south to Selvogur," he said, as if pleading for forgiveness for having ridden away—"I had to meet someone about buying land."

"Buying land," she said.

"Yes. Don't you think we ought to start buying some land?" he said. "It makes no sense at all to sell land and to buy none in its place. Now I've finally decided to buy some land. I've bought an estate in Selvogur."

"At what price?" she asked.

"Well, that's that, you know, dear Snæfríður," he said, and he drew closer and kissed her. "How wonderful it is for a man to come home to his wife, after he's been inundated for four days."

"Yes, how thoughtful of you to mention water," she said. "I was nearly drowned here at home."

"It won't be long before I've plugged all the holes," he said. "Everything will be perfect. You won't feel a drop. But first I've got to buy land."

"If you're planning to start buying land, Magnús mine," she said, "why don't you start by making a deal with me? How would you like to buy the estate from me? Bræðratunga is for sale."

"A man who is related by marriage to great aristocrats does not have to pay to sleep with his wife," he said. "And who needs to wait for the father-in-law to discharge the dowry?"

"Alright," she said, "then go ahead and buy your own land."

"Man and wife are one," said he. "The land I buy is yours. The land your father gives you is mine. Those who love each other share everything in common. Your father forced wealthy Fúsi to relinquish Bræðratunga and he gave you the title to the estate. You love me. That is why Bræðratunga is mine. I am going to buy an estate in Selvogur. That is why the estate that I am going to buy in Selvogur is yours."

"It's not a fair deal," she said. "On the one side we have a magnificent creditor, and on the other a poor female simpleton: though I love you a thousand times more than you love me it is still you who'll lose in a half-share partnership."

"General report has it that I'm the most happily married man in Iceland," he said.

"And one should always pay heed to general report," she said— "which reminds me, have you had anything to eat?"

The squire was in no mood to answer such an everyday sort of question: "In any case, Snæfríður mine, the deal is already done— except for a matter of a hundred rixdollars I need by tonight—and then the estate is ours. The seller's waiting for me south of the river."

"You're certainly not any more short of money now than you've been in the past," she said.

"You know it yourself, woman—you have absolutely nothing to do with a tenth or even twentieth part of the baubles you keep in your coffers. Out with the silver, out with the gold, woman, and show your husband you love him so that we can acquire some land. You yourself know that Bræðratunga was taken from me by fraud, and I won't stand for anything less than having an estate in my own name. How can a squire and cavalier look in other men's faces when he has no estate? Kiss me, my darling, and tell me the estate will be mine."

"When I was a child I was told that whoever swallowed a hock-bone would one day own land," she said. "Have you tried that? I was told a sheep's hock-bone brought a croft, a cow's an estate."

"I know there's only one type of land you wish was mine," he said. "A churchyard. I know you want to kill me."

"I didn't realize you were drunk, dear Magnús," she said. "But now I can see it. That's enough. No more. Go downstairs and get something to eat from Guðríður."

"I swallow whatever I please whenever I please with whomever I please," he said.

She said nothing; when he was in such a state it was difficult to predict his reactions.

"You can see it yourself, dear," he said, once again behaving clemently toward her. "Silver is not for great aristocrats, it's for misers' hoards, stashed away in trunks, of no use to anyone, losing its luster year from year."

"Many a man has taken great delight in sitting up at night, polishing his coins by the light of the moon," she said.

"Yes, but land is what makes great aristocrats," he said. "We are great aristocrats."

"You," she said. "Not I."

"You've always been so good to me, my Snjóka," he said. "If you'll just let me have a bit of a clasp-belt or a dented frontlet, and maybe three or four tarnished brooches, even if it's only worth fifty rix-dollars."

"I may not be much of a woman," she said, "but my silver was owned by great women in Iceland, some of whom lived as far back as the eleventh century. They adorned themselves with it on holy days, and it is their style, the spirit of their time, that resides in these things. Because of this they own them still, those old women before me, though they are in my keeping. Their material value makes no difference."

"Here, I'll show you the title deed to my new estate, so you won't think I'm going to drink away your silver," he said. "To tell you the truth, I've quit drinking, Snæfríður mine. I feel nothing but hatred for brennivín. At the very least I don't enjoy drinking any longer. My one and only comfort is to be here at home with you, my dear—to this I call my Creator as witness. Dear Snæfríður, a dented frontlet, a brooch, even if it's worth only twenty-five rixdollars—"

"I think you should go to sleep, dear Magnús. We'll see each other in the morning."

"—even just a couple of half-licked-away silver spoons from the time of the Black Death, just so they can see the silver, so they can see that I'm able to pay, so they can see that I'm a man and that I have a wife."

"I don't know whether you're a man, dear Magnús," she said. "Nor do I know whether you have a wife."

He recoiled from her and she continued to look aloofly, but unastonishedly, at this stranger.

"Open the chest," he said.

"Those are not your eyes that look at me, dear Magnús, nor is it your voice that speaks to me."

"I know what's in the chest," he said. "It's a man."

She kept looking straight into his eyes.

"I saw him riding ahead of me through the homefield. And I recognized him. I order you to open the chest."

"We'll allow the man to remain in peace," she said. "He's tired."

"He'll never have peace," said the squire. "I'll kill him; I'll hack the life out of him."

"Alright, my dear," she said. "Do that. But first we'll all go to sleep."

He walked over to the chest, kicked it with a booted foot with all his might, and screamed thief, dog, thief-dog. But the chest was made of oak, thickly planked and powerful; kicking it was most like kicking a boulder.

"Where's the book you stole from me—the half-finished one—the one whose covers you threw at me!?" he screamed at the man in the chest as he kept on kicking it.

The man in the chest did not respond.

"I demand my book back!"

Silence.

"All those golden illuminations and those sweet lais* you blotted out, all those lustrous white blank pages you ripped out, leaving me with nothing but the covers, stinking cold and empty! You vermin, give me back my book!"

He kept this up for a good long time, kicking the chest and shouting threats and curses at the man inside, but the chest didn't budge.

"Magnús," said his wife in a low voice. "Sit down beside me."

He quit his kicking and looked at her without lifting his head, his eyes white and red, like those of a bull foraging in the grass. It was her voice that touched him more deeply than anything else. When she spoke to him in this way, temperately, moderately, her voice soft and tinged with melancholy though its tones were woven with gold, it was always as if she hit one of his nerves, so quickly did the strength drain from him.

He sat beside her for some time and wept, and she stroked him several times with her slender hand, firmly, untenderly, somewhat distractedly, like someone petting an animal. Her touch relaxed him somewhat—but then he started in again.

"Snæfríður mine," he said, "lend me a tiny ring, even if it's worth only two rixdollars. I owe a man down in Eyrarbakki for some iron, and my manhood, my nobility, my pride, depend on my paying him back tonight; I'm certain, Snæfríður, that you who are even more of an aristocrat than me can't bear to see me so humiliated."

"Sleep here at home tonight, dear Magnús, and we'll pay for the iron tomorrow," she said.

"I beg you," he said. "Even if it's just a few measly pennies to throw at the lice-ridden riffraff who gather to jeer at vagabond aristo-crats."

"Tonight we should sleep," she said. "We'll go down to Bakki tomorrow and throw a penny at any lousy lad who makes fun of us."

He wept and sighed heavily.

"Has anyone seen a more wretched beggar than me?" he asked through sobs.

"No," she said.

He continued to weep.

The night was bright with moonlight. He had long since gone down to his room, but she was restless and lay awake in bed, tossing and turning. Moonbeams played across the floor. She rose and looked out her window; the weather was still and the earth sparkled, its wetness frozen before the next debacle began. She lay back down. She was lying there for some time when suddenly she thought she heard a creaking on the steps to the loft, the sound of furtive passage that is heard nowhere and at no other time than in an old house at night. This creaking, in such a graceless house, clapped upon her sleep-deprived and sensitive ears like a death knell. Finally there came a clumsy, secretive fumbling at the doorlock, the kind of sound that's exaggerated to shrill trumpet-blasts by anxious ears in the dead of night. The door was lifted from its posts. She watched him come prowling into the room, dressed in his shirtsleeves, wearing thin shoes, with an ax in his hand. He peered around in the moonlight, and she could see his face and his eyes, how he stared into the darkness of her bedcloset without seeing her. She was convinced that he would promptly take a swing at her, but this is not what happened; the chest was uppermost in his mind. He fell to his knees before the chest and poked at the lid and the lock, but soon discovered that it was shut fast. He groped about to find a place where he could thrust the ax-blade in under the lid and lever the box open, and in the end the woman realized that he'd succeeded in getting the ax-edge under in one place and was putting the lid to the test.

"Leave the chest alone, Magnús," she said.

He stopped and gave her a sidelong glance, somewhat hesitantly, and she could once again see the white and the red of his eyes. He rose slowly to his feet, pulled the ax free, and hoisted it up, gripping it more like a carpenter than a warrior, then reeled his way over to the bedcloset where his wife lay. Now everything happened in a flash. The curtains were half-drawn before the bedcloset and it was dark inside. He had to stoop at the knees and shoulders to strike at her through the low-lying bedcloset doors, but he'd forgotten that the bed was also open at the other end, and no sooner had he lashed out before someone came up from behind and threw a blanket over his head: here was the woman whom he had hoped to strike. She yelled as keenly as she could for her maidservant Guðríður, who shared quarters with another woman down the hallway at the other end of the loft. By the time the women arrived on the scene the squire had unwound the blanket from his head, and he had his wife in his grasp with his thumbs at the base of her throat. The ax had fallen to the floor. It was too late for him to accomplish the deed he had in mind—the two women rushed at him and overpowered him. In a short time he was sitting in a heap on the chest, dead-tired, his head hanging low.

"Everything goes badly for me and this is the worst," said the daleswoman. "And I'm certain that the madam my mistress will never forgive me for this. The only proper thing for me to do would be to ride home and lay my neck under the magistrate's heel."

When Snæfríður asked her where she'd gone wrong, all she could say was that it wasn't because of any virtue of hers that the blessed madam's daughter had survived. She said she wanted to ride west and tell her mistress to send her daughter a more faithful servant than herself. Then she wiped the tears from her face and begged merciful God to forgive her sins.

"I'm riding away, dear Guðríður," said the mistress of the house. "You will remain here in charge of the estate. Bring out my finest clothing and valuables and pack them well, and be quick about it. Put the rest in storage. I'll be in Skálholt for a while. Wake up some of the farmhands and tell them to fetch horses and prepare themselves to accompany me over the river tonight."

— 8 —

When Arnas Arnæus sent word from the east at the end of the summer that he expected to be in Skálholt around the time of the roundup and wished to spend the winter at the bishop's residence, the bishop set to work at once, summoning workers to refurbish the Grand Salon and the two smaller parlors behind it, where noble guests were customarily accommodated. The woodwork was repaired and painted or oiled, the locks and door-hinges mended, the stoves rebricked; in the interior parlor a bed frame was supplied with duvets and piles of pillows, and clean curtains were brought out, recreased, and hung up around it, while the outer parlor was prepared as a study and furnished with an imposing bureau, a writing desk, stools, two pretentious, antiquely carved easy-chairs, and a clothes-chest. Everything metal was polished: tin pitchers, copper pots, and silverware; then the house was scoured thoroughly. Finally juniper was burned in the study.

Toward the end of September one of the servants of the royal envoy transported his master's luggage on several packhorses from the south over the heaths, while Arnas himself came several days later from the east with a packtrain of thirty horses, along with his secretaries, valets, and attendants. Stacks of the books and papers he brought with him quickly filled the rooms.

Although the king's envoy was by nature a calm and placid man, a great bustle of activity arose around him quite soon after he set up his office in Skálholt. He sent servants on official business in various directions, carrying missives and messages, summoning folk to meet with him, while others came uninvited, some from remote districts. Everyone was curious to hear as many details as possible concerning his mission, since they were aware of the fact that he'd been ordered by our Highness to make a thorough inspection of the country's economic circumstances and afterward to submit proposals to the king as to how the huge impoverishment pressing upon the countryfolk could most successfully be alleviated. The letters he had published at the Öxará Assembly stated explicitly that he possessed full and complete access to the authorities' records and could demand that the authorities answer to him in any matter whatsoever, just as he saw fit, that it fell to his jurisdiction to investigate the cases that the Chancery deemed to have been dubiously prosecuted, and that he could demand retrials in cases he determined to have been misjudged and consequently bring those responsible to justice. He was open toward people about most matters and inquisitive about their conditions, but was unwilling to go into details concerning his mission and even less talkative when it came to his authority; instead he came across as the most self-effacing and soft-spoken of men, asking companionably about all sorts of things as if his closest neighbor for most of his life happened to be the person with whom he was currently conversing. He knew no less about the lives and families of hanged thieves and branded beggar-girls than he did of legislators and scholars, and he never held the things that he had seen and experienced over the heads of the persons he interviewed. It became apparent that his most cherished topics for conversation were old books and reminiscences, and those who had expected to be interrogated by some no-nonsense authority about the evil deeds that burdened their consciences were awestruck that his conversation should focus primarily on an old strip of parchment or some useless, miserable old booklet.

This particular autumn day all was quiet in Skálholt—no one had the slightest inkling that anything was afoot, except that it had started to freeze, causing the stench of rubbish and mire particular to the place to diminish slightly. She arrived between matins and prime, the time when folk lie sleeping most soundly, and because of her familiarity with the parish grounds she did not have to inconvenience anyone not belonging to her family; instead she rode straight up to her sister's window and rapped upon the pane with the head of her riding crop. The bishop's wife awoke and looked out the window to see who had come. By the time the madam reached the doors Snæfríður's attendants had left, leaving her standing alone with her luggage behind the house. They conversed quietly in the madam's loft the whole morning, until the moon sunk down and the housemaids started slamming doors and stoking fires in the front part of the house; then they lay down to rest. Around tierce, when the madam went downstairs, Snæfríður had just fallen asleep. She slept the whole day, and no one knew that a new visitor had arrived.

When the bishop's wife sent a message to the archpriest Sigurður that he was not to eat his evening meal in the servant's quarters, but rather at the bishop's table in the Grand Salon, the learned man of God began to grow suspicious, and he put on his old sleeved dress-cassock, threadbare and glossy, then fetched out his dusty and shrunken boots from under his bed and pulled them onto his feet. However, when he arrived at the Grand Salon at the appointed time, no one was there except for Guðrún, the bishop's adolescent elder daughter, who walked in and out and snorted when she saw him as if she'd caught a whiff of something rotten. The tables had been set with tablecloths and polished dishes and lustrous pitchers, and two candlesticks with burning three-stemmed candles. Presently the assessor's secretary walked in, a young man, graduate of the cathedral school at Hólar and baccalaureus* at the university in Copenhagen. He glanced at the archpriest but did not greet him, and instead started circling the room, flicking at the wainscoting with a finger, crooning vain refrains of Latin hymns.

The archpriest took heed not to look up, but could not refrain from muttering, "O tempora, O mores,"* as he gave a low cough.

Soon afterward the bishop made his entrance, his bearing exaggerated, his crucifix hanging from a chain round his neck, broad, sleek, flushed, and radiant, diffusing his evangelical charitable embrace to all in good faith, smoothing away every wrinkle, every knot, because the Lord's sufferings proclaimed joy, a friend to all because the Lord's will is that all men be redeemed, honoring each man's word because no heart remains closed to the Holy Spirit. By the time he reached his finale his cold gray eye had gained the upper hand. Of his smile nothing remained but the creases, like ripples left in sand after ebb tide; and thus was the bishop's comprehension of things made manifest, in a way profoundly precluded to most.

Arnæus emerged from his bedroom with hardly a sound and greeted the men respectfully. He was pale-complexioned, the gap in his chin wider than it had been sixteen years ago and his eyelids heavier, but his peruke was as carefully curled as ever, his clothing just as precisely tailored; when he looked at something he saw reflexively not only everything around it, but also everything beyond it and behind it. He apparently did not expect any surprises here and immediately took his seat, and the bishop, the master of the house, followed his example as if to sanction his action, and bade Reverend Sigurður take his seat opposite the assessor.

The bishop's wife and her sister Snæfríður walked together into the hall: he is situated opposite the doorway and sees her come in. When he realized who had come he immediately stood up and walked over to her. She was as slender as of old, though the clumsy and excessive suppleness of her childhood, when she had moved like a foal, had given way to an adult woman's dignity. Her hair was just as airy and lively, yet both her hair and her eyebrows had darkened by degrees. Her eyebrows were raised higher than before, and her lips, which before had been open, were now closed, while a semblance of mournful distraction appeared in the radiant azure of her eyes. She was wearing a laced mantle, pale of hue, as if both blue and red had been used to discolor the other. He reached out to her with both hands and in his soft, dim voice spoke words he had not spoken in sixteen years:

"Lady Snæfríður."

She extended a hand to him and bowed courteously, without a

trace of delight, looking at him with an air of remote blue grandeur. And he hastened to add: "I know my dear friend foregoes such plaisanterie,* but she was so young when we parted, though it seems to have been only yesterday."

"My sister has come to visit me," said the bishop's wife, with a smile. "She will be my guest for several days."

Snæfríður greeted all the men with handshakes and they stood up one by one, and her brother-in-law the bishop took her in his arms and kissed her.

"We must celebrate such a distinguished visitation," said Arnæus as the bishop embraced and kissed her. "We must drink to her health, with Madam Jórunn's permission."

The bishop's wife said that she did not dare to serve her empoisoned wine, least of all to the assessor and his dear friends, old and new, when she knew that he had claret at hand, and he asked his secretary to order the valet to bring in a bottle of claret. It was to no avail though Snæfríður begged to be excused from such an honor by claiming it improper for magnates to drink to the health of poor farmers' wives; the assessor bade her be unafraid, saying that in this gathering there would be no drinking to old maids. Then he filled their glasses, lifted his cup, and drank her health. His table-companions followed suit—all except the archpriest, who poured only a drop of soured whey into his own glass, saying that he did not partake of wine, least of all at evening, but he sincerely wished all those well who raised their cups, with God's blessing, in a happy hour. Their guest looked up, though she purposefully guarded her eyes against meeting theirs, lifted her cup once for all of them, moistened her lips, and opened them in a modest, maidenly smile, displaying just a touch of the instinctive sarcasm that ran in her blood; her teeth were slightly forward-jutting, but she still had them all, as white and even as ever.

When they had finished their toast they found nothing more to say, so the bishop closed his eyes and clasped his hands and started to say grace. The others bowed their heads silently, and the bishop's daughter sneezed. They all responded amen and the bishop's wife served thick raisin porridge from a polished tureen into small bowls painted with flowers, and though she enveloped the dining room with her winsome, motherly smile, her pupils were dilated and her eyes stingingly hot; red flecks appeared on her cheeks. The assessor glanced at the archpriest, who was ascetical, hunched over his whey.

"It would not harm your Reverence to have a glass now and then," he said with gentle joviality, "especially not at evening. It lightens one's mood."

"I thank my lord Commissarius,"* said the archpriest. "With blame I have enough to contend, even foregoing this."

"And yet, as our master has said, pecca fortiter,"* said Arnæus, smiling.

"Most of Luther's maxims abide closer to my heart than this one," said the archpriest, staring straight ahead, ever more stiffly, as if he were reading from a book placed before him. "It is not, however, out of fear of sin that I do not drink your wine tonight, Commissarius."

"Foul blather can also beget great sanctity," said the baccalaureus, but they all pretended not to notice this interjection, except for little Gunna, who hastily squeezed her nose. Then the bishop said, authoritatively:

"It would not harm our friend if he were to partake of the advice of the Commissarius, in this respect, for our friend need not fear sin to the same degree as most of those gathered here. Sometimes, when I reflect on his hard life and his long vigils, I feel that the Anabaptists may in some ways be correct, when they suggest that some men in this life attain to such status perfectionis* that they are no longer afflicted by sin."

"By your leave," said the baccalaureus, "isn't it proper theology to say that the devil never tempts those in whom he already has his hooks?"

"No, young man," said the bishop, laughing. "That is Calvin's error."

Now the guests were thoroughly amused, not least the commissary, who said to his secretary: "You deserved that—and take my advice, my boy, refrain from engaging in any more disputation during this meal."

Reverend Sigurður had not smiled in the least, but instead ate his porridge under the steadfast weight of earnestness. After the others had finished laughing to their heart's content, however, he took up the topic again.

"I certainly possess nothing approximating Anabaptist virtue, as my friend the lord bishop says, nor holiness in word and deed, something that learned modernity seeks to attribute to healthy old codgers. All the same it is my hope that I am not naturaliter* a child of the devil like this young cosmopolitan, the eminent royal ambassador, conjectured here at the table. One thing I cannot deny is that I am often compelled to contemplate the state of poor men, not least when I sit amongst the rich and powerful. And then I cease to desire dainties, especially wine."

"Each word rings more true than the next," said the bishop's wife. "Our beloved Reverend Sigurður often eats only one meal a day, for the sake of God's poor. When I complain that my pea soup is too meager he complains it is too grand—"

"—and he puts the meat back onto the platter on Fridays," said the bishop's daughter quickly.

"Guðrún," said the bishop's wife. "Will you leave this instant. Forgive us, Assessor, our children's discourtesy, but there is nothing that we can do about it here in Iceland—"

"Madame," said the archpriest, still looking straight ahead. "Allow Guðrún to remain. What she said was correct: sometimes I do put the meat back. On the contrary, that I do this on Fridays, following Catholic custom—this she heard from the schoolboys."

"Oh, never!" shouted the girl in agitation, and her cheeks turned crimson red, since schoolboys were precisely the sort of company that one was not allowed to suspect the adolescent bishop's daughter in Skálholt of having anything to do with.

"Now I would like to ask your Reverence one thing," said Arnæus, turning toward the archpriest, "for I have no doubt that within you exists the inner light that is the only thing that makes erudition sweet: are the indigent pleasing to God and are we obliged to imitate them? Or is poverty God's punishing rod against the evil deeds and muted faith of the countryfolk? Or shall the old rule still stand, that poverty is praised only by paupers?"

The archpriest: "My lord Commissarius is mistaken if he believes that I would use learning to pride myself over the learned and to extend my imperfectiones* beyond the essential. It should be no secret to any Christian, however, since Christians have always been privileged to hear it in their sermons and to read it in their books, that poverty produces a simple heart, which is more pleasing to God and which is far closer to status perfectionis than all the finery and wisdom of the world. And our Redeemer himself counted the poor amongst the blessed when He said, 'They shall always remain nearest to us.'"

The king's envoy: "If the Lord wills the existence of the indigent, so that Christians can benefit from their proximity and take their destitution as a lesson, is He not then opposed to the improvement of their pitiful state? If the day should come when the indigent have something to wear and to eat, whom then should Christians take as models for their lives? Where then should one look to find an example of the simple heart, which is so pleasing to God?"

The archpriest: "Just as the Lord made the poor so that the rich might gain from them instruction for a more humble way of life, so has He also placed the higher classes under His special protection and invited them to strengthen the condition of their souls through almsgiving and prayer."

"The sound of dialectic being pursued over the dinner table in Skálholt is long overdue," interrupted the bishop. "And there has seldom been more need than in our day and age to hear lessons of morality as conveyed and interpreted in books. Yet we should not dig so deeply into the porridge, my praeclari et illustrissimi,* lest our appetites be ruined before we get to the steak."

The bishop looked around, expecting everyone to laugh, but no one even smiled, except for the commissarius.

"We lads," said he, and he smiled at the sisters as he chose to begin with such homely words instead of saying something in Latin, "we lads are weak when it comes to sitting with beautiful women, for then we try to display ourselves as just a touch more intelligent than we really are, instead of listening to their beautiful voices."

"I am unable to comment on how beautiful our voices might be," said the bishop's wife, "but since the conversation turns to the poor, a memory appertaining to Skálholt comes to mind: one of my predecessors ordered the stone bridge that nature built over the Brúar River destroyed, and in doing so denied the indigent access to the diocese. That ugly memory has not infrequently visited me, as if I myself had been party to the deed. Nevertheless, it has occurred to me to have some sort of semblance of a bridge built there again so that almsmen would no longer have to die on the riverbank on the other side. It is assuredly a pernicious sin to destroy the bridge of Christian charity which, God willing, may be raised between the poor and the rich. And yet, when I contemplate the matter more carefully, I find that my old predecessor may have had an excuse: namely, Iceland's honor could hardly have been increased if the bishop in Skálholt were to have been eaten out of house and home, and the ravenous mob from every corner of the land allowed to lay the diocese low."

The red flecks on the madam's face had by now merged into one, and though she smiled amicably at her guests one could clearly read in her eyes that she had not spoken first and foremost out of love for philosophy. Her sister put her knife down and stared at her from an incredible distance.

"What does Snæfríður think?" asked the commissary.

She gave a slight start when he spoke her name, then answered hastily:

"I beg your pardon, I have been sleeping all day and am not yet awake. I am dreaming."

The bishop turned to his wife and said:

"My best beloved, tell me who is not an almsman in the eyes of our Redeemer? By my faith, how often have I envied the barefooted tramp who sleeps by the highways without sorrow, and wished that I might stay behind with the crowd of mendicants lying on the sand spit by the stream, watching the birds and praying to God, under obligation to no one. The burdens that the Lord has bestowed on us, the caretakers of this poor country, are heavy, in temporalibus no less than in spiritualibus,* though I doubt that the commoners would appreciate this."

Arnæus asked: "How then shall our lord king best respond to the tearful petitions that are forever pouring out of this land, if vagrants and tramps are more blessed than their overseers?"

"All creation complains and moans, my dear lord Commissarius," said the bishop. "Complaint is its distinctive sound."

"Each and every man complains to his lord and all men bemoan their own lot, yet we know that everything that happens to us, for ill or for good, has its origins in ourselves," said the archpriest. "It is not for men to alleviate the need of the people whom the Lord wishes to discipline with his justice: need cries out for the things that cannot be obtained through anyone's prayer vigils until it has paid the price for its evil deeds. Inexorabilia* is its life."

"You speak truly, Reverend Sigurður," said the commissarius. "Men should never be so conceited as to hinder God's justice, though naturally such a statement is no novelty. But I cannot agree, and presume it is certainly not your view, that this information lightens our obligation toward human justice. According to all Christian doctrine, our Lord granted to men the wisdom to discern right from wrong just as soon as the world began. Now, since good men have shown the king that it is not Sebaoth* who sells the Icelanders bad wares or else sells them too little for them to survive, nor whose judgments are too lenient for the vaunted rich and too severe for the indigent, ordering the hands of some cut off and the tongues of others cut out, hanging a third and burning a fourth for their bereavement and defenselessness, then it is not contrary to God's will that the king should wish to inspect this foul business thoroughly and investigate acutely the overly lenient as well as the overly severe judgments; rather, he works in harmony with the wisdom given to us by our Creator to discern right from wrong and to use that understanding to live our lives with a certain honorable and regimented deportment."

"Indeed, dear Commissarius, we owe you a great debt of gratitude for your vigorous admonition of the merchants, many of whom are in fact my good friends and some of them my true and faithful friends," said the bishop, "though unfortunately they are sinful men no less than we countryfolk. And may God grant that your dealings with them will serve to bring us better flour next year, and, if possible, compensation in silver."

The meal soon came to an end and the bishop began his prayer of thanksgiving, saying that all gathered should lift up their hearts, edified as they were by the conversation of our erudite and beloved table-companions: his friend the archpriest, who prays that God's justice may find its place, and his friend and Lordship the specially appointed commissarius to His Most Worshipful Grace, who prays that human justice might prevail over the Danes as well as the Icelanders, the learned as well as the unlearned, the high as well as the low—

". . . and that the illustrious men who protect the honor and dignity of this our destitute land might hold their heads high, along with their good wives, unimpeded until their final end—" the bishop's wife added her own pious voice to the prayer as she sat with her head bowed, her eyes closed, the palms of her hands clasped together.

"And, as my ardently beloved prays," continued the bishop, "let His divine grace strengthen the illustrious noblemen who uphold the honor of our destitute land. Let us thereby in conclusion raise our voices in singing the humble verse left to us by our dearly departed Reverend Ólafur from Sandar,* which we learned at our mothers' knees:

'May the grace of our Lord Jesus sublime
Protect us all throughout all time,
May God bless our comrades wracked with fear,
Whether they be far or near;
May the bounds of God's Christendom ever increase,
May His defense of authority never cease,
May He grant to all of us heaven's peace.'"

— 9 —

The next day Arnas Arnæus went around midday to visit the bishop's wife in her bower. Sitting there with her was her sister Snæfríður. Both were engaged in needlework and the sun shone in upon them this autumn day.

He greeted them companionably and begged that they excuse his intrusion, but he owed Madam Jórunn an apology for having instigated such frivolous table-chatter the previous evening; his imprudent citation of Luther's words had most likely given offense to that illustrious man their friend Reverend Sigurður, but he did not fully realize it until his puerile repartee, directed against the respectable servant of God, had excited that pert boy his secretary. He said that cosmopolitans were slow to reach a level of maturity sufficient to enable them to speak properly to those who hold the world in contempt.

The bishop's wife accepted the assessor's apology good-naturedly and said that it would certainly be something new to hear kings' courtiers in Iceland describe themselves as lacking in courtesy, but as far as the baccalaureus was concerned, it had simply been a case of youth's natural disdain for those who scorn the world—Reverend Sigurður had encountered such disdain before and understood it. Snæfríður, on the other hand, answered that it could hardly come as any surprise to champions of the faith like Reverend Sigurður, who would readily order men's tongues pulled out of their mouths and cut off, if these weapons struck out at them while they were still attached to their owners.

The assessor said that he was of course quite familiar with Reverend Sigurður's proposals, reiterated at ecumenical councils and the Alþingi and founded on his brimfully learned interpretations of Scripture and abstruse articles of law, that heretics should be tortured and sorcerers burned, but, he said, the archpriest did not deserve to be treated any less courteously by others on account of this.

Arnæus was still standing in the middle of the room, but now the bishop's wife bade him humbly honor two helpless females by remaining in their company for a short time.

". . . and let's stop talking about our friend the honest inquisitor and erudite tongue-cutter Reverend Sigurður; instead tell us some trifle about the realms of the world"—it was Snæfríður who spoke, casually and insuppressibly, her eyes radiant, a completely different woman than the one to whom they had raised their glasses last evening in the Grand Salon.

He said that although he was actually quite pressed for time, since people who had traveled long distances to meet him were waiting downstairs, he could not conceivably refuse such a noble invitation, and he accepted the easy-chair offered to him by the mistress of the house. After he was seated Snæfríður stood up and placed a footstool at his feet.

"Now then, I am of course unfamiliar with those delightful realms of the world which cause elegant ladies to feel homesick, but from those poor countries with which I am acquainted you may choose as you like," he said, and he produced little golden snuffboxes and handed them to the women. They took tiny pinches of snuff, in the manner of noblewomen, and Snæfríður sneezed and laughed and hurriedly wiped her nose and eyes with a handkerchief. "I am familiar namely with those countries to which my demon has drawn me," he continued, "compelling me, as it has done for so long, to search for my very own."

"My sister is well-educated, she may choose her country first," said the bishop's wife. "Perhaps she will choose for both of us."

"We would like to hear about all the countries where noble-women are skilled in the proper use of snuff," said Snæfríður.

"Then it seems to me that I could hardly offer women of that sort anything less than the city of Rome," said the royal commissarius.

Snæfríður was delighted, but her sister the bishop's wife felt that Rome was far too remote. Turning to her sister, she asked: "Oh, do you really wish to hear about the cursed pope now, Snæfríður mine?"

But the commissarius said that there was always a first time for everything, and that he finally found himself forced to disagree with the bishop's wife, since, in his opinion, there were few cities lying closer to Iceland than Rome, and in fact it was easy to recall the time when it lay closest of all cities, closer even than the city of Zion, which is on a height. As far as the pope was concerned, he preferred not to quarrel with the ladies about him, but it could not be denied, he said, that the further south one traveled in the northern hemisphere, the less remote one would find St. Peter.

"I am certain, though you would never admit it, Assessor," said the bishop's wife, "that there can exist two kinds of genuine truth, one for the south, the other for the north."

Arnas Arnæus answered slowly, in his droll, centrifugal manner of speaking, which sounded at times like mere rambling, but which never endangered solemn conversation:

"Up north in Kinn there is a mountain called Bakrangi by those who look to it from the east, but Ógöngufjall by those who stand to its west; sailors out in Skjálfandi call it Galti. And I am ashamed to say it, but I went to Rome not to search for the truth—though it certainly would have proven difficult for me, as for many others, to leave there without finding it. But now I am certain that I am confusing my ladies. Therefore I shall tell you exactly how it was: I went to Rome to search for three books—particularly one of the three. They all have something to do with Iceland, especially the one I desired most to find. This book gives much more accurate information than those mistily veiled fabulae* we know so well concerning how our people discovered America terra* and settled there shortly before the year 1000—and also how they abandoned the place."

When they pressed him for more details he said that a letter written in the Middle Ages, now stored in Paris, mentions that in the archives of an ancient cloister in Rome there exists a codex containing the writings of a certain woman from Hislant terra,* Gurid by name, who undertook a pilgrimage to Rome around the year 1025. The source says that when the woman went to make her confession, a monk discovered that she was neither more nor less than the most widely traveled woman who existed in all of Christendom at that time. As a youth she had dwelt for ten years with her husband and several of her countrymen in a land to the west of the world's ocean, beyond the world's boundary, and had borne a child for her husband there, but strange creatures had made war on them in that land, forcing them to take their infant son and leave. This woman related such great tidings in the sight of God in the city of Rome that the monk finally decided to put them down in letters, and his text could still be read there in the cloister long afterward. Later the cloister was torn down and its possessions were scattered or lost, but some were rediscovered and collected centuries later, when work began on the construction of the papal library after the papal seat was reestablished at Rome following its extended exile.

The two other books Arnæus tried to find in the papal collections were the *Liber Islandorum,* containing both genealogies and biographies of kings omitted by Ari in his Icelandic version, and the *Breviarium Holense,* which, under Jón Arason's initiative, was the first book printed in Iceland, and which had been laid upon the breast of Master Þorlákur in his grave as far as anyone knew.*

The pope is a great bookman and there is little doubt that he had all of these books in his possession at one time or another, and there is nothing more likely than that he still does. But a great many beautiful old books have been filched from the poor old fellow these days, and because of this he has become, as one might expect, somewhat suspicious of people who arrive from far and wide, wanting to rummage through his scraps of books. For years Arnæus had worked to secure the intercession of potentates: ambassadors, generals, archbishops, and cardinals, who for various reasons required him to be permitted entrance to the dark forest called the Papal Archives. Yet the entire time that he wandered in this earthbound recess of history he was never accorded such trust as to be allowed to search alone; a canon was ordered to stand at his side, with an armed Swiss guard behind him, to ensure that he neither stole a single slip of paper nor took it upon himself to make unauthorized copies of any of the memoranda that the evangelists could most likely put to good use in their ongoing struggles against the servant of the servants of God.

He wandered about for so long in this catacomb of the ages that the contemporary world turned into a remote dream. Many of the satchels containing deeds and schedulae* that here filled the halls, the narrow passageways, and the earthen tunnels had grown dusty in repose and had been chewed by termites throughout the march of time; from some of them crept worms and other vermin. Again and again the searcher was afflicted with a catarrh like some farmer out in Iceland who for years has had to pitch moldy hay out in the haymow; there were even times when he had to remain bedridden due to the obstruction in his lungs. In this place his hands uncovered as much important as unimportant evidence concerning every tiny detail ever mentioned in all of Christendom since its history began, everything except for the *Liber Islandorum,* the *Breviarium Holense,* and the

memoirs of the woman Gurid from Hislant terra. The leave of
absence granted to him by His Gracious Sire the King of the Danes
for the undertaking of his journey had long since expired. In the end
he became absolutely convinced that even if he were to search for the
rest of his days, no matter how many he had left, he would remain
equidistant from his goal until the hour of his death. And yet he was
as certain that the books were there as an insane tramp he recalled
seeing in his youth was certain that treasure was to be found hidden
under stones. In his own case, however, the solace inherent in God's
promise that all who seek shall also find seemed to have deserted him
completely.

"You found nothing at all?" asked Snæfríður. She had placed her
needlework on her lap and was staring at him. "Not a single thing?"

"I know," he said, directing his gaze at the bishop's wife, "that it is
a sin, when studying Scripture, to extrapolate or to interpolate, but
original sin, that abominable burden, always reveals itself. For a long
time I have been plagued by the suspicion that the passage I cited just
now originally read something like this: seek and you shall find—
something entirely different from whatever it is you were searching
for. But now I must apologize for my prattle—I feel I really have said
quite enough for today."

He made a move as if to stand up and leave.

"But you have forgotten to tell us of Rome," said Snæfríður. "We
chose this city and now you intend to neglect your duty to us."

The bishop's wife also pleaded that for the sake of courtesy he be
less hasty in his departure.

He remained seated. In truth he was in no hurry—it was quite
possible that he had never had any thoughts of leaving. They allowed
him to examine their cloths, and he unfolded them and expressed his
admiration for them, displaying his knowledge of women's needlework. His hands were delicate, with slightly declining fingertips, his
wrists slender, the backs of his hands smooth and covered with fine
dark hair. Afterward he leaned back again in his easy-chair, but he
still had not put his feet up on the footstool.

"Rome," he said, and he smiled distractedly, looking out into the
distance somewhere. "I saw two men there and one woman; of

course I saw several others, but always these two men and this one woman; morning and evening these three, two Icelandic men, one Icelandic woman."

The women's eyes opened wide—"Icelandic men, an Icelandic woman?"

He described for them a small, brisk woman, rather lean, traveling with a group of German pilgrims to Rome, an unremarkable individual in a group of gray folk, who appeared even grayer than usual in contrast to the residents of the city and who, to the natives, were as deserving of notice as a flock of migrant birds; even the beggars and thieves of Rome were like grandees compared to them. And alone amongst this drab company is, namely, this everyday, unattractive woman in a torn black smock of wadmal, with a cap tied to her head, barefooted like all of Europe at the dawn of the eleventh century, when Christians, due to indigence, were still little more than cannibals. But in a little scrip that this barefoot commoner carried under one arm she kept shoes that looked new, though she had had them for a very long time. They were made of colored, tanned hide, wondrously soft, with stubby toes and soles sewn up around the outside of the foot, the stitching covered over with delicate leaf-shaped cuttings and the vamps set with beautifully colored leather beads. Such shoes had never been seen in Christendom, nor in ancient Rome, nor during the days of any other distinguished nation of ages past; another such pair of shoes shall never be seen again in the world for the next four hundred years. These seldom-seen shoes, a token of a path longer than any other in the world, she had brought south to present to the pope in recompense for the sins she had committed in the land where she had acquired them, Vínland the Good. I tried to look into the eyes of this woman, who alone of all earthly women had discovered the new world, but they were only the eyes of a tired traveler; when I strained my ears I could hear clearly that she spoke to her fellow travelers in a Low German dialect, the language of pilgrims at that time. This woman was Gurid from Hislant terra, Guðríður Þorbjarnardóttir, from Glaumbær in Skagafjörður in Iceland; she had worked a farm in Vínland the Good for close to a year, and had there given birth to a son from whom generations of Icelanders are descended, Snorri the son of Þorfinnur Karlsefni.*

Next he told them the story of the two other Icelanders he had seen in Rome. One of them had traveled south upon a kingly steed, as noblemen do, in the company of other noblemen carrying silver and gold, accompanied by a troop of soldiers hired to protect them from brigands. He was a handsome and vigorous man, with wide but somewhat deep-set eyes; his countenance was like that of a curious child, yet nothing in his bearing indicated that he considered himself less than any other man in the inhabited world. Here come to Rome was the incarnation of the man who had as a merchant escaped from Constantinople and traveled to the land of the caliph while Europe lay in the grip of barbarianism; here was the man who had besieged Paris and Seville, set up kingdoms in France and Italy, brought his ship to the coast of Straumfjörður in Vínland—and composed the *Völuspá*. Now he had slaughtered his kinsmen in Iceland and brought his country to the brink of Ragnarök, as described in the poem, and he had come to Rome to receive shrift from the pope. Penance was ordered: he was led barefoot before the churches of Rome and chastised before most of the cathedrals, as the populace lingered in the streets and watched in amazement, lamenting that such a distinguished man should be so deplorably treated. The man's name was Sturla Sighvatsson.*

The other man had of course never visited Rome, but he had received a letter from the pope, a letter reminding him of his duty to defend with point and edge Iceland's church and its possessions against the Lutheran kings. And at that time, just as today, very few people gave a second thought to the passage of arms. It was Rome that lay before the eyes of this last remaining Icelander of antiquity, until he was led to the block. Arnas Arnæus said that he had often seen the image of this man as if in a vision, but in Rome he had beheld this presbyter as a kind of lucent mirage, the sort which transforms reality into shadows of doubt. It is night here in Skálholt. He stands vigil with his two sons. They appear older, more infirm than their father the elder, because they are more like average men. Misfortune, however, had made his shoulders so strong that they could never be overburdened, no matter how heavy the load, and his neck so stocky that it would never bend. Now it is morning: the seventh of November. Snow has turned the mountains gray overnight. Rime rests on the grassblades.

"These were the people I saw."

"And then no one else?" asked Snæfríður.

"Ah, yes," he said softly, and he looked at her and smiled: "Then the entire world."

"There is no doubt," said the bishop's wife, "that Jón Arason was a great champion, a true Icelander like the men of antiquity, but doesn't it make your blood run cold to think upon what might have happened if that ribald had won, and with him the popish heretics? May my Redeemer help me."

"During my stay in Rome the city celebrated a jubilee for all of Christendom," said Arnas Arnæus. "I was strolling along the river one day. The truth is, I was heavy-hearted, as happens to those who come to realize that a long chapter in their short lives has been squandered in idle labor, in the expenditure of effort and wealth, their health placed in jeopardy, the friendship of good men forfeit due to obstinacy. I was thinking about what sort of excuses I could make to my king and lord for having neglected my duties for too long. There I wandered, filled with misgiving, and before I knew it I met a huge crowd of people inching forward, heading for the bridge over the river. Neither before nor since have I seen such a throng of people: the lanes and highways were so packed that it was difficult to distinguish the bystanders from the procession's participants, and all of them were singing. I stopped in the midst of a group of Roman citizens to watch the stream pass by. They were pilgrims from different nations, come south to receive absolution for their sins during that special Christian year of grace. Within the throng were gathered a great many smaller groups, each group walking in procession, its members wearing badges emblazoned with the image of its shire's protective saint, or else carrying either the bones of its district's steward of God in a little shrine or a replica of its cathedral's holy statue. The images of Maria were distinctive to each place, for throughout the papal realms there are as many different Marias as there are cities and towns—some are associated with flowers, others with stones, still others with health-giving springs, several with the Virgin's seat, the particular configuration of the Christ child, or the color of the Virgin's mantle. It was remarkable to see representatives of so many different shires marching together over one bridge for the sake of their souls. When I was young and walked along Breiðafjörður I never would have thought that such a wide variety of people inhabited the world. Here were folk from the numerous city-states and counties of Italy: Milanese, Napolese and Sicilians, Sardinians, Savoyards, Venetians and Tuscans, along with the Romans themselves; here one could see the peoples of the six Spanish kingdoms: the Castilians, Aragonese, Catalans, Valencians, Majorcans, and Navarrans; gathered here were envoys from the different nations of the Empire, even from the nations that had adopted Luther's reforms: Bavarians, Germans and Croatians, Franconians, Westphalians, Rhinelanders, Saxons, Burgundians, Franks, Walloons, Austrians, and Styrians. But why am I reeling off the names of all these peoples? And yet, it was so: I watched them all going by, and many more. I saw people from nations I knew nothing about, their countenances, the textures of their clothing, their grimy faces and their eyes filled with passion and tenacity. Most often, however, I found myself thinking about their countless feet, bare or in shoes, most certainly tired, yet somehow lively and hopeful; and the old crusade-dance that resounded through their musica,* whether they struck the strings of the lyre or any other instrument, or blew into their folkish homeland-pipes: 'Fair are the fields, cloudless God's sky.' And suddenly I realized that Guðríður Þorbjarnardóttir was gone. Not a single Icelander remained."

The bishop's wife had also laid aside her handiwork; she too was staring at the storyteller.

"Thank God there were no Icelanders present," she said. "Or perhaps you didn't find it grievous to think upon all those ignorant heretics whom the pope prevents from hearing the message of Christ, denying them the privilege of salvation through faith?"

"When a man sees so many feet walking by, my lady, he unavoidably asks: 'Where are you going?' They march over the Tiber and stop in the square in front of St. Peter's Basilica, and the moment the pope walks out onto the balcony of his palace, *Te Deum Laudamus* begins while all the bells of Rome ring out. Is it right, is it wrong, my lady? I don't know. Well-informed auctores* tell us that the wealthy Giovanni de Medici, otherwise known as Leo the Tenth, was a wise aristocrat and student of the Epicurean school, and that it never once occurred to him to believe in the soul even though he sold indulgences for its redemption. Perhaps that's the very reason he did these things. Sometimes one gets the impression that Martin Luther was a peculiar sort of rustic, trying to dispute the liberty of the soul with such a man."

"Yes, but, my dear lord Commissarius, isn't it sinful to think such a thing about our master Luther?" asked the bishop's wife.

"I don't know, my lady," said Arnas Arnæus. "It may very well be. But one thing is certain: those learned and inspired reformatores* were quite suddenly situated far to the north of me. After I had been watching these immense numbers of feet for some time, I suddenly found myself thinking: 'You will follow this procession wherever it leads.' Then the only Icelander in the crowd walked over the Tiber River. We took our place before Sancti Petri Basilica and the bells of Rome rang and the pope, wearing his miter and holding his crosier, walked out onto his balcony while we all sang the *Te Deum.* I had been searching for old Icelandic books, and sorrow had gotten the better of me when I was unable to find them. Suddenly I realized that it did not matter at all that I had not found those old books. I had found something in their place. I left Rome the very next day."

The ladies thanked the assessor cordially for his stories about the chief city of Guðríður Þorbjarnardóttir, Sturla Sighvatsson, and Jón Arason. But since there were visitors awaiting him downstairs, folk who had traveled great distances to meet him, he could not take the time, just now, to describe more cities for them, and the bishop's wife, who was a fierce Protestant and therefore slightly less than content with the papacy, asked whether the assessor would allow her to choose her city at some later time. He granted them the right to choose any city they liked, at any other time they liked, then bade them farewell and walked to the door.

"Before I forget," said Snæfríður, springing up from her chair as he opened the door. "I have something to discuss with you, Assessor.

In fact I'd almost completely forgotten about it. But I must point out that it has to do with something else."

"Does it have to do with a book?" he asked, and he turned on the threshold and looked at her in earnest.

"No, a man," she said.

He said that her fondest wish was most welcome to him.

Then he was gone.

— 10 —

He asked her to sit down.

She sat down opposite him, clasped her hands in her lap, and looked at him aloofly; her bearing was restrained.

"I didn't want to come even though the old man begged me to do so," she said. "I told the old man that it wasn't my concern. All the same, I've come to you because of him. You mustn't think that I've come for any other reason."

"Welcome, Snæfríður," he said for the second or third time.

"Yes," she said, "I know that you're an expert in worldly complaisance. But there's really no avoiding it: this old man whom I don't know and who doesn't concern me, it's as if I've always known him and he does concern me. His name is Jón Hreggviðsson."

"Yes, old Jón Hreggviðsson," said Arnæus. "It was his mother who had in her keeping the single most precious treasure to be found in all the Nordic lands."

"Yes," said Snæfríður. "Her heart—"

"No, some old vellum leaves," interrupted Arnas Arnæus.

"I beg your pardon."

"We all owe a great debt of gratitude to Jón Hreggviðsson—because of his mother," said Arnas Arnæus. "This is why, Snæfríður, when he brought me the ring I gave it back to him, so that he could do himself some good."

"Oh, enough with your vanity now, after fifteen years," said Snæfríður. "It's both ludicrous and embarrassing to recall one's youth."

He leaned back against his desk. Behind him were thick books and bundles of papers, some bound and some opened. He was wearing a wide, black dress coat and white gloves. He hooked his index fingers together and spoke again.

"When I left and did not return despite my promised vow, because fate is stronger than a man's will as it says in the sagas, I consoled myself with the thought that the next time I beheld the fair maiden she would be a different woman: her youth vanished along with her beauty, youth's innate gift. The ancient philosophers taught that faithlessness in love is the only kind of betrayal that the gods look upon with clemency: 'Venus hac perjuria ridet.'* Last evening when you walked into the dining room after all these years I saw that there was no need for Lofn* to smile clemently upon me."

"I beg you, Assessor, enough with your worthless vanity," she said, as she unclasped her hands and raised them momentarily in defense. "For God's sake."

"Just as all men are poets when they are young, but never afterward, so are all fair for a time when young; youth connotes these two things," he said. "But the gods grant these gifts to some through a special grace that they sustain from the cradle to the grave, regardless of the amount of one's allotted years."

"You are without doubt a poet, Assessor," she said.

"I would like for what I have just said to serve as the preface to all that remains for us to discuss," said he.

She stared off into the distance as if she had forgotten the purpose of her visit. Her appearance was ruled by a kind of primal, empty calm that had more of a semblance of sky than earth. Finally, however, she looked down at her lap.

"Jón Hreggviðsson," she said—"the only thing I want to discuss with you is him. They say that an almsgiver is indebted to the beggars he supports. Whatever a man does once endures forever. Now this Jón Hreggviðsson returns after fifteen years and claims his debt."

"I thought you would have been proud to have saved the head of old Jón Hreggviðsson, who killed the king's hangman."

"But my father deserved more from me than to have me spirit away his convicted criminals," she said. "He has never wanted anything but the best for me. You are a friend of the king, and for his sake, you must be angry with me, since, as you say, he killed a man, he killed the king's man."

"There's no doubt that he did it," said Arnas Arnæus. "But with regard to our king, we can't be blamed for helping the man. Nothing was ever proven against him."

"My father does not pass false judgment," she said.

"How do you know that?" he said.

"I am a part of him," she said. "He is in me. I feel as if I myself could have justifiably condemned this criminal. That's why my conscience reviles me for having set him free."

"A man's conscience is an unsteady judge of right and wrong," he said. "Conscience is only a dog inside us, trained to varying degrees. All it can do is obey its master, the statutes laid down by its environment, and its master can be either fair or foul depending upon circumstance. Sometimes its master is nothing but a rogue. Pay no heed to what your conscience deems its obligation as far as Jón Hreggviðsson's head is concerned. You are not infallible and consequently neither is your father. Imagine that the court has erred, until it is proven otherwise."

"If the court did err, and Jón Hreggviðsson is innocent, isn't justice worth more than one beggar's head?—even though justice itself has been known to fail now and again."

"If the court proves a man guilty, he loses his head for it—even if he never committed the crime. It's a hard lesson; but without it we would not have justice. And this is exactly where the court seems to have erred in Jón Hreggviðsson's case, and actually in the cases of many other alleged criminals in this country—too many."

"Perhaps," she said. "But I've never heard anyone express any doubt as to whether Jón Hreggviðsson killed the man. And you yourself admit it. After all, the old man wouldn't be so worried about the case if he didn't harbor doubts about his own innocence."

"It would have been very little problem to arrest Jón Hreggviðsson and behead him—he's been sitting at home in Rein for between ten and twenty years now, utterly terrified of the authorities. But no one has touched a hair on his head."

"My father never condemns a man twice for the same crime," she said. "The old man returned to Iceland with some letters from the king."

"Unfortunately not letters confirming eternal life," said Arnas Arnæus, and he smiled.

"Letters of protection."

"One letter concerned a retrial of his case. But it was never published in court. And the case was never retried."

"My father never stabs anyone under the table," she said. "He's a compassionate man and has even felt sorry for this scoundrel."

"Is it right to be compassionate?" asked Arnas Arnæus, still smiling.

"I know that I'm foolish," she said. "I know that I'm so foolish that before you I'm like a little bug that has rolled over on its back and can't get to its feet to escape."

"Your lips haven't changed: two caterpillars," he said.

"I'm certain that Jón Hreggviðsson killed a man," she said.

"You sent him to me for safekeeping."

"That was coquetterie,"* she said. "I was seventeen."

"He told me that his mother came to see you," said Arnas Arnæus.

"More of the same," she said. "I have no heart."

"May I try to find it?" he said.

"No," she said.

"But your cheeks are flushed," he said.

"I know that I'm amusing," she said. "But it's unnecessary for you, my lord, to rub it in."

"Snæfríður," he said.

"No," she said. "Please do not speak my name. Just tell me one thing: if this case is pursued any further, will it really matter at all what happens to Jón Hreggviðsson?"

He had stopped smiling, and, assuming an official air, answered slowly and impersonally: "No decisions have been made. A number of old items, however, require attention. The king has ordered that they be taken into account. Jón Hreggviðsson came here the other day and we discussed his case freely for an hour. Things do not bode well in his case. But no matter how it goes for him, I believe that a reexamination of his case will prove beneficial to the countryfolk in Iceland in the future."

"And if he's found guilty—after all these years?"

"He cannot be found any more guilty than he was according to the old ruling."

"And if he's innocent?"

"Hm. What did Jón Hreggviðsson want from you?"

She ignored the question, but looked straight at the king's envoy and asked:

"Is the king my father's enemy?"

"I believe that it is impossible for me to say no," said Arnæus. "I believe that our Most Gracious Sire the king and my esteemed friend the magistrate are both equally devoted to the cause of justice."

She had stood up.

"I thank you," she said. "Your words befit a king's man: you reveal nothing, and instead concoct enticing stories when necessary, like the ones you told us today about Rome."

"Snæfríður," he said as she turned to leave. He was suddenly standing very close to her. "What else could I have done but give Jón Hreggviðsson the ring?"

"Nothing, Assessor," she said.

"I wasn't free," he said. "I was bound by my work. Iceland owned me, the old books that I kept in Copenhagen—their demon was my demon, their Iceland was the only Iceland in existence. If I had come out in the spring on the Bakkaship as I promised I would have sold out Iceland. Every last one of my books, every leaf and every page would have fallen into the hands of the usurers, my creditors. We two would have ended up on some dilapidated estate, two highborn beggars. I would have abandoned myself to drink and would have sold you for brennivín, perhaps even cut off your head—"

She turned completely around and stared at him, then quickly took him by the hand, leaned her face in one swift movement up against his chest, and whispered:

"Árni."

She said nothing more, and he stroked her fair and magnificent hair once, then let her leave as she had intended.

— **II** —

A poor man, chafed blue in the face and soaking wet from the rain, stands before the bishop's doors one day in the autumn and demands to speak with someone, but he is ignored. His clothing is tattered and shabby, though it was originally tailored for a man of higher standing. His boots are scuffed and coming apart at the seams, about as ragged as one could expect in the land where everyone shared a single common distinctive feature: wretched shoes. He is apparently sober. His face does not resemble a caricature but rather the relics of a man, displaying occasional traces of his youthful, manly mien. It is clear from the man's vigorous carriage that he has seen better days. He refuses to mingle with the common folk gathered here; his business, he says, is with the higher-ups.

The first time he knocked upon the bishop's door his only request was that he be allowed to see his wife. The door was slammed shut in his face. He stood at the door for some time, and when it was finally opened for other visitors, he was ordered to stay outside. He remained standing there and poked at the door now and then, but those within knew who it was and left it shut. He walked around behind the house and tried to get to the bishop's office through the main bedroom, and even made it as far as the hallway when he ran into angry housemaids who told him that he had to go around to the other side if he wanted to see the bishop. After numerous other attempts he was finally allowed to speak to one of the bishop's wife's maidservants, who informed him that the madam's sister was in poor health, and that the madam herself was preoccupied. He asked to be allowed to speak to the bishop, but was told that the bishop was at a meeting with his priests.

The visitor returns the next day and the events of the previous day are replayed, only now in a southwesterly gale and fierce hailstorms. In between the gusts of hail that tear into the visitor's clothing one can see that his legs are starting to quiver and his knees to bend, but his boots are still more dismally dry than wet. He wears no gloves and wipes his nose with his bare fingers, sneezing and snuffling. The third time he visits the place he knocks on the front door and hands over a letter addressed to the bishop, then dawdles and loiters until early evening, when someone comes and informs him that he is to appear before the bishop in the Grand Salon. The bishop addressed him, "Dear Magnús," then took hold of his cold hands, smiling and respectful and dignified; he was not at all angry, but rather patronizing, saying that he thought Magnús had come from more clever stock than this, to imperil himself in such a hazardous course by attempting to initiate legal proceedings touching upon his marital estate, as outlined in his letter. As far as the husband's wish to discuss the matter with his wife was concerned, the bishop's only answer was that it was entirely her decision to meet with him or not. And as for the letter's demand that the bishop impose his clerical power and authority and order the woman back home to her husband, he replied along these lines, that his sister-in-law was welcome to stay at the see whenever she chose. Magnús from Bræðratunga proclaimed that he loved his wife with all his heart and beyond measure, and that to drag her away from him was a tremendously evil deed. The bishop said that he was not a party to their affairs and asked his brother-in-law not to be offended though he could not offer any more advice on matters of the heart, especially since nothing had happened yet between husband and wife that might demand his special and immediate attention.

The husband continued nonetheless to hang about the place, day and night. He came up with various excuses to speak with the steward and persons in other low-level positions when the higher-ups refused to see him. He even took it upon himself to repair the riding gear of gentlemen who had business at the see and did odd jobs in the smithy for the steward. He stayed completely sober, even when surrounded by drunks, and when the louts on the premises invited him to join in their public drinking party after a supply trip to Eyrarbakki he staunchly refused to join in the fun and walked away.

One Sunday morning he planned to waylay his wife as she went to mass. He waited for a very long time but she never appeared, and finally when he went into the church he saw her sitting with her sister and other prominent women in the farthest corner of the women's pews. She was wearing a faldur.* She stared straight ahead, unmoving, paying close attention to Reverend Sigurður's sermon on people afflicted with palsy. He had lingered too long outside and when he went to take a seat in the choir he found them all occupied, as was every other seat in the side-nook—Arnas Arnæus was sitting there with his entourage and a number of aristocrats from other districts. The squire slunk back to the nave and sat down. After the priest intoned the collect he saw Snæfríður and the bishop's wife, along with the housekeeper and a maidservant, stand up and make ready to leave; but instead of walking out through the church after exiting the choir, they turned the other direction, following the parclose around the altar to the sacristy. From there an underground passageway used mainly during winter storms led to the bishop's residence. She would surely have to take off her faldur before venturing into that dirty hole.

One day not too long after this unlucky churchgoing the husband decides to speak to Arnæus, and is shown to the room where he and two of his secretaries sit working before a fire blazing in the fireplace. The abandoned husband placed his cold-benumbed hand in the warm and blessed hand of the royal envoy. Arnæus welcomed his visitor cheerfully and bade him sit. The husband sat down, glanced about quixotically, and scowled. Opposite the true gentleman with the fire burning behind him, the huge books and the carved chairs, the visitor looked more like a lanky, awkward youth who doesn't know for certain whether he's a man though he tries hard to act like one.

"Is there something I can do for you?" asked Arnas Arnæus.

"I wanted to say a few words to you—Your Lordship," he said.

"Privatim?" asked the assessor.

The visitor looked up with a smirk, baring his gaping teeth and gums. "Yes, just so," he said. "I haven't used Latin for a long time: privatim."*

Arnæus asked his secretaries to leave the two of them alone to talk.

The man's smirk remained both shy and forward at once, its sting directed both inward and out. He said:

"I was thinking of offering you a couple of old, worn-out books, if they haven't yet gone rotten out in my storehouse loft; they're from my blessed father's farm."

Arnæus said that he was always curious to hear about opera antiquaria* and asked him what books these were, but the squire wasn't quite sure, since he hadn't been much in the habit of digging around in the old fables about Gunnar of Hlíðarendi and Grettir Ásmundarson* and other highwaymen who lived in this country in the old days; he said he'd even give his Lordship the old rubbish if he wanted it.

Arnæus bowed in his seat and thanked the squire for his gift. The conversation halted for a moment. The husband's eyes had stopped wandering for the most part, but he sat downcast in wordless obstinacy. Arnas Arnæus looked silently at his broad, flat forehead, which resembled the crown of a bull's head. Finally, when the silence grew unnaturally long, he asked:

"Was there anything else?"

The visitor seemed to awaken suddenly, and he said: "I've been wanting to ask the assessor if he would lend me his support in a certain small matter."

"It is my duty, as far as I am able, to lend every man my support for righteous causes," said Arnas Arnæus.

The visitor paused for a moment, then began to explain. He was married to an outstanding woman whom he loved very much—she was an extraordinarily sensible woman. He said that he'd always treated this woman like an unhatched egg, watching over her night and day, treating her like a princess in her tower with her gold and silver jewelry and her beautiful embroidery, putting panes of glass in her windows, providing her with delicacies to eat and a stove, while he himself slept in a faraway wing of the house whenever it pleased her. He'd never considered anything too good for this woman, because she was from a noble family, besides the fact that many people considered her to be the most beautiful woman in Iceland. But such is the female race: suddenly she wants nothing more to do with her husband and runs away from him.

Arnæus carefully considered the man before him as he was speaking. It wasn't clear whether Magnús was telling this story out of naiveté, under the presumption that this dignitary from afar was unfamiliar with the particulars of such a private matter, or whether this was in fact sarcastic dissimulation, whereby a crafty cuckold was playing the fool for his old competitor in some sort of test of wits. Although there could still be seen in the eyes of the visitor distilled traces of the attributes that confirmed that he had once been a cavalier and a charmer, their luster revealed the astonishing torpidity of the man's mind, like that of a prisoner or a beast—it was highly doubtful whether a man was hidden behind them.

"Who is the defendant in this case, the woman herself or someone else?" asked Arnas Arnæus.

"The bishop," said the husband.

This required some explanation, which ran as follows: the bishop, the visitor's brother-in-law, and that entire side of the family had long been contriving to belie him to his wife. Now they'd finally achieved their goal—they'd cunningly lured his wife away from him and turned her into a kind of prisoner here at the bishopric, holding her against her will and standing guard over her day and night so that her rightful husband by the laws of God and man would never get the chance to meet with her. The husband said that he'd gone to the bishop to discuss the matter, but had gotten nothing back from him but excuses and hearsay. Now the husband hoped and prayed that the royal envoy would grant him his support in bringing a lawsuit against the bishop, in order to assert his rights and legally reclaim his wife.

Arnæus smiled affably, but said that he would prefer to be excused from bringing legal action against his host and friend the bishop, especially on account of another man's wife, unless of course a huge breach of justice was at issue in the case; as far as the husband's old books were concerned, however, he said that if the opportunity arose he would be delighted to have a look at them and assess their value. Then he stood up, took a pinch of snuff and offered some to the husband, then showed him to the door.

Snow is drifting outside. A chill wind presses in upon a wayward man standing in the dooryard of the bishop's residence one evening. He turns his back to the wind like a horse left outside, one blue hand at his neckline, holding together the collar of his coat since he's too aristocratic to wear a scarf, and stares up at the little windows just above the Grand Salon, but the curtains have been let down and it is dark inside; she is taking her twilight nap. He stands there shivering for a while before a man with a few dogs steps out from the passageway between the buildings and shouts at him through the snowstorm, saying that that damned villain Magnús from Bræðratunga was to vacate the premises of Skálholt immediately or he would sic the dogs on him; and if he tried to go on behaving in the same way, skulking around here day and night, he would be tied to a post and flogged the very next time he showed his face. It looked as if the steward, who up until now had acted benignly toward the husband and had frequently assigned him various jobs to do around the see, had recently received orders outlining the novel attitude toward this pilgrim that was to be adopted by the see's inhabitants.

The husband said nothing. He was too great a squire to bandy words with nobodies, especially when sober, and amongst other things he was hungry. He walked straight into the winds coursing between the estate's buildings and the gusts tore through his clothing; his legs had never felt more weak or his knees more bowed than now. Once upon a time he had ridden his horse over these lordly flagstones on late spring nights as fair as any described in the lais; horses were not allowed in the yard during the day. Unfortunately he no longer owned a single shoed horse. On the other hand, coming toward him now is a man riding a black horse with calked shoes; he has been out on the Hundapollur, giving his black minion a twilight run. The squire pretended not to notice the rider and continued on against the wind, but the latter stopped a short distance behind him and reined in his wild mount, which champed its bit, dripping foam. The rider turned in the saddle and called out to the walker:

"Are you drunk?"

"No," said the squire.

"Do you by chance have business with me?"

"No."

"Then with whom?"

"My wife."

"So she is still here in Skálholt," said the priest. "I hope that her visit has done my dearly beloved friend well."

"I wouldn't doubt it if you already knew best yourself how things are going for folk here in Skálholt," said the walker. He could be pert with the rider because they'd been schoolmates here a long time ago. "You've all done a good job of duping my wife into leaving me. And you certainly can't be said to have neglected your own interests."

"I always assumed that it was beyond my ability, dear Magnús, to lure a woman away from someone as charming as you," said the priest.

"I have it on good authority that you had a long conversation with her out in my homefield last summer."

"Oh, I never heard it was a crime, dear Magnús, for rectors to hold open conversations with their beloved parishioners out in a homefield in the light of day. If I were you I would probably consider more noteworthy those conversations that might be taking place elsewhere than out in the open in a homefield in the light of day."

"I'm cold, I'm hungry, I'm sick, and I have no desire to stand here out in the open in frost and storm and listen to your prattle. Farewell, I'm gone," said the husband.

"Otherwise I make no secret of the business that I had with your wife last summer, dear Magnús," said Reverend Sigurður. "If it is important for you to hear it I will be glad to tell it to you right away."

"Is that so?" said the husband.

"This summer people were rumoring that you have an excessive fondness for brennivín, dear Magnús," said Reverend Sigurður. "So I came to your wife, my dear Snæfríður, to learn whether there was any truth to the rumor."

"So what," said the squire. "What do you care if I drink? Who doesn't drink?"

"People have different opinions about brennivín," said Reverend Sigurður. "You know it yourself, dear Magnús. Some find it disgusting. Some do not care for more than a small sip. Others drink a bit to relax or perhaps to get tipsy, and then stop. There are also those who are able to drink themselves out of their wits and wisdom day after day, and yet do not admire brennivín so much that they will sacrifice the things they value for it. These men are not fond of brennivín."

"I see you haven't lost your old habit of going in circles around a question," said Magnús from Bræðratunga. "Just between us, I don't understand you and never have. What I asked was, who besides me really cares whether I've enjoyed a drink of brennivín in the past? No one knows it better than my wife and she hasn't once in all of our married life criticized me for it."

"A man who does not put much stock in brennivín," said Reverend Sigurður, "would not be prepared to let his estate crumble to ruins for it. And he would not be prepared to sell his wife for it, and his children if he had any. Even if his wife might fetch him the handsomest price of all the women in Iceland."

"It's a lie," said Magnús from Bræðratunga. "If there's one thing I despise, it's brennivín."

"I should think it to be the voice of the Lord and not your own that speaks these words, dear Magnús," said the archpriest. "People should be able to distinguish between the two. It is not a man's admission of certain deeds but rather the deeds themselves that reveal which voice he heeds."

"I've made a solemn vow never to let my lips touch brennivín again," said the husband. He had come all the way up to the horse and took its mane in both of his hands. Finally he looked up with fervent eyes at the mounted priest and said: "I've kept vigil and prayed to God every night since my wife left home, though I know you would never believe it. My mother taught me to read in the *Book of Seven Words.* And there no longer exists within me a single spark of longing for brennivín. I've been offered brennivín time and again these days, and what do you think I've really wanted to do? I've wanted to spit in it. If you speak to her, Reverend Sigurður, you can tell her that."

"I think it might be better if you tell her yourself, dear Magnús," said the priest. "But if you want to send her any messages, there are others more fitting to bring them to her than I."

"They've all slammed the door in my face," said the husband. "Finally I went to see the man who's even higher now than the householder himself, and they sicked the dogs on me as soon as I left him and threatened to hurt me if I ever came back."

"These men of the world!" said the priest.

The squire leaned up against the horse's neck and looked even more fervently into the rider's face as he asked:

"Tell me truthfully, my dear Reverend Sigurður: do you think that she's having an affair with him?"

Reverend Sigurður had given the horse rein.

"Forgive me for hindering you," he said as he prepared to ride away.

"I thought you might have had business with me. And when I saw you, I wanted to tell you that whatever might be happening now, it was as recently as when Snæfríður and I talked in the homefield that she was willing to overlook all of your faults, since she loved the man who would sell her for nothing more deeply than the man who would give everything to have her."

The squire stood there in the storm and called out after him: "Siggi, dear Siggi, I have some business with you, let's speak together for a moment or two!"

"I often keep vigil at night—after the dogs are asleep," said the archpriest. "I shall open the door for you if you stand by my window and say quietly, 'God be here!'"

— 12 —

Breiðafjörður is a beautiful region: eiderducks crowd the inlets, seals sleep on the rocks, salmon hurdle the falls, seabirds throng on the isles. The seashore is bounded by meadows, the slopes are covered with shrub and the mountain ravines with grass; heathery moors, streams, and falls fill the upper expanses. Farmhouses stand on grassy banks overlooking the pastures and the fjord, and in calm weather the holms and the skerries cast quivering, flossy-soft shadows, lucid like shade on springwaters—it is Arnæus, speaking to her one evening; she has come to him to ask what her husband wanted from him. "As I recall, you own a farm in the area?"

"So what?" she said.

"If you care to household there, I shall send you timber."

"The renowned cosmopolitan," she said. "Are you really such a child?"

"Yes," he said, "I am such a child. First impressions have a lasting effect. The first time I saw you we were at such a farm. In my mind I shall see Breiðafjörður around you forever; and I shall see the folk in Breiðafjörður, whose faces convey a nobility that can never be over-come by sorrow nor effaced by trial."

"I have no idea where I come from," she said emptily.

"May I tell you a story?" he asked.

She nodded her head, her mind elsewhere.

"Once there was a wedding feast in Breiðafjörður. It was late in the spring, around the time of the summer sun's return, when every-thing in Iceland that did not die quickens. Late one evening two travelers came riding into the yard. They were not allowed to con-tinue on their way until they had eaten. A tent had been set up in the homefield and the folk sat there joyously drinking their cares into oblivion. The travelers were invited into the farmhouse, where the more prudent farmers were sitting with their wives. Several young girls brought food and drink. These unbidden guests who had stopped for a short time at a nighttime feast were brothers, the first a man of some distinction, a bailiff from the far side of the fjord. The other was a young man who had dwelt an entire decade abroad. The elder brother had gone to meet his ship in Stykkishólmur, and they had planned to ride on through the night. The returnee once again beheld the gray folk he remembered from his youth, how their charming manners served only to make their grayness more poignant and their sorrow more unfortunate. A number of people tumbled down the grassy slope dead drunk. The travelers sat for some time in the farmhouse, surrounded by more sensible men, when it so hap-pened that a face passed before the eyes of the traveler from afar. The face immediately wakened in him such an intense astonishment that the others were transformed into specters at the same moment—and though he had previously been entertained in king's halls, he knew then that he had never before experienced such a thing."

"You frighten me," she said.

"I realize that when I say such things I violate all the rules of pro-priety governing polite conversation," he said. "But no matter how often the visitor has thought upon that vision, he has not yet found words propitious enough to describe the image, the aura in the veiled gleam of a summer night. He still asks himself the same questions he asked then: 'How can such a thing be? How can such a gulf exist between one person's countenance and those of all the others?' Later he often reproached himself, saying: 'Haven't you encountered enough illustrious women out in the world to enable you to withstand the aura of a single maiden from Breiðafjörður? Your derangement springs from within, from the kind of illumination that can fill the soul in a moment of bliss, though the intellect might seek false grounds for it in the outer world.' This glimmer, however, became ever more fixed as time passed by, until finally the illustriousness and beauty of foreign women were exiled from the visitor's mind into the realm of shadows: and only she remained."

"Perhaps this foreign traveler was most surprised at how widely a girl from Breiðafjörður could open her eyes the first time she saw a man!"

He did not let her interjection distract him.

"There is only one moment in a man's life that stays with him and will always stay with him throughout the march of time. Everything he does afterward, for good or for ill, he does in the reflected light of that moment, as he fights his lifelong battles—and there is nothing that he can do to resist it. For certain, it is always one pair of eyes that reigns over such a moment, the eyes for which all poets are born, and yet their poet is never born, for upon the day that their true name is spoken the world will perish. What happened, what was said? At such a moment nothing happens, nothing is said. But suddenly they are down in the meadow by the river, and the estuary is flooded. Golden clouds shine behind her. The night breeze breathes through her fair hair. Traces of the day remain in the pale blush upon her rose-petal cheeks."

"How did it ever occur to the friend of queens to ask this muddle-headed girl to walk with him out in the meadow? She had seen only fifteen winters."

"She had seen only fifteen springs."

"She herself scarcely understood she existed. She thought that because the visitor was a nobleman he was going to ask her to take a message to her father, who had left the feast. It wasn't until the next

day that she realized he had given her the ring—that he had given it
to her."

"What might she have thought of such a peculiar guest?"

"She was the magistrate's daughter and everyone gives gifts to the
rich. She simply thought that magistrates' daughters were given
gifts."

"When the ring came back to him he gave it to Jón Hreggviðsson
so that the farmer could buy himself a drink. He had burnt his ship.
Promises, oaths, our fondest wishes: ephemera. He had sold the
young rose petal of a fair spring night for shriveled parchment books.
They were his life."

"You told me that once before," she said. "But you've skipped
ahead, Árni. You've skipped over two summers."

"Tell me, Snæfríður."

"I don't have the words."

"The one who has the words cannot tell the tale, Snæfríður—the
only one who can is the one who truly breathes. Breathe."

She sat for a long time and stared straight ahead, trancelike,
breathing.

"When you came to stay with us to have a look at my father's old
books, I don't remember rejoicing; but I might have been just a bit
curious. I never dared to tell my mother that a strange man had given
me a ring, but that was because she had forbidden me to accept gifts
from strangers without her consent. She was of the opinion that an
unfamiliar man who gave a magistrate's daughter gifts harbored evil
thoughts. Actually, young girls have a hard time believing what their
mothers say, but all the same, I took precautions to make sure that
no unpleasant witness against me would reach her ears; so I hid the
ring."

"Please continue," he said.

"With what?" she said. "Am I telling a story?"

"I will not interrupt you."

She looked down and said distractedly, dimly: "What happened?
You came. I was fifteen. You left. Nothing at all."

"I stayed at your father's for half a month that summer to browse
through his books. He had quite a few paper editions and several
good vellum manuscripts. Some of them I copied, others I bought

from him, some he gave to me. He is a model Icelandic scholar and is particularly knowledgeable in genealogy. We spent many late summer evenings chatting for hours about the folk who have lived in this country."

"I often eavesdropped," she said. "Never before had I wanted to listen to adults. But then I couldn't tear myself away, though I understood little of what you were discussing. I was spying on you. I was terribly anxious to examine this man, how he was clothed, his boots, his bearing, to hear him speak no matter what he talked about, yet first and last to listen to the tone of his voice. Then you left. The house was empty. How lucky that he's not more distant than on the other side of the fjord, thought this fool; oh, who was to eavesdrop now in the evenings? One day in the autumn she heard that he had sailed from Hólmur."

"That winter the king sent me south to Saxony to examine some books that he wished to purchase. I stayed in the palace of a count. But in a country where even a fat, happy commoner could enter the concert hall for two shillings after his day's work, or could go and listen to great masters perform their cantatas on Sundays in church, where do you think the thoughts of the visitor were but in the one country in the world's north that was oppressed by famine, its folk labeled by learned men gens paene barbara?* While I was studying those precious volumina* made by the greatest printers, some by Plantino the arch-printer, some by Gutenberg* himself, ornate books, lavishly illuminated, beautifully bound, some with clasps of silver, the books my lord was planning to purchase for his library in Copenhagen, all my thoughts were in the country where the most precious treasure in the Nordic lands had its origin—and which was now consigned to rot in an earthen hovel somewhere. Every evening as I lay down to sleep, this was my insomniac thought: today the mold has fastened itself to yet another page of the *Skálda*."

"And in Breiðafjörður a little girl suffers through Þorri and Góa*— fortunately you weren't thinking about that."

"In the sagas one often reads that Icelanders at the courts of kings grew silent as winter came on. I booked passage on the first spring ship from Glückstadt to Iceland."

"She didn't understand the reasons why, but she was always thinking about only one man. There's an old niggard in Grundarfjörður who doesn't sleep at night—he just sits awake, staring at a gold ducat—maybe she was insane like this pitiful man. Why this disturbance? This trembling anxiety? This emptiness? This fear of a cold verdict, to be stranded, without ever again being able to return home, like the folk in Greenland. Old Helga Álfsdóttir sits on a trunk outside the couple's bedroom, stitching lace in the twilight while the others sleep. She has long since stopped telling me fairy tales, because she thinks that I'm a big girl. More often now she tells me stories about folk who have encountered hardships. Her own memory of the countryfolk goes back many generations, and nothing a man can experience in his life surprised her. When she told her stories, it was as if the history of the country and its people passed before my eyes. And finally I snuck to her bedcloset one evening, took heart, and bade her draw the curtain, since I was going to tell her a secret. I told her that there was a little something needling my mind, and because of this I could not live a happy day, and I begged her not to call me the magistrate's daughter, but instead to call me her dear child as she did when I was a little girl. And then she asked, 'What's the matter, dear child?'

"'It's a man,' said I.

"'Who is it?' said she.

"'It's a grown man who means nothing to me, whom I don't know. I'm most likely insane.'

"'God help us,' said old Helga Álfsdóttir, 'if it's one of the riffraff.'

"'It's the man who was wearing English boots,' I said, because I'd never seen a man wearing polished boots before. I showed her the ring you'd given me the night we saw each other. And then I went on, describing for her in detail how this man who meant nothing to me and whom I did not know and whom I would never see again would not leave my mind day or night, and how frightened I was. And after I told her all of my secrets, she placed the palm of her hand on the back of mine, leaned toward me, and whispered in my ear so faintly that I didn't grasp what she'd said until she'd leaned away from me again.

"'Do not fear, dear child—it's love.'

"I think I blacked out. I had no idea how I could escape. Love—it was one of those words one could never say; in the magistrate's family no such thing was ever mentioned—we didn't know it existed, and when my sister Jórunn married the bishop in Skálholt seven years prior there was nothing more preposterous than to connect that act with such an idea. When other folk married it was either like any other economic arrangement in the countryside, or else they did it in response to impulses foreign to a magistrate's family. My dear father had taught me to read from Cicero's arithmetic, and when I began to read the *Aeneid,* the farthest I ever got in the world of grammatica, it never occurred to me that Dido's overwhelming emotions were only poetry, contrary to reality. So when I learned from old Helga Álfsdóttir what had happened to me, it was no great wonder that it took me by more than surprise. I snuck back to my bed and of course dampened one or two pillows; then I prayed all the Bjarni-prayers and all the Þórður-prayers,* and finally when nothing else worked I prayed the Hail Mary twelve times in Latin from an old Catholic tome, 'Ora pro nobis peccatoribus nunc et in hora mortis nostrae.'* And then I was soothed."

Arnæus said: "My first day back in Breiðafjörður at your home, I knew it the moment we saw each other. We both knew it. On that day all other knowledge seemed insignificant and unnecessary."

"And," she said, "I came to you for the first time. No one knew it. I came in a trance because you had told me to, and because my will was not mine, it was yours. I would have come even if I had been forced to wade through powerful waterfalls or commit deadly sins. And then I had come to you. I didn't know what you did to me. I had no awareness of what happened. I knew only this: I was yours. And because of this everything was good; everything right."

"I remember what you asked that first time," he said. "'Aren't you the finest man in the whole world?' you asked, and you looked at me as if to see whether you would be safe. Then you said nothing more."

"Yes, I did—in the autumn," said she. "In the autumn when you left, when we said farewell here in Skálholt, I said to you: 'Now there is no need for me to ask, now I know.'"

"The moonlight shone in my little room. I made all the promises a man can make. I had seas to sail."

"Yes, I should have known," she said.

"I know what you mean," he said, "'Nulla viro juranti femina credat.'* Ships can be delayed and still reach home, Snæfríður."

"When the ships returned to Greenland," she said, "the people there were long since gone. The settlement was deserted."

"It's fate, the gods, that determine the return of ships," he said. "The sagas of Icelanders witness it."*

"Yes, it certainly is fortunate that both the gods and fate exist," she said.

He said: "I wasn't the finest man in the whole world."

"No?" she said. "Otherwise I wouldn't have married the squire in Bræðratunga; I would have married the archpriest in Skálholt."

"It was an autumn day. We were traveling, you and I, along with your sister and brother-in-law, on our way hither to Skálholt from the west; I was supposed to sail after a few days. It was one of those autumn days that are brighter than spring days. You were wearing red stockings. It seemed to me like I was living amongst elves, as it always did whenever you were near, and that my previous world across the sea was forgotten. We rode through Hafnarskógur. Just as soon as a traveler steps into the open spaces in this luminous country, with its sun and streams and the fragrance of the fields, he forgets that poverty rules here. The turf-grown farmhouses out in the countryside seemed to lie in a deep sleep, blessed and charmed. You were wearing a blue cloak, riding ahead of us, the wind blowing through your locks—to my eyes you were the undying woman for whom the heroes of the ancient sagas gave up their lives. She must not be betrayed though all else is lost, said the man riding after her through the copse. I was determined never to leave you. I knew that the king would give me whatever office in Iceland I desired most, and at that time the second magistrate's office was unfilled. But—there was a book called the *Skálda*. For years this book dominated my mind, and I sent men into every corner of the land to search for its leaves. A hundred years ago it had fallen to the heirs of a poor aristocrat, and they tore it into pieces that came to rest in the hands of inhuman beggars scattered throughout the land. It took me incredible effort, but I managed to scrape together much of it, though I still lacked fourteen leaves, the most valuable leaves of all. I had a vague suspicion that there were several pieces of an old manuscript in a cottage on Akranes and you let yourself be persuaded to make a detour there with me. The place was called Rein."

She said, "I remember when you led me inside."

"How true it was, that place was ill suited to a woman of heroic tales. I remember clearly how you cuddled up to me in front of everyone and said, 'My friend, why have you brought me into this dreadful house?' And then you were gone."

"You forgot me."

"In that hovel I found the most precious leaves from the *Skálda*. We searched around until we found them buried with the rubbish in an old woman's bed—this gem of books. I remember the moment when I stood there in the sitting room, the leaves in my hands, thinking about the folk who kept the crown of all that was precious to book-lore in the Nordic lands: the decrepit old woman and the simpleton, the farmer, a crabbed and disdainful cord-thief, his back swollen from the lash-strokes of the hangman whom he was accused of having murdered, the emaciated girl with the huge eyes, and the two lepers whose faces had been wiped away; but you were gone. I knew that I would leave and never return. At that moment I betrayed you. Nothing could force me to become the leader of a murdered people. Iceland's books reclaimed me."

Lady Snæfríður was standing.

"I never blamed you, Árni," she said. "Not with words, not with thoughts. You must have known that by the messages I sent you with the ring."

"I asked Jón Hreggviðsson to keep quiet," he said. "I never received your messages."

"I rode away from Skálholt," she said, "and came to Þingvellir by night. I was alone. I had decided to send this criminal to you. His mother came to me over mountains and streams. I knew that you wouldn't return, but I didn't accuse you; I murdered my love willfully the night before, when I gave myself to Magnús from Bræðratunga for the first time. As I rode to Þingvellir I composed the messages I was planning to send to you, and then you refused to hear them, because you didn't trust me. Now I'm going to say what I wanted to say, all the same, and ask that they be the last words between us tonight and every night as if it were the last."

Then she spoke the words that she had once, long ago, bidden her father's condemned criminal carry from Þingvellir by Öxará to her lover: "If my lord can save Iceland's honor, even if I suffer disgrace, his face shall still shine for this maiden."

—— 13 ——

One day the bishop's wife went to her sister to inquire after Snæfríður's health and to admire her embroidery, which was consistently masterful. The madam's cheeks were slightly flushed, and her eyes flickered with a peculiar gleam. She asked her sister, amongst other things, whether she was getting enough sleep at night, and whether her own daughter Guðrún, who shared a bedroom with her aunt, did not keep her awake with all her typically girlish noise and bustle. If this were the case, she said, she could find the girl another place to sleep. Snæfríður automatically became her sister's adversary whenever the madam showed up in a gracious mood. She said she needed nothing, and as far as the girl's residing with her, it delighted her to no end.

"And she goes to sleep at a decent hour?" asked the bishop's wife.

"She's generally asleep before me," said Snæfríður.

"But, my darling Snæfríður, I've always thought you go to bed so early."

"I always get a bit drowsy in the evening," said Snæfríður.*

"One of the girls in the weaving room happened to mention that she has noticed you downstairs sometimes at night," said the bishop's wife.

"Housemaids should sleep more at night," said Snæfríður. "And speak less during the day."

The bishop's wife hesitated slightly, then said: "Since we are on the subject of the proper time to retire, it is probably best if I tell you, while it is still fresh in my mind, the latest news: the bishop has started to receive letters written somewhere in this district, containing complaints about the nighttime activities of folk here in Skálholt and threatening inquiries and lawsuits."

Snæfríður acted, as expected, as if she were curious to hear more about these letters and their origins, and her sister informed her that a letter concerning the matter had been addressed to the king's proxy, Arnæus, naming him as one of the parties being accused of engaging in certain late-night habits; the other party was the madam's sister, Snæfríður herself. The bishop's wife said that it had crossed her mind that her sister might be more knowledgeable about the reasons behind such a letter than she herself. Snæfríður said that she had never heard mention of this before.

The bishop's wife then explained that Arnæus had very recently met with the bishop and shown him a letter sent to him by Magnús from Bræðratunga. The letter was written in a threatening tone in what nearly amounted to an open attack on Arnæus, accusing the royal commissary of pursuing, in Skálholt, a forbidden relationship with the letter-writer's wife—word of this relationship was already being circulated amongst the general public. Magnús claimed to have received trustworthy report that his wife had gone frequently to Arnæus's rooms when he was there alone, sometimes after noontime, when cunning men would be least suspicious, or else late in the evening when they felt sure that the others had gone to bed; she would then remain alone with him for an hour or so behind locked doors. In the letter Magnús testified that a long time ago his wife, then a nubile girl, had been discovered in some sort of liaison with the king's proxy, then Assessor in Consistorio, and that now the old thread must have been taken up anew, since the woman's obstinacy toward her husband had increased in the spring no sooner than she heard news of Arnæus's arrival in Iceland. In addition, Magnús from Bræðratunga claimed to be oppressed by the hateful tyranny of the authorities related to him by marriage; these authorities had, during the previous autumn, seduced his wife away from him, her lawful husband, and he asked God to strengthen him against the vexations of high-ranking men and to thwart their haughty behavior toward a poor man bereft of family and friends.

When the story reached this point Snæfríður could no longer contain herself and she laughed out loud. The bishop's wife stared at her in amazement.

"You laugh, sister?" she asked.

"What else can I do?" said Snæfríður.

"The Great Decree* is still in effect in this country," said the bishop's wife.

"I expect we'll all be put on the rack," said Snæfríður.

"All Magnús has to do is bring a charge of adultery against the see's caretakers and all the knaves and wenches and that whole ragtag lot of beggars will have more than enough to keep them entertained. We will all have to bear the consequences."

Snæfríður stopped laughing and looked at her sister. The woman was no longer in a gracious mood. When Snæfríður said nothing, the bishop's wife asked:

"What am I, your sister, matron in Skálholt, to believe?"

"Believe whatever you think is most true, dear woman," said Snæfríður.

"This news crashed over me like thunder," said the bishop's wife.

"If I really wanted to hide something from you, sister, do you think you would become better informed by asking me about it?" said Snæfríður. "You ought to understand your own kin better than that; especially one of your own gender."

"I am the housewife here in Skálholt," said the bishop's wife. "And I am your elder sister. I have before God and men both the right and the responsibility to know whether or not this is a false accusation."

"It was my understanding that the members of our family were great enough aristocrats that such a matter would be of little concern to them," said Snæfríður.

"What is it that you think I desire other than your honor and mine and all of ours, to know whether the accusation is true or false?" said the bishop's wife.

"It would certainly be a novelty if people here in Skálholt started making a fuss about something Magnús Sigurðsson has said," said Snæfríður.

"No one knows what steps a desperate man might take: we can understand drinkers when they are drunk, but not when they are sober," said the bishop's wife. "And how am I to defend my household if I do not know where I stand once the trials and testimonies have begun?"

"It may not matter one bit," said Snæfríður, "whether I swear yea or nay, now or later. And you might as well let it sink in, sister Jórunn: a woman will swear against her own better conscience everywhere and to anyone, once she decides to conceal a matter that is more precious to her than the truth."

"God have mercy on me, I am horrified to hear you say these things. I am the wife of a spiritual man."

"Ragnheiður the bishop's daughter swore an oath at the altar in the sight of God."*

"I could tell you all about myself, sister, under oath, without omitting a single detail, be it great or small," said the bishop's wife. "But whoever answers in absurd riddles awakens suspicion of an unclean conscience. Such a thing must never occur between sisters—each should instead act as confidante and refuge to the other if misfortune should befall them."

"Once there was an old woman who died of regret," said Snæfríður. "She'd forgotten to feed the calf. I'm certain that she had no sister."

"This is mockery, Snæfríður," said the bishop's wife.

"I regret only one of my deeds," said Snæfríður. "A deed so disgraceful that I can't even reveal it to my own beloved sister except in summary: I saved a man's life."

"You are lost within your sorcerer's storms, Snæfríður," said the bishop's wife. "But now I want to ask you to tell me a story, if not for your own sake and mine, then for the sake of our good mother and our father who upholds the honor of his country: is there any pretext in this affair for those who wish us ill?"

"One night in the autumn," said Snæfríður, "I came hither to you, sister. I told you that I was saving my own life. All the same, I wasn't in any more danger that night than I had been every other night for fifteen years. Magnús may be dextrous, but he doesn't know how to kill, at least me anyway, when he's drunk. I have no doubt that when he sobered up he must have found it strange that I'd decided to go to Skálholt that autumn, since I never went any other autumn, and he may have been right: I don't know where I am nor where I stand, and I can't make these things clear to myself though I try as hard as I can to do so. There is no artlessness in me. It may just as well have happened, though I can't recall it clearly, that I stayed for some small amount of time in the few instances that I had urgent business with the royal commissary. You yourself know what a master he is at engaging in pleasant conversation even with those who are not particularly clever themselves, men as well as women. And there is nothing more likely than that his secretary was in the vicinity while we were conversing, though I don't recall it clearly."

"Hardly," said the bishop's wife. A somewhat coarse pucker had appeared around her lips. "Don't you realize that his is the greatest family of philanderers in the country?"

Snæfríður's face turned blood-red and its lines slackened for a moment. She reached for her embroidery and in a voice slightly lower than before said:

"Spare me from vulgaria, madam."*

"I do not speak Latin, dear Snæfríður," said the bishop's wife.

They both sat in silence for a long moment. Snæfríður did not look up but instead attended calmly to her needlework. Finally her sister walked over to her and kissed her on the forehead. Her gracious demeanor had returned.

"There is only one thing that I must know," she said, "if my husband is to be held liable for the conduct of those who are within his keeping . . ."—when she reached this point she leaned toward her sister and whispered: "Does anyone know?"

Snæfríður stared coldly and aloofly at her sister, and answered emptily: "I swear it was nothing."

A little later their conversation ended.

One evening shortly afterward, Snæfríður went to visit the commissary and brought up, amongst other things, the matter of the letter that he was rumored to have received from Magnús Sigurðsson. He replied that as an officer of the crown he had felt it his duty to bring the letter to the bishop's attention; otherwise he considered the document to be inconsequential, since nothing could be proven to have happened.

She asked: "Then did nothing happen?"

"Nothing has happened unless it is possible to prove that it has," he said.

"We've sat here alone some evenings," she said.

"The ancient Icelanders were not idiots," he said. "They introduced Christianity, of course; but they did not prohibit men from engaging in heathen practices—as long as they did it in private. In Persia lying was not prohibited—every man was free to do so if he wanted, as long as he did it in such a way that no one could refute him for it. But whoever lied in such a way that it evoked suspicion was ridiculed, and if he lied a second time in the same way, he was labeled a scoundrel; if it was proven that he had lied a third time his tongue was cut out. The laws in Egypt were much the same: it was considered not only permissible, but also praiseworthy, to steal, but if a man was caught in the act of stealing, both his hands were cut off at the wrists."

"Shall our little acquaintance then be equated throughout eternity with a crime?" she asked.

The courtier's lively, cheerful mannerisms disappeared abruptly, and he answered darkly:

"When has human fortune ever been regarded as something better than a crime, or been enjoyed in any other way than in secret, directly contrary to the laws of God and man?"

She stared at him for several moments. Finally she walked over to him and said:

"My friend, you're tired."

It was silent throughout the house for quite some time before she left him. In the foyer of the Grand Salon a little lamp was left burning at night in case anyone should need to go out, as was the case now. Another door opposite the building's main doorway opened from the foyer onto the hallway that led to the pantry and the kitchen and then to the householders' bedroom; a set of stairs led from the foyer to a loft above. Now it so happens, as Snæfríður leaves the Grand Salon, and Arnæus, who has accompanied her from his rooms, stands at her back upon the threshold and bids her good night, that she catches a glimpse of a face, illumined by the glimmer of lamplight, flickering and hovering in the doorway to the hall. The man saw them but did not move; he stood there in the doorway, ashen and startled, staring at them with black eyes, his features etched with shadows.

She looked at the man in the doorway for a second, then glanced at the assessor, who only whispered: "Go carefully." She acted as if nothing out of the ordinary was happening and walked the few steps from the threshold of the Grand Salon to the stairway, then climbed silently up to her room. Arnas pulled the doors shut and returned to his rooms. The man in the hall doorway also drew his door quietly into place.

And all was quiet in the house.

— 14 —

The schoolboys quit their roughhousing and watched in dead silence as she walked, small-footed and slender within her wide cloak, through their quarters to the archpriest's office.

Hoarfrost glazed his windowpanes. He sat at his desk hunched over some books and morosely called out "Deo gratias"* when the knock came upon his door, but he did not look up when the door opened; he just kept reading, completely absorbed. She stepped across the threshold and stared at the abominable wooden crucifix hanging over his desk, then greeted him in a tone both pious and carefree: "May God grant you—good day."

Upon hearing this voice he looked up in bewilderment bordering on terror. When the light was particularly fickle, like now, his black eyes glowed like burning embers. He stood up, bowed to her and plumped the cushions in his armchair for her, then sat down midway between her and the crucifix, one cheek facing each of them.

"This is the first time a de-hm-destitute man is granted such an honor," he began, but he was so unprepared for this visitation, and found himself therefore at such a loss for the twisted, scholarly word-clinches so suited to the standards of courtesy necessary for such a meeting, that all he could do was cough.

"No, you can't call yourself destitute, my dear Reverend Sigurður," she said. "You who own all those acres of land. And it's a shame that you should have no stove here to keep you warm; it's a wonder that you haven't caught a cold by now. Besides, this isn't the first time: I came to you once before, when your blessed wife was still with us, and she gave me honey in a box—oh, I see that you've forgotten—but you've brought this horrid image into your home—" she gave a short-winded sigh as she looked toward the rood: "Do you really believe that the blessed Redeemer was so miserable?"

> "In cruce latebat sola deitas
> at hic latet simul et humanitas"*

—mumbled the archpriest.

"Now that was a poem!" she said. "I've completely forgotten what little I knew of grammatica. But I know that 'deitas' is divinity and 'humanitas' humanity, and that these two can be called enemies— am I right? But do you think that a man ought to pray the *Ave Maria* constantly in atonement, Reverend Sigurður, or should he behave like our dear master Luther, who had a pious wife?"

"I would be better able to answer if I knew your reasons for asking," said the archpriest. "Just now you reminded me of my dear wife. But when I gaze upon these wounds, I am filled with gratitude to God for the mercy He exhibited to me when He took my mortal comfort away from me."

"Don't take pains to frighten me, my dear Reverend Sigurður," she said, and she looked from Christ toward the man. "You still own a fat horse, however; and land. Call me mademoiselle now, as you did before, and be my companion; and my suitor."

He drew his cassock more closely about his frame and puckered his lips more tightly.

"You must be cold, my dear Reverend Sigurður. The frost clings to your windowpanes."

"Hm," he said.

"Do try to understand me," she said. "I know you think that I'm never going to get around to the matter at hand. But you must realize that it's difficult to discuss one's own paltriness with a man who has his eternal victory in the Lord."

"I once thought that I would be chosen to extend you my hand, Snæfríður," he said. "But God has His ways."

She asked suddenly: "Why were you standing in the hall doorway at the bishop's house two nights ago? And why didn't you wish me good evening?"

"It was late," he said. "It was very late."

"It wasn't too late for me," she said. "And even if you were tired, you were still up and about. I thought you could have at least said good evening."

"I was speaking with a sick woman in one of the bedrooms and it grew late," he said. "I was going to go out through the front door, but it was locked. So I turned back."

"I told my sister about it first thing yesterday morning. 'What do you think Reverend Sigurður thinks of you?' she asked me. 'Well,' I said, 'I expect he believes all those ugly fables. I must speak to him myself.'"

He said, "What men think does not matter. What God knows is the only thing that matters."

"Anyway, I'm not afraid of what God knows," said Snæfríður. "But I do care what men think, most of all what you think, dear Reverend Sigurður, you who are my confessor and my friend. I would take it sorely if such an excellent man as Arnæus were to fall into disrepute because of me, a wretched beggar-girl dependent on parish-alms. It was for this reason that I went to his room the night before last and said to him: 'Árni, wouldn't it be better if I left Skálholt and went home to my husband? I can't bear to know that you, an innocent man, might have to endure calumny on my account.'"

"If you are going to tell me something, then I ask that you tell me from your own heart, as you did so long ago when you were a girl. Do not speak in words that you have been given by others, especially by that man whom you named just now—he has a serpent's forked tongue."

"You who love Christ," she said, "how can you hate a man?"

"Christians hate the words and deeds of a man who has pledged himself to Satan. The man himself they pity."

"If I didn't know that you are one of the saints, my dear Reverend Sigurður, I might sometimes believe that you were jealous, and then what could I do but congratulate myself and end up a conceited spinster?"

"In some ways I am indebted to you, Snæfríður, for the fact that the soul's prayers for stigmata and the cross should have become the words that I hold closest to my heart, 'Fac me plagis vulnerari, fac me cruce inebriari.'"*

"Yet it wasn't any longer ago than last summer that you came to a married woman one day when her husband was away and as much as proposed to her," she said. "At least she couldn't understand the meaning of your words in any other way after she'd plucked the theology and Chancery jargon out of them."

"I deny, madame, that my visit to you last summer had any sinful purpose," he said. "If my thoughts toward you were ever in any way blended with sinful yearnings of nature, then it was long, long ago. The soul's love for other souls rules my thoughts for you now. I also pray that the evil mirages that confound you might pass away. Dear Snæfríður, is it not clear to you how disastrous your words were, when you said just now that you do not fear the eye of God watching over you? Or have you never tried to comprehend just how much the Lord is the lover of your soul? Do you know that His love for your soul is so overwhelmingly extensive that the entire world is as a grain of dust next to it? And have you ever considered that the man who does not love his own soul hates God? 'My precious soul, my beloved soul,' says our good psalmist when he addresses his soul, mindful of the fact that the soul is the part of the individual that God was born in a manger and crucified on the cross to redeem."

"Reverend Sigurður," she said, "will you just once push aside your great works of theology; will you place your hand on the heart and look in the face of a living individual for one moment, instead of gaping at the pierced wooden feet of the Redeemer, and answer me candidly one question: who has suffered more for the other in this world, God for men, or men for God?"

"Only someone who is inclined toward terrible sins would ask such a thing. I pray that this poison cup containing eternal death might be taken from you."

"I think that you're completely ignorant as far as my affairs are concerned," she said. "You lend your support to the servant-girls' drivel and rumor about me more by your ill will than by credible reasoning."

"Those are heavy words," said the priest.

"All the same, I don't threaten you with eternal death, which I'm told means Hell in your language," she answered, and she laughed.

His face quivered.

"A woman who comes to a man during the night," he began, but then stopped. He shot her a glance quick as a flame and said, "I so much as caught you in the act. It has gone beyond servant-girls' drivel."

"I knew you would think that," she said. "I've come to tell you that you're mistaken. And I would like to warn you about slandering him. His reputation will live on after they have stopped laughing at both you and me. He was eager to give his life and his happiness to increase the honor of his poor country. Nothing lies farther away from such a man than an ignoble, wayward female who comes to him to beg his help."

"A woman who comes to a man during the night has only one thing in mind," said the archpriest.

"A man who is never able to tear his mind away from his miserable flesh, fastening an icon of it to his wall, like an idol, with needles through its arms and legs, or who constantly witnesses to this carnal desire with citations from holy books, will never understand the man who has turned in body and soul to the service of the defenseless and the vindication of his people."

"It is the Enemy's habit to assume many different disguises and seduce women under one pretext or another; the first time was when he assumed the likeness of a serpent and deceived a woman by painting a flattering picture of an apple. He himself did not hand her the apple, but rather confounded her with words so that she took it herself, in violation of God's commandment. It is not in his nature to commit the act of defilement, for if it were so, mankind would get off free, and therefore he is called the Tempter, for he allures man's will into consent with his own. In the book *De Operatione Daemonum*,* which you see lying open before you here, his operations are witnessed in hundreds of exempla. For instance, a certain damsel, trapped in despair after Satan has inflamed her with fleshly desire and then slipped out between her fingers, asks: 'Quid ergo exigis carnale conjugium, quod naturae tuae dinoscitur esse contrarium?'— 'How can you allure me into carnal relations, being of no flesh yourself?' And he answers: 'Tu tantum mihi consensisti, nihil aliud a te nisi copulae consensum requiro'—'You consented to intercourse and your consent was all that I required.'"

By the time the archpriest finished conveying this lesson carefully in both tongues his guest's patience had shortened noticeably. She looked at the man for a while with the kind of wordless expression of shock that borders on complete vacuity. Finally she stood up, smiled aloofly, curtsied, and turned to go, saying:

"I sincerely thank my devoted friend and confessor for his charming obscenities."

The week after Easter a synod was convened in Skálholt, attended not only by clergy but also by cloister wardens, authorized agents, and others who managed church estates throughout the lowlands. Their discussions focused on rents and rental taxes, the ministration of lepers and the administration of hospitals, migrancy in the countryside, lawsuits against church administrators who exhausted their estates' chattel, the interment of vagrant folk who had given up the ghost on mountain tracks, sometimes in large groups, and of course they did not fail to haggle over their yearly petition to the king concerning the shortage of sacramental wine and lack of cord, which, as far as the latter was concerned, made it nearly as difficult for men to drag fish from the church's fishing-grounds as the former did to prevent men from successfully sailing the sea of mercy. These and many of the other issues normally discussed by clerics at their synods occupied their attention for three days. At the close of the synod the bishop ascended his throne before his priests and once again admonished them concerning the chief articles of the true faith, wording his admonishments gently and pleasantly so as to alarm no one. The congregation was ready to depart. Finally a hymn was sung for the journey home: "Let your spirit nourish us."

During the final verse of the hymn, however, the archpriest, Reverend Sigurður Sveinsson, rises from his seat, walks over and stands stock-still, gravely, in the choir doorway, waiting for the song to come to an end. He removes a letter from his cassock, unfolds it carefully, and holds it up with trembling hands. Then he lets his voice ring out throughout the cold church as the coarse chanting dwindles, announcing that it is not for him to hinder the petition of one of his parishioners, a respectful and beloved gentleman, who had written to this synod and entrusted the letter to his furtherance; the archpriest considered himself and the others even more duty-bound to comply with the petition since he knew full well that the petitioner had tried by all means possible to find a more convenient solution to his case.

He now began his monological delivery of the petition's massive quantity of text in a tone rich in edificatory spirit, with astonishing word-windings and entangled sentence constructions, so that his audience was for a very long time prohibited from determining where the text was headed. After a weighty lecture in praise of moral conduct and a description of the correct estimation of the proprietal worth of this exalted condition, which should furthermost be upheld by the servants of Christ as an exemplary model for the general public, reference was made to the dreadful tragedies that by now had become so common in this country, particularly amongst high personages, male as well as female, but which were concealed or passed over in chilling silence by the clergy, though they were so greatly ruinous to the commoners' moral life, that is, mores,* as one reads in the *Book of Seven Words*—it went on endlessly like this.

At first it was not surprising when one man or other opened his eyes wider, let his jaw drop, or thrust his chin forward, or when the old priests who were hard of hearing made trumpets round their ears with the palms of their hands. But as his endless prattle stretched on even longer, unwavering in its overwhelming sheen, the men's expressions became as dull as those of strung-up ling heads. Yet after a while the petitioner finally gained a slightly more stable foothold, as he began to reveal the terrible tale of woe so firmly affixed to his heart, how his wedded wife Snæfríður Björnsdóttir had during the previous autumn let herself be duped into leaving her own home. Then he repeated down to the last detail the story that he had told many times before whenever he had the opportunity, concerning his wife's departure, the rumors about her previous acquaintance with Arnas Arnæus and the recent report of the renewal of their secret, forbidden relations in Skálholt, his attempts to get highly placed members within the bishopric to act as go-betweens between him and her to persuade her to return home, and furthermore, how these said attempts had been completely rebuffed. Then the petitioner described how, when he finally tried to publicize his troubles in Skál-holt, the dogs were sicked on him and he was threatened with bodily injury. He knew full well of course that these threats did not come directly from the bishopric's landlords, but he did have a substanti-ated suspicion that they were descended from those who at the pres-ent time considered themselves to be even greater landlords than the true representatives of the bishopric. Now it was the petitioner's request, his public and tearful lament, that this worshipful council of priests take steps to put a stop to his wife's aforementioned reprehen-sible riot in Skálholt and grant him, the husband, assistance in drag-ging her up out of the ditch into which she had in the sight of God and Christianity fallen. The letter wound to a close with repeated ref-erences to the *Book of Seven Words* and intricate theological saluta-tions in which all the persons of the Trinity were invoked in prayer for the strengthening of morality throughout the country, followed immediately by the words "Amen, amen, Magnús Sigurðsson."

It was completely impossible to determine by the countenances of the men sitting there in church what they thought of this petition; their weatherbeaten faces evoked images of mountainous breccia for-mations chiseled with human features: some with oblong chins, overly large noses, or horrendous shocks of hair, but all immutable from any point of view, whether in sparkling sunlight or pelting storm and rain.

The archpriest stuck the letter back into a pocket in his cassock and walked out through the choir doorway. Mass had ended; the men stood up; one young chaplain stole forward to look into his superior's face, but his inquisitive glance was ignored. The men started chatting easily as they walked down the doorsteps and out of the church.

Someone brought this news to Arnæus, and he immediately sent his secretary to the archpriest to make a copy of Magnús Sigurðsson's letter. This he read aloud to his servants, to their great amusement. Even so, that same day he sent word to the bailiff Vigfús in Hjálmholt, requesting that the author of the letter be subpoenaed. He ordered his men to prepare their baggage for travel tomorrow, and to have the horses shod.

The sun's course had lengthened considerably, but freezing winds blew as they often do during the closing weeks of winter.

On a cold, cloudless morning a group of horses stands out upon the flagstones; several are fitted with riding gear, others with packsaddles. Trunk after trunk of the winter-sojourner's belongings was brought out and lifted to the pegs of the packsaddles. The entourage was to travel south, to the royal estate at Bessastaðir.

Arnæus himself, clad in great Russian furs and topboots, was last to exit the house. He kissed the bishop and his wife before their door, mounted a white mare, called to his secretary to follow him closely, and rode out of the yard. The two rooms he had occupied behind the Grand Salon were empty. The Grand Salon was empty. A maidservant came in and cleared the tables. The smell of roasted meat lingered in the house. Red wine remained in his cup—he had not drunk it dry.

— 15 —

His Majesty's royal commissarius and specially appointed judge over diverse lawsuits, Arnas Arnæus, summons your wise and noble honor, Magistrate Eydalín, to Þingvellir by Öxará on the coming 12 June to defend before his court and his fellow jurors a number of your past and recent sentences and decisions, videlicet,* various death sentences pronounced in cases of rapine, wanton acts of adultery, possession and handling of characteres,* etcetera, protracted incarcerations at Bremerholm, flogging, branding, and dismemberment of poverty-stricken men on poorly substantiated grounds, handed down particularly for crimes against the Handelen, such as smuggling, trade with Dutchmen, and the conduct of business transactions outside one's own trade district during the period when the delineations were valid, as well as for recalcitrance on the part of the lodgers in satisfying the demands imposed upon them by the landlords in general, and by the governor in particular. In generali:* you have, in a multitude of your official acts, overburdened the indigent, making it practically impossible during your term as magistrate for the commoners to maintain their rights against the affluent, and you have denied these rights entirely in cases connected in any way with the church, the merchants, or the crown. Some of your rulings appear not to have been made with complete disregard for justice, but rather, in all respects sine allegationibus juris vel rationum.* It is now the will of our country's patron and Most Gracious Royal Highness, so clearly communicated in my commission, that such rulings be subject to judicial inquest, and I am ordered by His Highness to accomplish the following: to bring to trial those authorities who have flaunted the law and destabilized the legal system; to annul the rulings that appear to have been handed down more to ensure that the name of the judge will be pronounced complacently by the powerful rather than to fully satisfy and comply with mortal justice and the laws of the land as they were sanctioned by our forefathers; and finally to penalize the authorities who are found guilty.

Following this, precedents were attested and specific charges enumerated.

Although around the country it was considered no insignificant bit of news when Arnæus implemented legal proceedings against the merchants during the previous spring, people were completely taken aback when they received report of the criminal trials that the royal commissarius was convening this spring against several of the highest authorities in the land, crowned by the arraignment of no less an authority than the magistrate himself.

The bishop's wife Jórunn goes to her sister one day in the spring and without a word hands her two documents, a copy of Arnæus's indictment of their father, and a letter from their mother.

Snæfríður read the indictment carefully, item by item. Amongst other things, their father was ordered to answer to a certain arrangement or contract he had made in court at the Alþingi with Jón Hreggviðsson from Rein, who had been sentenced to death for murder. The particulars of this arrangement specified that this Jón would be allowed to live his life a free man, uncharged and unindicted, in the district neighboring his judge the magistrate's own, provided that he did not publicize the Supreme Court appeal issued in connection with his prior sentence, as contained in the royal warrant that he had brought home with him from Copenhagen.

Snæfríður glanced next over their mother's letter, which was addressed to Jórunn.

After the madam in Eydalur had with several prefatory remarks suitably praised the Lord for the health of her life and soul, which was as good as could be expected in spite of the advance of old age, she turned immediately to the storm clouds now gathering over the peaceable household of husband and wife in the twilight of their lives. She mentioned the rewards in store for her bridegroom the magistrate Eydalín's long and altruistic service to his native country and Royal Majesty, now that an individual who was to remain nameless was making an attempt to drag him before some sort of drunkard's tribunal and to use the testimony of scoundrels to either dispossess him of his honor and reputation or even send him, a bedridden old man, to labor in chains for the king. And although the lawsuit had been cruelly implemented, the old woman had no misgivings concerning its outcome. She said that those who had lived upright lives would not be easily oppressed or forced to cower though it might suit the whim of knights-errant, native or foreign, bearing peculiar letters from Copenhagen; such visitations were not without precedent, but this country's providence had always proven to be too powerful for vagrant knaves, just as it would once again. The country's guardian spirits had never failed and would not fail now to defend the country's elders; instead they would strengthen and invigorate them in their adversity, promote their prosperity, and support them in their hour of need in quelling their enemies' fury.

The aged noblewoman wrote that she had feared only one thing more, that those who were closest to her and her husband by ties of blood and affection might superfluously awaken false report amongst the general public on account of their way of life; she could not deny that news of such report had been borne to her ears concerning her own poor and harassed daughter Snæfríður, who had recently been accused of engaging in disgraceful intimacies with a despised individual. Certainly there was nothing more preposterous than for the magistrate's couple to take any stock of the drunken gurglings of Magnús Sigurðsson, whether written or spoken, but the causes of these accusations were not at issue here: no matter what, it was a blight to the honor of a noblewoman for her private life to become fodder for the public imagination. She said that her daughter had saddled crime to misfortune by pursuing further, for whatever reason, righteous or unrighteous, her association with her father's reviler, the man who was as much a curse to his motherland as the endless death-dealing winters and the fire-spewing mountains. She said that she grieved for her long-suffering offspring and that she would never be able to enjoy peace until the reasons for this lawsuit were truthfully confirmed. She bade Jórunn reply candidly and offered to send Snæfríður horses and attendants if she wished to ride west to Breiðafjörður, then, bidding farewell for the time being, wished her two girls the same, though sorrow might rage or the world's false fortunes smile, and prayed their forgiveness for this tearstained, hastily written missive, their faithful and simple mother.

Snæfríður stared out the window for some time. The countryside was silent but for the sound of thawing streams. "Now then," said her sister, the bishop's wife.

The younger sister's mind cleared, and she glanced at their mother's letter lying open on the table and with a flick of her finger sent it tumbling into the lap of her elder sister.

"This is a letter from our mother," said the bishop's wife.

"We poets recognize letters written by our own kin," said Snæfríður, and she smiled.

"And you have not a single word of compassion for our father, either?" asked the bishop's wife.

"It seems that our father has committed the one act that will cost him dearly in his old age," said Snæfríður.

"Am I also to listen to you speak poorly of him, sister?"

"Very poorly," said Snæfríður. "He has fathered daughters."

The journeyman who had delivered the letter was planning to travel west again early the next morning.

"What am I to write?" asked the bishop's wife.

"I send my greetings," said Snæfríður.

"Is that all?"

"Tell our mother that I am the matron in Bræðratunga and will not ride west. On the other hand, if my father wishes it, I will be at his side at Þingvellir by Öxará on the twelfth of June."

That same day she dismantled her loom, rolled up her tapestries, and packed away the belongings she had brought with her in the autumn, taking about the same amount of time it took for Jórunn the bishop's wife to write her letter.

"Well, sister," said Snæfríður. "The nights of respite draw to a close. I thank you for the winter: you're a hospitable woman. Kiss the bishop for me and tell him that he shouldn't be held liable on my account. Finally, I know you'll loan me horses and attendants for this short stretch over the Tunga River—home."

— 16 —

It had been a long time since the buildings at Bræðratunga had been in such good condition. Magnús worked throughout the entire winter repairing the timberwork on the farm, sometimes with the help of other carpenters, and as soon as the ground thawed in the spring he employed stonemasons to repair the walls. Now only the doors needed mending. One day he and the others caught sight of someone riding up from Sporður, where the ferry to Skálholt was anchored, and Magnús, who was keen-eyed, recognized immediately who it was. He climbed down from the wall where he'd been busy troweling, went into the farmhouse, washed himself as quickly as he could, put on a clean shirt and new trousers, and combed his hair. Just as he stepped outside his wife rode into the yard.

"Welcome home from your trip, Snæfríður my dear," he said, and he helped her dismount, kissed her, and led her by the hand into the farmhouse.

Her loft was much the same as it had been when she left, except that the roof had been repaired and planks added where water had leaked in during the previous autumn. Another window had been added, and the fragrance of planed wood filled the room. The floor had been scrubbed clean. She lifted the coverlet to find creased snow-white linen bedsheets. The curtains had been aired and dusted so that the images upon them shone, and someone had used a small paintbrush to touch up the paintings on the dowry-chest, to brighten the roses. Snæfríður kissed Guðríður, her nurse.

"I've not yet received any word from the madam my mistress that I'm to stop scrubbing this cubbyhole," she said respectfully.

The housewife ordered that her luggage be brought in, then she opened the chest and bureau and placed her silver and other jewelry, her embroidery, and her clothing within. That same day she set up her loom again, to make altar-cloths for the cathedral in a heartfelt show of gratitude from a woman who had left home to dwell in Skálholt, but who had now come home.

No man was as skilled at repentance or better understood other's regret as Magnús Sigurðsson from Bræðratunga. He never mentioned a single thing that had occurred. Neither asked forgiveness of the other for anything. It was as if nothing had happened. He lay silently in her loft for hours at a time, staring at her with a compliant, timorous, obliterated look. He was like a child that's been spanked after having fallen into a puddle—after exhausting itself with tears it becomes placid once again, its tranquillity deep and glorious.

A few days after her homecoming she sent a man to Seigneur Vigfús Þórarinsson in Hjálmholt, to deliver to the bailiff the message that she had business to discuss with him. It wasn't long before this tried and true friend of noblewomen appeared at her door, his face drawn, his upper lip long, and his jowls covered with patches of gray stubble; he had coarse black eyebrows and limpid, watery gray eyes. He kissed the housewife carefully, and she offered him a seat and asked him the current news.

He said: "I brought the foal along again."

She asked, "What foal?"

He said that although he was certainly unskilled when it came to choosing gifts for noblewomen, her foremothers had never thought it a discredit to receive a saddle horse from a good friend.

She recalled the horse he had left tied to the horseblock in the yard the last time he visited, and thanked him for the gift, but said it was her understanding that the horse had been killed and cut up to provide alms to the beggars last spring, when things had been so difficult.

He said that the horse came from stock out west in Breiðafjörður, and after it had bolted from the Bræðratunga pastures last year it had been brought back to him. Since few people had known about the gift, he had simply kept it with his own saddle horses over the winter; might she have need of it this spring?

She said that a poor woman could take a great deal of encouragement from enjoying the protection of such a cavalier, but that the time had come to discuss her business rather than horses.

First she wanted to mention the kindnesses that his son-in-law Jón from Vatn had bestowed upon her husband Magnús last year, when he had not only bought Bræðratunga from him, but had also paid in cash, at a time when others amused themselves by trying to swipe all of her husband's estates from him by plying him with brennivín, or by engaging him in wagers, dice games, or other ruses so easily used to chicane helpless men. There was no need for her to narrate the rest of the story to the bailiff: he himself knew best how he and her father had haggled over the purchase of the estate later at the Alþingi. The one thing she knew was that she had inherited the estate from her father, as a legal bestowment—she had the title deed in hand. Later in the autumn certain events occurred that by now had become public knowledge: she had left her husband, with the unexpressed understanding that she would not return home until she could be certain that Magnús had given up the habits that had made their cohabitation so strenuous. Now, after residing at Skálholt for half a year, she had received trustworthy report that during that whole time Magnús had never once picked up his old crutch, so she had come home, determined to pick up where she had left off, hoping that her husband would live fully resuscitated for the rest of his days. It was therefore her request that the bailiff invalidate the previous year's contracts, which stated that the estate, patrimony, and allodium of Magnús Sigurðsson was to be entirely her own possession. She asked instead that the estate and control of its revenues be transferred in full to her husband, following the procedure commonly used by married couples for property that was not specifically covered in written contracts.

Seigneur Vigfús Þórarinsson's eyelids drooped shut as he sat murmuring and rocking in his seat, stroking his chin with a bony hand.

"I dare say, good madam," he said finally, "that although Magistrate Eydalín and I have not always been able to come to felicitous terms at assemblies, I count myself amongst the authorities who look with undivided reverence toward our dear friend and chief, who took over the magistrate's office when he was a bankrupt bailiff in an inferior district twenty years ago and is now counted amongst the wealthiest of men, having purchased more estates, under more favorable terms, from His Majesty than any other Icelander not consecrated bishop. And since Her Virtue has now deigned to invite me into her presence, it is my wish that I might offer her one piece of good advice: that she discuss this matter with her illustrious and well-learned father before she invalidates the deeds that were made in connection with this estate and signed by his own hand last summer."

She said that she had no desire to haggle with her father over this matter, since she hadn't been a child for quite some time. And even though he had intervened in the case the previous summer it was doubtless primarily due to the fact that he reproached himself for having withheld his daughter's dowry for fifteen years.

The bailiff asked whether she thought it urgent that this case be resolved before men met at Þingvellir in the spring.

She said that she did indeed.

Then Vigfús Þórarinsson started in on the same old story: the country was in danger of being swamped by torrential streams, the pox was on the rise in Denmark, and the authority of highborn men was being rebuffed in that country; the burghers and upstarts had broken through the shield-wall raised around the monarchy, thus forcing the king to answer to them; after the head the limbs would be dancing here in Iceland. The air was tinged with malignancy, as the old saying goes,* and it had come to such a pass that no one knew how things could be rectified. One of this century's novelties was that the authorities could now be indicted, and whoever struck out at an emissary of the crown would sacrifice his life and honor. He said that one particular case of this sort of aspersion against a king's man had been sent to his court and that a hasty ruling had been demanded. "But," he said, "since my friend the magistrate's daughter is possessed of such eminent virtue, it is certain that the prejudicial report contained in the letter that her husband had read aloud in the choir doorway in Skálholt can never be verified. And because of that, the householder in Bræðratunga is now being held liable for serious crimes against an exalted personage."

Snæfríður said: "Now you've cut right to the heart of the matter, my dear bailiff: I would like you to complete this deal and give Magnús total control of Bræðratunga before he is prosecuted for his slander, not just at the Alþingi, but also in your district court. If the penalty for my husband's words is to be complete forfeiture of his property, then I would prefer that he incur it as a man of means rather than as a pauper."

He said that it was her choice, but that he would take her saddle horse home for the time being and let it continue to convalesce throughout the spring. Afterward Magnús Sigurðsson was summoned and in the presence of witnesses was once again made the full and lawful owner of Bræðratunga. The bailiff kissed Snæfríður farewell and departed.

It was spring in Iceland, the time between hay and grass when the livestock falls most quickly. The beggars had begun their tottering migrations throughout the countryside to the east. The first two had already been found dead in Landeyjasandur, a man and woman who had lost their way in a fog. Ravens led the way to their remains.

The householder at Bræðratunga rose early each day and woke up his workers. He had stone slabs transported home to the farm, since he wanted to repave the footpath up to and in through the main doorway. He had already torn down most of the barn, leaving no other entrance to the house but the hole at the back of the kitchen where peat was carried in and dung and ashes thrown out. One day around midmorning, after the farmer had been working zealously since dawn, he was gripped by a sudden urge to see his horses and sent someone to round them up. They seemed to him to be in poor condition, and he pronounced them unfit for work and said that two were to be shod at home and allowed to graze in the homefield and brought milk to drink. The daleswoman brought the daughter of her mistress the madam this ominous news.

"Has anyone heard anything about a ship?" asked Snæfríður, and sure enough, there was a dubious story about a ship anchored in Keflavík.

"What would the blessed madam say if she were to hear that the horses were now to be given those few drops of milk I've been eking out to give to the workers to keep them alive," said the daleswoman.

"The master of the estate in Bræðratunga is a nobleman; it does not beseem him to own thin horses," said Snæfríður.

The horses were given the milk.

That evening the farmer complained, in his wife's hearing, that some unspecified band of vagrants, at least as far as he could determine, had stolen a copper rod that he kept in his smithy. He'd been planning to use the copper to make a handle for the new farmhouse door. Now, because of this, he had to go south to Ölfus to make a deal with an acquaintance of his who had some copper.

Snæfríður said: "This is the sixteenth year we've lived here, and we've managed to get on well enough without having had so much as an iron handle in the door, not to mention a copper one."

"How well I know that you've made it out," said he.

"And you in," said she.

On the next day he clipped his horses and brushed them. He was never satisfied with the way the flagstones were lying and was constantly ordering that they be torn up. He ordered his workers to crawl through the hole in the kitchen wall. The daleswoman said that it was only great southern aristocrats who had to crawl through the dung-gap in their houses. The squire said that there was no use complaining about things that didn't concern her, and that he didn't pity her or any of her kind for having to slip through holes in walls.

Late in the afternoon he took two short rides, and a snatch of verse was heard being hummed quickly out in the yard. The sky was red.

Next day he was gone. Heaps of earth blocked the main doorway, and a gap in the roof was left unthatched. The house had no front door. He had left his hammer and his ax lying in a pile of woodchips.

— 17 —

As evening came on a rainstorm approached from the south. It rained all night and throughout the next day. The main doorway became completely impassable; only wind and water had free passage through the house. Later that evening the storm subsided.

Several days passed and then a visitor arrived, riding a fat black horse. He inquired after the housewife. When she heard that the archpriest was outside she sent word that she was not entirely healthy and was therefore uninclined to receive guests, but she ordered that he be given whey. His response was that he had not come for a social visit, and would willingly speak to the housewife by her bedside if she was too weak to stand. She said in that case it would be best to drag the archpriest in through the hole in the wall at the back of the kitchen, then show him into the houseroom. She continued to embroider for some time. When she finally came down she was wearing a lace-trimmed mantle, beneath which could be seen a belt of golden bands.

The whey stood untouched where the housemaid had left it upon the table before the guest. When she came in he stood up and greeted her.

"I am delighted to see that my friend from youth is not too sickly to come down," said the archpriest.

She bade him welcome, but said she regretted that visitors could not be invited in through the front door; she would have had the entryway cleared out if she had expected the archpriest, but he had come without warning. Would he please take a seat?

He bent his head, coughed slightly, and let his eyes wander about the room, though his gaze never reached any higher than about knee-high off the floor. Finally they came to rest on the pitcher on the table before him. He said:

"Will my friend please have this whey removed."

She took the pitcher immediately and splashed its contents out through the door.

He remained seated, letting his eyes wander. She did not sit down.

"Hm—I had planned to start with a suitable preface to this business," he said. "But I can no longer find the words. When a man beholds you, a man forgets what he was going to say."

"Then it must not have been important," she said.

"It was," he said.

"Then you reduce the damage by forgetting the preface," she said. "I never understood prefaces. What do you want?"

"It is very difficult," he said, and he took a deep breath to gather his strength for this trial. "But I am here. Therefore I must speak."

"Cleverly spoken," she said. "Sum, ergo loquor."*

"It is useless to mock me though I might deserve it," he said. "You know that I stand defenseless before your ice-cold innuendo. I have come to you after keeping long vigil."

"People should sleep more at night," she said.

"The petition, hm," he said, "which I was persuaded to read in the choir doorway at the synod: for that I owe you my apologies. It was, however, not done out of the blue, but rather after long invocation of the Lord, who most definitely withholds His grace from you, but who preserves your beauty in order to honor a destitute land."

She fell silent and looked at him from such an extreme distance that she might have been a man looking down upon an overturned giant's ox.

It did not take him long, however, to right himself and continue, though he was careful to look in any direction other than where she was sitting so that he would not forget what he had been planning to say: he said that above all else he wanted to assure her that the words he had spoken to her in the winter, concerning the nature of the Tempter and women's dealings with him, according to Holy Scripture and the auctores, had not in truth been spoken in order to reproach her, but had sprung from sorrow, "or should I say, rather, from resentment," over the fact that she, Iceland's sun, should run the risk of putting her soul's health in jeopardy by taking delight in the presence of sin. Despite his grief and resentment it was his belief that as far as she was concerned nothing had occurred in Skálholt that could be viewed as disgraceful for an esteemed female personage or that divine grace would be unwilling to repair, especially if faith and repentance were to take its place. Then he turned back to the petition. "If," said he, "your confessor intervened in this case in a manner disagreeable to you, he did it only out of concern for your beloved soul. Though all hope of gaining your favor might have been spoiled because of it, he was with God's support eager to pay even this price, if it meant that it would work to drive the sinful presence away from the soul he esteemed above all other souls—which did indeed happen the day after the letter was read."

Afterward many things had been tangibly proven by the occurrence of certain events, just as he had tried to explain to her before concerning the nature of things, though she had always turned a deaf ear to his teachings. As a case in point he named the attacks now being made upon Iceland's honor, with summonses being served against the country's elders, our overseers, so beloved by God.

By the time he reached this point in his story his rhetorical skill had blossomed, and he delivered a sermon about what would happen in the country if the Christian authorities were to be forced from their seats, where they had been placed by God to discipline the masses, who invested themselves in nothing other than the satisfaction of their wicked lusts, searching for opportunities to perpetrate sedition and trample morality underfoot. He proved, with examples from the doctors and other sources, that only one man out of a thousand was worthy of redemption, and even so, that this would happen only through grace. He cited the example of the Greeks and Romans, under what impossible circumstances their republics arose, and said that one could draw analogies from this to what would happen to our miserable people if thieves, murderers, and beggars were to gain power, while the Christian authorities suffered attack, injury, and ruin, and were finally held captive in infamy and shame. "If the rabble succeeds in rising against its overlords, it is always due to the work of one man sent by Satan to confound the simpletons and betray the king. No one doubts the intelligence of Arnas Arnæus. But his mission is the same. He wants to wipe his wretched fatherland from the face of the inhabited world, and he shirks from any other remedy. First he sheared the land of any remnant of its golden age by duping our penniless scholars into giving up the literary gemstones that comprise our crown, offering payment for some and allurements for others, mostly for a mere pittance, as if they were old frocks or worn-out perukes; these he shipped off or had sent to him in Copenhagen. Next in line are our ancient laws and our fathers' ordering of our government, and the evil spirit has appeared here as well, this time with judicial authority the likes of which no one has ever seen in this country, carrying letters that no one dares to impugn, letters that supposedly give him the right to appoint himself litigator in whatever case he chooses and to adjudge one and all according to his whims. Consequently, the authorities shall be overthrown, the aristocrats' estates seized and they themselves hounded into ignominy, the courts' rulings annulled, lawbreakers and vandals exalted. And it is plain who will be first to be forced to bow down in the dust before the rabble's feet."

She said: "I would be terribly disappointed if my father were to feel any consternation over the fact that the king sends a man to make inquests into the proper fulfillment of his duties; he will remain standing upright though he might have faltered once. That is only human. Otherwise, he has conducted himself in his lifelong work in a manner beyond reproach."

"The court will deprive your father of his estates and his honor within a few weeks," said the archpriest, and his mouth quivered as he glanced sharply at her face. They said nothing for several minutes. His face continued to quiver.

"What do you want from me?" she asked.

"I am your suitor," he said—"the black sheep in the fold."

"I have come home to my husband Magnús," she said.

"District court has already passed sentence against Magnús Sigurðsson for his letter," said the archpriest. "He is an ignominious man. His assets, including this estate given to him by you, have been seized by the king."

"Then it's good," she said, "that it was a man who appeared in court."

"Yesterday a messenger came to me from Flói to request that I see to it that Magnús Sigurðsson be held liable for his conduct there the other night. This is of course not the first time that I have acted as arbitrator in such matters—on behalf of the person who respects me least of all men."

"On my behalf?" she asked.

"On behalf of her beloved personage, cotters have occasionally been done slight favors by good men in order to prevent cases such as this from undergoing further litigation. However, mercy of this kind can most certainly be reckoned according to philosophy as an unreasonable act of charity, equivalent to sin."

The archpriest then explained to the housewife how her husband had, two nights ago, ridden down to a certain cottage in Flói, thrown the man out of bed, and committed adultery with his wife.

She smiled and said that the money being used to prevent such good news from reaching her was being wasted; her husband had always been a great cavalier. "And I am proud to hear," she said, "that I am wed to a man who still enjoys women after submersing himself in brennivín for thirty years."

The archpriest stared into the distance, without moving or giving any other sign to acknowledge that he had heard this frivolous answer.

"My dear Reverend Sigurður," she said. "Why don't you ever smile?"

"This so-called marriage," he said, "has scandalized good men in this country for too long, and it is high time for it to be dissolved by the grace of God and the church's consent."

"I can't see how that will change anything," she said. "I'll always be saddled in the public's eyes with a charge of adultery, with no possible chance to refute such calumny—divorcing my ignominious, plebeian husband will do nothing to rectify that. And it is useless to seek support from my father, since, according to you, even he is going to be reduced to the level of pauper—a miscreant in the sight of all in his old age."

"Last winter I stood in anguish outside your window by night, often in frost and storm," he said. "I offer you my wealth and my life. My last hundred of land is yours to use to reclaim your father's honor, if you so desire."

"What does that pierced troll say, whom you wished to appoint as my judge last winter?"

Her blasphemy seemed to touch him no longer:

"My Redeemer's immortal witness, Reverend Hallgrímur Péturs-son, had a pagan wife.* I am not in a worse position than he was."

"And what do the church ordinances say, which are far more bind-ing than the crucified one himself ever was?" she asked. "How long can a priest retain his vestments, when he is wed to a runaway wife with a reputation for adultery on top of everything else?"

"May I speak to you in confidence?" he asked.

"Do as you please," she said.

"I have come here with the full support of the man who is second only to your father in his embodiment of our country's honor, the aristocrat to whom both you and I can safely entrust our lots."

"The bishop?" she asked.

"Your sister's husband," he said.

She laughed coldly. Then, silence.

"Ride back home to your troll, Reverend Sigurður," she said. "My sister Jórunn and I are better able to converse without a go-between."

A few days later the squire was carried home on a horse-drawn stretcher. His body was stark with blood. His internal organs, or at the very least several ribs, had likely been damaged. He could move neither his body nor his limbs, and he did not have the power to speak. He was edged carefully in through the hole in the kitchen wall and put to bed in his houseroom. It had been a cruel turn of events.

When he had recovered enough to speak he asked to see his wife, but was told that she was ill. He demanded to be carried up to her, but was told that she had ordered that her door be bolted from the inside.

"That doesn't matter," he said. "She'll open the door anyway."

He was told that the daleswoman Guðríður never moved from her place beside Snæfríður's bedcloset, night or day.

Things were not looking well for him. He asked what his wife's symptoms were and the answer came back that she had gone down bedecked in finery to receive a visitor a week ago, had chatted with him for some time and had cheerfully bidden him farewell, then had stepped lightly back up to her room. She hadn't been up and about since then. She could endure neither the sunshine nor the incessant noise of birds twittering around the farm day and night at this time of the year, and so she had a curtain of black wadmal drawn before her window.

— 18 —

On either side of a crag in Almannagjá stand two old tents, battered-looking and torn in places, though imprinted with the crown of our Most Gracious Majesty. Men occupied the tent on the Brennugjá side, women the one nearest Drekkingarhylur. Some of these people had been summoned to Þingvellir to testify in court, but most were convicted criminals who'd been punished physically, either recently or at some time in the past: they'd been branded, flogged, had their hands chopped off. The king's special envoy had called them hither this time to retry their cases. Today they were waiting for their portion of the king's soup, prepared by a cook from Bessastaðir.

"This company's far too sluggish for my liking, considering justice is finally about to be done," said one man. "I'm amazed no one's even up to giving us a ballad."

Most were in tatters, their feet either bare or wrapped with layers of rags, their chins shaggy, their scraps of clothing bound with bits of rope-ends or bands of unspun wool. They had no belongings, though some who still had hands carried broken rake-shafts for walking sticks. Some individuals in the group actually owned milch cows, wranglers who had at some time or other been punished by the authorities and who had never been able to forget it—these stayed up at night muddling over their lot, relentless in their ability to complain, lay blame, and curse. One of these men now said, since it looked as if he was about to be exonerated:

"I demand a day's wages for being torn away from my spring work and dragged up here."

Another man felt that the costs of the trip to Þingvellir would never be fully compensated until he got the chance to watch his bailiff being flogged.

A holy man who'd been branded for stealing from the poor box said:

"In my opinion, these demands are being made out of little love for the folk who were burned here in Brennugjá, hanged at Gálga-klettur,* or sunk in Drekkingarhylur, alone and abandoned, either because they couldn't swear a counteroath against false charges or because the devil showed up in a dogsbody and testified against them. Are we more pitiable than them? Why not you and I?"

Jón Hreggviðsson from Rein, who was sitting out in front of the men's tent with a gray beard in place of his black one, wearing muddy skin-stockings, a thick wadmal smock begrimed with dirt and horsehair, and a piece of cord about his waist, cried out:

"A long time ago they brought me here eastward over the heath, along with one Jón Þeófílusson from the Westfjörds, who was burned after the devil testified against him. And I've got one thing to say about that: a ladies' man like him, who could sit up in the gables an entire night holding on to a Blusterer while his girl was in bed with another man, didn't deserve any better, and that's why I told him so many times in the black pit, 'You'll definitely be burned, dear Jón.'"

"A lot of folks might say there'd never have been such trouble these days if they'd have cut your head off back then, Hreggviðsson," said a handless thief.

"Why wasn't my head cut off, why wasn't I hanged? I wasn't better than any of them," said the saint who'd stolen from the poor box.

A certain soft-spoken man who'd been spared execution for incest said this:

"My sister was drowned, as everyone knows, and by God's grace I was sentenced to outlawry and banished to another quarter where I had to lie about my name. My first job was to snitch on thieves to the bailiff, and he flushed them out and stoned them. Of course my identity finally came out, and for ten years everyone's known it was me. For ten years I've been walking repentantly from house to house, and the countryfolk have long accepted me as their own and God's lawbreaker and have treated me kindly. And now, after ten years, it turns out it was a completely different man and a completely differ-

ent woman who'd had the child that they drowned my sister for supposedly having had with me. Who have I been all these years and
who am I now? Will anyone treat me charitably after this? Will anyone take me in in the spirit of mercy and forbearance after this? No,
they'll laugh at me throughout all of Iceland. No one'll ever throw
me as much as a single fish-belly. They'll send the dogs after me. My
God, my God, why did you take my crime from me?"

"When I was a child I was taught to look up to the gentry," said an
old tramp who was on the verge of tears. "And now in my old age I
have to watch four of the good bailiffs who had me flogged dragged
into court. If there's no one around to flog us anymore, who's a man
supposed to look up to?"

"To God," said someone.

"Well said," said a blind criminal. "What did Reverend Ólafur
from Sandar mean in his venerable verses when he begged our Lord
Jesus to defend the authorities?"

"I would never think to put all authorities together in the same
boat," said the man missing a hand. "I was flogged at Rangárvellir for
the same crime they cut my hand off for down south by the sea."

"Are you suggesting," said the blind man, "that our Redeemer
ought to defend certain authorities, certain good authorities, for
example those authorities who allow men's hides to be tanned, but
not those who cut off men's hands? I don't think the dear reverend in
his fair verse meant to leave anyone out: his prayer was that the
Redeemer might defend all the authorities, those who chop off men's
hands no less than those who tan men's hides."

"Reverend Ólafur from Sandar can eat shit," said one man.

"It's not for me to say what Reverend Ólafur from Sandar can
eat," said the blind criminal. "But I know for certain that when Master Brynjólfur had grown so old that he couldn't understand Greek
and Hebrew any longer, and had also forgotten all his dialectic and
astronomy, and couldn't remember how to decline mensa* in Latin,
he always used to recite this verse by Reverend Ólafur from Sandar,
which his mother had taught him when he was a child."

"Whoever trusts the authorities isn't a man," said Jón Hreggviðsson. "I've walked across Holland."

"My king is just," said the old, oft-flogged tramp.

"Whatever a man doesn't take for himself a man never takes," said Jón Hreggviðsson. "I've landed in adventures with the Germans."

"Blessed is the man who serves his sentence," said the oft-flogged man.

"I spit at The Grandees when their sentences are unjust," said Jón Hreggviðsson. "But I spit at them even more when their sentences are just, because then I know they're scared. You think I don't know my king and his hangman? I've chopped down Iceland's bell, worn a Spanish Jacket out in Glückstadt, and had the Paternoster put on my head in Copenhagen. When I came home my daughter was lying on her bier. I wouldn't trust them to bring an innocent child over a brook without getting it drowned."

"Jón Hreggviðsson is the very picture of Satan," said the oft-flogged man, and he quivered like an aspen leaf. "God have mercy on me for my sins."

The blind criminal said:

"Let us keep the peace dear brothers, while we await the king's soup. We are the rabble, the lowest creatures on earth. Let us pray for the health of each and every authority who comes to the aid of the defenseless. But there will never be any justice until we ourselves become men. Centuries will pass by. The reprieve granted to us by the last king will be taken from us by the next. But our day will come. And upon that day, when we become men, God will come to us and fight on our side."

— 19 —

On the same day that the king's poor innocents sat waiting for the king's soup at Þingvellir by Öxará this newsworthy event occurred in Bræðratunga: the housewife rose from bed, summoned her farm-hands and ordered them to round up some horses, then announced that she was leaving. They said that the master of the house had ridden from home for the time being and none of the horses remaining was ridable. She said:

"Do you remember the horse that stood here tied to the horse-block last spring, the one I ordered you to slaughter?"

They looked at each other, smiling sarcastically.

"Go to Hjálmholt, where you will find this horse in the bailiff's pastures, and bring it to me," she said.

They returned with the horse around midnight, to find her waiting and ready to leave. She ordered them to bring out her saddle and put it on the horse, then threw on a great, hooded wadmal cloak to protect herself against the incessant rain and assigned one of the men to accompany her westward over the river. She planned to ride the rest of the way alone that night. The weather was calm and mild, with dense drizzling rain.

No sooner had her attendant crossed back over the Brúar River than her horse grew restive. She lashed at it for a short time before it suddenly jumped with a start into a gallop, nearly throwing her off. It tore along at a tremendous pace for a while and it took her everything she had just to stay in the saddle, her hands locked in a death-grip around the saddle horn. Finally it pulled the reins from her grasp, ran out onto the moor, and stood still. She started beating the horse with her crop again, and when it grew annoyed at the beating it snorted and lashed its tail, giving warning that it was going to rear. In the end it did no such thing, but instead galloped away, just as before. This time it tried to catch her off guard with some old tricks, taking eccentric turns and doing as much as possible to throw her off. She dismounted and caressed the horse, but it refused to acquiesce to her kindnesses. Finally she managed to get it moving again, but only in a fast gallop, and in between spurts of galloping it stood stock-still. Maybe she was a bad rider. In the end it entered a hollow divided by a stream and turned sharply to one side. She was thrown forward off the saddle and in a flash found herself lying on the ground. She stood up and wiped off the dirt and the mud; otherwise she was unhurt. A whimbrel cried out sharply and energetically through the haze. The horse grazed by the bank of the stream. She remounted halfheartedly, struck at its groin, jerked at the reins, and shouted "Ho!" but it was all for nothing. Maybe she knew nothing about beating horses. One thing was certain: it wasn't going to move.

It went against everything in its constitution to continue on in this way. It gave a few ponderous starts, then reared. She dismounted, walked up along the shoulder of the hollow, sat down upon a moss-covered hillock, and stared at the horse through the rain.

"I should've known that a horse given to someone by a crook as compensation for injury wouldn't turn out to be any better than you, you sluggard," she said to the horse.

Luckily there was no one to witness her stop-and-start journey, since it was near daybreak and the countryside was asleep. It seemed to her as if the haze was brighter than it had been a short time ago, so she knew that the sun must have risen.

She straightened out her cloak and pressed onward. A fog lay over the hills and the heather glistened with moisture. A gray web of mist glistened upon the turfless patches. The birch was partly in bud and smelled almost sickly sweet in the warm and tranquil drizzle. She was poorly prepared for walking: her boots quickly became waterlogged and her skirt soaked and heavy as her feet were entangled by the dripping copsewood, besides the fact that she had only newly risen from her sickbed and was lacking somewhat in strength. She fell several times, but forced herself up again and pressed on. She was thoroughly drenched by the time she made it through Bláskógar.

When she finally reached Öxará it was late enough that the drunks had gone to sleep. The purl of the cold river seemed to be frozen in the break of the fog-enshrouded day, distant even to the ears of someone standing at its bank. Several sleeping horses stood hobbled in the pasture, their heads drooping.

Standing here and there near the courthouse were a few tents, and she spied the canopied magistrate's booth and made her way toward it. The booth had a double canopy of a protective outer tarp and an inner lining, and its walls had been rebuilt. Three stone steps led up to a practical door set in a comely doorway in the paneled front wall. She rapped on the door. One of her father's attendants came out, drunk with sleep, and she bade him wake the magistrate. The old man turned over in bed and asked hoarsely who was outside.

"It is I, dear father," she said softly, in a melancholy tone, and she leaned up against the doorpost.

The tent's inner lining was dry in spite of the rain and there was a removable wooden platform for a floor. Her father was lying in a sleeping bag made of skin, beneath him a pad smelling of manured hay, which was a princely fragrance on spring days when no one had any hay. He raised himself halfway, clad in a thick wadmal night-shirt, with a scarf around his neck, blue-faced, quite bald, his nose overly large and his eyebrows appallingly thick. Old age had made him noticeably emaciated and his cheeks were sagging; a dewlap had replaced his double chin. He looked at her apathetically.

"What do you want, child?" he asked.

"I wish to speak with you in private, father," she said, the same dusky tone in her voice. She did not look at him, but continued to lean tiredly against the doorpost.

He told his attendant to go to the servants' tent for the time being, then asked her to wait at the threshold while he dressed. When she was finally allowed in, her father was on his feet, having put on his boots and thick cloak and peruke. She noticed the heavy golden ring on his right ring finger as he took some snuff from a silver box. She went straight up to him and kissed him.

"Well now," he said, after she finished kissing him.

"I've come to you father, that's all," she said.

"To me?" he said.

"Yes," she said, "one has to be able to lean against someone, other-wise one dies."

"You always were an unruly child," he said.

"Dear father, will you permit me to stand at your side?" she asked.

"Dear child," he said. "You are no longer a child."

"I've been lying ill in bed, father," she said.

"I heard that you were ill, but I see that you must be feeling well again," he said.

"Father," she said. "One day this spring I saw nothing but dark-ness. It engulfed me and I lost my strength and gave in to its power. All I could do was lie there in the darkness. And yet, I didn't die. How can it be that I didn't die, father?"

"Many people fall ill in the spring and live to tell about it, good child," he said.

"Yesterday I heard a voice whispering to me that I should go to you. Someone said that the verdicts would be handed down today. I suddenly recovered. I arose. Dear father, in spite of this dreadful poverty, our family is still of some worth, isn't it?"

"Yes it is," he said. "I come from excellent folk. Your mother comes from even better folk. God be praised."

"They haven't succeeded in confounding us," she said. "Not entirely. We're still standing upright. Are we human or aren't we, father? I'm certain that if I'm bound by any obligation, it's to you."

"You have proven to be a great challenge to your mother, child," he said.

She said, "Now I'm going to ride home to her with you, as she asked me to do."

He looked away.

"Father," she continued. "I hope that they're not still disputing the verdicts in court."

He said that he wasn't entirely sure what she meant by verdicts, since things had reached such a state that no one knew any longer where justice was to be found in this miserable country. He himself didn't know what name he should give to the buffoonery taking place just now. Then he asked what sort of grudge she bore that could have persuaded her to transfer control of Bræðratunga back to Magnús Sigurðsson after it had become clear that he would be defamed for his libelous censure against her, instead of declaring herself divorced from the man with legal documents and witnesses. "Yet you knew," he said, "that those who were more heedful of their reputation and honor than Magnús Sigurðsson would be prosecuted here and deprived of their names and their estates though they might have done far less to offend the country's newest ruling power." He said that a vice-magistrate and two bailiffs had been appointed and invested with the power of magistrate to make a ruling in the lawsuit against him, because Arnæus had announced that he could not perform his official duties until his name was cleared of this aspersion, and he had demanded that this be accomplished not just by means of the judgment of one district court, but also by means of a magistrate's judgment. The verdict was to be announced early this morning, and then Arnæus would take over in court.

"Father," she said. "What sort of penalty will be imposed if Magnús's accusations are verified?"

He answered: "If a married man takes a married woman, the punishment is loss of reputation and respect, and a pecuniary fine to be paid to the crown is imposed upon each of them—and of course the fine may be paid with skin in place of cash."

"Father," she said, "will you permit me to come forth in court and say a few words?"

"Words are worth nothing here," he said. "What do you want?"

"I'll force a mistrial—the court will be brought to ruin and the judges vitiated, and good men will have the chance to send their advocates to council with the king. Perhaps if this man is forced out, they'll think twice about appointing a successor to prosecute you into ignominy next summer."

"I don't know what sort of dream it is you're living in, child," he said.

"I'm going to request a hearing," she said, "and demand to be called as a witness in the case against Magnús Sigurðsson. I'm going to explain to the court that Magnús was justified in writing the letter he had read in the choir doorway in Skálholt cathedral."

"It shocks me to hear you say such things," said Magistrate Eydalín. "Both your sister and her husband the bishop sent word to your mother that this calumny was the blackest lie that any man could conceive of. And just who is supposed to confirm such testimony?"

She said, "I'll swear an oath to it."

"My honor wouldn't be worth much if I were to consider saving him from the trampling of the reputation-thieves by putting my daughter's life and honor on the line in this judicial dispute," said the magistrate. "Particularly and especially since the oath that you intend to swear in praejudicio Arnæi* in this case must necessarily be perjurious."

"It's not your business," she said. "It's our fatherland's. If the few of you who stand upright throughout this time of need are to sit upon the outlaws' bench and be condemned, if our family is to be trampled down into the mire, if there are no longer to be men in Iceland, then what was all this for?"

"If you believe that I am prepared, good child, to let someone swear a false oath in order to promote my own advantage in a lawsuit involving me, then you do not know your own father. I shudder to hear such support being offered by my child, support that even the most dishonest man would refuse to accept from a bandit. The ideas that a wretched female can come up with are incomprehensible to sensible men. I readily acknowledge that my senility has caused me to make one or two mistakes; but I am a Christian man. A Christian man holds his soul's well-being above all other things. If someone swears a false oath with another's consent and on behalf of that person, then both of them eternally forsake their souls' well-being."

"Even if by committing this crime they're able to save the honor of the entire country?" she asked.

"Yes," he said, "even for that, or so it seems."

"You taught me once, father, to call such hairsplitting ars casuistica,"* she said. "Fie upon that art."

He said huskily and coldly: "Your words dimly remind me of a confused girl who has through her own self-imposed tribulations forsaken her luck, lost hold of her ability to perceive the difference between disgrace and honor, and who now speaks in desperatione vitae.* This conversation must end now, good child. But since you are here, God knows why, I shall now call for the boys and bid them light the fire and heat some tea, since day is breaking."

"Father," she said. "Call for no one. Wait. I didn't tell you everything: not the truth. But now I'll tell it. I don't need to swear a false oath: throughout the entire winter Árni and I regularly engaged in forbidden relations in Skálholt. I went to him by night"—she spoke quietly and darkly down into her lap as she sat there cowering at the door.

He cleared his throat and bellowed in a voice huskier than before:

"Such testimony would carry no weight in court, and therefore you would never be allowed to swear an oath! There are plenty of examples of married persons telling just such lies in order to obtain a divorce! In this case the court would require witnesses!"

She said: "A man working in complicity with my sister and my sister's husband came to me in the spring to discuss this case with me. It was one of the exalted personages of the see of Skálholt, the man who read the document containing the charges against me in the choir doorway, and I wouldn't be surprised if he even played a part in writing it, with the full consent and approval of my sister Jórunn. One thing is certain, the archpriest, Reverend Sigurður Sveinsson, is too crafty a man to read such a document in a holy place on a whim—he had good reason to do so, since he so much as caught me in the act one night. Besides this, I gleaned from both his and my sister's comments earlier in the winter that they had sent one or more of the see's housemaids to spy on our movements. It will be easy to find witnesses."

He remained silent for a long moment before answering.

"I am an old man," he said finally. "And I am your father. No such thing has ever been proven to have occurred in our family. On the other hand some of your mother's folk did lose their wits, and if you say anything more along these lines, I'll know that you belong to this group."

"Árni will never deny this against me," she said. "He'll drop the case."

Her father said: "Even if Arnas Arnæus were to father a beautiful boy with you, and even if not only the archpriest and the housemaids, but also the bishop and his wife, were to catch him in the act, that same man would stop at nothing until he had acquired decrees from princes, emperors, and popes confirming that you had begotten the child with some hangabout. I know his kind."

"Father," she said, looking straight at him, "would you rather I say nothing? Does your honor mean nothing to you? Are your sixty estates worth nothing to you?"

He said: "I consider it far less disgraceful to stand upright in opposition to a fop at a daytime assembly than to have a daughter who has fallen before a fop during a nighttime rendezvous, even if I knew this blemish to be a self-imposed lie. And this you know, child, that when you ran off and married the greatest scamp in the southerners' quarter after one of the richest clerics in the land, the exceptionally learned poet Reverend Sigurður Sveinsson, had asked for your hand, I of course remained silent over this indignity; and when he sold away his patrimony and brought you to the brink of poverty I bought the property in silence. And then, when your mother found out that you had been sold to a Dane for brennivín and threatened with the ax, I excused myself from answering such foolishness. Even when you went back to him, transferring to your executioner the property that I had deeded to you, I did not open my mouth, nor for that matter my heart, to anyone. Now as before I may well have to endure the churls' mudslinging in this the seat of my power, Þingvellir by Öxará, but that makes little difference: no one will laugh after a time. But of all the indignities that you have forced your mother and me to endure, you would do well to remain silent in this last one, if you would rather not turn your people into the greatest laughing-stocks in the history of this destitute country throughout the ages."

In repose he still appeared to be the most active of men. But when he stood up, took hold of his staff, and walked out to order his servants to their morning work, one could see how decrepit he really was. He tottered out along the platform, short-stepped and haltingly, stooping to such a degree that the lap of his cloak dragged along the floor, and gritting his teeth to help suppress the arthritic casts that gripped him after his graceless rest in this damp, cold shed so early in the summer.

—— 20 ——

Shortly after the magistrate went to wake his servants his daughter also stood up and left the booth. She was tired and wet after her nightlong march in the rain and she was immediately gripped by the cold. She hurried away from her father's booth and in no time at all found herself standing in Almannagjá, its sheer edges and crags leaning in and closing over her, the projecting rock face above her disappearing into the fog. She roamed for some time beneath the ravine walls. Her feet were in pain. Misted horses stood in the fields at the foot of the ravine, causing droplets of dew to fall as they grazed. The river murmured in the fog somewhere close by. Soon she was standing by the great women's pool, where the river turns back on itself and drains from the ravine. She watched the water billow like eddying black velvet, deep and cold and clean at the break of day, and she noticed that her mouth was dry.

After gazing at the pool for some time she heard a pounding sound rising over the water's murmur, and she spied a woman clad in gray with a handkerchief wound round her head standing upon a flat rock at the water's edge, beating socks with a battledore.* She walked over to the woman and greeted her.

"Do you live here?" she asked the woman.

"Yes and no," said the woman. "I was once supposed to have been drowned in this pool."

"I've heard people say that the moon is sometimes mirrored in it," said Snæfríður.

The woman straightened up and looked at her, took note of her dark-colored cloak, which was made from good, thick wadmal, then went right up to her and lifted the cloak's hem, revealing a blue skirt of foreign cloth and a silver belt with a long ornamental endpiece; upon her feet she wore English boots that were rather grimy, but which would still fetch her two or three hundreds of land. The woman examined her face and eyes.

"You must be an elf-wife," said the gray woman.

"I'm tired," said the stranger.

The gray woman explained that there were three beldames sharing a tent here, each from a different district. One had been branded for having run off with a thief, another was to have been drowned here for having sworn she was a virgin despite the fact that she was pregnant, and the third had disburdened herself of a child north in Sléttuhlíð, but since the likelihood existed that it had actually been stillborn she had been sent from Drekkingarhylur to the Spindehus* in Copenhagen. She had labored as an inmate there for six years and had been set free when His Most Benevolent Majesty and Grace took his queen to wife. Now these women had been summoned to Þingvellir to witness the sentencing of their heaven-sent authorities to ignominy. They planned to go home today. "But," said the woman, "since you have for some reason come to me, dear daughter-in-law, and are in need of hospitality, come into my tent with me."

The woman's two companions looked over the elf-wife in pious silence, and she allowed them to touch her. They wanted to treat her as hospitably as possible, since treating elves well is guaranteed to bring good luck. They were very eager to tell her their life stories, as usually happens when commoners come into contact with supernatural beings and aristocrats, but she listened to them distractedly as if their stories were wind blowing on the opposite side of a mountain. Now and then she shuddered. They asked her why she had cast off her misty veil and come here.

"I'm doomed," she said.

They said: "Go to Arnæus, sister, he will acquit you no matter what you have done."

"The court that will acquit me does not exist, neither amongst elves nor men," she said.

"It exists in heaven," said the woman who had disburdened herself and labored in the Spindehus.

"No, nor in heaven," said Snæfríður.

They looked at her wordlessly, incredulous that the court that could acquit this criminal existed neither in heaven nor on earth nor in the world of elves.

"Don't let that trouble you," said the woman from the Spindehus. "The only women who were lucky were those who took their rest in the pool."

They had gathered moss to lie upon, but had received coverlets from the king. Now they prepared a bed for her. And because she was soaking wet, they undressed her and exchanged clothing with her— she took a smock from one, a skirt from another, and a shirt from the third. The woman who had gone to the Spindehus removed her own kerchief and tied it round her head. They fetched tea and bread from the Bessastaðir cook and shared it with her. Finally they wrapped a coverlet marked with the king's seal around her and tucked her into the moss.

In a moment she was asleep, finally. One of her many burdens during this torpid spring was that she could find no rest in sleep. But now she slept. She slept deeply and tranquilly. She slept for a long time. Slept.

When she awoke the three innocents were gone, along with any sign that they had ever been there. The tent was empty. She stood up and gazed out through the opening: the grass was long since dry, the sky was clear, the sun was sinking in the west. She had slept the entire day. She hadn't seen the sun since sometime last year, but now she saw it shining over Þingvellir by Öxará: over Skjaldbreiður, Bláskógar, the estuary, the lake, and Hengill. Something was irritating her skin beneath her clothing and when she looked down she found that she was wearing the three innocents' clothing: a patched-up gray smock with white bone buttons but no belt, a muddy and tattered short skirt with a frayed hem and a tear up the side, rust brown goat's hair socks with newer foreparts knitted onto older sock-legs, shoes of untanned cowhide with holes at the toes and slits in the seams, and a gray wadmal rag tied around her head. Her legs jutted out below the hem of her skirt and the sleeves of the smock covered only her upper arms. These tatters smelled of all the unclean stenches that best distinguish a destitute folk: smoke, horsemeat, whale oil, stale body odor. She looked to see what was irritating her skin, and found it red and swollen with lice.

A lice-ridden woman in gray rags staggers away from her sleeping place. She stopped at the riverbank and drank water from the palms of her hands, then redrew her kerchief before her face. She ambled in the direction of the courthouse, but didn't dare to enter the building; instead she stepped off the stairs and sat down in the peat a short distance from where a horse nibbled at the grass. The courthouse, Iceland's Hall of Justice, had succumbed to ruin: its walls had collapsed, its bargeboards were broken, every single plank was out of place, the door had fallen off its hinges, the frame was warped. And there was no bell. Several dogs were fighting out front. The evening sun gilded the budding copse.

Finally a little handbell was rung within the house: court was adjourned. The first to exit were three men wearing wide cloaks, top-boots, and feathered hats, and one was girded with a sword: the governor's proxy. The others were the vice-magistrate and finally our Most Gracious Majesty's specially appointed commissarius, Arnas Arnæus, Assessor Consistorii, Professor Philosophiae et Antiquitatum

Danicarum. Following these three noblemen came their secretaries and adjutants, along with several armed Danish soldiers. The vice-magistrate and the governor's proxy were conversing in Danish, but the commissarius followed them silently, restively, legal documents in hand.

Next came Magistrate Eydalín, tottering out of the courthouse with a servant at his side to support him. In all actuality he had grown feeble: he stretched out his hand like a child to the man leading him, instead of offering his arm. His cloak dragged along on the ground behind him.

Several middle-aged authorities followed him out of the house. They were apparently quite agitated, if one could tell by their cursing—some of them were drunk and wove about on the path. Finally came several men who had previously fallen under grave sentences but had not been executed only by sheer coincidence. These men had now been acquitted, but even so, they didn't look any more joyful than any of the others who had come out of the house.

One of the commoners in the group turned from the path in the direction of the ragged woman sitting in the peat. He swore. She thought he might be drunk and might try to harm her, but he didn't come over to her after all. He didn't even look at her, but instead walked up to the horse grazing nearby. This workhorse was somewhat obstinate and at first it showed its master only its hindquarters. The obstinacy was apparently only for show, however, because in just a few moments the latter was rope-bridling the former, reciting as he did so a peculiar prefatory stanza from the seventh canto of the *Elder Ballad of Pontus:*

> "March on, spare none, let there now resound
> The gale of a battle mercilessly fought,
> The gale of a battle mercilessly fought,
> A whale white in color is the last to be caught."

Then he took the horse from its hobble.

"Jón Hreggviðsson," she said.

"Who're you?" he said.

"How did it go?" she said.

"Their injustice is bad, and their justice is worse," he said. "Now they've ordered me to get a new Supreme Court appeal from the king, and on top of that threatened to send me to Bremerholm right after the Alþingi this summer for not having published the old one. I don't suppose you're one of those they acquitted?"

"No," she said, "I'm one of the guilty. The innocents stole my cloak."

"I don't believe in any justice except my own," he said.

"What was the verdict in the case of the squire from Bræðratunga?" asked the woman.

"Those kinds of men condemn themselves," he said. "They were grumbling something about me killing my son. So what? Wasn't he my son? There's only one crime that avenges itself, and that's betraying the hidden people."

"I don't understand," she said.

"Two gentlemen stand opposite each other and each condemns the other, but they don't know that they're both guilty. Both betrayed the fair maiden, the slender elf-body. The squire calls the commissary a whorer in the choir doorway, the commissary answers by seizing the squire's estate for himself and the king. But where's my lord Arnæus's fortune? Jón Hreggviðsson's been a rich man ever since he entered that house. If you want I'll give you a ride to Skagi and put you to work for me, my dear woman."

She refused his offer and said: "I would rather beg for alms than work to support myself; I'm one of those. Give me some more news so that I have a bit of a story to think about wherever I find a bed for the night. How did it go for the authorities?"

He said that Magistrate Eydalín and three bailiffs had been deprived of their honor and rank, and that all of their property had been transferred to the king:

"There's little left of him apart from his mouth and his voice. It's a shame to pity a man—I'm not talking about the gentry, mind you— but today when I was sitting next to the old man, I in a new jacket and he in the old cloak he was wearing when he sentenced me all those years ago, I thought to myself, well, I guess you shouldn't have been so good to Jón Hreggviðsson's ugly old head after all."

"Did you kill the man?" she said.

"Did I kill him? Either you kill him or he kills you," said Jón Hreggviðsson. "Once I had black hair. Now it's gray. Soon it'll be white. But whether it's black, gray, or white, I spit at any justice other than the justice that's in me, Jón Hreggviðsson from Rein, and the justice that's behind the world. Here, let me give you a rixdollar, good woman. But I can't save your head."

He took a silver coin from his purse and threw it into her lap as he mounted his horse. Then he was gone. The beggarwoman sat there on a hillock for quite some time after he'd gone and turned the coin over in her hands absentmindedly. Then she stood up, her face veiled by her kerchief. She felt uncomfortable in the innocent's skirt, because it revealed not only her feet with their high insteps, her thin ankles and long slender tendons, but also how her leg grew more stocky and became the strong feminine calf that no one had ever seen before. The woman felt naked. But the men whom she met at the riverbank were too caught up in their own concerns to take any notice of whether the skirt of a woman of the road was an inch too short or not. And when she saw that they weren't thinking about her but rather about themselves, she turned her head and called out to them:

"Has anyone seen Magnús from Bræðratunga?"

But these were prominent individuals who had come here explicitly to take part in the court proceedings, and they were insulted that a beggarwoman should dare to question them about a man, if a man he could be called, especially after they had already convicted him on charges of calumny and deprived him of his estate and title, and they did not answer her. There was one young man amongst them, however, who apparently had less to think about; he simply waited on the riverbank with two saddled horses while his father bestowed parting kisses upon the cheeks of the other gentlemen close by, and he answered her thus:

"The squire in Bræðratunga is precisely the sort of man virile enough to lie down with you—he who slandered his wife, Snæfríður, Iceland's sun, as a whore in the choir doorway."

After this she didn't dare mention the squire again, but when she met an old, gray-bearded groom, she came up with the clever idea of asking the whereabouts of Magnús Sigurðsson's horses.

"Magnús Sigurðsson?" asked the bearded man. "Isn't that the man who sold his wife to a Dane for brennivín?"

"Yes," she said.

"And then tried to cut off her head with an ax?"

"Yes," she said.

"And then accused her in the choir doorway in Skálholt of having slept with her father's enemy?"

"Yes," said the woman. "That's him."

"I'm pretty sure that the grooms at Bessastaðir have taken charge of his horses," said the bearded man. "If you were planning on trying to catch them, they're hardly on the loose anymore."

She roamed for some time throughout this holy place, Þingvellir by Öxará, where poor men suffered so greatly that finally the cliffs themselves began to speak. The sun gleams off the black walls of the ravine and the columns of steam on the mountain across the lake ascend high into the sky. A short distance away a dog howls, cutting through the calm, its tones drawn-out, false and drawling, broken only by an apathetic bark now and then. This miserable drone had probably been sounding for quite some time before she noticed it. She caught a glimpse of the dog sitting upon a hillock at the foot of a cliff; it lowered its head, let its eyelids droop, stretched its snout upward, and howled against the sun with its mouth almost fully closed. Behind it lay a man faceup in the grass, perhaps dead. When the woman drew near, the dog stopped howling and opened its jaws wide several times with a look of despair that only a dog can make, then stood up and dragged itself toward her. Its gut was stretched tight from hunger. As it came closer it recognized who she was despite her attire, and it tried to fawn on her. She had the feeling that this was the dog from Bræðratunga.

The squire lay there in the grass, sleeping. He was bloody and grimy, his face swollen from a beating, his clothing torn so much that his bare body showed through. She bent down over the man and the dog licked her cheek. His hat was lying a short distance away in the grass and she picked it up and used it to fetch riverwater to wash him off. He awoke and tried to rise, but gave a cry and fell back to the ground.

"Let me die in peace!" he shouted.

When she looked more closely she discovered that one of his legs was broken at midcalf and powerless.

"What hussy are you?" he said.

She lifted the kerchief from her face, revealing the golden complexion and the blue eyes that were like no others in the Nordic lands.

She said: "It is I, your wife, Snæfríður."

Then she set to work treating her husband's wounds.

FIRE IN COPENHAGEN

— I —

There is a celebration in Jaegersborg.*

The queen is hosting a banquet for her husband the king, her mother the German princess, and her brother the duke of Hanover. The highest-ranking men in the land, as well as the most renowned foreigners, have been invited to take part in this gala affair.

The queen had ordered the construction, in Hamburg, of more than fifty exquisite bows and four exquisite arrows for each bow, for today the king would be hunting a stag.

In late afternoon the nobles gathered in a glade encircled by tall beech trees and strewn with canopies. The nobles took their seats and our Most Gracious Highness and Majesty appeared at the edge of the glade, wearing crimson hunting garb, an ell-long feather bobbing above his black velvet beret. The queen and her esteemed brother followed, also outfitted for the hunt; stepping lightly along behind them were the ladies-in-waiting and other honorable ladies of the realm, dressed as huntresses.

Erected on the right side of the field was a kind of counter, a hundred feet long; displayed upon this were the silver trophies that were to be awarded at the conclusion of the contest. Near one end of the counter hung a curtain strung between two wooden posts, and opposite this canopy were the seats for the grandees and their ladies and ladies-in-waiting. The cavaliers, however, were obliged to stand— the same went for the members of a certain delegation outfitted with kalpaks, long sabers, and black beards; this, folk said, was the Tartar delegation.

Now the trumpets are blown, the verdant curtain raised—a stag appears and prances away, gamboling from one tree to the next. The Tartars were given the opportunity to shoot first, but their arrows went quite astray. Then the graceful ladies-in-waiting shot, and the entire company praised their elegant style. Next came the cavaliers, and some of them hit rather close to the mark, though none close enough, and everyone there delighted in this marvelous entertainment. The king and queen were the last to shoot. And without further ado, the king hit the stag with his first shot and thereby claimed the title Most Agile Archer in the North. The other prizes were distributed amongst the cavaliers and ladies, but the queen deferentially and courteously accepted no prize herself.

Alongside this outdoor gaming field a hill had been raised by extraordinarily artful means. Up along the hill ran an archway, the pillars on either side fashioned to resemble lemon or golden apple trees. The king and queen's seal had been carved into the wooden posts here and there, as well as imprinted upon the vault of blue cloth strung over the archway. Centered on top of the hill was a radiant pond teeming with fish and swarming with tamed ducks and other birds. In the center of the pond a crag had been fabricated, and from this crag sprouted four fountains. Each fountain was nearly half the length of a lance and sent arcs of water shimmering over the pond. Encircling the pond was a bench built of turf, its surfaces covered with grass. A beautiful cloth had been spread over the top of the bench, transforming it into a banquet-board. Chairs were distributed and arranged so that royalty sat beneath the king's canopy, while the ambassadors, the nobility, and the courtiers sat facing one another across the table. Official functionaries and other dignitaries representing the bourgeoisie, along with their ladies and other invited guests, including merchants, feasted alongside the Tartars on the greensward at the foot of the hill. The king's table was laden with over two hundred varieties of dishes and close to two hundred types of preserves and fruits in golden bowls. These delicacies stretched away in two rows as far as the eye could see—it was a magnificent sight to behold.

"Ein Land, vom lieben Gott gesegnet."*

The distinguished, potbellied German who had greeted the Assessor Consistorii et Professor Antiquitatum Danicarum Arnas Arnæus during the hunt, and who had introduced himself as Kommerzienrat Uffelen from Hamburg, took his place at the table beside Arnæus and addressed him companionably.

"Our gracious lady the queen, your compatriot, is a noble and generous woman," said Arnas Arnæus. "In her grace's villa, which she calls her summer sanctuary, she and her maidens often costume themselves as wood nymphs and elves. And in the evenings they dance upon the meadow to the strains of fiddles and flutes or bagpipes and shawms. A man can sail in the moonlight out upon her little whimsical Furusee.* And the evenings are concluded with fireworks."

The German answered: "I see that my lord enjoys more favor than a German commoner could ever hope to receive from his compatriot. I, however, was granted the privilege of entering the palace of the king's two daughters in Amager, since, out of sheer galanterie,* I had brought along two hummingbirds for their volières.* As it turned out, unfortunately, the day when young princesses learn to bestow love on little birds is far, far away. The little graces said they weren't too pleased to have been given small birds in place of the beast they'd really been dreaming of: a crocodile."

"Ach ja mein Herr, das Leben ist schwer,"* said Arnas Arnæus.

"My attendants and I also shared in the honor of being invited by His Highness to partake in a hunters' breakfast out at Hirschholm, his summer palace," said the German. "We dined there in his splendid arbor, which is fifty feet square and enclosed by twenty columns and adorned within with gold and velvet and silk. Hanging inside the cupola are over eight hundred imitation lemons and bitter oranges—you'd have to go all the way south to Welschland to encounter such style again."

"My queen, your compatriot, recently received a most remarkable monkey, purchased for two hundred special-dollars," said Arnas Arnæus—"and I won't even say how much her outstanding parrots cost. If my lord had, instead of giving the princesses two small birds, presented his compatriot with a second pair of Spanish horses as fine as the pair purchased last year for her for two thousand special-dollars burgled from Eyrarbakki, the largest trading station in the Danish realm, the queen's grief over not owning a four-horse team might have been soothed. And my lord might have spent a grand evening with the nymphs in the sanctuary by the Furusee—and been bidden good night with a fireworks display."

"I rejoice that my compatriot should finally have found in Iceland an admirer who considers no earthly creature too good for her if it can give her genuine pleasure," said the German.

Arnas Arnæus said: "We Icelanders would certainly present to her grace a team of four blue whales, if we did not esteem another queen even higher."

The gentleman from Hamburg glanced inquisitively at the Professor Antiquitatum Danicarum.

"The woman you mention can scarcely have her kingdom on earth if you would presume to place my compatriot in a lower position at her banquet table," he said.

"You are correct," said Arnæus, and he smiled. "She is the queen of Iceland."

The German continued to look askance at his table-companion, his coldly sapient eyes gleaming through folds of flesh, shoving food without pause into his mouth, leaving no tidbit untasted, doubtlessly thinking something completely contrary to whatever he was saying in the meantime. He reached for a crab and tore off one of its legs with these words:

"Isn't it about time that the woman to whom you refer descended from the airy halls of concept onto solid ground?"

"Things have been very difficult for us lately," said the Icelander. "The aforementioned queen is more blessed up in the air than she is down on the ground."

"I hear that the pox has done ferocious damage in Iceland," said the German.

"The country was poorly equipped to handle epidemic," said Arnas Arnæus. "The pox sailed in in the wake of famine."

"I hear that the bishop in Schalholt and his wife have perished," said the German.

Arnas Arnæus looked with surprise at this stranger. "Very true," he said. "My friends, hosts, and illustrious countrymen, the bishop and the madam in Skálholt, were called away from us last winter by the pox, along with twenty-five others in their household."

"My lord has my condolences," said the gentleman from Hamburg. "His country deserves better."

"I am delighted to hear you say this," said Arnæus. "Icelanders are grateful to meet foreigners who have heard of their country. And even more grateful to hear someone say it deserves better. But perhaps my lord should take note—sitting across from us, directly behind the roasted pig resting comfortably there upon its silver plate, is the Bürgermeister in Copenhagen, formerly a ship's-boy on a merchantman to Iceland, but now the highest ranking man in the Company, the Iceland merchants' league—it might be unwise to provoke him at this pleasant hour by speaking too loudly of Iceland. To wit, he has been forced to pay several thousand rixdollars in compensation for selling the Icelanders maggoty flour—and for overvaluing it by weight."

"I hope I don't seem too audacious," said the German, "if I mention the old days when my fellow townsmen and predecessors in the Hansa sailed to the island; times were different then. Perhaps after the meal is finished we can find a comfortable nook where an old man from Hamburg can share good memories with the Icelander whom the Danes in the Iceland trade claim to be Satan in the flesh— preferably a place where these our friends can't overhear us."

"There are a number of people in Iceland who would probably be willing to admit that the Iceland merchants' opinions of me are not entirely unwarranted," said Arnas. "But unfortunately for my countrymen, I have been defeated. I am the serpent that the Iceland merchants crush beneath their heels. Yes, we did get them to pay compensation for the flour, and the king will continue to send something of a grain supplement as long as there is a threat of famine. But it was not compensation that I wanted for my people, and not grain supplements, but rather, better trade."

The queen had stipulated that no strong liquor was to be found upon her banquet-board. Instead one and all would drink light

French wine, served in moderate proportion, so that the celebration would be marked in the very least by coarseness of character, which in her eyes was characteristic of folk from the Nordic lands and which always reared its head whenever these people drank.

Around sunset the tables were cleared. For after-dinner entertainment several small dogs were thrown into the pond upon the hill, and the dogs made quite a show chasing and biting to death the tame ducks and other wing-clipped birds swimming there, to the great amusement of the Royal Majesties and their illustrious guests.

Afterward they paraded with great ceremony to the palace in Jaegersborg, where the dance was scheduled to commence within a short time. Since this was to be a family dance, the court custom of wearing masks or other special costumes was abandoned for the evening by all except the queen and her ladies, who donned black gowns before joining the dance.

After the meal acquaintances amongst the guests spent a few moments chatting. Arnas Arnæus had always been a sought-after guest at all sorts of high-class gatherings due to his immense learning, but now it seemed to him as if various noblemen and other erudite men with whom he was familiar had either forgotten to greet him or else had disappeared sooner than they had a chance to do so. He felt of course that some of the gentlemen in the city government, shareholders in the Company like the Bürgermeister, could be excused for being unable at present to exchange a few words with a man who very recently had been instrumental in obtaining convictions against them on charges of fraud and deceit. On the other hand he found it utterly astonishing when two highborn judges from our Majesty's Supreme Court hastily looked down and walked away instead of returning his greeting. Even less did he understand why two of his colleagues from the Consistory flinched when they saw him. Even his comrade and old friend, the royal tutor and librarian in Worms, spoke to him distractedly, with a nervous expression on his face, and ended up being the first person to leave the party. He also noticed it quite clearly when a number of cavaliers drew together and fixed him with the mocking stare usually reserved by inhabitants of the Nordic lands for Icelanders—it was a stare that Arnas Arnæus himself had not experienced for a very long time.

He let the throng of people streaming into the palace carry him along. And just as he arrives in the foyer along with the others, and the piping of the minstrels commences, the royal entourage rushes by on its way to the ballroom, and our Most Gracious Highness's eyes come to rest on the Icelander. An elated gleam spreads over the illustrious face with its bird's beak and the derangedly mischievous eyes of a lewd, impotent old man as he starts vocalizing in the Low German tongue acquired from his foster parents:

"Na, de grote Islänner, de grote Schöttenjäger"; that is to say, the great Icelander, the great skirt-chaser.

Someone burst out laughing.

The guests bowed to His Highness as the sublime entourage swept by. The Icelander stood apart by himself. When he glanced around at the other guests it seemed to him as if no one had taken any notice of what had just occurred, which only served to increase his doubts as to who he was or where he stood in the eyes of this company. Finally the fat, glib German from Hamburg reappeared at his side.

"I beg your pardon, but my lord did not outrightly refuse to discuss with me a trifle someplace where no one could hear. If you please, my lord."

Instead of continuing onward into the palace's inner hall they walked from the foyer out into the orchard. Arnas Arnæus remained silent as the gentleman from Hamburg talked. He talked about Denmark's grain and livestock, about Copenhagen's enviable location and the excellent alabaster imported here from Asia. He mentioned the numerous costly palaces in the kingdom and said that His Highness was such a galanthomme* that his equal was not to be found in all of Christendom—one would have to search throughout all the realms of Islam to find his match. To illustrate his point he told the following story, which had earned the king the admiration of folk everywhere: a great feast was held for him in Venice, and His Grace danced continuously for sixteen hours, while the knights and legates from three empires and four kingdoms, as well as others who had come from city-states and princedoms, turned pale or fell over from overexertion. Around dawn they had to send men into town to waken some of the big-boned wenches who sold vegetables and carried barrels of fish on their heads and to decorate them with silk and gold and peacock feathers to dance with this king from the land of the polar bear, as Denmark is called in Venice, since by then the noble ladies of that city-state were either on the verge of collapse or had already sunk to the floor.

"All the same," continued the German, "a man must pay for his entertainments, even a king. I know that my lord is more familiar with the Treasury of this realm than I, and that therefore it is unnecessary for me to inform him of the growing difficulty the government is having in approving the subsidies needed to defray the costs of the fancy-dress balls, which are not only increasing in number but are also becoming more bombastic year by year. In Hamburg we have received confirmed reports that during the last few years the rents from the Iceland trade have been used to subsidize the court's entertainments; but now the cow has been milked down to its blood, and famine is on the rise in Iceland, as no one knows better than my lord. In the last several years it has taken a great deal of effort to squeeze out of the Company and the governor the rents the king is supposed to be receiving from the island. And now, after having been forced to pay compensation for the flour, the merchants are reluctant to sail—just one more tiny punishment to add to your people's misery. No matter what, however, the balls must be held, more palaces must be built, the queen must have another pair of Spanish horses, my gracious princesses must have a crocodile. And above all, the war must be financed. Sound counsel is a rare thing here."

Arnas Arnæus said: "I'm afraid I don't understand precisely what my lord Kommerzienrat is getting at. Might he have been entrusted by my king or the Danish Treasury with the duty of procuring funds?"

"I've been asked if I would like to buy Iceland," said the gentleman from Hamburg.

"By whom, might I ask?"

"The king of Denmark."

"It is reassuring to hear that the country is being offered by someone who cannot be accused of treason," said Arnæus, and he smiled—he had suddenly become quite carefree. "And has this offer been validated in any way with warrants?"

The German removed from his cloak a letter imprinted with the name and seal of our Highness. The letter was an invitation to several merchants from Hamburg to buy the island called by men Islandia, situated halfway between Norway and Greenland, along with all rights and privileges for their full and free ownership, with a guarantee of the complete and total relinquishment of any claims to the aforementioned island by the Danish king and his descendants throughout eternity. The price was set at five barrels of gold, to be paid to Our Royal Treasury upon the occasion of the signing of the contract.

Arnas Arnæus ran his eyes over the document under the light of a lantern burning in the orchard, then handed it back to Uffelen with thanks.

"I am sure that it is unnecessary for me to point out to you," said the German, "that by showing you this, I only desire to extend my special confidence to the man who is principal amongst those bearing the name of Icelander in the Danish realm."

"At this time," said Arnas Arnæus, "my name is of such worth in the Danish realm that I am the last man of all to hear news of matters concerning Iceland. I have been allotted the great misfortune of desiring prosperity for my native country, and such a man is an enemy of the Danish realm: this is how fate has shaped these two countries. It has certainly never been the custom in Denmark to mention the name of Iceland in good company; but ever since I was gripped by a desire to quicken the hopes of men's lives in place of contenting myself with my country's ancient books, my friends pretend not to know me. And His Highness, my Royal Grace, mocks me in public."

"Might I then hope that this proposed offer would not be unwelcome to you, considering the cause that you have chosen to pursue?"

"Unfortunately, it appears that it really matters little what part I choose to play in this affair."

"And yet it is in your power to decide whether the transaction is concluded or not."

"How can this be, my lord, since I am in no way party to the affair?"

"Iceland will not be bought against your will."

"I am grateful that you trust me enough to inform me of your secret. But concerning this matter, I lack the conviction to take any part in it, whether in word or deed."

"You desire Iceland's prosperity," said the German merchant.

"Absolutely," said Arnas Arnæus.

"No one knows better than you that a worse fate could not befall the inhabitants of that island than to remain the milch cows of the Danish king and the other usurers to whom he's given shares of the country, the governor and the monopolists."

"Those are not my words."

"You know very well that the wealth gathered here in Copenhagen has been garnished for successive generations from the Iceland trade monopoly. The road to the highest rank in the Danish capital has always run through the Iceland trade. Scarcely a single family in this city doesn't have a member who hasn't earned his bread from the Company. And no one would think of Iceland being granted as an emolument to anyone other than the highest-ranking nobleman, preferably royalty. Iceland is a good country. No country has supported so many wealthy people as Iceland."

"It's unique to hear such great empathy coming from the mouth of a foreigner," said Arnas Arnæus.

"I know several other things," said the German. "I know that Icelanders have always had warm feelings for the men of Hamburg, which is not incredible, since old tax registers attest that in the same year that the Danish king drove the Hansa off the island and monopolized the trade for himself and his men, tariffs on domestic goods for exportation were reduced by almost sixty percent, whereas tariffs on foreign wares were raised by almost four hundred percent."

And after a short silence: "I would not have been so bold as to mention this matter to Your Lordship had I not made absolutely certain, by my Christian conscience, that we men of Hamburg could offer your countrymen better conditions than our Most Gracious Sire and Host."

They strolled silently for some time through the orchard. Arnæus was lost in thought. Finally he asked, pensively: "Has my lord ever sailed to Iceland?"

The gentleman from Hamburg answered no, but was curious to know why he asked.

"My lord has not seen Iceland rise from the sea after a long and arduous voyage," said Arnas Arnæus.

The merchant did not understand him clearly.

"Storm-beaten peaks and glacier caps slung with storm clouds arise from angry seas," said the Professor Antiquitatum Danicarum.

"Yes, and?" said the German.

Arnas Arnæus said: "I have stood to the lee in a cog following in the path of those weatherbitten pirates from Norway, who ran before the winds for so long at sea; until suddenly this image arose."

"Of its own accord," said the German.

"There is no sight more awesome than that of Iceland rising from the sea," said Arnas Arnæus.

"I'm not so sure of that," said the German, somewhat astonishedly.

"At this single sight one can fathom the mystery that the greatest books in all of Christendom were written in Iceland," said Arnas Arnæus.

"Is that so?" said the German.

"You must realize by now," said Arnas Arnæus, "that it is not possible to buy Iceland."

The gentleman from Hamburg thought for a moment, then said:

"I may be nothing more than a merchant, but I think I can grasp your reasoning a little. Forgive me for admitting that I'm not entirely in agreement with you. It is certainly not possible to buy or sell the sublimity residing upon those high peaks; nor the masterful leaps that have been made by the land's champions; nor the ballads that have been sung by its folk; and no merchant would ever make an offer for these things. The only thing we merchants care about is how profitable a thing is. In Iceland can be found great peaks and the poison-spewing mountain Hekla, which causes the entire world to tremble in fear. And Icelanders in ancient times composed remarkable Eddas and sagas. All the same, what matters most to Icelanders is whether they have something to eat and to drink and whether they have clothing to wear. All we ask is whether it is more profitable to the Icelanders for their island of Islandia to remain a Danish slave-house, or to become an independent barony—"

"—under the dominion of the emperor," added Arnas Arnæus.

"Icelandic noblemen did not consider such an idea too far-fetched in years past," said Uffelen. "There are some remarkable old Icelandic letters in Hamburg. The emperor would undoubtedly grant his Icelandic barony autonomy; as would the English king. In return, the administration in Iceland would concede fishing harbors and trading rights to the merchants' league in Hamburg."

"And the baron?"

"Baron Arnas Arnæus will govern the island as he pleases."

"You are a most delightful merchant, my lord."

"I would prefer it if Your Lordship would not look upon my proposal as mere prattle, especially since there is no reason for me to mock my lord."

Arnas Arnæus said: "I think that there is scarcely an official position in Iceland that has not been offered to me by the Danish king. For two years I possessed the highest authority of any man who has ever lived in that country: I had power over the Iceland bureau in the Council of the Crown, over the Company, over the judges, over the governor's proxies; and to a certain degree over the governor himself. Besides that I was the man most willing to work for his fatherland. And what was the result of my work? Starvation, my lord. More starvation. Iceland is beaten. The baron of such a land would become the laughingstock of the world even if he were in the service of the good men of Hamburg."

Uffelen answered: "Of course you had the king's mandate in Iceland, my lord, but you yourself have previously stated the reasons why it was useless. You had neither the power nor the authority to carry out what was most required: the expulsion of the royally sanctioned monopolists and the establishment of fair trade."

Arnas Arnæus said: "My Most Gracious Majesty has repeatedly dispatched envoys to foreign princes to beg them to buy Iceland from him or else to loan him money, taking Iceland as collateral. Every time the Company found out about these propositions it offered to pay the crown higher rents on the Iceland trade."

"I would prefer," said Uffelen, "that this deal be made swiftly, so that the Iceland merchants get no wind of it before it's made public. It all depends on whether you wish to act as our proxy to the Icelandic people. If you give me your promise today, we can close on the deal tomorrow."

"First we must be sure," said Arnæus, "that this offer is not just one of the king's schemes contrived in order to squeeze a higher rent out of the Iceland merchants at a time when he's doing everything he can to raise money to finance what follows the dance: the war. Nothing will be ruined though my answer might be delayed for a day or two."

— 2 —

Arnas Arnæus did not have to wait long before he discovered the reason for the peculiar behavior of the aristocrats at the queen's banquet. When he arrived home that night he found a letter waiting for him. He had been convicted. The Supreme Court's verdict in the so-called Bræðratunga case, which had been in the courts for almost two years now, declared Magnús Sigurðsson innocent on all charges.

The case originally centered on two letters that the aforenamed Magnús had written in Iceland; one letter contained a complaint against Arnæus for a suspected intimacy between him and the letter-writer's wife, and in the other, intended for public reading at the synod in Skálholt, the letter-writer accused his wife of engaging in forbidden relations with the royal commissary and implored the clergy to intercede in the matter. The king's envoy claimed to have been maligned by the letters and he had subpoenaed their author on charges of libel. A ruling was handed down in district court by the bailiff Vigfús Þórarinsson two weeks after the second letter was read aloud in the choir doorway, and Magnús Sigurðsson was dispossessed of both his honor and his property for his disgraceful attack on Arnæus. The commissary immediately transferred the verdict to Öxará and appealed the ruling before a higher judge whom he himself had specially appointed, since the acting magistrate Eydalín was

disqualified from any involvement in the proceedings due to his rela-
tion to the accused by marriage. The court at Öxará stiffened the district court's sentence and stipulated that besides forfeiting his estate
at Bræðratunga, Magnús was to pay the royal commissary the sum of
three hundred rixdollars as penalty for the malignant insinuations
found in his letters, along with alimentary fees to be paid to the court
for its own particular difficulties in handling the case.

The Supreme Court ruling reversed the former verdicts. The
premises stated that the pitiful wretch Magnús Sívertsen had been
subject to stringent and unchristian treatment by the prosecutor
Arnas Arnæus and the courts. He had been prosecuted for writing
two letters: firstly, to defend his honor, and secondly, in the letter
addressed to the ecclesiastical council, to try to compel Arnæus to sti-
fle at their source the rumors and hearsay running rampant at that
time, since it was prejudicial not only to the matron at Bræðratunga
and her husband but also to the diocese of Skálholt that such lewd
report should have its foundation and origin in the watchtower of
Christian admonition and the bulwark of Christian morality. As an
indication that these letters were not written on a whim nor dis-
closed to the public in vain was to be considered the fact that Arnæus
packed his belongings and transferred his residence from the bishop's
estate to Bessastaðir on the very next day after the second letter was
read publicly. The premises stated that it was difficult to justify how
these letters had set in motion such an unrestrained attack on a poor
man, resulting in such severe verdicts and stiff fines. It was quite clear
that Monsieur Sívertsen had sufficient grounds for writing his letters,
if by doing so he could silence the persistent rumor of his cuckoldry
that was making its way throughout the country. The woman had
used Magnús's drinking bouts as an excuse to rendezvous with this
man, Arnæus, who was responsible for the rise of her public reputation as a slattern while still in the flower of her youth. And now she
had run away from home and sojourned beneath the same roof with
this her lover from youth for an entire winter in an entirely reckless
relationship, which, according to court testimony, was evidenced in
the ceaseless intimate conversations that took place between her and
the commissary as often in the light of day as in the darkness of night

behind locked doors, and it was difficult to see otherwise than that her husband had from justo dolore* written the letters in the terms that he did. The twenty-seventh chapter of the civil law corpus, concerning defamation, confirmed that there was no justification for the type of penalty imposed upon Sívertsen according to the judgment of the court at Öxará, since the condemned's words had not been spoken as positive testimony, and even if they had been, they did nothing other than echo what was already public knowledge, the private conversations between Arnæus and the woman. This being the case, the former unjust and unchristian verdicts affecting Magnús Sívertsen's honor and reputation were hereby proclaimed invalid and absolutely unbinding. And whereas Arnas Arnæus has in accordance with the same verdicts had the defendant's property and possessions assessed and confiscated, this sequestration and appropriation is hereby declared invalid, and his assets, both fixed and liquid, are ordered to be returned to Magnús Sívertsen along with all of his earnings and dividends payable from the date of seizure. Item, whereas in the court's opinion Arnas Arnæus is causa prima* of the husband's jealousy, as well as of the court's persecution of him, it followed reason that the aforenamed Arnas Arnæus should pay to Magnús Sívertsen, for the costs of the proceedings as well as for the ridicule and trouble he had suffered, a fee equal to the one awarded to him by jure talionis* and the former judges from Magnús's assets. And whereas Arnas Arnæus has by his thoroughly unchristian conduct, his iniquity, and his insolence throughout this entire affair instigated exorbitant scandals and aroused the indignation of the common folk in Iceland, subjecting the isle's kingly administration to reprobation, so shall this oft-named personage be forbidden from sailing to Iceland and denied the right to reside upon the same island for an undetermined period of time, unless he should first procure special permission from our Most Benevolent Grace and Majesty.

On the morning after the banquet, around the time that the first carriages were to be heard rattling down the cobblestone streets and the vegetable seller had begun shouting behind the house, Arnas Arnæus, pale from insomnia, rose from his armchair. He walks into his library. His secretary, the studiosus antiquitatum* Joannes Grindvicensis, is sitting at his desk, sobbing. The man did not realize immediately that his lord had come in, and he continued to sob. His lord hemmed several times to see if he could call the attention of the studiosus away from his work. The secretary looked up hastily in confusion, but when he beheld his master he finally became so overwhelmed that he pounded his forehead against the desktop as a shaking seized his shoulders, which were sunken from the heavy burdens of erudition and guilt.

Arnas Arnæus paced the room several times and gazed with a touch of impatience at this novel and troubling sight of a man sitting sobbing within the heavy silence of the library. And when he saw that the man's sorrow would not be abated he said, somewhat gruffly:

"Now, now, man, what in heaven's name is this?"

A short time passed before the learned man was heard to groan the following words between sobs:

"J-jó-jón Ma-marteinsson—"

He continued harping on these words for several moments, and was unable to get any further.

"Have you been drinking?" asked his lord.

"H-he was here," stammered the scholar from Grindavík. "He was certe* here. God help me."

"Well now," said Arnas Arnæus. "What are we missing this time?"

"God grant me mercy for my sins," said the man from Grindavík.

"What are we missing?" asked Arnas Arnæus.

Jón Guðmundsson from Grindavík stood up from his stool at his desk, threw himself down upon his knees before his master, and confessed that the book of books itself, the gemstone of gemstones, the *Skálda,* was gone.

Arnas Arnæus turned away from the man and walked over to a cabinet in a side compartment where the library's most precious items were kept locked up. He took out a key, opened the cabinet, and stared at the spot where for the longest time he had stored what he considered to be the most valuable artifact in the northern hemisphere, the book that contained the ancient poetry of his race, in its proper tongue; now there was only a gap where it had stood.

Arnas Arnæus stared for some time at the open cabinet's empty shelf. Then he closed the cabinet. He walked across the hall once, returned and stopped, and looked at the old studiosus antiquitatum, who remained crouched there upon his knees with his haggard hands raised before his face, trembling so much that he was nearly in convulsions. His patched-up shoes had come off his feet and lay on the floor behind him. There were holes in his socks.

"There now, stand up. Let me pour you a drink," said Arnas Arnæus, and he opened a little corner cupboard and poured from a bottle into an old tin tankard. He helped his secretary to stand and handed him the drink.

"God's thanks," whispered Jón Guðmundsson from Grindavík, but he lacked the courage to look his master in the face until he had finished a second drink. "And I'm here almost all night on watch," he said. "Last night I came downstairs around matins to continue copying *Maríusaga** for you, and when I checked on the cabinet as I usually do, there was no *Skálda*. It was gone. He must have come during the one hour I was asleep, around midnight. How could he have gotten in?"

Arnas Arnæus stood there holding the bottle, and he took back the empty tankard from the secretary.

"Would you like more, my dear man?" he said.

"My lord, I may not drink so much that I let the wine take the place of the true comforter, the spirit of the muse," he said. "Not more than one more glass, my blessed man—though I should think that I deserve far more to feel your wrath for letting that veritable devil in the guise of a man slink past me again while I was sleeping. And I'm reminded of something I heard yesterday from a trustworthy man, that this scamp and gallows bird was seen several evenings ago driving with Count du Bertelskiold to the City Hall Tavern itself. He was dressed in a newish-looking dress coat, and there's word out that the count ordered grilled partridge and punch for him. What am I to do?"

"One glass more," said Arnas Arnæus.

"God reward you for your kindness to this wretch from Grindavík," said the secretary.

Arnas Arnæus raised his hand and said, "Vivat crescat floreat—

Martinius,"* as the secretary drank. Then he stuck the cork in the bottle and locked it and the tankard back into the corner cupboard.

"I know that my lord speaks such false words with a bleeding heart," said the secretary. "But I ask you in all earnestness, my lord: are the town watchmen and the local militia not stronger than Jón Marteinsson? Are not the Consistory, the clergy, and the military in any position to form an alliance against this man? My lord, you who are so highly favored by the judiciary must surely have the authority to send such a man to the Rasphus."*

"Unfortunately, I think that I'm no longer in favor with anyone, dear Jón," said Arnas Arnæus, "and especially not with the judiciary. Jón Marteinsson has the better of me everywhere. Now he has also won the Bræðratunga case, which he litigated against me on behalf of the Iceland merchants."

Grindvicensis was immediately dumbfounded and could do nothing but repeatedly open and close his mouth like a fish, until he finally regained his senses and sighed:

"Can it be the will of Christ that all the inhabited world has been placed at the disposal of the devil?"

"The Iceland merchants' wealth serves him well," said Arnas Arnæus.

"It should come as no surprise to anyone that he should have sold himself out to the Iceland merchants to bring an unjust case against his manifold patron and favorite son of our fatherland, since he was capable of traveling to Iceland to buy books and copies of books for the Swedes—of all the evils that could befall an Icelander the worst would be to serve the Swedes, who deny that we are men and claim that Icelandic books appertain to the Gotlanders and West Gotlanders. Is the *Skálda* going to belong to them now too, and be called a West Gotlandic poem?"

Arnas Arnæus had taken a seat and was leaning back, his face pale, his eyelids drooping. He stroked his unshaven chin distractedly and yawned.

"I'm tired," he said.

The secretary remained standing in the same spot for several moments, stooped, bony-shouldered, snorting and gaping and watching his employer and master. He started to rub his nose and lift one instep, but suddenly the tears flowed once again from the eyes of this poor scholar. He dispensed with all the quirks that distinguished him from others, and again placed a bony hand with its backward-bending thumb over his face.

"Is there something else, Jón?" said Arnas Arnæus.

Jón Guðmundsson from Grindavík sobbed:

"My lord has no friends."

— **3** —

Around midmorning, when the vegetable seller behind the house had grown hoarse from shouting and the brushmaker had become quite drunk and the knackerish knife-grinder was busy displaying his grindstone at people's doors, a certain man came strolling down the streets of Copenhagen. He was wearing his tattered walking-jacket, an aged top hat, and shriveled shoes, and he loped along with a peculiarly rhythmed, austere stride. His facial expression was so remote from its environs that the city and its spires, its eddies of humanity, and its contemporaneity all seemed to have disappeared within it. He looked upon neither the dead nor the living, so insignificant and hallucinatory to him was this city that had become his home only by chance.

"There goes that crazy Herr Grindevigen," whispered his neighbors to one another as he passed by.

The gentleman stopped at a side street near the canal and looked around to make sure he was headed in the right direction, then he passed through a gate, traversed a courtyard, and followed a dim passageway until he found at the ground floor of a house the door he was looking for, which he rapped on several times. For a long time not a sound of life emerged from within, but the Grindavíkian continued knocking on the door and trying to open it, until he lost his patience and shouted through the keyhole:

"You can go on pretending to be asleep, you fox, but I know you're awake!"

The house's occupant wasted no time in opening the door after hearing this voice. It was drab within and the strong stenches of decay and fermentation came wafting through the doorway.

"What, shark meat, it can't be anything but," said the Grindavíkian, and he snorted and rubbed his nose, thinking he had caught a whiff of the fragrance of the most succulent of Icelandic delicacies, which is eaten only after it's been buried in the ground for twelve years, or even better, for thirteen.

The master of the house stood in the doorway in a filthy nightshirt, and he pulled the visitor in through the threshold and kissed him carefully, then spat. The scholar from Grindavík wiped away the kiss with his coat sleeve and walked inside without removing his top hat. His host struck a match and lit a candle, barely illuminating the room. In one corner was a cot covered with an Icelandic sheepskin, before it a large chamber pot. One of the distinguishing features of this particular householder was that he never left his belongings out for all to see, but kept them packed up in sacks and bags. On the floor was a puddle so large that one could just as well call it a flood, and at first the Grindavíkian suspected that its source was the chamber pot. However, when he looked more closely in the half-light he saw that this was not the case—its source was actually closer to the opposite wall, beneath an oaken table upon which lay the drenched body of a drowned man, water dripping from him everywhere, especially from both ends. Off one end of the tabletop hung the man's head and its shock of wet hair, off the other dangled his feet, in boots that had apparently been full to the brim when the corpse was dragged here. No matter how much the visitor had previously suffered similar outrages, and no matter what sort of relentless sermon he had conjured up to admonish Jón Marteinsson, it went now as it always did: the gallows bird had caught him by surprise.

"Wha-what are you doing with this corpse?" asked Grindvicensis, instinctively removing his top hat out of respect for the dead.

Jón Marteinsson laid a finger to his lips to signal that they should speak quietly, then carefully locked the doors.

"I'm planning to eat it," he whispered.

The scholar from Grindavík shuddered and stared tremblingly at the householder.

"And here I thought it was shark, only to find it's corpse-rot," he said, and he snorted loudly as his trembling increased with agitation. "You must open your doors!"

"Don't carry on that way, my boy," said Jón Marteinsson. "Do you think it's that poor devil's corpse that smells, when I dragged him up just this morning at dawn—still warm? Quite the contrary: if you smell something, it's probably my sweaty feet."

"What do you think you're doing pulling dead people out of the canal?" asked the visitor.

"Aw, it was so pitiful to see him lying there dead—he's one of our countrymen," said Jón Marteinsson, and he lay back down upon his cot. "To tell you the truth, I hate being wakened so early—it makes my flesh crawl. What do you want?"

"Are you telling me that this is our countryman? Do you think you can just steal dead men and go right back to sleep?"

"Take him then," said Jón Marteinsson. "Take him with you if you want. Take him wherever you want. Take him to the devil."

Grindvicensis took the candle, approached the corpse, and held the light up to it. It was of a tall, thin man, middle-aged and graying, wearing decently tailored clothing and good boots. The corpse's face had a feeble expression like a sailor drowned at sea, the eyelids half-open in the head as it hung there off the end of the table, revealing only the whites of its eyes. Water dripped steadily from the corpse's nose and mouth onto the floor.

The Grindavíkian gaped several times, snorted, rubbed his nose with the index finger of his free hand and scratched his left calf with his right instep, then his right calf with his left instep.

"Magnús from Bræðratunga," he said. "How did he wind up here dead?"

"This man is hosting a banquet, can't you see that?" said Jón Marteinsson. "He won his lawsuit yesterday, the poor beggar, and went to a tavern to celebrate."

"Good, good," said the gaping Grindavíkian. "You've drowned him."

"I helped him win his lawsuit in life, and dragged him up in death," said Jón Marteinsson. "Can anyone do more for his countryman?"

"A true devil is fiendish to all, including those whom he pretends to help," said the Grindavíkian. "First you pushed him in."

"You don't say," said Jón Marteinsson. "And it was about time I did poor Árni a little favor. Now Snæfríður Björnsdóttir is a widow, so Árni can divorce Gilitrutt* and marry Snæfríður and they can go live in Bræðratunga, which she now lawfully inherits—all through my agency."

"Damn you, double damn you, and damn you forever for throwing your lot in with the Danes in a lawsuit against your countryman and patron, and for getting him convicted, which will surely make him the laughingstock of the rabble!"

"Pff, I'll get right to work on the Supreme Court appeal if Árni wants me to," said Jón Marteinsson. "But only if you've got enough money for beer, which of course you never do. Hey—see if there's anything in the corpse's pockets."

"Go ask the Company for beer. Go ask the Swedes," said the Grindavíkian. "Or maybe you think you're the only one in this whole city who wants beer? You could probably get me to do a lot of abominable things, but I would never rob the dead for you."

"If he's hiding any coins, he owes them to me. Whatever small amount of honor there is that might cling to this corpse's name was restituted by me, due to my long acta, petitiones, and appellationes—"* and with these words Jón Marteinsson jumped up from his cot and went over to search the corpse. "Do you think I have any respect for this man's corpse, when in the life of the living he allowed others to deprive him of both his honor and his estate?"

"The least I could expect from a murderer would be for him to refrain from speaking cruelly of the man he has murdered," said the Grindavíkian. "Such a thing was unheard of in the sagas. Not even the villains spoke cruelly of the men they killed. And even though this man was my master's opponent in the life of the living, you'll never hear me say a disrespectful word about soulless flesh. Requiescas, I say, quisquis es, in pace, amen.* But finally I come to the matter at hand: what have you done with the book *Scaldica Maiora*, which you stole from my lord's bibliothèque?"

"The *Skálda*," said Jón Marteinsson. "Did you misplace it?"

"My master knows only too well that there's no one to blame but you," said the Grindavíkian.

"No sane man would ever steal that book. If anyone were found with it he'd be arrested," said Jón Marteinsson.

"What wouldn't Satan steal to sell to the Swedes?" said the Grindavíkian.

"My dear Árni's been naive for so long: he thought he could put food on the Icelanders' tables by indicting the Company; he thought he could redeem Snæfríður Iceland's sun by defaming her beloved; he thought he could save the honor of his fatherland by duping starved dimwits in Iceland out of the few books they still had that hadn't gone rotten, and by piling them together here in Copenhagen in a place where they're in serious danger of burning up altogether in one night. And now he thinks the Swedes aren't as clever as he is. Let me tell you something: they are far more clever than he is, so clever that no power on earth will ever convince them that that collection of lice-ridden beggars on that shithole up north who call themselves Icelanders, and who will all be dead in a very short time, God be praised, wrote sagas. I know Árni impugns me for not gathering up and shoving into his bag every single scrap I can find. But can't he take some comfort in having acquired the best of a bad lot of books? All I did was sell von Oxenstirna and du Bertelskiold some totally useless old rubbish; de la Rosenquist, however, has asked me for a genealogical table so he can trace his family back to trolls."

"Even so, you'll be labeled the *Skálda*-thief no matter whether the scholars in Lund call it an old West Gotlandic text—and now tell me truthfully where you've hidden the book or I shall write to a man west in Arnarfjörður who is skilled in the handling of characteres."

"That'll just get you burned," said Jón Marteinsson.

By the time the story reached this point, he had found neither more nor less than the better part of two rixdollars on the corpse, and, thinking he would undoubtedly find more, he placed the coins on the windowsill beneath the carefully drawn curtains, and began trying to pull off the deceased's boots. The Grindavíkian realized, as he had realized many times before, that words meant very little to Jón Marteinsson, so he let the matter drop and stood there gaping and staring.

When Jón Marteinsson completed his task he started putting on assorted pieces of clothing, then combed strong-smelling fat through his hair in place of washing it. Finally he put on a cloak that most resembled an ancient bishop's frock in its expansiveness. He stuck Magnús from Bræðratunga's boots into the cloak's two pockets. Next he brought out his hat. Upon it were several half-dried spots of grime that he spat on and rubbed with his sleeve, then he smoothed out the worst of the crown's dents and placed it upon his head. The man had a kind of crib-shaped mouth that enabled him to suck on his upper lip with his lower one, and since his upper gums had been toothless for many years his chin was all the more inclined toward kissing the spike of his nose, which had flattened with age. The corners of his mouth sunk down below his cheeks on either side of his chin. His eyes, however, were incredibly lustrous and the man needed only a few moments' sleep in order for their gleam to be restored. He always spoke in a typically Icelandic tone of voice: a feeble, discontented whine.

"Aren't you going to do something about the corpse, man?" said the Grindavíkian, as Jón Marteinsson locked the door behind them.

"There's no rush," he said, "he'll still be lying there by the time we get back. The living shall drink. If I remember I'll tell them tonight that I've found an Icelander in the canal—they'll hardly be in any hurry to bury him."

This being said, the two men went for a drink.

— 4 —

In their books scholars have recorded some of the diverse portents that occurred in Iceland prior to the great smallpox epidemic. Foremost amongst these must be reckoned the hunger and famine that affected all corners of the land, causing tremendous loss of life, especially amongst the poor. Widespread shortage of fishing line. In addition, unusually high incidences of robbery and thievery, along with incest and earthquakes in the southern part of the country. Various rare phenomena as well. In Eyrarbakki an eighty-year-old woman married a twenty-year-old man the autumn before the epidemic, and in the spring she wanted to divorce him, impotentiae causa.* On the seventeenth of May seven suns were seen. That same spring, in Bakkakot in Skorradalur, a ewe gave birth to a misshapen lamb: it had a pig's head and a pig's bristles, its upper jawbones were missing beneath its eye sockets, and its tongue hung out quite some distance over its lower jawbones, which appeared to be disattached from its skull. It had nothing at all resembling eyes. Its ears were long like a hunting dog's, and hanging from the front part of its skull was a little ewe's teat with a hole in it. When it was born the lamb was heard to speak clearly, saying these words: "The devil has his claws in the children of the faithless." News came from Kirkjubæjarklaustur the winter before the epidemic that one evening the cloister steward and another man walking with him through the churchyard heard a howling beneath their feet. Uproar in the air in Kjalarnes. Fished up from the sea in Skagafjörður was a skate so odd that it started wailing and howling as soon as they brought it on board, and even after they had cut it up on shore each and every piece screamed and howled in the same way. As if that was not enough, after the pieces had been brought home each piece continued howling and screaming in its own way, so finally they all had to be thrown back into the sea. Men in the sky. And finally, mention must be made of the egg a hen laid at Fjall in Skeið. The egg was clearly inscribed with a certain dark pattern, apparently the mark of Saturn in reverse, meaning "Omnium rerum vicissitudo veniet."*

Thirty years had passed since the last outbreak of smallpox and fifty years since the outbreak preceding that when the great smallpox epidemic hit the country.* Most of the Icelanders who lived into their thirties were marked by the disease: the hands or feet of many were withered, some had bulging eyeballs, others disfigured faces or scalps. Besides this the majority of people bore the scars of one or another of the chronic illnesses affecting the population: rickets left people doubled over and crippled, their limbs askew; the lepers were ulcerous and nodous; hydatids distended the abdomens of others. Many could barely keep themselves going, having suffered the ravages of consumption. Due to prolonged famine people's growth was

so stunted that anyone who reached a decent height became fodder
for folktales. Such giants were not only considered the equals of
Gunnar of Hlíðarendi and other ancient Icelanders, but were also
thought to possess strength to match that of the Negroes sometimes
found aboard the Danish ships.

The pox overwhelmed these folk once again, and now with such
an unimaginable vehemence that nothing but the Black Death could
have equaled it. The disease came out on a merchantman that had
arrived in Eyrarbakki near the start of the moving days in the spring,
and within one week three tenant farms in that district were laid
waste. On a fourth farm all that survived was a seven-year-old child,
and the cows were no longer milked. After ten days forty people in
that poor district had lost their lives.

The decimation continued on in this way. Sometimes thirty
people at a time were buried in the tiny churchyards. Heavily popu-
lated parishes recorded losses of two hundred or more people. The
clerical ranks were hit so hard that divine services were no longer
held. Many a married couple went hand in hand to the same grave,
some lost all of their children at once, and in one particular case, the
only surviving member of a very large family was the half-wit. Many
became phrenetic or demented. Most were called away before they
reached the age of fifty—the most youthful, healthy, and promising
folk—while the aged and decrepit lived on. Great numbers lost their
sight or hearing, others were bedridden for a long time afterward.
The outbreak deprived the episcopal seat at Skálholt of its head and
the head of its crown, when the bishop, that shining witness to the
faith and friend to the poor, and his beloved wife, this country's radiant light of piety and beneficence, passed away just one week apart
and were laid together in one grave.

This was two years after His Royal Majesty sent hither his special
envoy, with the full authority to take whatever steps were necessary
to alleviate the people's suffering. When Arnas Arnæus returned to
Copenhagen he was met with the news that our then-reigning Highness lay upon his bier, and that the magnates were making prepara-
tions to crown the new king. The commoners were treated to soup
and steak, beer and red wine, in the square before the palace on the

day of coronation. It was the dawn of a new age in Denmark. The goodwill toward Icelanders that Arnæus, due to his long acquaintance with the court, had been able to awaken in the heart of His Highness was now benumbed along with Denmark's sleeping king. Arnæus's reports concerning conditions in Iceland, along with his proposals for the improvement of trade, industry, the judiciary, and the country's government, were received unenthusiastically by the Chancery, and it was doubtful whether they would ever be given a reading; everyone knew that the new king's thoughts were directed toward more valorous deeds than looking after the Icelanders. It would soon be necessary to renew the struggle against the Swedes. The functionaries gave little thought to anything but remaining in their posts after the crowning of the new king. In any case, it had never been of great advantage to advancement, and hence was not much of a temptation for the finest men in Denmark, to trouble oneself concerning that outpost of the Danish realm, that remote ulcer in the shape of a country whose name alone, Iceland, could nauseate any man in Copenhagen, even if everyone knew that from that country ran the whale oil that fed the lamps of their city.

Concerning the Icelanders there is this to say: although the members of the country's criminal class might have been Arnæus's friends, with one or two exceptions, including some of those whose brands he had invalidated, and although many Icelandic paupers rejoiced at the compensation he had forced the merchants to pay for their shoddy flour and at the grain supplements he had been able to importune from the crown, and although huge numbers of them were grateful to him for his willingness to carry to His Most Merciful Heart their petitions for fishing line, pig iron, and sacramental wine, not to mention more lenient taxes, which the governor had been shoving under his seat for seven years, there was scarcely less animosity directed toward Arnæus by the gentry in his fatherland than there had ever been at any time in Denmark. In addition, whereas the merchants had brought Magnús Sigurðsson from Bræðratunga to Copenhagen and financially supported his lawsuit for two years in order to get back at Arnæus, there now came word that the Icelandic bailiffs themselves were preparing litigation against him, with the goal of having the verdicts he handed down at Öxará, the so-called Commissarial Verdicts, overturned, thereby allowing them to recover the property that had been confiscated and vindicate the honor that had been defamed by the very same judge.

This bookman, who had let himself be lured away from his books for a time and who had for the sake of righteousness heeded the call to become the savior of his native country, now reaped what had once been sown, the reward of the eternal dolorous knight. The man who heeds this call never gains another opportunity to return to the books that are his entire world. And thus on the morning when he received news of the disappearance of the crown of all his books, all he could do was let himself sink back down, pale with insomnia, and say these words:

"I'm tired."

He sat there for a long time after the Grindavíkian had gone, and finally started to doze off. He shook himself awake and stood up. He hadn't undressed since leaving the queen's banquet, but now he washed and tidied himself and changed his clothes. He bade his coachman prepare his carriage, and then they drove away.

— 5 —

Arnæus acted as arbitrator in countless cases involving Icelanders, and thus he often visited the Chancery in order to keep informed of current events.

The statesman in charge of Icelandic affairs had sent for a barber to come to his office in the Chancery, and several times during his shave he raised himself up to eat fruit preserves from a crock standing upon his desk amidst the piles of reports on floggings, brandings, and hangings that had been sent to him from Iceland. The reek of coiffeur's unguents filled the room.

When the Professor Antiquitatum Danicarum opened the door, the statesman gave him a sidelong glance out from under the razor, said "My lord" in German or Low German, and motioned for the visitor to take a seat. Then he said in Danish: "I hear that there are plenty of pretty girls out in Iceland."

"That is so, your grace," said Arnas Arnæus.

"But they supposedly smell like whale oil beneath their clothing," said the supervisor of Icelandic affairs.

"That I have never heard," said Arnas Arnæus, and he took out a stubby clay pipe.

"Item, I've read that there's not a single virgin to be found in your country," said the statesman.

"Where might you have read this?" asked the Professor Antiquitatum.

"The good auctor Blefken says this."

"I wonder if the good auctor might not have misread his sources," said Arnæus. "The best auctores tell us that Icelandic girls remain chaste virgins up until they've had their seventh child, Your Benevolence."

The statesman lay dead still and spoke not a word as the barber shaved his throat. When this procedure was finished he sat up in his seat, not to eat preserves, but instead to express his sincere indignation at the outcome of a rotten case:

"Though we two have not had the good fortune to come to terms in most matters concerning Iceland, there's no making a secret of it: I do not understand how any righteous court can condemn an esteemed nobleman like yourself for his contacts with shameless persons. Das ist eine Schweinerei.* I have here the documents from a case prosecuted the year before last involving an Icelandic girl in Keblevig who was raped by two Germans. When the Germans were sentenced by the regent to fines and flogging, the girl's mother burst into tears and begged God to let fire and blood rain down over the judge."

Arnas Arnæus had lit his pipe.

"In my opinion," asserted the statesman, as the barber continued his work, "if honorable noblemen are not allowed to have mistresses, what are our lives worth? Surely no one can expect a man to be in love with his wife. My lord is well-versed in classicis* and therefore knows better than I that such a thing was unheard of amongst the ancients—they took wives out of duty, mistresses out of necessity, and boys for their pleasure."

The Professor Antiquitatum Danicarum leaned back contentedly

in his chair, his facial expression tranquil as he watched the smoke
rising from his pipe—"Oh, I'm not so sure about that—what does
the barber have to say?"

"As beseems a simple townsman, the barber doesn't care for irregu-
larity," said the statesman. "Just before my lord came through the
door he was telling me that early this morning our Most Gracious
Lord happened to be in that infamous house, the Golden Lion,
where he and his entourage of cavaliers were engaged in some sort of
coarse commerce that ended in nothing less than a scuffle with the
watchmen."

"I would never utter such words in the presence of two witnesses,"
said the barber, "but since it pleased Your Excellency to ask me the
news, and since it so happened that I had just come from the baron's,
and sitting there were two drunk lieutenant-generals who'd been present in a certain unnamed house, and who'd joined forces with our
Grace against the master of the watch, then, Lord forgive me—I who
merely attend to the lords and ladies, how could my ears have helped
but learn German?"

"The barber may apply the perfume and pomade," said the statesman.

The man being addressed immediately fell silent and bowed quite
elegantly, then started opening small boxes of pomade and gave his
perfume atomizers several test sprays. Arnæus sat quietly in his chair
and smoked enthusiastically while the barber sprayed and anointed
the statesman's head.

"By the way," he said quite casually as he gazed at his smoke: "Did
the shipment of fishing line make it onto the Hólmship, like we discussed last time?"

"Why should the king always have to be supplying these people
with more and more cord? Lying there in front of you is yet another
petition for cord. What are these people doing with all that cord?"

"Yes, I've heard that the petition to the king that I managed to get
back from Gyldenløve two years ago, after he'd been napping on it
for seven years, has finally been rejected here."

"It's of no concern to us whether the Icelanders dredge up more
fish than we have use for. When we recommence the war with the
Swedes they'll get more cord; and hooks as well."

"Your Benevolence would rather have the king send these people grain supplements than allow them to fish?"

"I never said that," said the statesman. "In my opinion what we have always needed in Iceland is a beneficent despot, to see to it that the underhanded gang of tramps that's forever roaming about the country would disappear once and for all, so that those few men possessed of any sort of pluck might be untroubled by thieves and beggars in doing their jobs: pulling in the fish that the Company needs now and then and smelting the oil that Copenhagen must have."

"May I convey the opinion of your Benevolence to the Alþingi?"

"You may speak as poorly of us to the Icelanders as you wish, my lord. It matters not one whit what Icelanders say or think. No one knows better than you yourself, my lord, that the Icelanders are plebeians. May I offer your Excellency some preserves?"

"I thank your Benevolence," said Arnas Arnæus. "But if my people are plebeians, what good are preserves going to do me?"

"No man sent by the king has ever defamed the honor of this folk as much as you have, my lord."

"I endeavored to make sure that the Icelanders are treated fairly and justly."

"Oh, do you think it matters what laws are used to adjudge the Icelanders? The Chancery has proof that this is a degenerate race: all of its better men in the old days killed each other off, until there was nothing left but this collection of beggars, thieves, lepers, lice-infested nobodies, and drunkards."

Arnæus continued smoking unconcernedly and mumbled several words in Latin, his voice low, like someone absentmindedly quoting poetry: "Non facile emergunt quorum virtutibus obstat res angusta domi."*

"Yes, I know, there's not a single poor excuse for a priest in Iceland who doesn't know his Donatus* backward and forward, quoting the classics day and night, besmirching petitions to His Majesty with so much out-of-place pedantry that it's a damned job to get to the bottom of it all, and then it turns out that all they really want is cord. In my view it's a vice for a cordless man to know Latin. Which brings me back to what I wanted to say in the first place: there were still a few people in Iceland who could be reckoned men, and you deprived them of their honor; people like old, honorable Eydalín, who was loyal to his king—you pounced on him in his old age and sent him to his grave an ignominious pleb."

"It's true—one result of my trip was that a number of regal Icelanders lost their honor; but defenseless men recovered theirs. If the folk there could hold on to the fruits of this victory, their lives would be more secure against the authorities in the future."

"All the same, you were not entirely satisfied, my lord. To top it all off you took it upon yourself to use all sorts of litigious pretexts to chase after the island's very own benefactors, the Iceland merchants, those honorable Danish citizens and honest men who place themselves in great mortal danger by transporting provisions to these people—so many of them perish out on the dreadful sea surrounding that miserable land. This slanderous rumor starts making the rounds, instigated primarily by you, that the Iceland trade should be made to hand over part of its profit. Forgive me, my lord, though we who know best are of a different opinion. We Danes have always been charitable in our trading operations with Iceland. And when our deceased Highness monopolized trade with the island it was only in order to prevent outsiders from extorting those pitiable people."

As the statesman spoke the barber continued to massage his face with one pomade after another, while his guest sat there quite contentedly, continuing to gaze at the smoky output of his pipe.

"It's true," he said finally, in his calm, almost entirely lackluster voice, "the tariffs set by the Hamburg merchants were never considered favorable in Iceland in the old days. But well-informed men reckon that things have in fact worsened since then, under both the Hørmangar and the Helsingør trade leagues as well as under the Company. And as far as monsieur's colleagues and partners in the Iceland trade are concerned, there's no need to bemoan their lot since they still enjoy the support of the Icelanders whom they rate most highly."

"We don't have any particular Icelanders in our employ or service beyond any others; we do, however, take pains to be faithful servants and true benefactors to the whole island."

"Hm," said Arnas Arnæus. "Jón Marteinsson certainly feels quite well these days."

"Joen Mortensen," said the statesman. "I don't recognize the name."

"The Danes claim not to know him when he's named," said Arnas Arnæus. "But he is the only Icelander whose door they can find. Representatives of several other countries also know the way to his door."

"There are no Danish books that say that the Icelanders are descended from traitors and pirates, at least the ones who aren't descended from Irish slaves—this comes from your own books," said the statesman, and he positioned himself better under the barber's hands. "By the way, what is your business here, my lord?"

"I've been asked to become Iceland's governor," said Arnas Arnæus.

"Wigmaker!" yelled the statesman as he tried clumsily to get up from his chair. "Enough! Take your grime away from me!—it stinks! Get out! What are you waiting for? Whom are you spying for?"

The barber was terrified and hurriedly attempted to towel off the statesman's face and clear away his pomade boxes, bowing repeatedly in the meantime, saying that he was a simple man who neither heard nor saw anything, and even if he did hear or see anything he understood nothing. After he backed out of the room, the statesman rose from his seat, turned toward the calm and recalcitrant master of Danish antiquities, and expressed his shock at the news his guest had delivered:

"What was that you were saying, monsieur?"

"I don't think I was saying anything of particular interest," said Arnas Arnæus. "Unless I might have said something when we were talking about Jón Marteinsson, the Iceland merchants' litigator, the great conqueror."

"What were you saying about a governor? Who's supposed to be governor where and for whom?"

"Your Benevolence knows much more about all of this than I do," said Arnas Arnæus.

"I know nothing!" yelled the statesman, who was standing in the middle of the room.

When it looked likely that there was no possible way that Arnas Arnæus was going to add anything, the highly placed gentleman grew all the more curious and gesticulated violently in self-pitying surrender.

"I know nothing," he repeated. "We here in the Chancery are always kept in the dark. Everything's taken care of by the Council of the Crown or by the Germans on the Council of War; or else by the queen in her bedchamber. We don't even get paid. I spend fifteen to sixteen hundred rixdollars a year for my maintenance, and in three years I haven't received a single two-shilling piece from the king. They cheat us; they don't talk to us; all sorts of schemes are going on behind our backs here in the city; and I could very well believe that we'll wake up one morning only to discover that that beast of a king has sold us."

"As I'm sure your Benevolence knows, our Highness has tried many times to sell or to pawn the oft-mentioned island of Iceland," said Arnas Arnæus. "Twice before in just over a decade, for example, he sent a legate to discuss the same matter with the king of England, as one can read in the court documents. The wealthy merchant from Hamburg, Uffelen, informed me yesterday that it has pleased our Grace's Most Clement Heart to put that country, if it can even be called that, up for sale once again."

At this news the statesman slumped back down into his chair, stared stiffly ahead, and turned pale. Finally he stammered, from somewhere within his gloom:

"This is caprice, this is treachery, this is a wicked deed."

Arnas Arnæus continued to smoke. Finally the statesman was able to summon the strength of will to stand up, and he fetched a bottle and glasses from a cupboard and poured wine for himself and his guest. After taking a drink he said:

"Permit me to impugn the king's right to sell the country behind the backs of those of us in the Chancery. That would amount to stealing the country; and not only from the Chancery, but also from the Company. What does the Ministry of Finance have to say about this? Or Gyldenløve, the governor of Iceland?"

"Your Benevolence must surely be aware," said Arnas Arnæus, "that after the papacy was defeated in Iceland and replaced by Lutheranism, the king became the owner of all church property in his kingdom; thus all of the greatest estates in Iceland, in addition to thousands of smaller farmsteads, have come under his control. Just one more command from him and he would also own whatever lands are left. What our Most Benign Grace does with his estates is entirely up to him. And would it not significantly lighten the load resting upon the High Chancery if this miserable land were taken off its conscience? The Iceland merchants would no longer perish on the arduous sea voyage. The Company would be relieved of a great deal of its burdens in providing charity to my needy folk."

The statesman was beginning to rage. Now he stood right before his guest, shook a quivering fist in his face, and said:

"This is another one of your damned deceptions; false; a scheme; a plot; you've duped the king; there's not a single Danish counselor or dignitary who would advise the king to sell Iceland, for the simple reason that no matter how high a price he could get for it this once, he could make much more profit from it in the long run through fair trading practices."

"We must first attend to our most pressing needs," said Arnas Arnæus. "The costume balls must go on; this costs money. An excellent costume ball gulps down all the revenues gathered in one year from all the Icelandic cloisters, your Benevolence. In addition, our Grace must make war upon the Swedes in order to increase Denmark's renown; this also costs money."

"And the Icelanders themselves," gasped the statesman, somewhere between rage and terror, "what do they have to say?"

"Icelanders," said Arnæus. "Who wants the opinion of an ignominious folk? Their one and only task is to retain their stories in memory until a better day."

"Your Excellency must excuse me," said the statesman in conclusion, "but urgent business calls me out into the city. I have, to wit, come into possession of a new mistress. Would my lord perhaps like to ride with me?"

Arnas Arnæus had stood up, and had stopped smoking.

"My carriage is also waiting outside," he said.

"By the way, with regard to the shipment of fishing line on the Hólmship," said the statesman, as he put on his cloak, "I shall look into the matter. The Chancery has always been willing to take into consideration the Icelanders' requests for pig iron, sacramental wine, and cord. It might even be possible to get more ships to sail this year than last."

— 6 —

In the spring following the epidemic the Alþingi was so poorly attended that the court cases were left unadjudged. From many districts not a single man came to the assembly. It became necessary to postpone the executions of criminals, since their Christian executioners had also been swept away by the sudden terror of the pox, and the offers made by crazed youths to behead the men and drown the women for their own amusement were not taken seriously there by the river that takes its name from the ax of justice. One woman from the Múli district out east was done away with, however, a certain Hallfríður who had had a child by a man named Ólafur who had been beheaded the year before, but no others from the same district had shown up except for the man who had escorted the woman to the assembly, and he absolutely refused to take her all the way back to the opposite end of the country alive, over so many lakes and rivers. Prudent men solved his problem by drowning the woman in Drekkingarhylur.

Now the story turns back to old Jón Hreggviðsson, sitting at home at his farm on Rein. It was no great wonder, considering the current circumstances, that he was in no hurry to obtain a new Supreme Court appeal as he'd been ordered to do by the Commissarial Court. Other things occupied his mind. Those blundering authorities who still showed signs of life also had other matters besides Jón Hreggviðsson to attend to for the time being. Seasons passed. Finally, however, when the decimation slackened and the countryfolk's pain was momentarily alleviated, the farmer heard rumor that the authorities who had replaced their fallen comrades hadn't completely forgotten his old case. No one in the country doubted that the commissary's mission had been of a peculiar nature:

he'd been made the judge of judges, and his verdicts could not be appealed. Those whom he convicted had no hope whatsoever of being exonerated. Those whom he exonerated were to suffer no further harm. Things proceeded in such a way that by the time his work was concluded it was more obvious who had fallen than who had been redeemed. The redeemed had disappeared. The fact that they had been freed was evidenced nowhere. The man who had lowered the high to raise the low was accorded not a single public show of gratitude. People did, however, bemoan the repudiation and fall of Magistrate Eydalín.

At the conclusion of the Commissarial Court convened at Öxará during the spring before the epidemic, Jón Hreggviðsson was the only man who returned home less sure of his fate, since he'd been both acquitted and convicted at the same time. His case was without a doubt the basis for one of the heaviest charges made against Eydalín and nothing else played such a significant role in the magistrate's repudiation than the death sentence he had passed ages ago against this man, based on evidence that could be considered dubious at best. On the other hand, there was not a single shred of positive evidence to support the charges made by the commissary against Eydalín, that he had, sixteen years ago, made an arrangement with Jón Hreggviðsson not to make public the Supreme Court appeal that he'd brought home with him from Copenhagen. And because there were no witnesses to testify to this arrangement, Christ's farmer had been ordered to procure a new Supreme Court appeal so that his case could be reopened and retried.

After Eydalín had fallen and the pox had sheared the see of Skálholt of its adornment and honor by putting to rest the bishop and his wife, the magistrate's daughter, and after a number of other noblemen who were in any position to prosecute him further had disappeared, Jón Hreggviðsson felt that there were few remaining who would blame him if he were to take his time in procuring a new appeal. As it happened, however, things didn't turn out quite as the farmer expected.

The second spring after the epidemic an assembly was held at Öxará, and this time enough manpower was present to facilitate the execution of criminals and the drafting of a new petition to the king. The country's high court was presided over by Jón Eyjólfsson, vice-magistrate and bailiff, as well as the regent Beyer from Bessastaðir.

The assembly was drawing to a close and there was still no sign that old lawsuits would be reviewed this session. The spring was cruel and cold; apathy and reluctance characterized the few members of the court who had taken the trouble of riding to the assembly over the half-dead countryside, throughout which the surviving remnants of stricken humanity managed to totter along, dizzied from the force of the blow. But one night toward the end of the assembly, after the members of the court had crawled under their sheepskins, a visitor on horseback arrived at Þingvellir. It was a woman. Her entourage, consisting of three grooms and a good number of horses, had ridden in across the plain from the east, from Kaldidalur, the natural boundary between the country's quarters. The pilgrimess dismounted near the regent's booth and went straight in to meet Beyer, the governor's proxy. She was there only a short time before a servant was sent to wake the vice-magistrate and escort him back to the regent's booth. Whatever happened at this meeting was never discussed with outsiders, and the visitor rode away from Þingvellir a short time later.

One other event occurred that night: two of the vice-magistrate's servants were woken and sent with papers west to Skagi to find the farmer Jón Hreggviðsson from Rein and to bring him to the assembly.

It was a rather beggarly set of authorities that reinstated the charges against Christ's tenant two days later at that dreary place, Þingvellir by Öxará. Even the Danish proxy's booth was a shambles, as if the royal power no longer gave any thought to protecting its image of authoritarian splendor against Iceland's storms of wind and rain, which were so inseparable from its folk, crooked and frostbitten pieces of timberwood in the shape of humans. Iceland's weather was a mill that left nothing unpulverized but for the country's basalt peaks. It uprooted and demolished all human works, wiping away not only their color but also their form. The florid bargeboards of the royal lodging were either splintered or torn off, anything iron corroded, the door thin and warped, the windowpanes cracked, the window shutters wrenched off their hinges, the king's seal for the most part washed away. And the governor's Danish proxy, the regent Beyer, was completely drunk almost every day throughout the course of the assembly.

The high court was convened in the dilapidated cottage that had once been called a courthouse. Its roof had been torn off, giving wind and rain free range throughout the hall. Mire that had run from the turf walls onto the rotten floorplanks hadn't been mucked out. Inward along the floorboards hobbled Jón Hreggviðsson from Rein, gray-haired, groaning, and puffing.

The vice-magistrate Jón Eyjólfsson asked how it came about that he had not heeded the duty prescribed to him by the Especial Royal Judiciary here at Öxará, that he appeal his case to the Supreme Court.

Jón Hreggviðsson removed his knitted cap, revealing his white hair to the bench. He stood bowed and humble before his judges, not presuming to look up at them, said that he was an old man, weak-eyed and eared and laid up by rheumatism; whatever sense he'd possessed as a youth was by now completely benumbed. He begged, due to his inability to defend himself, to be assigned an advocate. His request was denied but his response registered. They then moved hastily on to the next case, since it was now the final day of the assembly and it was urgent that the proceedings be concluded as quickly as possible before the judges became too drunk, as they usually did around nones. Jón Hreggviðsson felt fairly sure that nothing more would be done in his case at this assembly, so he took his jade and rode north toward Leggjabrjótur and home. When the judges did indeed find time to return to his case he was nowhere to be found. A ruling in his case was called for in his absence, without further argument, and the verdict issued was worded as follows: whereas this man Jón is renowned for his boorish, wicked, and dishonest behavior, and whereas he, accused of murder, has failed to comply with the stipulations set down in the letter of safe-conduct issued by His Royal Majesty and in the travel pass issued by the king's military, and has likewise neglected to publish the old Supreme Court appeal, and finally has recalcitrantly refused to procure a new appeal as

ordered by the Commissarial Court, but instead has abandoned the
assembly, showing his unwillingness to fulfill his obligation to wait
and defend himself in his case, the said Jón Hreggviðsson is hereby to
be lawfully arrested and placed under the custody of the bailiff in
Þverá and put aboard ship and transported, at the first opportunity
this summer, to the Bremerholm workhouse, there to spend his days
in penal servitude to the castle commandant; in addition, half of his
property is hereby forfeited to His Royal Majesty.

— 7 —

One day Jón Hreggviðsson, dressed only in his underclothes, was
standing out in the homefield at Rein mowing, when two men came
riding in toward him over the unmown grass. The farmer stopped
and stormed toward them, brandishing his scythe and threatening
them with murder for trampling down the grass. His ferocious dog
followed suit. The men were unmoved, and informed the farmer that
they'd been sent by the bailiff in Skagi to arrest him. He shoved the
scythe blade-up into the grass, walked over to them, stuck his fists
together, and proffered his wrists.

"I'm ready," he said.

They said that they wouldn't be shackling him for the time being.

"What're you waiting for?" he asked, annoyed at the typical Icelandic sluggishness that made them act as if they had nothing better
to do than waste the day in his meadow.

"You want to go dressed like that?" they said.

"That's my business," he said. "Which horse do I ride?"

"Don't you want to say good-bye to your family?" they said.

"What's it to you?" he said. "Let's go!"

This was a completely different man than the one who had stood
bent and shaking, sighing heavily and on the verge of tears, before his
judges at the Alþingi.

He jumped up onto the spare horse that they'd brought, and his
dog bit at the horse's hock.

"There will be no abductions today," announced the man in

charge—they would ride to the farmhouse and report their errand to the farmer's kinsmen.

The farm was nestled up against the foot of the mountain, its windows as sprightly as eyes peering out from the thick, grass-grown turf walls, its doors low enough that folk had to stoop to go in or out, a paved footpath out front. Smoke reeked from the chimney. His wife was long since dead. The half-wit was nowhere to be seen—people believed that the farmer, its father, had killed it. The leprous sisters had also passed away, leaving no one on the farm to praise God. The farmer had had another daughter to replace the one whom he'd found lying on her bier when he returned from abroad, and this nearly nubile girl came out from the kitchen and stood upon the footpath; she was grimy with soot and scarred from the pox, dark-lashed and dark-browed with her father's gleam in her black eyes, barefoot and sunburnt and clad in a short smock of wadmal, her knees fat. Her smock was decorated with ash, specks of manure, and gnarls of peat.

The men said: "We've been ordered to take your father into custody and to put him aboard ship in Ólafsvík."

The dog had grown even more agitated—it bristled and yelped and pissed on the wall.

"I'd rather see you dead," said the girl. "Can't you see how old this man is? Look at his white hair."

"Shut up, girl," said Jón Hreggviðsson.

"Papa," she said. "Don't you want to put on your trousers?"

"No," he said. "But bring me some cord."

She knew where he kept a small amount of fishing line hidden, and returned in a moment with a decent-sized hank of this precious commodity. The bailiff's men looked on in awe and respect. His daughter also brought her father's jacket, which reached down to midcalf, and persuaded him to put it on as he sat there on horseback, then he wove the cord around himself a number of times with quick hand movements. His daughter stood watching him. He finished girding himself by tying a knot in the cord.

"Papa, what shall I do when you're gone?" said the girl.

"Put the dog inside!" he ordered violently.

She called to the dog, but the dog wouldn't be fooled and walked no more than half the distance toward her, its tail sinking. She put on a gentle face and went to try to grab it, but it slunk out to the home-field with its tail between its legs.

"I'll kill you, Kolur, if you don't stay!" said the girl.

The dog lay down and started trembling. She walked over to it, grabbed it by the scruff of the neck, and dragged it whining down the path to one of the outer houses, then shoved it inside and bolted the door. By the time she finished this task the men had ridden from the yard.

"Bless you, papa," she called out after him, but he didn't hear her. The horses trotted out along the lane leading up to the farmhouse; her father rode in front, kicking at his stirrups. Two farmhands work-ing in the homefield, a man and a woman, stopped and watched in silence as their householder was taken away.

They stopped for the night in Andakíll at the home of the parish administrator and were given lodging in a storehouse. The two men stood guard over their prisoner and late that night tried to engage him in small talk, but he said he was old and tired of people. He said he regretted that the pox hadn't killed everyone in the country. They asked him whether he knew any ballads.

"Not for entertaining others," he said.

Early the next morning they pressed on. They rode with the farmer west over Mýrar, then out along Snæfellsnes, taking the path over Fróðarheiði to Ólafsvík. They arrived late in the evening in a drizzling rain. A merchantman lay at anchor in the harbor. They dis-mounted in front of the trading booth, announced their business to the merchant's servants, showed their papers, and asked to see the ship's captain. This particular individual came in his own good time, and he asked them what was new. They said they'd been sent by the bailiff in Þverá and had brought a criminal sentenced to hard labor at Bremerholm. They handed the captain the bailiff's letters confirm-ing this. The skipper was fat, blue-faced, and illiterate, and he sum-moned someone to read and translate the letters for him. When the recitation was finished he asked, "Where are the court transcripts?"

This they didn't know for sure.

The Dane pointed at Jón Hreggviðsson and asked, huskily and sullenly:

"What has this man done?"

"He killed the king's hangman," they said.

"This old man," said the Dane. "Where does it say that?"

They said they thought it would have been in the letters, but no matter how these were read they could find no corroboration for such a charge. The Dane said that no bailiff in Iceland could get him to take folk on pleasure cruises on his ship.

"What's a pleasure cruise?" said the men.

The captain said that if an Icelandic man sailed out on his ship without it having been proven that he was a thief or a murderer, it was a pleasure cruise. "It's quite a different case," he said, "if along with the man come the proper court documents affixed with the seal of the authorities at Bessested, as well as a signed receipt from the Treasury, guaranteeing payment for transport." As far as the man whom they'd dragged hither was concerned, there wasn't a single word in these letters that said he'd stolen as much as a lamb, much less murdered a man.

The captain could not be persuaded. The only way he'd take the man was if they first rode to Bessastaðir and secured the proper documents. And with that he walked away.

The journey from Ólafsvík to Bessastaðir would take no less than three days each way. The prisoner's wardens decided that their best alternative would be to try to appeal to the local district authority, the bailiff on Snæfellsnes, and see if they could get a warrant from him confirming that the man they were transporting had been sentenced at the Alþingi. They tried to find lodging for the night in Ólafsvík, but Snæfellsnes was under the grip of famine and hospitality was somewhat lacking in the few places where there was fish to be found in the shed or butter in the pantry; in fact many of the farms there had been cleared out by the pox, the inhabitants dead and buried.

The Company was the only entity on Snæfellsnes that owned a house made of wood instead of turf. Usually the house stood empty, its window shutters closed, except during the few weeks in the summer when trade was carried out. Jón Hreggviðsson's wardens went to see the merchant and asked whether he could house one prisoner and two men. The merchant answered that the Danes were under no obligation to house any Icelanders other than convicted criminals; this was certainly not the case here; they were fools and liars; they should look after themselves. They asked whether they could shove the prisoner into an outhouse or storage shed, since it was raining. The merchant said that the Icelanders defecated wherever they felt like it, besides the fact that they left lice behind wherever they went; such people weren't good enough for a Danish outhouse. With that the merchant was gone. A pleasant Danish warehouse-boy, however, gave the Icelanders plugs of tobacco, though they had no food. It was late in the evening. A little later the captain boarded his ship and went to his cabin to sleep. The merchant's house was locked. The wardens stood on the gravel outside the trading booth and talked things over. The prisoner stood a short distance away, clad in his cord, drops of water leaking from his knitted cap onto his hoary head. In front of the booth was a horseblock, fastened to the ground with a massive iron hook. Finally the wardens turned to their prisoner, pointed at the stone to indicate that he should come over to it, and said:

"Here's where we're going to tie you."

They unfastened the old man's cord and used it to bind his hands and feet, then looped the remainder around the hook and tied it. When they were gone the farmer moved slowly around to the sheltered side of the stone and leaned up against it, but he made no attempt to free himself though it would have been an easy thing for him to do, since the fetters were more symbolic than real; he was no longer as energetic a fugitive as he'd been twenty years ago, nor did he curse troll-women in his dreams at night. Now sleep sank over the exhausted man as he sat unmoving against the horseblock before the Danish booth during the night. And as he sleeps there against the stone in the night rain, a messenger, mild and gentle, appears to him, just as books describe the way that angels come through prison walls to visit captives, and it puffed in his beard and licked his closed eyes. It was the dog.

"Aw, is that you there, damn it all," said the man, as the drenched dog jumped on him and trampled him and wagged its tail and whined and licked his face. Since the man was bound, he couldn't beat the dog away.

"You've eaten a foal, you piece of shit," said Jón Hreggviðsson, and there is nothing worse that one can say to a dog. But the dog's joy remained the same, and finally it started running in rings around the stone to which the man was tied.

At dawn the man was sleeping against the stone and the dog against the man. Other men and dogs started moving about: lordly Danes stood upon the booth's steps bulging and satisfied after their morning brennivíns and their breakfasts, but the dreary residents of Ólafsvík loitered at a distance like wraiths, wearing tattered jackets, shoulderless and too long in the back, looking like fish-skin scarecrows out in the nesting grounds. The latter folk stared vacantly at the dog and the man; one said he knew all about the captive and his kin, another couldn't resist estimating the length of the cord binding him. Both spoke in shrill, rasping falsettos that bore no resemblance to human voices. The Danes standing in the doorway of the booth made witty remarks and laughed haughtily.

The wardens were nowhere to be seen and no one had a clue as to their whereabouts. Presently the Danes went off to their various tasks, but the locals remained behind and stared apathetically at the man and the dog. The idea that they should walk over and free the captive never crossed their minds, any more than anyone had ever thought to go and free the Fenris Wolf* or attempt any other task appertaining to the gods. On the other hand, one Dane who worked as an apprentice textile trader wanted to set the man free in order to harass the authorities and to watch him run, but when he came near, the dog bristled and made ready to defend its master and the cord binding him. Soon the locals returned to their work of loading the stockfish the fishermen had brought in, and no one gave any further thought to the murderer secured to the stone, except for a poor woman who, by the grace of God, came over and held a pail of milk to the man's lips and gave the dog slices of fish-skin.

And the day passed by.

It was late in the evening and the loading was finished. The ship lay prepared for departure. The wardens had returned and untied the farmer. They waited, loitering by the house of the merchant in Ólafsvík in the hope that a message from some royal personage or other would be brought, and that the ship's captain would accept it as valid. They had sent a dispatch during the night to the Snæfellsnes bailiff to procure written testimony that Jón Hreggviðsson was a convicted criminal.

Around midnight the prisoner's dog started barking, and in a moment came the din of hooves at full speed. The wardens straightened up in anticipation of the arrival of the bailiff, but instead watched as a number of foaming horses came galloping over the gravel, bearing a noblewoman and her attendants. The woman was darkly clad and wearing a hat. She jumped down from the saddle without any help, grabbed up a handful of her full-length riding frock to avoid trampling the hem, hurried lightly over the gravel, and went straight in to join the Danes in the merchant's house without knocking upon the door. Her attendants set about catching hold of the unsaddled horses to lead them to grass.

The stranger remained in the house for some time. When she emerged her hat was at her neck, and the night breeze blew in her hair. The merchant and the captain followed her outside and bowed to her, and her teeth gleamed as she smiled in the twilight. Her attendants walked her charger over and held it steady as she mounted, a few arm lengths away from where Jón Hreggviðsson sat upon the stone.

The prisoner opened his mouth:

"My lady rides higher tonight than the time when Jón Hreggviðsson threw a rixdollar into her lap," he said.

She shot back from the saddle:

"The one you give alms is your enemy."

"Then why couldn't I get my head chopped off twenty years ago when it still had black hair on it and when my neck was thick enough to be pronounced fit to offer to your father and the king's ax?" he said.

She said: "You try to do good for a pauper out of pity, but as soon as you turn your back your birthright is sold away. That was my error. I gave you your head in charity: and my father's head, the country's head, was forced to droop dishonored. Now the foot's going to kick back, even though it's weak."

"I'm an old man," he said.

"You will never have power over my father in this country," she said.

"I won't beg for mercy," he said, suddenly standing up from the stone, his knitted cap hanging down over his hoary head and his cord around his waist. "I have a friend, as I'm sure my lady his elf-wife knows."

"His whore," she corrected, and she laughed and rode away.

When she was gone the captain called out to the wardens and told them to bind the prisoner and bring him aboard.

— 8 —

And when the ship arrives in Copenhagen in August, the captain sends word to the civil authorities that he has a villain from Iceland aboard. Armor-clad soldiers were immediately sent from the castle to take custody of the man, to seize his accompanying papers, and to escort him to the place in Denmark most familiar to Icelanders at that time. The castle of Bremerholm stood, as its name indicates, upon what was once an islet in a harbor of the city, its thick walls rising up out of the sea and its deep cellars full of water, with artillery men stationed on top to fire cannons at the Swedes. The criminals' quarters in the castle were reserved exclusively for men, who lay there in a vast common room by night and slaved away in a workhouse by day. If the men were timid and behaved well, they earned the trust of their jailers and were allowed to spend the nights unshackled, but if they were intrepid and expressed their opinions or talked back, they were immediately shackled by their masters and kicked at and chained to the wall, each next to his own sleeping place.

It was not long before the Icelanders in the city started rumoring that the Öxará court's sentencing of the farmer from Rein to incar-

ceration at Bremerholm had been out of the ordinary, and that the
decision to retry the aforementioned farmer there at home had been
an improvidential one, to say the least. The rumors quickly found
their way to the Chancery. And when a certain party who found it
somehow worthwhile to make a fuss about this knave's ugly head
investigated the court documents, all that turned up in the farmer's
case was a cursory and unauthorized copy of the haphazard and hasty
verdict that had been passed over him in the spring at the Alþingi in
an unprosecuted and undefended case. The document said that since
the farmer was renowned for his rude treatment of others and was in
fact accused of murder, but had fled the assembly without having
answered the accusations, he was to be sent to Bremerholm. That
was all.

As a rule, the only way that anyone could escape from the castle of
Bremerholm was through a dead-ended opening: namely, the grave.
Very few at all who came to Bremerholm were able in the long run to
stand the weight of the burdens bound to them by justice. A few Icelandic prisoners incarcerated for various crimes thought it was high
time that Jón Hreggviðsson had come to join them for good, and
that it was unlikely that this old lash-scarred rascal, infamous for his
numerous misdeeds, would ever get the chance to get out now that
they'd been able to drag him this far. It was therefore not astonishing
that his fellow inmates' eyes widened when the chief warden walked
into the labor ward one day and called out for Regvidsen, the rogue
who had killed the king's hangman, an act tantamount to cutting off
the right hand of His Grace our Most Clement Highness. The warden ordered Regvidsen to follow him.

Jón Hreggviðsson wasn't taken to the mainland by way of Dybets-
gade, but instead was ferried from the castle over the Bremerholm
canal. The Danes had given him a shabby pair of trousers to put on
over the underclothes he was wearing when he was arrested, but his
cord had been confiscated. He was busy pestering the ferryman
about getting his cord back when they made land on the city side of
the canal, and he was ordered like a dog to go ashore. Standing there
was a lanky man in a patched-up dress coat, stooping forward and
twitching nervously. He stepped forward to meet the farmer and

extended a blue hand with a gigantic backward-bending thumb. He seemed slightly distracted, but otherwise was the very picture of seriousness in his bearing.

"Greetings, Jón," said the dress-coated man in Icelandic.

Jón Hreggviðsson looked at the man scowlingly and scratched his head—"Who're you again?"

"Studiosus Antiquitatum am I, and am called Joannes Grindvicensis, Jón Guðmundsson, born and raised in Grindavík."

"Oh, right, you'd think I would've recognized you, the man who came to the door of that renowned mansion when one of the king's soldiers was standing there—and greetings and best wishes to you also, my dear Jón."

The scholar from Grindavík snorted a few times and rubbed his nose for a moment.

"My lord and master wishes to grant you succor, Jón Hreggviðsson," he said. "And I've been standing here, at his request, since the bell in St. Nicholas's churchtower tolled the Angelus this morning. Soon they'll be ringing the Spiritus Sanctus. You must know that I am cold and thirsty."

"They took me away from my scythe as I was standing there in my underwear and I haven't got a single tuppence for beer," said Jón Hreggviðsson. "And the Danes have stolen my cord."

"Good, good," said the scholar, thus destroying this thread of conversation. "In the name of Jesus then, and with our throats dry, what's the news from Iceland?"

"Oh, you know, things are decent enough over there," said Jón Hreggviðsson. "Though it was pretty stormy during the fishing season last year. But the grass came up a little better in the summer."

"Good," said the scholar. He thought for a moment, then added: "I hear that you're still the same old criminal."

"Is that so," said Jón Hreggviðsson.

"Is it true?" asked the Grindavíkian.

"I'd say I'm something of a saint," said Jón Hreggviðsson.

The scholar from Grindavík did not find this amusing at all: "It's a dreadful shame to be a criminal," he said, in a tone of moral probity.

"Actually, I'm just a thief," said Jón Hreggviðsson.

"That is exactly what one should not be," said the man from Grindavík.

"I stole a tiny piece of cord from someone almost twenty years ago," said Jón Hreggviðsson.

"That is exactly what one should not do," said the Grindavíkian.

Jón Hreggviðsson said: "When's there ever been a decent saint who didn't start out as a thief?"

The scholar snorted and gaped for some time and stood upon his left leg in order to scratch his left calf with his right instep.

"As I was saying, good," he said finally, like a schoolteacher. "But what I really meant to ask was: has nothing happened in Iceland, nothing come to pass?"

"Not that I recall," said Jón Hreggviðsson. "At least not anything in particular. Not these past few years."

"Nothing at all remarkable?" asked the scholar from Grindavík.

"No, nothing remarkable's happened in Iceland for a long time," said Jón Hreggviðsson. "Not one single thing. Unless someone wants to call pulling up a howling ray last year in Skagafjörður news."

"I would call that more than just a little newsworthy," said the scholar. "What did you say, it was howling?"

"Oh, so maybe you haven't heard about this either, pal: three years ago men appeared in the sky over Iceland," said Jón Hreggviðsson.

"Men appeared in the sky," said the scholar, slightly less enthusiastically. "Good." After performing his tricks several times, including once wryly rubbing his nose, he spoke up again, saying:

"Might I remind my compatriot, that since you are just a common knave speaking with a learned man, even though I might be, as the lay brother Bergur Sokkason* phrased it, the most insignificant deacon in God's Christendom, it does not suit you to comport yourself too freely toward me and address me informally like I am some dog, or to call me your pal. And I am not speaking now on my behalf alone—I know that my lord and master would never tolerate such effrontery from a commoner toward a member of the learned class. And when he sent me home to Iceland last year to copy those twelfth-century apostles' lives found at Skarð, and when those Skarðsmen said that they would never allow it even for gold, he gave me a letter to carry with me, specifying that I should never be addressed with a title lower than monsieur there at home."

Jón Hreggviðsson answered:

"I'm nothing but a feebleminded cotter who's never met a decent man outside of my householder Jesus Christ, since I can't rightly mention that fleabag of a dog who followed me all the way west to the Ólafsvík trading-station horseblock where I lay tethered to a hook. But since Your Highly Learned Lordship wants to do me some favors, then I promise to henceforth comport myself according to the example of Your Learnedness except at those times when my unmanageable unwisdom gets in the way."

The Grindavíkian said:

"Though you and your kin are entirely under Moria's power,* my master would never hold it against you; he has always had a soft spot for your mother, who blindly saved what others had lost. Because of this he has gone to a great deal of trouble and expended no little energy negotiating with the authorities to have you pulled out of that castle, from which no man emerges alive; because of this he invites you now to come to see him. Now it remains to be seen what sort of man it is he has saved. However, I will warn you right now, for the safety and health of your life and soul: have no dealings whatsoever with Jón Marteinsson while you are here in the city."

"Oh, did I hear Your Learnedness right? Is he still above ground, that fiend who drank the king's boots off me here all those years ago when I served under the king's flag?" said Jón Hreggviðsson.

"Yes, and what's more, he has stolen the *Skálda* itself, fourteen pages of which were discovered in your deceased mother's den at Rein on Akranes."

"Hopefully at some point he's stolen something a little less good-for-nothing," said Jón Hreggviðsson. "My mother couldn't have used that rubbish to make as much as one patch for my jerkin."

"My master has offered Jón Marteinsson the book's weight in gold if he returns the stolen booty; he has offered to procure for him an estate and an official post in Iceland. He has had spies out for days on end to keep steadfast vigil over the thief, to catch him in a drunken moment and see if he says anything about the book; but all of this has come to nothing."

"Hm," said Jón Hreggviðsson, "I wonder if I, with God's help, wouldn't be able to make a little profit by becoming a thief here in Copenhagen."

The scholar from Grindavík gaped like a fish several times, but said nothing.

"I mean," said Jón Hreggviðsson, "since such men are offered gold, official posts, and estates; and are given brennivín to boot."

"He who pledges his soul to Satan will surely be rewarded as a lucky thief, until the day comes when mankind awakes to the sound of trumpets," said the scholar. "How else does it happen that no one ever catches Jón Marteinsson naked in bed? It is because he clothes himself in the skin of a dead man."

"Oh, yes, the poor fellow—it doesn't sit well with me to criticize him even though he drank my boots off me, because it's pretty clear he had something to do with getting me out of the Blue Tower here a few years ago. And word's gotten around in Iceland that he managed to get that pitiful scoundrel Mangi from Bræðratunga acquitted, after he'd been rejected by both God and men."

"And I say he drowned the man in the canal the same night he got him acquitted," said the Grindavíkian. "Anyone saved by Jón Marteinsson is lost."

"All the same, I remember pretty clearly that Your Learnedness thought it might be nice to stop in at a tavern with our namesake," said Jón Hreggviðsson.

"Good, good," said the scholar from Grindavík, and he performed all his stunts one after another: he snorted, gaped, rubbed both sides of his nose, stood in place and rubbed his left instep against his right calf and vice versa.

"I'm just going to stop in at St. Nicholas's," he said, "to say my prayers. You stand out here in the meantime and try to recollect something worthwhile."

In a short time the scholar stepped out of the church and stopped on the doorstep to put on his hat.

"Did you say that men appeared in the sky in Iceland?" he asked.

"Yes, and birds to boot," said Jón Hreggviðsson.

"Birds? In the sky?" repeated the scholar. "I would call that rare—sine dubio* with iron claws. I must put this down in my memoranda. And as far as your saying that I've gone to a tavern with Jón Marteinsson, it is neither dignum neque justum, true nor correct, for a common scoundrel from Bremerholm to say such a thing to my lord's scriba and famulus.* And let me tell you this: my lord is the kind of lord and master who ever and ay forgives his servant of his frailties, knowing, as he does, that I have very little money and that Jón Marteinsson clothes himself in a dead man's skin."

— 9 —

Over verdant lowlands cut by the deep streamwaters of the south hangs a peculiar gloom. Every eye is stifled by clouds that block the sight of the sun, every voice is muffled like the chirps of fleeing birds, every quasi-movement sluggish. Children must not laugh, no attention must be drawn to the fact that a man exists, one must not provoke the powers with frivolity—do nothing but prowl along, furtively, lowly. Maybe the Godhead had not yet struck its final blow, an unexpiated sin might still fester somewhere, perhaps there still lurked worms that needed to be crushed.

The center of domestic prosperity, the head and glory of the life of the nation, the see of Skálholt, tottered in its foundations. The inhabitants of the south were known to grumble from time to time about their episcopal seat depending upon who occupied it, but come what may, the office of bishop belonged here and would never be diminished though the king might strengthen his grip around it: here was the school, the hearthfire of learning and the learned, here the tithes of the diocesan estates were paid, here travelers were given alms so that they might cross over the streamwaters. Even when the wife of one particular bishop ordered the stone bridge over Hvítá demolished, impoverished men and wayfarers died on the river's eastern banks in the belief that the light of Christianity still shone on the river's western side.

But the sins of the nation had grown so great that not even the diocese could be defended. In its wrath the Godhead had also struck down the episcopal throne. When simple underlings at the see were forced to bend their necks beneath the scythe of punishment it was not beyond most people's comprehension. But now, when both its clerics and its learned teachers, its promising schoolboys and virtuous young damsels were whisked speedily away, and when the country's Christian patriarch, the bishop himself, and finally the perfumed honor of our land, the bishop's wife, who in her one person represented a consolidation of all the best lineages in the land, were called away to sleep in the bloom of their lives, it was clear that the rose had been cruelly cut down by this sudden storm, and all of clerkdom's foremost teachings on mankind's sins and God's wrath were turned into prophecies proven true.

A synod of the surviving priests in the diocese has entrusted the archpriest Sigurður Sveinsson with the custodianship of the office of bishop, and he has moved his books and other belongings from his small cold room within the servants' quarters to the bishop's residence. The abominable wooden crucifix hangs now in the green room, the Grand Salon.

Autumn brought cloudless days and hoarfrost at night. One day snorting horses stop upon the dry flagstones outside the bishop's residence; they rub their bridle bits impatiently against their legs after their riders slacken the reins and dismount. There is no knock upon the door. The one visitor who does not knock at others' doors has arrived. The outer door is jerked open as if by a sharp wind; there are light footsteps in the vestibule; the door to the Grand Salon is shoved open.

"Good day."

She stands in the doorway, slim and straight, wearing a dark riding frock wet with her horse's sweat and muddied somewhat at the hem, crop in hand. This full-grown woman's face has of course lost its blossomy texture, and her teeth jut out just enough to prevent her mouth from being called lovely, but her elegance has assumed the type of authority that arises when the particular is discarded and replaced with the absolute. And just as before, day dawns anew wherever her eyes shine.

The electus* looked up from his books toward her. He walked over to her and greeted her ceremoniously.

"What bonis auguriis*—?" he asked.

She said that she had ridden to Hjálmholt a week ago at the invitation of old Vigfús Þórarinsson the bailiff, and was now returning to her home, out west in Breiðafjörður; since she was passing this way she thought it a good idea to pay her old friend and suitor a visit.

"Besides," she added, "I have some small business with you, my dear Reverend Sigurður."

He proclaimed it to be the happiest of days when she required his services in any way, made enquiries concerning the condition of her life and soul, and expressed his sympathy that she should now be forced to mourn as a widow, recounting for her the news carried to Iceland last summer, that Magnús, his schoolmate and close acquaintance, that extraordinarily unfortunate man, had passed away in Copenhagen, though he had indeed won his lawsuit first.

She smiled.

"One man was certainly defeated in that lawsuit," she said. "But in times like these it's hardly worthwhile to trouble oneself with small details. That's why I haven't bothered to secure compurgators to support my abjuration of the charges brought against me by the Supreme Court. And you, my dear Reverend Sigurður, dishonor my disgrace by refusing to have me prosecuted according to the laws of the church and drowned in Öxará."

"Misdeeds that are repented no longer exist," said the episcopal vicarius.* "Any type of mortal punishment for them would only be conceit, since the Lord has erased them from His book."

"We'll put aside all this conceit," she said. "On the other hand, there's one thing that I find amusing in all this mess: the cottage at Bræðratunga here east of the river was reconfiscated from the king, along with its chamber pots and churns. Old Fúsi gave me a valid deed for all of it."

"The defeat of the powers that work affectionately for the Lord is but a momentary deception," said the episcopal vicarius. "The course that these affairs have taken is doubtless more in accord with God's will now than ever before. It may also be that the measure intended by the Lord for this poor land has already been filled up and poured out."

"Doubtless," she said, "since only I, a degenerate, am to survive my kinfolk."

"A certain itinerant poet hid a little maiden in his harp," said the episcopal vicarius. "Her noble kin had been wiped out. And when the maiden cried the poet struck the harpstrings. He knew that it fell to her lot to uphold the honor of her people."*

"I only hope that you won't be carrying an old pox-scarred widow, especially one who's been branded a whore, in your domiciled harp of Latin poetry, my dear Reverend Sigurður," she said.

"The true poet loves the rose of roses, the maiden of maidens," said the episcopal vicarius. "She whom my master Lutherus was never allowed to see, neither awake nor in dreams, never a daylight or midnight visitation, the poet loves her and her alone, the eternal rosa rosarum and virgo virginum who is virgo ante partum, in partu, post partum, so help me God, in Jesus' name."*

His guest said:

"I have known for quite some time that there is no field of study more obscene than theology, if it is taught correctly: a girl before she gives birth, a girl as she gives birth, a girl after giving birth. I blush— the old widow. In Jesus' name, help me back down to earth, my beloved Reverend Sigurður."

He had started to pace the room, his hands gripped together palms downward, his eyes fiery and black.

It was she who started the conversation again:

"Once you came to me eastward over the river, Reverend Sig- urður, three years ago, and spoke words that meant nothing to me at the time. But since then events have occurred that once again con- firm the old saying that the greatest exaggerations are always closest to the truth. You said you knew for certain that my father would be deprived of his honor and possessions. I laughed. And then you spoke those words."

He asked what words these were.

"You said, 'I offer you my wealth and my life; my last hundred of land.'"

"What do you want from me?" he asked.

"I need money, cash, silver, gold."

"For what?" he asked.

"I didn't think my friend would need to ask," she said. "Especially a friend of my father."

"I was once of the opinion that you yourself possessed a certain amount of ready cash," he said.

She said: "I did have a tiny bit of minted silver. When news got out about Magnús's death and his success in winning his lawsuit, people came flocking to me from various directions with claims for payment. I repaid whatever was demanded of me. I've already spent far too much. But still my blessed husband's creditors continue to arise."

"Men have always been in the habit of trying to extort money from women whom they know to be defenseless," said the episcopal vicarius. "The claims should have been investigated. You would have been much better off by coming to me earlier. Truth to tell, I doubt that you are the appropriate party to close on some of the deals made by the blessed Magnús."

She said that she had no desire to discuss this topic any further—these obligations were trifles compared to others she still had to fulfill. And with that she turned to the purpose of her visit.

She desired that her father's case be reopened and that a new investigation be made into the so-called execrable cases, the cases involving landlopers and skulkers that her father had supposedly been too rigorous in adjudging, and for which he had been prosecuted and condemned. Now as far as most of these men were concerned, if they were not already dead then they were such small-fry that it was absolutely pointless to retry their cases, except for one of them, the murderer Jón Hreggviðsson, whose case had weighed so heavily in the judgment passed against her father. She said that certain men well versed in law had assured her that his guilt in the matter had never been in doubt, but his case had been poorly prosecuted, and if it were possible to try him properly, even at such a late stage, it might provide sufficient pretext to force a retrial of Magistrate Eydalín's case. She now informed the electus that last spring she had

been able, under no small financial burden to herself, to persuade the
country's high court to convene a hearing concerning the old man's
case, but of course he'd slipped out of their grasp just as he'd done in
the past, without having been examined, though in the end they
handed down some sort of pro forma ruling and sentenced him to
incarceration at Bremerholm. "But as one might have expected," she
said, "that dismal congregation of drinking partners wasn't able to
write up a formal document spelling out the court's conclusions, so
that when the old man was brought to the ship, the best the Danes
could understand from his papers was that he was supposed to be
taken for a pleasure cruise. After negotiating with the bailiff on
Snæfellsnes I rode by night to Ólafsvík," she said, "where I had to
bribe the Danes to transport the old man abroad."

Then she told the vicarius that folk aboard the newly arrived
autumn ship had brought news of the old man's lawsuit. Powerful
forces in Copenhagen had worked long and hard to try to exonerate
this old lawbreaker who had been treated so leniently by her father, a
mistake that cost her father his honor and the honor of his country.
Jón Hreggviðsson hadn't stayed but a few nights in Bremerholm Castle before these intercessors managed to secure his release, and the
last she heard was that the old man was having a grand time of it in
the home of a renowned man in Copenhagen. Everything that she
had worked so hard to accomplish by manipulating this man's case
had been ruined. Those who preferred to see her father convicted
and Jón Hreggviðsson acquitted still wielded more power.

To sum up, it was her intention to travel to Denmark as soon as
expediency allowed, to meet with the lord whom the king had
granted Iceland as an enfeoffment and whom she believed to be Iceland's friend, to ask him to persuade the king to retry the case involving Magistrate Eydalín's honor before a valid court of law. "But," she
said, "to defray the costs of such a voyage I need silver."

The episcopal vicarius stood with his head bowed as she spoke.
He raised his eyes a few times from the floor up along the person
conversing with him, though never any higher than just above her
knees. Again and again an involuntary contraction gripped his upper
lip, and he clenched his fingers so tightly that the knuckles on his
blue hands whitened.

When she finished stating her case he cleared his throat in all earnestness, pulled his hands apart once, then locked them together again. He gave her face a glance quick as fire, his eyes burning, his own face quivering—he looked like a beast on the verge of howling. Yet when he started speaking his words came slowly and sedately, with an immense weight of gravity suited only to the most extreme sorts of reasoning.

"Forgive me," he said, "that the immutable lover of the health of your soul by our Lord God's holy name asks this one question before any other: Have you at any time in your life kissed Arnas Arnæus with the so-called Third Kiss, the kiss that the auctores have named suavium?"*

She gave him a capitulatory look, like a man who crosses a vast stretch of desert and finally finds a pool whose waters are putrid. She bit her lip and turned away, looking out the window to where her attendants had hobbled their horses on the flagstones while they waited for her. Finally she turned back toward the bishop-elect and smiled.

"I ask Your Piety not to misunderstand me—I have no intention of denying the charges made against my pitiable flesh," she said. "Just a few days and nights, and this dust will cease to stir. But, my dear Reverend Sigurður, since you are the lover of my soul, and since my soul is now defenseless, would it really matter at all whether the dust is kissed with the first, second, or third kiss?"

"I must warn you again, beloved soul, against giving answers that imply heavier sins, if true, than the sins you might deny," he said.

"A man is instantly reduced to a clawed imp by engaging in debate with such a holy man as Your Piety, Reverend Sigurður," she said. "I have long known that the more words I spoke with you, the more steps I would take down to deepest Hell. But just as before, I have come to you."

"My love for you remains the same, now and forever," said the electus.

"I have come to you because no one can find a more secure refuge in your pierced Christ than the lowest child of Hell. If I ever spoke disrespectful words about your idol in your ears it was not because I misunderstood his might. And it is my belief and my sincere acknowl-

edgment that if this dreadful redeemer exists anywhere in our country, it is in your heart."

"You have made a pact with all the forces of nature to oppose me,"
he said, as he kneaded his fingers together more tightly. "You have
enjoined the blossoms in the fields into swearing oaths against me.
Even the sun shining through cloudless skies—you have turned it
into the enemy of my soul."

"Forgive me, Reverend Sigurður," said she. "I thought that you
were my father's friend, and that those words of yours that I repeated
to you earlier had been spoken in all sincerity. Now I see that I was
mistaken. All I do is anger you. I will ride away as quickly as I can.
And we will forget everything."

He stepped in front of her and said: "What moment should I have
waited for all these years but that one when the most noble woman
in the land should come to this poor eremite?"

"The most wretched woman in the land," she said, "a true picture
of a pitiable woman: a she-creature opposed to all your theology.
Now you should allow this castaway to continue on her way, my dear
Reverend Sigurður."

"I-it's in a cask in the wall," he whispered. He unhooked his fingers and stood before her with his hands in the air. "Besides what little there is in the top compartment of the chest in the loft. Here are
the keys. And there are two hundred rixdollars in this bureau. Guard
this oblation of Satan, these faeces diaboli* which have burdened my
conscience for too long; use them to drive yourself southward into
the world to meet your lover. And if something is lost, whether he
treats you well or poorly, it is I."

— 10 —

Gyldenløve, the king's kinsman and Baron of Marselisborg, Postmaster
General in Norway, Governor of Iceland and Revenue Comptroller,
or, as he titled himself, Gouverneur von Ijsland, owned numerous
splendid estates and beautiful palaces in Denmark. He took his
greatest pleasure during the summers at Fredholm Palace, due to the

abundance of game to be found in the forests that began just beyond the palace canal. He had christened this palace Château au Bon Soleil, which in Danish meant Palace of the Good Sun or Villa of the Sun. The lane between the highroad and the palace bridge was nearly a mile long, and as everyone knows, the distance between highroad and palace gate is an excellent indicator of a man's nobility. Only highborn guests riding in carriages visit such places.

On a lovely midsummer afternoon in Denmark, an old tarnished carriage, its axles poorly oiled, comes creaking down the stately palace lane. The carriage is held together in places with bits of cord, and it looks as if one of the two horses pulling it is hobbling.

At the gate to the bridge over the canal stands a dragoon armed with a musket and sword; his steed stands near a stable some distance away. He asks, "Who goes there?" and the coachman opens the carriage door for him. Sitting within is a pale woman in a dark cloak, unadorned but for an old silver spangle fastened through a buttonhole at the neckline, beneath a white ruff. She wears a silver-colored wig so finely coiffured and radiant that it appears to have been bought the day before, perhaps for this visit. On top of the wig rests a somewhat rustic wide-brimmed hat, as if she had not had enough funds for a stylish feathered hat after the purchase of such a costly wig. The woman's bearing was magnificent. When the dragoon heard her speak stiffly in Danish, he bowed deeply to her and said that he could understand German, the language of better men, if she would rather speak unimpededly in that language. Then he marched, musket presented, salutatorily before the carriage over the canal bridge and sounded a trumpet on the palace square. A dignified-looking servant in red livery came out onto the square, opened the door of the carriage, and helped the visitor step out. She said:

"Inform the baron that the woman who wrote to him has arrived, bearing a letter from the regent Beyer."

The palace facade consisted of two tremendously high towers, one cylindrical, the other quadrilateral, linked by a four-story building with a portal broad enough for a carriage to pass through. The visitor was taken through a little door at the base of one of the towers and up a long, winding staircase that led to a dimly lit vestibule on an upper floor. Double doors are opened, and the woman is invited to proceed into the governor's hall, which is near the center of the palace, with windows overlooking the courtyard. The hall had a vaulted ceiling and its floor was of stone. Glorious weapons bedecked its walls: hanging here were not only a splendid variety of muskets, fuses, and powderhorns, but also spears, swords, and lances in bunches like flower bouquets. Coats of armor topped with helmets stood unsupported in the corners like giants. Over the doors and windows hung heraldic shields inscribed with dragons, birds of prey, and other fantastic wild beasts. The windows were fashioned from hundreds of tiny panes of glass joined together with lead and displayed images of knights upon strong-loined horses, fighting famous battles. Affixed to the walls were great racks of stag's antlers, some with incredible numbers of points, and attached to the antlers were the skulls of the beasts to which they had belonged. Expansive benches and ironclad chests were situated along the walls, stout oaken tables before them, and on the shelves above the benches stood burnished copper tankards and enormous stone pitchers embossed with bawdy ballads and the words of God in German. On one table lay two thick books, a Bible with clasps of copper and a medical textbook on diseases of horses, as thick or even thicker. Lying on the books were two gloves and a dog-whip.

The woman stood there for some time, regarding the hall and its contents, when in walked a man clad in silken clothing and golden cords. He announced to the guest in an extremely affected tone that the Durchlaucht* had arrived.

Gyldenløve, Baron of Marselisborg, Gouverneur von Ijsland, was a tall man with a sagging chest and a large paunch, his thighs slim in close-cut trousers, resembling two fir-twigs stuck into a bowl of punch. His face was long and his cheeks slack, and a green-tinted wig hung out over his shoulders. He wore a doublet embroidered with golden thread and soiled with splotches of grease and wine. His eyes, like those of his kin, were quick and watery-clear, similar to a pig's eyes. He was a reticent man, in every way a loner, tired-looking and slightly troubled, and he held a ramrod in one hand. He spoke in a rather abstruse language, characterized mainly by a kind of German normally used to berate soldiers, slung together with various glosses derived from other tongues. His voice was a brennivín-bass, and he rolled his "r" somewhere deep in his throat, making the rattling noise animals make as their throats are being cut.

"Bonjour, madame," said Iceland's governor. "Na, du bust en isländsch Wif, hombre, hew nie een seihn—so you are an Icelandic woman, man alive, I have never seen such a sight."

He walked over to her and poked at her, rubbing bits of her clothing between clammy fingers, asking where she had bought the cloth, and who had sewn her cloak, and here was a remarkable silver pendant, he had never seen silver embossed in such a way, do they do this in Iceland? Who gives them the silver to make such things? "Hombre, now I am completely astonished, would she like to give me this necklace?"

She said that all of her silver was his if it would please him to accept it but gave no indication whatsoever that she was about to remove the brooch and give it to him. Instead she turned immediately to her errand and took out the letter she had brought from the regent Beyer at Bessastaðir. As soon as he saw the letter he was overcome by an official weariness and apathy, and he asked dispiritedly:

"Why has this not gone through the Chancery? I look at nothing that has not gone through the Chancery. I am hunting."

"This letter deserves close attention," she said.

"I have long since stopped reading, except from my medical text when something is wrong with the horses," he said. "And I have no one to read it for me here. Besides, everything sent to me concerning Iceland can be learned from one book, since it's always the same whine about cord; all my life, nothing but cord. And it's not every year that we need fish here in Denmark. We are not predisposed toward letting people drag endless amounts of fish with endless amounts of cord."

"I," said she, "am the daughter of the magistrate over Iceland, who was innocently deprived of his honor and his estates in his old age. Your Excellency is governor of Iceland."

"Yes, my old friend, your father, was a great chicaner," said Gyldenløve. "Even so, things went for him as they did. There came an even greater chicaner. It has always been like this in Iceland. I'm tired of thinking about Icelanders."

"I have traveled all this way to meet with Your Excellency," she said.

"You are a splendid woman," he said, and he cheered up again as he looked her over and forgot about his official duties. "If I were in your shoes I would not return to Iceland. I would settle down in Denmark and find a husband. Things are going very well for us—it is very pleasant here. In my time the stock here in the forest has increased to more than three hundred animals. Look at this head, isn't this lovely?"—he stood up and pointed to the largest stag's head hanging on the wall—"there are twenty-nine points on these horns, hombre. I killed this deer myself. Not once has His Majesty my kinsman ever shot a deer with so many points."

"This is indeed a beautiful head," said the visitor. "I know, however, about a certain beast that has even more points. It is called justice. I have come to speak to you about the type of justice that affects an entire country: your country."

"Iceland, my country? Pfui deibel,"* said Gyldenløve, Baron of Marselisborg.

He did, however, agree to give the letter from his servant in Bessastaðir a hearing, if she wished to read it.

The letter stated that the woman who delivered it was the sole surviving member of the greatest aristocratic clan in Iceland. The letter's author recapitulated the scandal that had occurred on the island when this woman's father, the most distinguished man in all of Iceland, as well as a faithful and beloved servant of His Royal Majesty, was forced to endure the slander of that bizarre envoy Arnæus, who had been appointed by his deceased Majesty of praiseworthy memory to act as his plenipotentiary in Iceland. The letter described Arnæus's methods, how he had tyrannized the aged magistrate and several of his colleagues by invalidating the magistrate's rulings long after they had been made and by seizing his estates, until this aged and faithful servant of the king was reduced to an ignoble slave and pauper, and was laid upon his bier several weeks later.

The regent then stated that it had been the resolute intention of the bishop in Skálholt, the son-in-law of the old aristocrat, to travel to Denmark to attempt to persuade the highest authorities in that country to redress the situation. But the pox had swept over Iceland and had sent to their graves just over a third of its inhabitants, including a substantial portion of its clergy. The bishop in Skálholt, one of the king's most venerable friends, was one of those called away, along with his respectful wedded wife, the gentlewoman Madame Jooren.

Of this family there remained standing, alone to pursue her father's case, only the young lady Snefriid, the widow of the unlucky aristocrat Magnús Sívertsen. This particular lady had come to meet the letter's author at Bessastaðir and had informed him that her duty to her honor would drive her, a destitute hermit, over the storm-tossed sea, to deliver to the governor or even to our Highness himself her most humble petition that the so-called Commissarial Verdict in her father's lawsuit be reexamined by a higher court. Commending this honorable lady to the most charitable goodwill of the Baron of Marselisborg and Governor of Iceland, requesting that he examine carefully and take into consideration the dangerous currents introduced into Iceland by the conduct of the commissary Arnæus, and put a stop to practices whereby knights-errant were glorified for trampling down auctoritas, molesting the king's servants, and beguiling the common folk, I remain Your Excellency's most humble and très obéissant serviteur.*

Gyldenløve stuck the ramrod into his boot to scratch his ankle. He said:

"I have always said this to His Majesty, my kinsman: Send the Icelanders to Jylland where there is enough heather for their sheep-creatures, hombre, and sell Iceland to the Germans, the English, or even the Dutch, the sooner the better, for whatever decent sum you can get, and use the money to fight the Swedes, who have snatched your good land of Skåne away from you."

She sat silently for a long moment after hearing his answer.

"There is a verse by an ancient Icelandic poet," she said finally, "which goes something like this: Though a man loses his wealth and his kin, and in the end dies himself, he loses nothing if he has made a name for himself."

"Hew ick nich verstahn,"* said the Baron of Marselisborg, Governor of Iceland.

She continued, and though she hesitated slightly at first, her spirit strengthened as she spoke:

"I ask Your Excellency: Why are we deprived of our honor before our lives? Why won't the king of Denmark leave us our names? We have done nothing against him. We deserve no less respect than he does. My forefathers were kings of land and sea. They sailed their ships over storm-wracked seas and came to Iceland at a time when no other race on earth knew how to sail. Our skalds composed poetry and told stories in the language of King Óðinn himself, who came from Ásgarður when Europe still spoke the language of slaves.* Where are the poems, where are the stories composed by the Danes? We Icelanders even gave life to your ancient heroes in our books. Your ancient tongue, the Danish tongue that you have ruined and lost, we preserve. Do as you please, take my foremothers' silver—" at this point she unfastened the silver pendant from her neckline, and her black cloak fell from her shoulders: she was dressed in blue with a golden band encircling her midriff—"take all of it. Sell us like livestock. Send us to the heaths of Jylland where the heather grows. Or, if it suits you, keep beating us with your whips back at home in our own country. Hopefully we have done enough to deserve it. A Danish ax rests upon Bishop Jón Arason's neck throughout eternity, and that is fine. God be praised that he did enough to deserve all seven of the strokes it took to separate his trunk from his hoary head and his short, thick neck that would never bend. Excuse me for speaking up, excuse us for being a race of historians who forget nothing. But do not misunderstand me: I regret nothing that has happened, neither in words nor thoughts. It may be that the most victorious race is the one that is exterminated: I will not plead with words for mercy for the Icelanders. We Icelanders are truly not too good to die. And life has meant nothing to us for a long time. But there is one thing that we can never lose while one man of this race, rich or poor, remains standing; and even in death this thing is never lost to us; that which is described in the old poem, and which we call fame: just so my father and my mother are not, though they are dust, called ignoble thieves."

The Baron of Marselisborg pulled an empty cartridge from his purse and peered into it with one eye.

"If anyone has deprived the Icelanders of their honor and reputation, it is they themselves, ma chère madame,"* he said, and he smiled so widely that his eyes sunk back and several yellow buckteeth jutted out. "When their laziness and drunkenness bring them to the brink of starvation, my kinsman His Majesty has to send them grain supplements. When they think the grain is not good enough for them they go to court and demand gold and silver. And as far as justice is concerned, ma chère, it is clear to me that the Icelanders have chosen their man, the man whom they consider best. And from what I have heard, it was this very galanthomme who deprived the honorable old magistrate, your father, of his estates and honor. It's the same old story for you Icelanders. Learned men have informed me that Icelanders' books say that in the old days all the better men in Iceland set about beating each other to death until no one was left but oafs and barbarians. Now, for the first time in my life, an Icelandic woman comes to me—wearing, might I add, a golden belt around her waist—and she begs for more justice. Is it not to be wondered that I ask: Wat schall ick maken?"*

"I ask for nothing more than the honor and the estates befitting my father's name," she said.

Gyldenløve put down the ramrod and picked up his golden snuffboxes.

He said: "There are two forces in the Danish realm. When the one that works in collusion with sorcerers and thieves is in power, many a good man is forced to bow down. But if those who demand full rights for good, highborn men are raised up under my kinsman, the new king, then life will be better; it may be that certain knavish brewers and libertines will be shown the noose, with God's help. There are no contracts made between good and evil men. Unfortunately, ma chère, many a man must bide his time."

"There is an Icelandic criminal named Jón Hreggviðsson," she said. "He killed the king's hangman. The entire country knows it. My father sentenced him to death twenty years ago, but an infant amused itself by freeing him the night before his execution. The law still has not caught up with him. The royal commissarius convicted my father because of this case, and he acquitted the lawbreaker. At the last Alþingi the old man's case was reopened and he was sentenced to prison at Bremerholm. But he barely passes through the castle gate before the magnates drag him out of there and offer him refuge. And while this oft-sentenced convict, this murderer of a servant of the king, lives in luxury in the capital, my parents lie in their graves, branded as thieves."

"Icelanders are, shall we say, quite shrewd, and crafty when it comes to law," said the governor. "They'll leave no stone unturned to prove that whatever law-article is used to convict them comes from a corpus that some fool of a Norwegian king invalidated hundreds of years ago; or from some Danish laws never recognized in Iceland; or that it is at variance with some valid prescript given in the laws of St. Ólafur; or is from their *Gray Goose,* that collection of utterly heathen statutes.* They presume that the only laws valid for them are the ones that acquit them of all criminal liability. I can tell you for certain, madame, that many a fine Danish functionary has sweated over the case of this despicable Icelandic rogue."

The same distressed official look came over this huntsman's face as he started explaining to her how there were few others more knowledgeable than he concerning just how worthy a servant her deceased father had been on behalf of the king and the realm, though he had actually been quite overzealous when promoting his own interests in the Treasury, and thus had been able to appropriate, dirt-cheap, several large estates that had been taken over by the Danish king during the Reformation. But the government in Copenhagen put up with that excellent old aristocrat since he was a trustworthy individual. And it was a cause for great sorrow amongst his friends in the city when they received news of the conviction and the disgrace that he was forced to suffer in his old age. Gyldenløve said that he wished the magistrate's daughter could know, understand, and acknowledge the fact that neither the government nor he himself, Gyldenløve, nor any other Danish functionary serving under him had anything to do with the case—that the only party responsible was, in fact, as he put it, "the man whom madame doubtless knows much better than I."

She said:

"Even though my name has been disgracefully connected with the man to whom Your Excellency refers, through a reprehensible lawsuit certain merchants duped my poor husband into pursuing, the so-called Bræðratunga case, I do not know Arnas Arnæus. The discredit that I have incurred in the case is of no consequence to me; I have not once felt the slightest desire to ward off this drivel—which hardly becomes any more noteworthy just because it has found its way into the trial records here in Denmark. I would like Your Excellency to understand that it is not on my own account that I have come to ask you for justice."

When Gyldenløve heard what his visitor had to say about Arnæus, he let loose concerning this dangerous enemy, proclaiming the man hateful and treacherous: he had long pretended to be a friend of the king, but had always been planning to betray him, having despised him with all his heart; he said he knew for certain that Arnæus had once in the presence of witnesses spoken words to the effect that there had never been a criminal in Iceland except for the king of Denmark. He said that Arnæus hated every respectable Dane, no less than he hated those compatriots of his who affirmed their sincerity and earnestness in their service to their Royal Highness: he wished the deaths of such men wherever they could be found and would string them all up if he got the chance, so that he and his henchmen could take control of the country ad arbitrium.* He was convinced that her departed father would never be vindicated until this man and his comrades were hanging from the gallows. "One of them," he said, "was wrong in principio,* either your departed father or Arnas Arnæus." He asked whether her father's reputation was so valuable to her that she would prefer it if he, Gyldenløve, were to subjugate this man, and if she would lend her testimony and oaths to support his case.

She thought for a moment, then answered in a voice more deep and melancholy:

"And yet, I will not bear false witness against anyone."

—— II ——

Nearly half a year had passed since Jón Hreggviðsson, farmer from
Rein, had been fetched from the castle and elevated from enchained
evildoer to tranquil water bearer and woodcutter at the residence of
none other than the Assessor in the Consistory and Master of Danish
Antiquities. When the scholar from Grindavík brought him home to
the mansion from the castle, the erudite master greeted him and
smiled indulgently at him, and said that while they were still in the
process of finding a solution to his case he would be permitted board
and bed here in his home, but only if he conducted himself with the
utmost dignity, otherwise he would be sent to serve under the king's
standard, to fight with the king's soldiers in foreign lands.

Every time his countryman and master came upon him in the garden or met him as he was delivering buckets of water from the well,
he greeted him by name, asked him amicably how he was getting on,
and gave him snuff. On the other hand, he wasn't accorded any
excessively propitious respect by the resident rabble. Since the Danes
found the Icelandic odor so disgusting that they could barely stand
to mingle together under the same roof with a single Icelander, the
steward assigned Regvidsen a sleeping-place in the hayloft over the
stables. The coachman, however, prohibited him from coming too
near the horses, for fear that the beasts would pick up lice or some
other sort of vermin from Iceland's farmer of Christ. This chariot-
eer paid such close attention to his four-footed friends by washing
them and clipping and combing their hair morning and night that
even those unmarried homebodies in Iceland who were thought to
be most suitable for marriage, the daughters of better sorts of men,
could hardly have been described as being better tidied and decorated. At first the farmer thought it would be best, to help set the
others' minds at ease, if he were to eat elsewhere than at the servants'
table, since in Iceland it was customary for commoners to eat elsewhere than at table except during important feasts; instead they all
sat upon their own beds with their own wooden dinner pots. Thus a
girl was sent to bring the farmer's bowl of food out to the woodshed,

where he spent most of his day, except when he went to eat with the beggars, ragamuffins, and rascals who were fed twice a week in the vestibule of the main doorway in order to buttress support for the king.

One day toward the end of summer the farmer was granted something of an unexpected honor when there came to his woodshed no less a person than the housewife herself, his housemistress, the assessor's eminently virtuous and honor-bedecked wedded wife, Dame Mette. She greeted the Icelander. It had been twenty years since this gentlewoman cursed Jón Hreggviðsson to Hell in soldier's German through her own front door, and during that time her chin had sunk even further away from her mouth. Besides this so much fat had piled up on the woman that she looked similar to a clay statue that has fallen from a shelf and compressed itself into a lump before being put in the kiln. She had dabbed her face with white powder and bore upon her head a broad lace mantle that reached down to her hump, and she wore a wide, extremely wrinkled, full-length black skirt. Jón Hreggviðsson tore his hat off his head, wiped his nose, and declared his praise for God. She looked with a housemotherly expression at his pile of wood. He asked whether she wanted the sticks shorter than around three spans, or approximately, might he be permitted to say, the length of one medium-sized horse's penis, but she said that that would be a suitable length. Concerning water, he asked whether she would rather have it from the well on the west side, where the Danish boy was drowned last year, or from the one on the east side, out of which a German woman was fished in the spring.

She told him that the water and the wood were not laughing matters, and that there was one thing even more important: he had conducted himself in an exemplary manner here at the mansion. She said that her husband Arnæus customarily assigned someone to keep an eye on new recruits to the ranks of the mansion's servants, to see whether they might be cheaters or complainers; if so, the newcomers were swiftly driven away. Now, since Regvidsen had shown during the past year that he was not one of these undesirables, she felt that the time had come for her to look in on him and to inquire about his health. Jón Hreggviðsson replied that he'd never had any physical or spiritual health, neither good nor ill—he was an Icelander, after all. Everything depended on what the king wanted. He said he hoped that the good king, whom he could never praise highly enough, might have the heart not to let one fool from Skagi remain, for the rest of his days, an encumbrance to Christian countesses and baronesses in Denmark, and to their husbands, especially since this could very well result in the noble and honor-bedecked horses in Denmark contracting lice.

Whether the madam understood the farmer's courtesies or not, it turned out that she was quite eager to talk to him about something, not least due to the fact that her lord and wedded spouse belonged to the same race. She said that she had been casting it about in her mind for quite some time as to whether she should ask Regvidsen the news from Iceland, which certainly was a peculiar country—some even said that the mouth of Hell was located there, but since her dearest was a good Christian man, even though he was Icelandic, she would not believe it without further proof.

Maintaining his modest attitude for the sake of his country, he said that his exceptionally virtuous countess, baroness, and madam should not make the mistake of thinking that there was much in the way of news to be had from that cursed dog's ass that people call Iceland, except for that old bit of news that is and will always be the truth, even if good folk do themselves an injustice by even mentioning it in words, that Hell is and will always be located in that country throughout eternity—for those who deserve to be punished.

The madam asked, "How does it go for the Icelanders now that our Lord has sent them the merciful and blessed pestilence?"

"Oh, they've been slaughtered like sickly lambs and have gone straight to the devil," said Jón Hreggviðsson.

"Their pest-masters should have bled them," said the woman.

"Oh, all the blood was drained out of those scum a long time ago, good woman," said Jón Hreggviðsson. "Ever since they killed my kinsman Gunnar of Hlíðarendi there hasn't been any blood in Iceland."

"Who killed him?" asked the woman.

He looked away and scratched his head.

"I'm not going to go into that again," he said. "When a man's dead, a man's dead and gone to the devil. It's no use crying about it. But Gunnar of Hlíðarendi was a great and respectable man when he was alive."

"Yes, you Icelanders think we Danes have killed you all," said the woman. "But may I ask who it was that planned to kill my husband Magister* Arnæus when he went there to help them? Not the Danes—it was the Icelanders themselves."

"Yes, you see how those folk are," said Jón Hreggviðsson. "First I stole a bit of cord. Then, when I couldn't stand my son any longer, I killed him. And what's more, some people say I drowned a royal official in a waterhole."

"Even though my husband is called an Icelander, he is as fine a Christian as any other Danish man," said the woman.

"Yes, all the worse for him," said Jón Hreggviðsson. "He's been running around all over the place trying to save those Icelanders, first from the noose, then from the ax; or else from eating Danish maggots, which I for my part feel are just about right for them, and too good for them when they complain. And what's he gotten out of all this? Shit and shame. No, woman, you mustn't think I have any pity for those Icelanders. As for myself, I've always tried to keep some cord for fishing line up my sleeve. That's the only thing that pays. I'd gotten together a little fishing operation at Innrihólmur, in defiance of the Innrihólmsmen. A six-oared boat, woman, that's three oars a side, one two three four five six. I called it Hretbyggja, understand that, woman? Reetbygge in Danish. That's because southwesters crash against the shore on that side. In Skagi, good woman, understand? Akranes. Rein—under the mountain up from Innrihólmur, which is owned by the Innrihólmsmen. What more should I tell you? Oh, twice I've had daughters. The first one, the one with the big eyes, she was on her bier when I got back from the war. The other one's going to live, the pox didn't stick to her, she'd started sleeping with the farmhand sometimes at night, and she stood in the doorway when I left. She didn't look after the dog well enough, though, and it chased me west to Ólafsvík. It's Christ's farm. Jesus Christ owns the farm, understand that, woman?"

"How lovely of you to say that Jesus Christ owns the farm," said the woman. "It shows that your heart is contrite. He who repents shall be forgiven his sins."

"Sins," said Jón Hreggviðsson, and his nostrils flared. "I've never committed any sins. I'm a great and honorable criminal."

"God forgives those who admit that they are criminals," said the woman. "And the scullery girl has told me many times that you've never shorted them even a quarter of a rixdollar after they send you to market. That's another reason why I'm speaking to you like a man of honor even though you're an Icelander. Now what was I going to say? Oh yes, by the way, who is this whore of Babylon who has come to Copenhagen from Iceland?"

Jón Hreggviðsson looked away somewhat sheepishly and tried to solve this riddle, but since he found no clues in anything they'd just been discussing, he gave up.

"Babylon," he said. "You've put me in check with that one, good madam. I'll stop lying now."

She said, "Oh, that woman in Iceland who could have cared less even if they'd murdered my husband because of her; but of course they knew that she was worse than murder, so they kept on trying to implicate him with her until the king himself started believing their stories and ordered them to condemn this good Christian man, who could be a Dane or even a German—that woman. What kind of woman is she, anyway? And how could my husband, this good Christian man who is always lying amongst his old books at night, have had any interest in chasing after her?"

Jón Hreggviðsson scratched himself in likely as well as unlikely spots as he puzzled over this question, until he started to thread together an answer.

"Although my mother's side of the family has always had books, I've never read one," he said. "And I can't write any letters except for runes. So I wouldn't blame any man for it if he exchanged a book for a woman, if he's determined to stay up all night delving into things, because there's no two things that can be read as alike as those two."

"There is no excuse for an Icelandic man to cheat on a Danish woman," she said. "But luckily, as my dearest says, nothing is true that cannot be proven—and therefore, it's not true."

"Yes, as for me and myself, when I was in Rotterdam, which is in Holland, where the doggers come from, I met a priest's wife there one night. Mmhmm, what can I say? I had an ugly, boring old woman back in Iceland—"

"If you are insinuating that I am ugly and boring, in an attempt to excuse my husband for sleeping with that whore of Babylon, then let me tell you, Regvidsen, that even though he, Arnæus, thinks he's a man, he doesn't fetch criminals out of Bremerholm Castle without my giving him leave to do so. And this I can tell you, Icelander, you who emit such a stench of rotten shark and whale oil and all that other shit that one finds out in Iceland that it turns all the perfume of all the lavender in Denmark into powerless vapors, that my former husband, who was a real man even though the king never invited him to dinner, said that I knew well how to please a man. And where would this man be now, the one who's supposed to be called my husband, if I hadn't put up the money and the house and the carriage and horses? He didn't own a single book. So I have every right to know what sort of woman it is out in Iceland who's supposedly come here to Copenhagen."

"She's thin," said Jón Hreggviðsson.

"How thin?" asked the woman.

"Almost clean through, almost nothing," said Jón Hreggviðsson. "Not like anything I've ever seen."

"Like what then?" asked the woman.

He closed one eye and peered at the woman.

"Like the plant called the reed—the thinnest and most flexible of all plants," said Jón Hreggviðsson.

"Are you insinuating that I'm stout?" said the woman. "Or that she's some sort of switch to be used against me?"

"My magnificent dame mistress and baroness mustn't credit one Icelandic Bremerholmer with more wisdom than he really has; and she mustn't take offense at his dim-witted babble. If this ragamuffin didn't have a mouth, if you could call it that, which has so often been the cause of injury to God and men, he would kiss her esteemed toes."

"Now what was that nonsense about the switch?" said the woman.

Jón Hreggviðsson said: "All I really meant was a kind of staff that can't be broken—a staff that rights itself when you let go of it; it becomes as straight as it was before."

"I order you to answer," said the woman.

"You'd do better asking Grindavík-Jón," said Jón Hreggviðsson. "He's a learned man and a philosopher."

"The insane Joen Grindevigen," she said. "The kind of people Icelanders call learned men and philosophers are here in Denmark called village idiots and it is against the law for them to take one step outside of their own villages."

"Or Jón Marteinsson then," said Jón Hreggviðsson. "He knows what kind of women there are in both Iceland and Denmark, because he's slept with bishops' daughters. I would never ever compare to such a man."

"My house is a Christian house—hen-thieves are not permitted here," said the madam. "And if you don't tell me this instant everything there is to tell about this woman you'll be going to Jón Marteinsson yourself—then he can look after you."

"The long and short of what I know about this woman is that she rescued me from the ax at Öxará and tied me to a horseblock in Ólafsvík."

"Does she have money?" asked the woman. "And how does she dress?"

"Did you say money? She's got more money than any woman in Denmark," said Jón Hreggviðsson. "She's got all the money in Iceland. She's got silver and gold from throughout the ages. She owns all the estates in the land and all the cottages along with them, whether she's able to steal them back from the king or not; forests and salmon-rivers, woman; all those beaches so rich in driftage—a man could build his own Constantinople from just one of those tree trunks if he only had a saw; marshy meadows and sedged morasses; pastures up in the highlands with streams full of fish and grazing land right up against the glaciers; out on remote stretches of ocean islands so full of seabirds that you wade up to your knees in eiderdown, woman; eddying bird-cliffs sheer to the sea where on midsummer's eve one can hear happy egg-hunters cursing at the ends of their ropes sixty ells down. But that's just the least of what she owns—I would never reach the end counting it all up. But she's richest of all on the day when all her wealth has been seized by the court and the murderer Jón Hreggviðsson throws her a rixdollar as she sits there by the road. How's she dressed? She's got a golden band around her waist, where the red flame burned, good woman. She's dressed like the elf-wife's always been dressed in Iceland. She comes clad in blue and adorned with gold and silver to the place where one blackhaired murderous dog lies beaten. But she was never dressed any better than when she was put in wool socks and a shift of wadmal by beggarwomen and whores, when she turned those eyes upon Jón Hreggviðsson, those eyes that will rule over Iceland upon the very day when the rest of the world falls under the weight of its own evil deeds."

— **12** —

Late one autumn evening, at Goldsmith's guesthouse in Nyhavn, a sojourning gentlewoman and her maidservant prepare for departure. Moored ships from faraway places bob gently in the narrow canal outside, their bows touching the embankment momentarily before swinging out again. They pack their belongings, their valuables, and their clothing into boxes and trunks, the lady assigning everything its particular place, yet distractedly. She even forgets her task for a time, and turns away to stand lost in her own private vision at the window. Her middle-aged maidservant follows suit: she stops what she is doing and watches her mistress in secret, compassionately.

Finally everything is packed, with the exception of one item. Lying upon the windowsill, half-wrapped in a red silken handkerchief, is an ancient, shriveled parchment book, darkened by soot, begrimed by the oily fingers of men dead for so long that no trace of their lives on earth remained except for these fingerprints. Again and again the maidservant hesitantly picks up this artifact, fumblingly unwraps the red silk and wraps it around anew, or else puts it down in another place before returning it after a moment to where it had originally lain. Still her mistress has not told her where this book is to go; in fact she hasn't mentioned it at all. Night falls and the streets grow silent; the seagulls that hover back and forth around the rigging of the ships increase in number, and the lady still stands at the window, staring out.

Until finally the maidservant pipes up: "Would you like me to venture out onto the streets, though it's so late, and return the book to where it belongs?"

"Do you have any idea where this book belongs?" asked her mistress in a low voice, its tones golden-dusky and distant.

"I remember you saying before we left Iceland that this book belonged in only one place; hm; with one man."

"That man is more distant from us in Copenhagen in the fall than he was in Iceland in the spring," said the lady.

The maidservant busied herself with some small task or other and answered, without looking up: "My deceased mistress, your blessed mother, often told us girls a story about one of your foremothers, a woman who kissed no man more warmly than her father's enemy, nor treated anyone more openhandedly than she did him, though she sent a man after him to kill him after he'd ridden out of the yard."

Snæfríður did not look at her maidservant, but answered lukewarmly, from somewhere deep within her distraction: "It may be that my sagalike great-grandmother killed her father's enemy after having first given him gifts. But she did not send him gifts after having had him killed."

"And my deceased mistress's daughter hasn't killed anyone yet," said the maidservant. "And now we have nothing left but one night in this city, and there's not much left of this night either, and it's fall and any kind of weather is possible, and in just a few moments we're supposed to sail out onto that raging sea that most resembles the rushing rivers in the south of Iceland. And whether we perish or not, time is running out, and if she doesn't pull herself together and take advantage of this final night then she'll never return the book to him; his book."

"I have no idea what you're trying to imply," said the lady, and she looked with surprise at her maidservant. "I don't expect that you're talking about the rigger who's been going back and forth, back and forth, this entire day and all day yesterday and all day the day before yesterday, all day, all night, doing his work on the far side of the canal?"

The maidservant said nothing. After a moment she started gasping and panting as she stood stooping over an open trunk, and when her mistress looked over she saw the woman's tears falling.

"I have succeeded—he is to be convicted by my friends Beyer and Jón Eyjólfsson at Öxará in the spring," said the gentlewoman coldly. "The rescript from the king is in that trunk."

"He hasn't been convicted yet," said the maidservant. "Those papers didn't come until today. He won't hear about it until after you've gone. You can give him the gift tonight."

"You are a child, dear Guðríður, though you are twenty-five years older than me," said the gentlewoman. "Do you really imagine that he didn't know everything about my errand from the moment I stepped on shore here in the summer? He is not deceived by baubles."

"But you yourself know best why you brought this book with you from Iceland this summer," said the maidservant.

"If I had been rebuffed and forced to sail back to Iceland having accomplished nothing, I might have given him this gift," said the lady. "But the victor cannot give gifts to those whom he defeats. And in the end I almost gave the book to that devil Jón Marteinsson, who showed up here today while you were out. He tried extortion: he said I had him to thank for Bræðratunga."

"God be with us! What would your dear departed mother have said?" said the maidservant as she wiped away tears. "I'm sure you would have preferred to die rather than to give that miserable lout gifts! He's put your name in who knows how many documents here in Copenhagen, all to the amusement of the Danes."

"We'll let the Danes laugh, dear Guðríður. Put the old book under the lid of that trunk there and lock it up well. It's bedtime for us travelers."

The lamp flame had dwindled, but it was useless to clip the wick: they would shortly extinguish it and go to sleep. In the morning they would be gone. Their room was divided into two, the walls of the outermost chamber paneled halfway up with green-painted wood and whitewashed the rest of the way. Hanging on the walls were embossed bronze bowls and enameled dishes decorated with colorful paintings, as well as two copperplates, one obtained from Romanian Jews, the other from the Cathedral of St. Mark in Venice. Stacked upon the shelves of an open, painted cabinet against the wall were the dishes, bowls, cups, and other tableware that they had used for their meals. The lady did not join her host at his table, but rather requested that her meals be brought to her room. Further in was the bedroom, where the lady's bed, made up with snow-white bed-clothes, was located beneath a window; the maidservant slept upon a bench near the doorway.

Although the lady had said it was bedtime, she continued to stand lost in thought at the window, forcing the maidservant to find something to do in the meantime since she would not retire before her mistress. It was midnight. The silence was so deep that they were nearly shocked when a knock came upon the door. The drowsy night watchman had come up to inform the lady that a foreign gentleman was standing downstairs, wishing to speak to her Excellency.

She turned pale and her pupils widened. "Go and make sure that it is indeed me he is searching for," she said, "and if that is the case, then show him in."

As he stood there now at her doorway in this guesthouse in Copenhagen on her last night in the city, after all that had happened and all the trial of distance, he felt as self-assured as if he had left this room just a short time ago to take a stroll in the king's park in pleasant weather.

"Good evening," he said.

He held his hat in his hands. The man was still clothed in his fine old style, but he had grown stouter, the lines in his face had deepened, and the shine in his eyes had been dimmed from overwork and exhaustion. His carefully curled argent peruke glistened.

She did not immediately return the visitor's greeting as she stood there at the window, but instead looked sharply at her maidservant and said:

"Go down to your friend the cook and say good-bye to her."

He waited just beyond the threshold until the maidservant walked out past him, then he stepped over and entered her room. She said nothing, but went to the door and shut it, took one step forward and welcomed her guest with a kiss, then wrapped both arms around his neck and pressed her face to his cheek. He ran the palm of his hand over her long, fair hair, which had started to pale. She buried her face in his chest for some time before looking up at him.

"I didn't think that you would come, Árni," she said. "Yet somehow I knew that you would."

"Some come late," said he.

"I have a book for you," said she.

"That's like you," said he.

She asked him to sit down upon the bench. Then she opened the lid of the trunk where the book lay wrapped in red silk, took it out, and handed it to him.

"This was my blessed father's dearest book," she said.

He started unwrapping the silk gently and slowly, and she waited anxiously to behold the gleam that newly acquired antique books always ignited in his eyes. Suddenly he paused in his unveiling, looked up, smiled, and said:

"I've lost my dearest book."

"Which one?" she said.

"The one we found together," he said—"in Jón Hreggviðsson's house."

He explained to her casually and resignedly how he had lost the *Skálda*.

"It's a terrible loss," she said.

"Most terrible," he said, "is when a man loses his love for precious books."

"I thought that a man could love a lost treasure for as long as he missed it," she said.

"A man doesn't know precisely when the longing disappears," he said. "In its own way it's like a wound that's been healed; or like death. A man doesn't know precisely when the wound ceased to cause him pain; nor does he know precisely when he dies. Suddenly a man is healed; suddenly dead."

She looked at him aloofly.

Finally she said: "You have the countenance of a dead man who appears to his friend in a dream: it is he and yet it is not he."

He smiled. And in the silence that followed he began again to unwrap the book.

When he was finished he set the silken cover aside, nodded his head, and said, "I know this book. I offered to acquire Holt in Önundarfjörður for your father in exchange for this poor lawbook— it is namely considered to be the most important source in existence concerning Germanic society, even more important than the old *Lex Salica** of the Franks. Yes, that was at the time when the Treasury considered my counsel about as useful as a leak in the roof. I had also intended to wait and offer him Viðey* if he didn't think Holt sufficient enough payment for this poor old thing. But although he seldom refused an opportunity to acquire real property if he could get it for a reasonable price, he knew as well as I that all the estates in Iceland are worth next to nothing compared to old Icelandic manuscripts; so he would not let himself be persuaded in this case. Later I wrote to him and offered to deposit into his account with the Company here in Copenhagen as much silver or gold as he decided, whatever the amount, for this worn-out old book. The following spring he sent me as a gift a copy of the book, made in the customary haphazard way that such things are done in Iceland: either the scribe himself misreads the original text, or else he works himself into difficulties trying to correct his predecessors' mistakes. I myself already owned several higher quality copies of the book."

"Are you still of the opinion that no Iceland exists any longer except for the Iceland that's preserved in these old books?" she asked. "And are we, the inhabitants of that country, only an ache in your heart that you would be happy to get rid of in any way possible? Or perhaps we aren't even as much as that any longer?"

He said: "The soul of the Nordic peoples is to be found in Icelandic books, but not in the folk who currently live in the Nordic countries or in Iceland itself. On the other hand, a sibyl once prophesied that the golden game pieces of old will be found in the grass before it all ends."*

"I hear that there's been talk here of sending us to the heaths of Jylland," she said.

"If you wish, this can be prevented," he said, and he smiled.

"If I wish," she repeated. "What can one pitiable woman do? The last time I saw you I was a beggar at Þingvellir by Öxará."

"I was in the service of the defenseless," he said. "I saw you sitting out by the path—"

"—wearing the rags of those whom you had exonerated," she added.

He spoke darkly, without looking up, entirely lost in his own thoughts as if reciting an old refrain:

"Where are the lowly whom I wished to raise? They are lower now than ever. And the defenseless whom I wished to defend? Even their sighs are no longer heard."

"You have Jón Hreggviðsson," she said.

"Yes," he said. "I have Jón Hreggviðsson. And that's all I have. And it's possible that he'll be taken away from me and hanged before the winter has passed."

"Oh, no," she said, and she inched herself closer toward him. "We're not supposed to be talking about Jón Hreggviðsson. I'm sorry that I mentioned his name. I'm going to go wake the landlord and ask him to bring us a pitcher of wine."

"No," he said. "No wine from the landlord; nothing from anyone. As long as we are sitting here together we have everything."

She leaned back and quietly repeated the final word:

"Everything."

"In any case, only one thing exists in our lives," said he.

She whispered: "One thing."

"Do you know why I have come?" he asked.

"Yes," she said. "So that you will never part from me again."

She stood up, went over to a sturdy medium-sized ironclad trunk, and took out from a small end compartment some impressive-looking documents affixed with the seal of the supreme governmental authority.

She held out the documents, gripping them between her thumb and index finger like a man holding a rat by its tail.

"These rescripts," said she, "these orders and subpoenas, dispensations and permits, are nothing but vanity and hypocrisy."

The king's seal hung by a thread from one of the documents, and he went over and weighed it in the palm of his hand. His hand movements were like those of a man who dangles a spider by its silken line and says, "Up, up if you know something good, down, down if you know something bad."

"Your business here has been successful," he said.

"I came here in the hope of finding you," she said. "Nothing else matters. Now I can tear up this rubbish."

He said: "It doesn't matter whether these deeds are intact or torn to pieces. All of the decrees made by the Danish king will no longer be valid in Iceland before the next Alþingi is convened at Öxará."

"Do you mean that from now on we're to be governed by dreams and fables?" she asked, and her face brightened.

"Control over Iceland has been offered to me," he said. "I am to become its lord, and you will be my lady. I have come here precisely to tell you this."

"High treason?" she asked in a low voice.

"No," he said. "The king wants to sell Iceland. The Danish kings have always been terribly eager to sell or pawn off this possession, but only foreign princes have been considered to be suitable buyers. Until now, that is. Some Germans from Hamburg intend to buy the country. But they don't trust themselves to control it unless they can appoint a governor who is popular with his people. They are of the opinion that I am this man."

She stared at him for several moments.

"What are you going to do?" she asked.

"Rule the country," he said with a smile. "The first step will be to reestablish our civil liberties based upon a foundation of law similar to the one that was established when the covenant was made with Hákon the Old in Norway."*

"And the judiciary?" she asked.

"One of my first tasks will be to remove all of the Danish king's functionaries. Some I will banish, including the regent Páll Beyer and the vice-magistrate Jón Eyjólfsson. We must cleanse the legislature of Danish pollution and establish it anew."

"And where do you plan to have your seat of power?" she said.

"Where would you like me to have my seat of power?"

She said: "At Bessastaðir."

"As you wish," he said. "The residence shall be rebuilt and constructed in no less a splendid manner than the palace of any landgrave within the empire. I'll order a library constructed of stone and will return to their rightful home all of the precious books that I saved from rotting away in the hovels of folk who have been ravaged into utter misery by the Danes."

"We'll have a magnificent banquet hall," she said. "The walls will be hung with the weapons and shields of ancient champions. Your friends will sit with you in the evenings at an oaken table and recount ancient sagas and drink tankards of beer."

"The people of Iceland will no longer be punished for trying to earn a living through trade," said Arnas Arnæus. "Commercial centers based on foreign models will rise around the harbors and a fleet of ships will be fitted out for fishing. We'll sell stockfish and woolen goods to cities on the mainland, just as the Icelanders of old did until the death of Jón Arason, and from those same cities we'll buy wares befitting civilized men. The earth will be mined for precious minerals. The Kaiser will shake his fist at the Danish king and demand that he return to the Icelanders the artifacts that the Danish king's men stole from the cathedral in Hólar and from the monasteries at Munkaþverá, Möðruvellir, and Þingeyri. The ancient estates that the Danish crown seized after the downfall of the Icelandic church will be recovered. And we shall build in Iceland a splendid university and collegia,* where Icelandic scholars will once again live the lives of men."

"We'll build palaces," she said, "no less great than those that Governor Gyldenløve built in Denmark using the taxes from Iceland."

He said: "A splendid courthouse shall be raised at Þingvellir, and another bell hung there, larger and more melodious than the one that the king demanded from Iceland and that the hangman ordered Jón Hreggviðsson to cut down."

"The cold moonlight gleaming upon Drekkingarhylur will no longer be the one and only merciful consolation for destitute women in Iceland," said she.

"And famished beggars will no longer be strung up in the name of justice at Almannagjá," said he.

"They'll all be our friends," said she, "for the folk will be contented."

"And the Þrælakista at Bessastaðir shall be torn down," said he. "For in the land where the folk are contented no crimes are committed."

"And we'll ride throughout the land on white horses," said she.

— 13 —

Seagulls still hovered peaceably over the streets and canals of the sleeping city when from outside came a heavy clattering of hooves and the rattling of carriage wheels, and finally the screech of brakes being pulled. A moment later there was a quiet knock upon the door, like a secret sign. Snæfríður, clad only in a nightshirt, peered out through the doorway. Her face was flushed and her eyes softly lustrous. Her hair hung loosely about her shoulders.

"You knock upon the door and stand unmoving outside," she said. "Why don't you come in?"

"I thought I might be a nuisance," said the maidservant.

"To whom?"

"Are you alone?"

"What's that to you?"

"They've come from the Company with a carriage to fetch the luggage," said the maidservant.

"Where have you been all night, woman?"

"You told me last night to go to my dear Trine," said the maidservant. "I didn't dare come in again. I thought someone might be there."

"What do you mean? Who do you think might have been here?"

"I never heard anyone leave."

"And who might it have been leaving?"

"But the man who came to fetch the book?"

"What book?"

"The book."

"No one has come to fetch the book, as you will see if you look under the lid of the trunk where you put it last night."

The lady opened the trunk as a sign of proof for her maidservant, and indeed, there lay the book, just as she had left it, wrapped in red silk.

"No one has ever heard of him leaving behind a book," said the woman.

"I have no idea whom you're talking about," said the lady.

"But the man who was standing here on the threshold when you told me to leave last night!"

"It's true, last night I asked you to go downstairs and bid farewell to our host's cook, who has been a friend to you. But tell no one that you saw a man here—people might think you were out of your mind."

The massive buildings of the Iceland Trade Company out on Slotsholmen appeared in silhouette against the dawn. The Iceland merchantman lay at anchor; it was to sail today with the grain supplements that the king believed would help alleviate Iceland's burden of famine.

The staff at Goldsmith's house had risen although it was still early. Servants loaded the lady's luggage onto the carriage and the landlord's wife helped her to dress for travel, weeping that a woman with eyes such as hers should have to set sail across the dreadful sea where in winter only God has command, on her way to the land where the funnel of Hell burns below ice.

That same morning the assessor Arnas Arnæus was up and about in his library much earlier than he'd been for quite some time. He wakened a servant and ordered him to light the fire in the stove and bring him hot tea, then asked him to dust in the library and tidy up the foyer because he was expecting a guest sometime before noon.

After he had shaved, combed his peruke, and applied ointments and colognes befitting a nobleman, he paced the room in true Icelandic fashion, smoking from a large pipe.

Around midmorning a huge foreign carriage stopped outside the gate, and from it stepped a giant man in an immensely capacious

cloak. He was potbellied and his jowls hung down over his shoulders:
it was Uffelen from Hamburg. The German was shown to the assessor's study, where he began bowing as soon as he reached the door.
Arnas Arnæus invited him in and bade him sit. They began by
exchanging general news and paying each other flattering compli-
ments. Then the visitor turned to his business. He had returned
according to the agreement that they had made earlier in the year, to
hear his final answer to the question that he had brought up with his
lord on several occasions concerning his native country Islandia,
especially and particularly in connection with the proposal affecting
the island's future that had insistently been conveyed to the Hamburg merchants by the envoys of His Highness the Danish king; a
swift reply was imperative now, since it appeared that the war with
the Swedes could not be delayed much longer. The Hamburg merchants had now investigated as carefully as possible various relationes* regarding this land inasmuch as opportunity had allowed,
and reiterated and reaffirmed the stipulations previously agreed to,
that they would take the purchase of the island from the Danish king
into consideration only if they were able to convince a certain Icelander who was trusted and accepted by the poor inhabitants of the
island to become their chief man over Islandia. This man, moreover,
had to have the ability to be able to act as the representative of the
Kaiser in Iceland, which they hoped would someday develop into a
republic, while the Kaiser himself would bear the title of Supreme
Majesty of this country like so many other countries in the
Holy Roman Empire, whether they were autonomous or semi-
autonomous. Uffelen said that both he and his colleagues, acting upon
the assessor's advice, had tried to find another man amongst the Icelanders who might be more likely than the assessor, or perhaps might
be just as likely but much more eager, to accept the position and
responsibility of governor of the island. They had not been able to
find such a man. They would neither trust their island to some
retired Danish court official nor dress up as their servant some uncul-
tured boor of a farmer, and they knew well that all of the foremost
men on the island were infected with an inconvenient, old-school
loyalty toward the Danish king, secured through years of bribes and

promises of emoluments. On the other hand, they had received verifiable reports that the lord Assessor Consistorii was the favorite and darling son of the inhabitants of the aforementioned island, a folk so helpless that they were incapable of raising their standards of morality and culture on their own.

Arnas Arnæus, who had been pacing the room during the German's speech, asked whether they had discussed with the Danish envoys the plan that was now uppermost in the minds of various ministers in the Chancery, though it had not yet been put down on paper: to send the surviving band of starving Icelanders to the heaths of Jylland and afterward sell the empty land.

Uffelen said that as far as the Hamburg merchants were concerned, such a plan was out of the question, since they were in no position to hire and transport the manpower necessary to make profitable use of the island. There were no human works to be found in Iceland no matter how much one searched, and the native inhabitants had the talent, unknown amongst the members of any other race, of being able to live inside piles of turf or holes in the ground instead of houses; it was likely that no race of people other than the one already acclimatized to Iceland could sustain itself there. The Hamburg merchants would aim to increase the Icelanders' prosperity and help them to shape as quickly as possible a way of life no more inferior to the one that was in vogue while the Hansa controlled commercial enterprises there in the old days.

Arnas Arnæus asked whether the Hamburg merchants might not have considered whether it was advisable to appoint a German as governor of Iceland, if a clement and righteous German could be found.

To this Uffelen said that he could give the same old answer as found in the letters and memoirs of Hinrik the Eighth and his advisors, made in response to the Danish king's persistent offers to the English king for the purchase of the aforementioned island. The English had replied that they had no desire to purchase a country that would cost so much to safeguard as Iceland if the foreign authorities were to carry out their work there secure of life and limb. According to an investigation into the history of the island carried out by the

English king's advisors, the native islanders were well known for their barbaric attacks against foreign envoys to whom they did not take a liking. This had always been one of the principal reasons why it was so difficult for the Danish king to sell the country. Uffelen knew the names of famous foreigners whom the Icelandic commoners had executed without benefit of trial or law, kings' agents and governmental proxies, governors, bishops, and regents, amongst them a number of men of noble birth. Icelandic women had consistently spearheaded such attacks. He could just as well mention the time when one Icelandic woman had ordered an illustrious Danish nobleman boiled in a kettle along with sixteen of his servants—the Danish king was never able to exact revenge for this murder, nor even so much as indict the murderers. One lofty German baron who had been in the service of the Danish king was also found encairned like a dog under some scree a stone's throw from the Schalholt bishopric's vegetable garden. A celebrated, right honorable Swedish archbishop, whose coat of arms could still be seen hanging in the cathedral in Uppsala, was made bishop of Iceland, but the rabble drowned him in a bag like a dog. "We men of Hamburg," said Uffelen, "do not conduct ourselves with kingly arrogance. We are judicious merchants, goodwilled toward the Icelanders, and we wish to conduct trade with them through the intercession of one of their own friends."

When he reached this point Arnas Arnæus stopped pacing. He stood facing the German and said:

"There is one reason why it is impossible for me to serve as your representative in Iceland: namely, the man who is offering to sell the country does not own it. It is true that I was appointed to my current office, though I may not have merited it, by a king who became ruler of my native country as a result of intractable events and accidents long before my time; and therefore, the latter error would be even more despicable than the former if I were also to become the confidant of those to whom he would wrongly sell this country."

The gentleman from Hamburg answered: "My lord knows that stored in Hamburg in a secret coffer are the letters that the bishops Augmundus and Jona Aronis,* in their own ways two of the most eminent men in Iceland during their day and age, wrote to our Kaiser, Karl the Fifth of praiseworthy memory, asking him for his support in their struggle against the Danish king, who at that time had sent out mercenaries on warships to plunder Iceland of its chattel and valuables and to take over the estates owned by the Icelandic church. In their letters Their Excellencies the Icelandic bishops express their hope that the Kaiser will protect and assist their country by granting Iceland status as either a confederate state within the Holy Roman Empire or else as a member, with full duties and rights, of the Hansa's republican alliance. Your office, under German patronage, would only represent a continuation of the endeavors of these outstanding Icelandic devotees to their fatherland who lived during those proud times before the islanders were thoroughly broken beneath the yoke of the Danish crown."

Arnas Arnæus said that things had been completely different at that time. The Danish king had waged war against a strong authoritative power in Iceland, a power that was firmly rooted in the land and its people: the Icelandic church, an institution that was in many ways equivalent to and synonymous with Icelandic self-determination, yet which was also an inseparable part of the Catholic Christianity represented by the Roman church; therefore the Icelandic church had no choice but to act as a votary to the German Kaiser, who, in accordance with the origins and nature of the empire, was a confederate of the holy seat at Rome. No such institution existed any longer in Iceland, since the Danish king had wiped out the Icelandic church as a temporal authority and obliterated it from its place in human hearts as a moral authority, introducing in its place the Lutheran heresy, as it is called, which aims to make the pillage and rapine of princes canon law. "Therefore you can see," said Arnæus, "that in Iceland there exists no power, institute, public opinion, or any other sort of backing that would serve to morally buttress or legally justify my entering into the service of a new foreign overlord."

Uffelen said that the Icelanders were obligated to remember that the greatest Icelanders of their time, those two elders who had sought the support of Kaiser Karl the Fifth, had both been arrested by the Danish king's agents—one, blind and decrepit, had been exiled to a foreign country, the other, seventy years old, had been brought out and beheaded in his very own country by the Danes.

Arnas Arnæus said: "Herr Uffelen! My heart is truly moved when

I hear that a foreigner has such an excellent knowledge of events that have taken place in Iceland. Our Redeemer has withheld from us many of his gifts of love, but I never once thought that I would be forced to doubt my countrymen's ability to remember. The fates of Bishop Ögmundur of Skálholt and Bishop Arason of Hólar are and always shall remain fixed in the memory of each and every Icelander throughout the centuries. And although the Danish king has not yet actually managed to sell us into slavery despite his best intentions, enough has already occurred to ensure that His Most Clement Heart will have its own deserved place in Icelandic history and lore in times to come.

"A man who tries to strangle a small animal with his hands eventually grows tired. He holds it an arm's length away and tightens his grip around its throat as strongly as he can, but it does not die. It stares at him; its claws are out. The animal expects no help, though a cheerful-looking troll might come along and offer to free it. Its only hope is that time is on its side and that its enemy's strength will wane.

"If a small and defenseless nation is granted somewhere in the midst of its misfortune the fortune to possess a sufficiently powerful enemy, time will fight on its side just as it does for the animal in my example. If in its dire need it assents to the troll's protection it will be swallowed up in one bite. I know that you men of Hamburg would send us Icelanders maggot-free grain, and that you would never consider it worth your while to try to swindle us by tampering with the weights and scales. But when German fishing villages and German market towns have been built on Iceland's shores, how long will we have to wait before German castles with German barons and mercenaries are raised there as well? What then will be the lot of the Icelanders, who wrote such celebrated books? They will have become nothing more than the fat servants of a German puppet state. A fat servant is not much of a man. A beaten servant is a great man, because in his breast freedom has its home."

— **14** —

During the autumn and the following winter Arnas Arnæus no longer spent as much time in his library as he was normally accustomed to doing. He had for the longest time been the most diligent of men when it came to rising early, often starting work between matins and midmorning, though he always complained that his mornings scarcely sufficed him to make, for the benefit of future generations, the necessary annotations concerning the contents, origins, and composition of the thousand or so old Icelandic manuscripts that he had in his keeping. Now it happened that on some days he was not to be found in his study until well past noon, and on other days not at all. If anyone came asking his whereabouts, his staff usually replied that he was ill, or else had gone to bed late and decided to sleep in. Once or twice they answered that he'd been out of the house since the day before, but they weren't sure where he'd gone. He paid little heed to the official duties he performed for both the ecclesiastical court, the Consistory, and academia, at the university.

Sitting alone in the study is the studiosus antiquitatum Grindvicensis, working at his livelihood, copying out faded vellum manuscripts. He often finds himself compelled to stop to scribble down various ideas or notations that spring to mind, bending over the learned texts that he himself has authored in his spare time, texts concerning Iceland's incredible natural wonders, especially its mysterious energy. In addition to this work, he had been entrusted to guard the house against Jón Marteinsson, a task that burdened him with such grave responsibility that he had no peace, day or night. Much of the Grindavíkian's time was wasted in dashing from his desk to check to see if he really had heard a rustling in the foyer or at the back door, or the sound of footsteps outside the window. On many nights he was plagued by the suspicion that this unwelcome visitor was on the prowl in the vicinity, and he would neither take off his clothes nor go up to his room to sleep; instead he would sprawl himself out on the floor of the study with a thick volume in folio under his head, wrap himself in a woolen coverlet from Auðnir on Vatnsleysuströnd, and either sleep with one eye open or lie there awake amongst the books that were the life of Iceland and the soul of the Nordic lands.

One evening he was working on his great grammatical treatise, attempting to prove that Icelandic, otherwise known as the Danish tongue, had never been heard spoken in the garden of Eden, but rather had come into being as a mixture of Greek and Celtic around the time of the Great Flood. He had started to drift into sleep over this significant work of scholarship, and had even, though it might come as some surprise, leaned over, head on his arms, as he sat there at his desk. A westerly was blowing that evening, thoroughly uncompromising and bitter, with intermittent sleet. The fire in the stove had died out and the house had grown cold. A gate that hadn't been locked properly rattled in its post in a neighbor's wall, and muffled hoofbeats and the rattling of carriage wheels could sometimes be heard coming from nearby streets, as soldiers rode home or the king drove out to take his pleasure. There was nothing suspicious afoot anywhere—until suddenly a peculiar wailing sound, both tenuous and deep, gruff and tuneless, comes from somewhere out in the garden. The Grindavíkian jumped up with a start and was instantly wide awake.

"Could a cat be in heat in this wind?" asked the studiosus antiquitatum fearfully. He involuntarily started in on an old hymn for comfort in distress that he had learned at his mother's knee:

> "While Satan eternally howls and rages
> There in his foul pit groveling
> My Lord reigns in heaven throughout the ages
> With harp-song and angels hovering."

He crossed himself for protection against evil spirits and hurried out of the study toward the back entrance, then lifted the door from its posts and peered out. And naturally, who should be there but Jón Marteinsson himself, with his bag of tricks.

When the studiosus antiquitatum saw what sort of thing it was standing there he hissed through the doorway and against the wind:

"Abi, scurra."*

"Copenhagen's burning," mumbled the visitor, and the wind carried his words away. The house's occupant was just about to start in on a Latin jingle he kept handy for moments such as this, and had even opened his mouth to begin, when the brim of a wind-squall snuck in through the doorway, bearing a shred of the visitor's words to his ears. Once again Jón Marteinsson succeeded in taking Jón Guðmundsson completely by surprise.

"What? What did you say?" said the latter.

"Nothing," said the visitor. "Except when I said that Copenhagen's burning. There's a fire in Copenhagen."

"In that case I know you're lying, you wicked fiend, unless you yourself started it," said the Grindavíkian.

"Deliver my message to Árni and tell him I want a piece of a saga."

"First tell us where the *Skálda* is, which you doubtlessly sold to the Swedes for brennivín."

At that moment the air glimmered: the fire could not have been far away.

"No brennivín," said Jón Marteinsson. "And I got so cold standing out by the wall watching it. It's past midnight. I went down to the Golden Lion to ask about Árni, but the girls said he'd be drinking at home tonight since his carriage left there this morning, with him in it sleeping."

"If you dare once more to connect the name of my lord and master with that whores' den I'll call for the master of the watch," said the studiosus antiquitatum.

"The place isn't that bad—just now the king himself was riding down there on all fours. But you wouldn't be used to anything better, coming from Grindavík," said Jón Marteinsson.

"The king does not ride on all fours—he rides in a four-horse carriage," said the man from Grindavík. "He who slanders the king shall be flogged with eighty strokes of the rod."

The glimmer continued to play about the vault of heaven. To the west one could see the roofs of nearby mansions and the tower of Our Lady's Church silhouetted against the dull red glow of embers in the darkness of the night.

The Grindavíkian shut the door carefully and turned the key. He didn't go straight to his master to report the news; instead he went to where Jón Hreggviðsson was lying, woke him, ordered him to get up immediately and go out into the garden and stand guard over Jón Marteinsson, who had set the city of Copenhagen on fire and who was now planning to take advantage of a good opportunity, when everything was in confusion, to steal books from the householder and chickens from the madam. He told the farmer that the flames loomed over the tower of Our Lady's Church.

Then the Grindavíkian went back into the house and up the stairway, stopping outside the assessor's bedroom. The door was locked. He knocked several times, and when he received no answer he called in through the keyhole:

"My lord, my lord! Jón Marteinsson has come! Flames are looming over Our Lady's Church. Copenhagen is ablaze!"

Finally the sound of a key turning in the keyhole came from within, and the door opened. A dim light burned in the bedroom. Arnæus stood in the doorway drunk with sleep, still wearing yesterday's clothing. He was unshaven and wore no wig. The bedroom reeked of the stenches of alcohol and settled tobacco smoke. He stared out at the man in the doorway, his gaze strangely aloof, giving the appearance at first as if he had neither heard what the Grindavíkian had said nor understood its significance.

"My lord," said his famulus once again, "Jón Marteinsson has set the city on fire."

"What does it matter to me?" said Arnas Arnæus in his dusky bass.

"Copenhagen is on fire," said the Grindavíkian.

"Don't you suppose that that's one of Jón Marteinsson's lies?" said Arnas Arnæus.

The Grindavíkian answered, without giving himself any time to think: "My lord himself knows full well that Jón Marteinsson never lies."

"Is that so," said Arnas Arnæus.

"On the other hand, I am absolutely convinced that it was he who set the city on fire," said the man from Grindavík. "I myself saw the red glow behind Our Lady's Church. I woke Jón Hreggviðsson and told him to keep an eye on Jón Marteinsson."

"Take your drivel about Jón Marteinsson and get out," said the assessor, and he started to shut the door.

"The books, the books," stammered the man from Grindavík. His voice had gone falsetto and tears flowed from his eyes. "For God's sake and in Jesus' name: the precious membrana, Iceland's life!"

"Books," said Arnæus, "what do you intend to do with them? The precious membrana—let them be."

"They'll burn," said the Grindavíkian.

"Not tonight," said Arnas Arnæus. "Didn't you say that the fire was on the other side of Our Lady's Church?"

"But the wind is from the west, my lord. Shouldn't I try to bring the most valuable ones over the canal immediately, just to be on the safe side?"

Arnas Arnæus said: "The *Skálda* is in the hands of thieves. And I left the good magistrate's book behind, though it had been given to me as a gift. Now it's best to let the gods decide. I'm tired."

"If the fire reaches Our Lady's Church, it's just a stone's throw from us," said his famulus, refusing to give in.

"We'll let Our Lady's Church burn," said Arnas Arnæus. "Go on up to your bedcloset and sleep."

—— 15 ——

The fire started at approximately nine o'clock on Wednesday evening down below Vesterport, its cause thought to be a child's carelessness with a candle flame. The fire brigade arrived quickly on the scene, but because of strong winds the fire spread so rapidly that nothing could be done; the conflagration leaped from house to house along the narrow streets. At first the fire pursued a northward course along the wall and cut slantwise into the city. Around ten o'clock the wind shifted direction, driving the fire across the city along Vestergade and Studiestraede; it was now so ferocious that no mortal power could control it. For no apparent reason other fires started springing up in various places in the neighborhood, for instance in a brewery on Nørregade later that night; this new blaze also spread quickly in both directions, making the work of the firemen ever more difficult. On Thursday morning, around dawn, the houses on both sides of Nørregade were burning; the wind now blew from the northwest and drove the firestorm further down into the city. The branch of the fire burning in Vestergade had by then laid waste to the entire street and the neighborhood all the way down to Gammeltorv. At about the same time the fire reached the bishop's residence and from there moved to Saint Peter's Church—unfortunately many city residents thought that the Lord would spare the churches and brought all of their belongings there, filling the churches with flammable material and thereby fueling the fire. Around ten in the morning both the city hall and the orphanage burned down together—the children from the latter were brought down to the king's stables, while the horses were driven out to Frederiksberg. At around eleven the fire reached Our Lady's Church. Before those gathered there knew it a cloud of smoke gushed from the church's high tower, followed immediately by massive flames; a little later the tower and the spire collapsed together. At the same time both the academy and Our Lady's School burned to the ground, and thus the fire arrived at the neighborhood where the scholars had their homes. At three in the afternoon one could watch the capital's diverse exalted and age-old buildings and mansions being devoured by the flames, and the same went for the students' dormitory and the collegia. The fire continued to burn throughout the rest of the day. Near midevening Holy Trinity Church caught fire and shortly afterward the academy's magnificent and irreplaceable library did the same, followed by the Church of the Holy Spirit and its exalted organ. All the next night the fire burned in Købmagergade and then throughout the lower parts of the city all the way down to Gammelstrand, where it was finally extinguished with water from the canal.

The inhabitants of the city rushed panic-stricken out into the streets, much as in Iceland when loads of worms crawl out of rotten lumpfish when it's grilled over the embers to give to the shepherd boys. Some people cuddled children, some carried bags of various belongings, others were naked and ashamed, hungry and thirsty, or else had lost their senses, emitting shrieks and howls of grief. One

woman was unable to save anything but her fire-poker, and she stood
in the street buck-naked; many were lying like sheep on and around
the walls, as well as in the king's park, in the driving rain and wind.
Many of them might never have gotten up again had not His Kingly
Majesty taken pity on his poor people's torment and need. His Most
Gracious Heart rode out in person to where folk lay weeping upon
the ground, and had bread and beer distributed to them wherever he
went.

Early in the morning on the second day of the fire a number of
Icelanders gathered at the home of Arnas Arnæus. These included
both gentlemen's sons studying at the university and several poor
yeoman apprentices, as well as one penniless sailor. They sent for the
assessor, announced that the fire was swiftly approaching Our Lady's
Church, and offered their help in rescuing the renowned Icelandic
books. But Arnas refused their help, claiming that the fire would
soon be extinguished; he would rather offer them beer. The men
were restless and didn't want to drink, but they lacked the determina-
tion to pressure the erudite nobleman and walked dejectedly away.
They didn't go far, however, but rather loitered in the vicinity of the
assessor's residence, feeling the heat from the conflagration and
watching as the fire spread from house to house, coming ever nearer.
Finally when flames shot up from the tower of Our Lady's Church
and started to flow over its roof, the men went back to Arnæus's
home, and, abandoning modesty, rushed into the house through the
back entrance and past the horrified kitchen wenches, not stopping
until they reached the library, where they found Jón Guðmundsson
from Grindavík, tearfully singing from a Latin hymnbook. One of
the men searched for the householder and found him in his room,
standing on a dais at the window, watching the fire. The man said
that he and his companions had come to the rescue. By this time the
housemistress and the servants were in a rush to save the furniture.
Finally Arnæus came to his senses and told the men to save whatever
they wanted and whatever they could.

The bookshelves in the library reached from the floor to the ceiling on all four walls, and besides this there were books stored in
two side compartments. The Icelanders made a rush for these, since

everyone knew that the library's treasures were stored in locked cabinets in these two corners. But now they were faced with disaster, as always happens in nightmares: the keys to the cabinets were not at hand. Arnæus himself went to search for them. By then the heat from the firestorm had started to leak through the walls of the house, and since the men feared that the house would be engulfed in flames before the assessor could find his keys they took to the cabinets with whatever they could find as cudgels. When they had smashed open the cabinets they made the assessor's secretary show them which of the books were most valuable, then they grabbed up handfuls of these most famous manuscripts containing the handwritten stories of the ancient Icelanders and the kings of Norway and carried them out. They didn't make more than one trip. When they turned to go in and fetch more books the fire entered the house. Blue smoke gushed from the two side compartments and soon a dull red tongue of flame licked out from the smoke. The men wanted to try and grab whatever they could get their hands on from the shelves of the main reading room before it was consumed, but Arnas Arnæus, who had returned with the keys to the cabinets that now stood unimpressively awash in flames, stopped in the doorway of his library and waved his hands at the men, preventing them entrance. Just as the surf crashes against sheer cliffs, or as the plant called parmelia quickly fastens its roots and spreads with speed in all directions, but withers in the place where it was first sown, so too did the fire spread over the precious bookspines covering the walls of the hall. Arnas Arnæus stood in the doorway staring in, the Icelanders helpless in the foyer behind him. Then he turned to them, pointed in through the doorway at the flaming bookshelves and smiled as he said:

"Never again shall such books be found, anywhere, even unto Doomsday."

— 16 —

Night. Two Icelandic Jóns stagger waywardly through a burning city. The learned Grindavíkian is bawling like a child. The farmer from

Rein plods silently behind. The fire of Copenhagen is at their heels, driving them on in the direction of Nørreport. The sea of flames turns terrified folk into frantic silhouettes, fleshly phantoms.

"What are you whining about?" said the man from Skagi, completely neglecting to address his learned namesake respectfully. "You could hardly be mourning for Copenhagen."

"No," said the scholar. "This city, built with the blood of my destitute people, is bound to perish. For God is just."

"Well, then I think you'd better start praising him," said Jón Hreggviðsson.

"I would give much to be illiterate like you, Hreggviðsson," said the scholar.

"I think there'll probably be enough old books left in the world even if your rubbish burns, if that's what you're crying about," said the farmer.

"Even if my life's work were to perish," said the studiosus antiquitatum, "even if the flames were to consume all those texts that I diligently compiled for four decades, mostly by night after I'd completed my day's work, I would still eternally weep for a poor man's poor books. I weep for my lord's books. His books, which burn even as we speak, contain the life and soul of the Nordic peoples, who spoke the Danish tongue ever since the Flood and all the way up until the time when they abandoned their origins and adopted a Germanic mien. I weep because now there will no longer exist any books written in the Danish tongue. The Nordic countries no longer have a soul. I weep for my master's sorrow."

Passersby could hear by their speech that they were foreigners, and thinking that they were Swedish spies were eager to string them up without delay.

Suddenly they ran straight into a man wearing a dress coat and a top hat, carrying a bag upon his back. Jón Hreggviðsson greeted him warmly, but the scholar from Grindavík pretended not to notice the man and tearfully continued on his way.

"Hey you Grindavík dimwit!" called Jón Marteinsson after him. "Don't you want beer and bread?"

The third Jón who now joined their company was as crafty as ever no matter where he went. Even here at the Nørrevold he knew of a woman who could provide a man with beer and bread.

"But I'll tell you this right now," he said, "if you don't stare up at me like beaten dogs while you're drinking the beer that I'm going to get for you, then I'll take it right back."

He led them to this particular wench's kitchen and told them to take a seat. Jón Hreggviðsson sneered and grimaced in a variety of ways, but the man from Grindavík did not look up.

The woman was terribly affected by the fire in Copenhagen and wailed and begged God for mercy, but Jón Marteinsson grabbed hold of her, gave her a quick tweak in a spot just above her hams, and said:

"Give these old farmers here flat beer in poor mugs and brennivín in tin goblets; but give me fresh Rostocker beer in an enameled stone pitcher, preferably with a silver lid and inscribed with one of Luther's bawdy lyrics; and brennivín in a silver goblet."

The woman gave the man a clout, but cheered up slightly.

"Cheers lads and tell us a lie," said Jón Marteinsson. "And bring us bread and sausages, my good woman."

They gulped down the beer.

"It's horrendous to think," said the woman as she smeared the bread, "what trials God sets before our blessed king."

"Screw the king," said Jón Marteinsson.

"You Icelanders are heartless," said the woman.

"Make sure you put a lot of smoked blubber on that," said Jón Marteinsson.

After they had slaked the worst of their thirst he continued:

"Well now, old Árni's gone and gotten all of Iceland's books burned—"

The scholar from Grindavík looked with tear-filled eyes directly into his enemy's face and said only one word: "Satan."

"—except for the ones I managed to rescue in time and bring to the Swedish count du Bertelskiold and his brothers," said Jón Marteinsson.

"You've conducted business with men who call Iceland's books West Gotlandic," said the Grindavíkian.

"Yet here in the bottom of my bag is something that will ensure that the name of Jón Marteinsson will never be forgotten as long as the world exists," said the other.

They ate and drank for a short time, saying nothing, except for Jón Marteinsson, who directed flirtatious comments at the woman in between mouthfuls. The scholar from Grindavík had stopped crying, and he had a spot of jam on his nose. By the time they were well into their third pitcher Jón Hreggviðsson had become adequately drunk, and he started reciting a stanza from the *Elder Ballad of Pontus* at the top of his lungs.

As they finished the food and drink and the festivities started winding down, Jón Marteinsson, the party's host, started peeking quickly and furtively beneath the table in order to take stock of his guests' shoes. Typically Icelandic, as he might have guessed. He also examined the buttons on their jackets: neither brass nor silver, just bits of bone. Jón Marteinsson asked the woman to loan them cards or dice. Both of the guests declined their host's invitation to a game of craps, but Jón Hreggviðsson said he wouldn't mind a bit of arm wrestling. He said that even though he might be an old geezer, he'd still be able to fend off each and every man whom Jón Marteinsson sent to remove him from his shoes. The blubbery woman, flat-footed and knock-kneed, her face swollen from crying, stood at the stove and watched the three men. She soon gathered what sort of people these were, then stopped lamenting the king's misfortune and said that these insane Icelanders would always be more akin to themselves than to human beings, and that anyone who did as much as extend his little finger to them would regret it, even if the city were burning around him and the pit of Hell gaped open beneath his feet—even if the inhabited world were destroyed, she said, their lies and trickery would remain. Jón Marteinsson tried pinching her again but she would not be appeased and instead announced that she was going to send for the master of the watch.

Jón Marteinsson said that in that case there was nothing left to do but open up his bag and hand over its contents as payment or ransom for the hospitality, and he pulled out a large, age-old vellum manuscript and handed it to the woman.

"What am I supposed to do with this?" said the woman, looking contemptuously at this heap of blackened, tattered, and shriveled patches of skin in the faint light of the inn's coal stove. "I couldn't use this thing to light the fire under my kettle even once. And I'd be surprised if the plague's not lurking in it."

The two Jóns stared wide-eyed at the book: one of them beheld before him the lost chief treasure of his master, and the other felt for sure that what he saw were the parchment pages that had belonged to his blessed mother from Rein. It was the *Skálda*. Without a word, both of them reached down and removed their shoes.

— **17** —

The Alþingi sentenced Jón Hreggviðsson to prison at Bremerholm for having at one time concealed the Supreme Court appeal contained in the royal warrant that had been issued in connection with his case. Arnæus retrieved the old man from the castle at the same time as he concluded arrangements to have the farmer's original case finally tried before the Supreme Court. His case was contested once again throughout the first winter of the farmer's present sojourn in Copenhagen and on into the summer. Almost all of the litigation took place behind the farmer's back, except for once when he was summoned to appear before the judge. He repeated all the answers he had made to the old charges; he wasn't about to deny anything. He also knew well how to put his wretchedness on display before the court: an old white-haired rustic stands with drooping shoulders, tearful and trembling before foreign judges in a distant land, overcome by the tremendous and difficult journeys of past and present that he'd been forced to make because of a long-past accident that had made him an innocent man to the dismay of the authorities.

The lawsuit dragged on, not because of any prevailing interest in Denmark in the fate of a farmer from Akranes, but rather because it was an essential part of the conflict being waged between two opposing camps within the government, both equally strong in many ways. Arnæus served as litigator on behalf of Jón Hreggviðsson and employed the uncompromising logic and learned pedantry that had always been the Icelanders' strength against Danish courts. In a lawsuit such as this, in which the indictments were long since obsolete, the grounds banal, and none of the evidence against the accused legally admissible, it was easier than usual for Arnæus to use philosophy and logic to unravel the prosecution's arguments. The court documents, both old and new, for and against, had become so muddled that nothing was more likely than that they were the incarnation of the Icelanders' evil propensities for chicanery and quibbling, and it was deemed impossible for anyone to attempt to learn the truth from them as to whether or not the aforementioned Regvidsen had, twenty years ago, finished off his executioner in a black bog on a black autumn night in the black land called Iceland.

For a time during the summer it had looked likely that the case would continue to expand in size, that the two contestants on this field of battle would increase the force of their exertions, and that the old entanglements would be transformed into a matted mass that could never be unraveled. The main reason for this was that the daughter of Magistrate Eydalín from Iceland wanted Jón Hreggviðsson's case to be made the touchstone for determining her departed father's integrity as a judge. The knot continued to be hacked at by the highest authorities until the king decreed that the two cases were to be tried separately: the Supreme Court was, as originally planned, to pass judgment in the case of the farmer from Rein, but the Commissarial Court's harsh judgments against the departed Eydalín and numerous other officials were to be disputed before Iceland's high court at Öxará.

And now as spring approached and human life in Copenhagen was returning to normal after the fire, news came which many people, the Icelanders least of all, could scarcely believe: a verdict had finally been issued by our Majesty's Supreme Court in the much-despised and seemingly endless lawsuit against Joen Regvidsen paa Skage.* Due to a lack of positive evidence the man was acquitted of the old charge brought by the magistrate that he had murdered the executioner Sívert Snorresen, and he was therewith released from the burden of any other penalties he had accrued in connection with his case and pronounced free to return home to our Royal Majesty's country of Iceland.

One day in the spring, Arnas Arnæus, who now resided on Laxagade in the midst of the throng, sends for his woodcutter and hands him a new jacket, breeches, and boots, and lastly places a new hat upon the man's hoary head, telling him at the same time that they would ride together today to Dragør.

This was the first time that Jón Hreggviðsson had ever been driven anywhere without having to sit up front with the driver. He was allowed to sit inside the carriage next to the scholar from Grindavík, and on the rear seat opposite them sat their lord and master, who gave them snuff and chatted with them pleasantly, though somewhat distractedly.

"Now I shall teach you an introductory verse from the *Elder Ballad of Pontus* that you have never heard before," he said.

Then he recited this verse:

> "Folk will marvel at the story
> There on Iceland's shore
> When Hreggviðsson's old gray and hoary
> Head comes home once more."

After both Jóns had memorized the verse they all sat in silence. The road was wet, causing the carriage to sway from side to side.

The assessor remained lost in thought for some time, then finally looked at the Rein farmer, smiled at him, and said:

"Jón Marteinsson saved the *Skálda*. You were all that fell to my lot."

Jón Hreggviðsson said: "Does my lord have any messages he would like me to deliver?"

"Here is a rixdollar for your daughter in Rein, who stood in the doorway of your farm as you rode away," said Arnas Arnæus.

"I can't understand why that devil of a girl let the dog out," said Jón Hreggviðsson. "Like I hadn't already told her to keep her eye on it."

"We shall hope that Rover found his way back home," said Arnas Arnæus.

"If you should ever hear of anything unusual in Saurbær parish," said the scholar from Grindavík, "peculiar dreams, trolls, elves, monsters, or any remarkable abnormalities, then please ask my dear Reverend Þorsteinn, and give him my greetings as well, to put it down in letters and send it to me so that I can add it to a book I've just begun writing, *De Mirabilibus Islandiae: Concerning Iceland's Wonders.*"

They arrived at the trading station at Dragør. The merchantman to Iceland dawdled at anchor in the harbor, a few of its sails already hoisted.

"It is auspicious to set sail for Iceland from Dragør," said Arnas Arnæus, and he extended his hand in farewell as Jón Hreggviðsson stepped down into the rowboat that would take him out to the merchantman. "Old friends of Icelanders linger here. Saint Ólafur* was known to loan Icelanders his ferryboat here, after the other ships had gone, especially if he thought it important that they arrive home in time for the Alþingi. If it so happens now that the holy King Ólafur enables you to reach home before the thirteenth week of summer, then I would like to ask you to pay a visit to the Alþingi by Öxará and show them your head."

"Should it say something to them?" asked Jón Hreggviðsson.

"You can tell them from me that Iceland has not been sold; not this time. They'll understand later. Then you can hand them your pardon."

"But shouldn't I convey your greetings to anyone?" said Jón Hreggviðsson.

"Your old ruffled head—that shall be my greeting," said the Professor Antiquitatum Danicarum.

The easy breezes from Øresund blew through the white locks on the head of the old Icelandic scoundrel Jón Hreggviðsson as he stood there in the stern of the rowboat midway between ship and shore on his way home, waving his hat to the tired man who remained behind.

— 18 —

At one place in Almannagjá the Öxará River turns back upon itself as
if in consternation, then breaks crosswise out of the ravine. There it
forms the great women's pool, Drekkingarhylur, and a little further
out there is a footpath up between the sheer cliff walls.

Sitting below the footpath upon a grassy patch near the pool were
several criminals, rubbing the sleep from their eyes in the morning
sun. Nothing stirred in the aristocrats' booths, but on the plain to the
east black horses were being driven toward the bishop's booth. A man
wearing a Danish jacket and a hat, his boots hanging over his shoulder, comes up over the low ravine-slope from the south and is greeted
by the sight of the morning sun shining down on the drowsy criminals alongside Drekkingarhylur.

Their eyes open wide. "Can I believe my eyes? Is it really Jón
Hreggviðsson come home from the king? With a new hat? And wearing a jacket?"

He had arrived in Eyrarbakki the day before, and when he heard
that there was only one day left in the assembly at Öxará he had
someone in Flói make him some shoes, then he slung his boots over
his shoulder and walked all night.

It seemed to him that his old friends' luck, if it could be called
that, had taken a turn for the worse, since the lawbreakers now had
to lie around under the open sky. Years ago, when he had spent a
night here just like them, the king had lodged him in a tent imprinted
with the crown and the king's servants had brought him tea.

But they weren't complaining. The Lord had been as merciful to
them now as always. Sentences had been passed at the Alþingi yesterday. The new madam at Skálholt, the wedded wife of the bishop-elect
Sigurður Sveinsson and daughter of our dear departed magistrate, had
during the previous summer inveigled royal permission to have her
father's case retried before Iceland's high court: yesterday Beyer, the
regent at Bessastaðir, was convicted along with the vice-magistrate
and twenty-four other authorities involved in the case. The departed
magistrate Eydalín was acquitted of all charges brought against him

by the royal envoy Arnæus and the deceased's name was exonerated. His estates, amongst them the sixty farms that the king had seized, were restored to him and thereby made the lawful inheritance of Snæfríður, the bishop's wife. The so-called Commissarial Verdict in the case against the magistrate was declared null and void, and the commissary himself, Arnas Arnæus, was ordered to pay pecuniary penalties to the crown for his violence toward and desecration of the law. Most of the people acquitted by Arnæus were once again convicted by the high court, excluding Jón Hreggviðsson, who had been granted beneficium paupertatis* to appeal his case before the Supreme Court in Denmark. Eydalín's judgments in the so-called execrable cases, which the commissary had annulled, were either reinstated or pronounced unfit for hearing by any worldly court, amongst them the case of the pregnant woman who had sworn that she was a virgin: such cases were left to the spirits to pursue. The only other verdicts annulled were the ones that the blessed magistrate had pronounced in cases that in reality lay beyond the bounds of his jurisdiction.

"God be praised that a man has someone to look up to again," said the old sorrow-bitten criminal who several years ago had lamented seeing dragged before the court some of the good bailiffs who'd ordered him flogged.

The saint who'd stolen from the poor box said:

"No man is blessed but the one who has served his sentence—"

"—and the one who's recovered his criminality," said the man who'd been deprived of his criminality for some time.

This man had been a criminal for ten years before the authorities ruled that it was an entirely different woman and an entirely different man who had had the child that his sister had been drowned in the pool for having had with him. Up until then everyone had given him alms. But after he was acquitted of the crime he was scorned throughout all of Iceland. Not one person ever threw him a single bite of fish. People sicked their dogs on him. Now the case had been retried before a new judge: he had unquestionably committed this hideous crime and was once again a true lawbreaker before God and man.

"Now I know that no one in Iceland will laugh at me any longer," he said. "The dogs won't be sicked on me, and they'll throw me bits of codfish. God be praised."

The blind criminal who'd been sitting silently on the outskirts of the group now spoke up like the others: "Our crime is that we're not men even though we're called men. What does Jón Hreggviðsson say?"

"Nothing except that I plan to walk over Leggjabrjótur today, home," he said. "When I came home from my first trip my daughter was lying on her bier. The daughter who was standing in the doorway when I left for my latest trip might still be alive. Maybe she's had a son who'll tell her grandson the story of their grandsire Jón Hreggviðsson from Rein and his friend and lord, Master Arnas Arnæus."

Now the sound of hoofbeats came from beyond the eastern wall of the ravine, and when the criminals walked out through the rocks they saw a man and a woman riding in a great group of horses and attendants along the earthen pathways over the plain toward Kaldidalur, the boundary between the country's quarters. They were both darkly clad and all of their horses were black.

"Who's that riding by?" asked the blind man.

They answered: "Snæfríður Iceland's sun rides in black; as does her husband Sigurður Sveinsson the Latin poet, bishop-elect in Skálholt. They're on their way west to appraise her inheritance, which she recovered from the king."

And the criminals stood beneath the cliffs and watched the bishop and his lady ride by; and the dew-drenched, black-maned horses glistened in the dawn of the day.

NOTES

The events of the novel take place during the late seventeenth and early eighteenth centuries, at a time when Iceland was severely oppressed by famine, plague, and the Danish monopoly on trade. Most of the characters in the novel, including officials, criminals, scholars, and farmers, are based on actual historical figures. The farmer Jón Hreggviðsson lived at Efri-Reynir on Akranes and undertook almost the same sort of difficulties as described in the novel in order to clear himself of the charge of murdering the king's hangman (the flogging described here took place in 1683, and he was finally acquitted of the murder charge in 1715). Arnas Arnæus is based on the great scholar and book collector Árni Magnússon (b. 1663); the manuscripts that he collected are stored now at institutes bearing his name in Copenhagen and Reykjavík. Snæfríður Björnsdóttir Eydalín is loosely based on a woman named Þórdís Jónsdóttir, the sister of the wife (Sigríður Jónsdóttir) of the bishop of Skálholt (Jón Vídalín), and the wife of the historical Magnús Sigurðsson from Bræðratunga. The supposed affair between Árni Magnússon and Þórdís Jónsdóttir became the grounds for extensive legal wrangling between Árni and Magnús, similar to how this legal case is described in the novel. The characters whom Jón Hreggviðsson meets in Copenhagen, Jón Grindvicensis and Jón Marteinsson, are based, respectively, on Jón Guðmundsson from Grunnavík and on two or three other individuals who worked for Árni Magnússon (including one actually named Jón Marteinsson). The Great Fire in Copenhagen occurred in 1728, and while it is realized now that the damage to Árni Magnússon's collection was not nearly as extensive as first thought, it was a tragic blow to him and precipitated his death in 1730.

There were two "official" languages in Iceland during the time when the events of this novel took place: Danish and Latin, used respectively for secular and ecclesiastical affairs. Learned Icelanders often interspersed their own Icelandic with words or phrases from these two languages, as can be seen in historical documents from the time period (such as Árni Magnússon's letters). Laxness occasionally mirrors this linguistic potpourri in *Iceland's Bell,* sprinkling people's speech with Latin words and phrases where appropriate, or using or having certain speakers use different forms of proper or place names, such as Danish Joen Joensen for Icelandic Jón Jónsson, Icelandic Jes Ló for Danish Jens Loy, Danish Sívert Snorresen (with an Icelandic diacritical *í*) for Sigurður Snorrason, Danish Bessested for Icelandic Bessastaðir. Similarly, when Jón Hreggviðsson travels throughout northern Europe, he encounters both a wide variety of languages and people who can speak a wide variety of languages, and his own name is occasionally transformed by various speakers (Joen Regvidsen for example). The various forms of names have not been specifically noted, but the reader should be aware that the spelling variants are intentional.

p. 3 Þingvellir: The site of the Alþingi, the general assembly that was held for two weeks in June throughout most of Iceland's history (it was held for the last time at Þingvellir in 1798; after being held in Reykjavík in 1799 and 1800 it was abandoned, until it was reconvened in Reykjavík starting in 1845). Lawsuits were settled and laws enacted beneath the cliffs of Almannagjá, a dramatic ravine formed by the separation of tectonic plates. Öxará is a river that runs partly through Almannagjá and empties into Þingvallavatn, Þingvellir Lake. The area around Þingvellir, to the north and east, was in older days given the name Bláskógar, from the birchwood copse growing there (*skógur* meaning "copse" or "forest"); in the novel Magistrate Eydalín says that the copse bears the name Bláskógar or Bláskógaheiði, and on maps Bláskógaheiði is the extensive heath running northward from Þingvellir, on the western side of Ármannsfell, toward the passes Uxahryggir and Kaldidalur. Peaks that can be seen from Þingvellir include Ármannsfell, Hrafnabjörg, Súlur or Botnssúlur, Skjaldbreiður, and Hengill.

At the time that this story takes place, the king of Denmark had absolute power over Iceland (absolute monarchy was established in 1662 by Frederik III, who reigned 1648–1670; Christian V was king from 1670–1699, and Frederik IV from 1699–1730). Iceland's government was controlled by the Danish *Rentekammer* (Ministry of Finance) and the *Kancelli* (Chancery). Answering to these ministries was the *stiftamtmaður,* the highest governmental authority in Iceland (the post was actually established in 1684); following him, in descending order of executive power, were the *amtmaður* (established in 1688), the *landfógeti* (established 1683), the *sýslumenn, umboðsmenn sýslumanna,* and *hreppstjórar.* In *Iceland's Bell,* Gyldenløve performs the function of the *stiftamtmaður,* although he is called *lénsherra, landstjóri,* or *gouverneur;* thus his title has been translated as "governor." Laxness refers to the character Páll Beyer variously as *landfógeti* and *amtmaður* (combining the two separate offices), and as he reports directly to Gyldenløve, or acts as Gyldenløve's representative in the governor's absence (he is also called at times the *umboðsmaður lénsherrans,* or "governor's representative"), both *landfógeti* and *amtmaður* have been translated as "regent." The *sýslumenn* are district authorities who have executive and judicial authority; these are rendered as "bailiffs." *Umboðsmenn sýslumanna,* or representatives of the bailiffs, are not really seen in this novel; mention is made, however, of *hreppstjórar,* the authorities of *hreppar,* or parishes; this term is translated as "parish administrators."

The *Kancelli* was in charge of the ecclesiastical government of Iceland; in the latter part of the seventeenth century Iceland's highest ecclesiastical authorities, the bishops of Skálholt and Hólar, answered to the bishop of Sjaelland in Denmark. Below the bishops on the hierarchical ladder in Iceland were the *prófastar* (deans) and then *prestar* (priests); Reverend Sigurður Sveinsson occupies a somewhat unique position in this novel as the *dómkirkjuprestur,* or archpriest (literally, "cathedral priest"), the assistant to the bishop.

The legislative and judicial branches of Iceland's government also answered directly to the king of Denmark; the main legislative assembly in Iceland was the *Alþingi,* with eighty-four representatives, thirty-six of them serving in the *lögrétta,* or judiciary body. The highest native Icelandic legislative and judicial authority was the *lögmaður,* literally "lawman"; in *Iceland's Bell* the *lögmaður* is shown primarily in his role as a judge, and he has been given the exclusive title "magistrate." Two men could hold the office of *lögmaður* at this time and Arnæus mentions that the "second magistrate's office was not filled," although later he appoints a second *lögmaður* to help him judge Magistrate Eydalín; this office is called by Laxness *vísilögmaður* or "vice-magistrate." The highest court in Iceland, which was subordinate to the Danish Supreme Court (*hæstiréttur*), was the *yfirdómur* (translated as Iceland's "high court"), consisting of twenty-four *lögréttumenn* ("legislators" or "jurists") and under the control of the *amtmaður.* After this was the *lögmannsdómur* (magistrate's court), consisting of six, twelve, or twenty-four *lögréttumenn* chosen by the *lögmaður,* and then the *héraðsdómur* (district court), with *dómsmenn* (judges) appointed by the *sýslumaður* (bailiff). Jón Hreggviðsson's case obviously goes through all of these courts, beginning with district court and ending up in the Supreme Court in Denmark.

In 1602 the king of Denmark established a monopoly over trade in Iceland. In 1620 the Iceland trade company (*Det Islandske Kompagni,* called in the novel "Compagniet" and translated "the Company") was set up and given the opportunity to pay rents to do business in Iceland. In 1662 Iceland was divided into four commercial districts, and the number of these districts was increased in 1684. Each district was controlled by a Danish *kaupmaður,* translated here as "merchant." The value of goods and the taxes imposed on them fluctuated during the seventeenth century; prior to 1684 merchants had to pay a high tax on Icelandic wool and other domestic products but not on fish, and had to sell grain for a price less than could be made elsewhere; hence the Icelanders could sell little and there was little grain to be bought. After 1684 taxes on goods imported into Iceland were raised and on domestic goods for export lowered (as is mentioned in the novel), which was another policy that provided no benefit to the Icelanders. Further harmful policies at this time included laws preventing the Icelanders from trading with foreigners other than the Danes (such as the Dutch or English), as well as from doing any commercial business outside of their own district; examples of these various prohibitions are found in the novel.

p. 4 Gunnar of Hlíðarendi is one of the heroes of *Njáls saga* (also known as *Brennu-Njáls saga*), which is considered by many to be the greatest of the medieval Icelandic sagas. Gunnar was regarded as the peerless hero of his age; he is renowned for his prowess and elegance, as well as for his dramatic death.

p. 4 Bessastaðir, just south of Reykjavík, was the site of the Danish headquarters in Iceland, and is the current residence of the president of Iceland. The Þrælakista was a workhouse for criminals.

p. 5 Hólmship: A ship that sailed to and from the trading station of Hólmur (Hólmurinn), which was set up at Reykjavík.

p. 6 There was no farm named Fíflavellir in the Þingvellir area listed in the Icelandic census of 1703, though apparently there was a farm of that name, near Skjaldbreiður, at an earlier time.

p. 6 The *Elder Ballad of Pontus:* Beginning in the fourteenth century, balladry, the composition and singing of heroic or romantic epic poems, was

the most popular literary form in Iceland. Icelandic ballads were characterized by the use of intricate language and complex meters. The *Ballad of Pontus* (Icelandic *Pontusrímur*) was composed in the sixteenth century by
Magnús *prúði* ("the Courteous"), with additions by the legislator Pétur
Einarsson and Reverend Ólafur Halldórsson. The ballad is based on the
fourteenth-century French romantic epic *Ponthus et la belle Sidoine*. In this
epic (which is derived from the older Anglo-Norman poem *Horn et Rimen-
hild*), King Thibour of Galicia is defeated by a sultan's son, but Thibour's
son Ponthus, along with other noblemen's children, are sent into hiding in
Brittany. Ponthus grows up at the court of the king of Brittany and falls in
love with the king's daughter, Sidoine, but in order to win her hand, and
recover his kingdom in Galicia, he must undergo a number of dangerous
adventures. The *Elder Ballad of Pontus* referred to in *Iceland's Bell* is a
creation of Laxness: Jón Hreggviðsson is inspired by the heroic Pontus,
but the verses he sings are taken mostly, and anachronistically, from other
nineteenth-century ballads.

p. 6 Axlar-Björn is an infamous Icelandic criminal who lived at Öxl on
Snæfellsnes. He killed eighteen people, mostly travelers to whom he had
granted hospitality, and sunk their bodies in a pond near his homefield; he
was executed in 1596.

p. 8 The westernmost point on the Akranes peninsula, where the town of
Akranes is now located, had the old name of Skagi (later changed to Skipa-
skagi). Modern residents of Akranes are often called "Skagamenn" (people
from Skagi). In *Iceland's Bell* Akranes and Skagi, as well as the name of Jón
Hreggviðsson's farm, Rein, are used interchangeably as the names of Jón
Hreggviðsson's home. When Laxness writes of Jón Hreggviðsson going "out
to Skagi" he means the farmer goes west from his farm toward the headland.

p. 8 The "six-cow inventory" (in Icelandic, *sex kvígildi*) is a term for the
value of the farm. The farm that Jón Hreggviðsson inherits comes with
chattel to the value of six cows, that is, either six cows or thirty-six sheep, or
a combination of both.

p. 8 Skálholt (in southern Iceland), where much of the action of the novel
takes place (especially in the second part), is the site of the episcopal see in
Iceland, established in 1056 by Iceland's first bishop, Ísleifur Gizurarson. A
second episcopal see was established at Hólar in the north in 1106 by Ísleifur's son Gizurr.

p. 10 Rixdollar (Danish *rigsdaler*): A type of Danish silver currency.

p. 12 Wadmal (Icelandic *vaðmál*): Thick, woolen homespun cloth (used as payment in Scandinavian countries before coined gold and silver came into use).

p. 13 Brennivín: A distilled spirit flavored with angelica root or caraway seeds.

p. 18 Beneficium (Latin): Assistance.

p. 19 Njáll Þorgeirsson is the eponymous hero of *Njáls saga*. He was a great lawyer and, according to the saga, tried everything he could to maintain peace in Iceland, though in the year 1011 he was finally burned alive in his own home along with his family.

p. 19 The *Graduale* is a book of plainsong that gives the words and music to the parts of the mass sung by the choir. The *Kross School Hymns* were actually composed by Reverend Jón Einarsson in the late seventeenth century. The character of Reverend Halldór from Presthólar is also based upon the well-known psalmist Reverend Sigurður Jónsson of Presthólar (1590–1661).

p. 20 Örvar-Oddur is the eponymous hero of *Örvar-Odds saga* (*Arrow-Oddur's saga*), one of the so-called legendary sagas (in Icelandic, *fornaldarsögur;* these are mainly fantastical tales composed during the thirteenth to the fifteenth centuries). He traveled widely, battling with giants and sorcerers, and did indeed live to be three hundred years old. Haraldur *hilditönn* (Danish *hildetand,* "Battletooth") was a semi-legendary eighth-century Danish king who was purportedly killed by the god Óðinn at the Battle of Brávalla; for the story, see for instance the *Gesta Danorum* of Saxo Grammaticus (ca. 1150–ca. 1220).

p. 22 Auro carior (Latin): More precious than gold.

p. 22 Involucra (Latin): Bindings; wrapping.

p. 23 Professor Antiquitatum (Latin): Professor of Antiquities.

p. 24 Membranum (Latin): Parchment.

p. 24 Pretiosissima, thesaurus, cimelium (Latin): Most precious, a treasure, a jewel.

p. 24 The name *Skálda*, in Old Norse paleographical studies, is normally used for a collection of philological treatises, dating from the twelfth to the fourteenth centuries, that are attached as an appendix to the *Ormsbók* manuscript of the *Edda* of Snorri Sturluson (1178–1241). Two texts in Icelandic literature bear the name *Edda:* the first, the *Poetic Edda* (referred to also as the *Elder* or *Sæmundar Edda*), is a collection of mythological and heroic poems recorded in Iceland probably in the twelfth century. Snorri's *Edda* (also referred to as the *Younger* or *Prose Edda*) uses older Eddaic poems as the foundation for a treatise on poetry consisting of three main parts: *Gylfaginning* (mythological tales), *Skáldskaparmál* (poetical arts, primarily diction), and *Háttatál* (poetic meters); the second part, *Skáldskaparmál,* is also often referred to as *Skálda*. Arnas Arnæus's description of the *Skálda* manuscript that he finds in Jón Hreggviðsson's house as containing the most beautiful poems in the northern hemisphere suggests that it contains specimens of Eddaic poems, although the nonspecific description suggests that this manuscript should be taken as a representative of any or all of the precious manuscripts that preserve the literature of the ancient Icelanders (and, as is suggested in the novel, the soul of the Nordic lands).

p. 25 Minutissima particula (Latin): The slightest particle.

p. 25 Sine exemplo (Latin): Unique; exceptional; phenomenal.

p. 25 Antiqui (Latin): Antiquity; days of old.

p. 25 Litteras (Latin): Literature, letters.

p. 31 Bishop Jón Arason (1484–1550) was the last Catholic bishop of Hólar (see note to pages 3 and 8 above), and a great opponent of the Lutherans. The Danes beheaded him at Skálholt on November 7, 1550.

p. 31 Þórir Steinfinnsson *jökull* ("Glacier") was a character in *Sturlunga saga* (thirteenth century). He received a mortal wound at the battle of Örlygsstaðir and recited a stoic verse just before he died.

p. 33 Bremerholm: Beginning in 1620, dangerous male criminals were sentenced to hard labor at the naval dockyards at Bremerholm in Copenhagen.

p. 33 Suðurnes is the name of Iceland's southwesternmost peninsula, although in older days the name was used to indicate all of the area in the southern part of Faxaflói (including Romshvalanes, Álftanes, and Seltjarnarnes).

p. 35 A *sending* is a ghost conjured and sent by a sorcerer to an enemy; there are many examples of these in Icelandic folktales.

p. 38 Moving days (Icelandic *fardagar*): Four days at the end of May when working folk in Iceland changed abodes.

p. 38   Grótta is the westernmost tip of the Seltjarnarnes peninsula.

p. 38   Hólmur: see note for page 5.

p. 42   Egill Skallagrímsson is the eponymous hero of *Egils saga*. He is considered by many to have been the greatest Viking and poet to have lived in Iceland.

p. 43   Parce nobis domine (Latin): Spare us, O Lord.

p. 46   Bakkaship: A merchant ship that sailed to and from the trading station of Eyrarbakki in southern Iceland.

p. 48   Mary Stuart, Queen of Scots, was beheaded February 8, 1587.

p. 56   Credo in unum Deum (Latin): I believe in one God.

p. 56   I can conjugate "amo" in most modi and tempora: I can conjugate "to love" in most moods and tenses.

p. 60   Hallgerður *langbrók* ("Long-breech") was the wife of Gunnar of Hlíðarendi, and one of the main characters of *Njáls saga*. She was well-known for her independent-mindedness.

p. 61   Drekkingarhylur: Drowning Pool, the name of the pool in Almannagjá where women were drowned (primarily for the crimes of adultery, incest, and infanticide).

p. 62   Amo, etc. (Latin): I love, you love, he loves, we love, you (two) love, they love.

p. 63   Brynjólfur Sveinsson (1605–1675) was bishop in Skálholt. His daughter Ragnheiður had a son by a man named Daði Halldórsson, but nine months earlier the bishop had made her swear an oath that she was a virgin.

p. 65   Curae (Latin): Concerns.

p. 65   Property in Iceland was for a long time taxed by "hundreds," a term for the value of the land, and reckoned according to an old duodecimal hundred, that is 12 x 10 = 120.

p. 71   Brennugjá: Burning Ravine, the ravine at Þingvellir where men were burned (for sorcery).

p. 72   Skyr: A unique Icelandic milk product, curdled and fermented skimmed milk.

p. 73 Illugi *Gríðarfóstri* ("Gríður's Foster-son") was a great champion who freed the troll-woman Gríður and her daughter Hildur from a spell (as told in *Illuga saga Gríðarfóstra*, one of the *fornaldarsögur;* see note to page 20 above).

p. 86 Welschland: Normandy.

p. 100 Aus Ijsland buertig (Low German): from Iceland.

p. 107 Doctus in Veteri Lingua Septentrionali (Latin): Doctor in Old Norse. Scientia mirabilium rerum (Latin): The study of marvels.

p. 108 Assessor Consistorii, Professor Philosophiae et Antiquitatum Danicarum (Latin): Assessor at the Consistory (the Danish high court), Professor of Philosophy and Danish Antiquities.

p. 108 The "mistress of the house," Arnas Arnæus's wife, although described in fairly grotesque terms, is based on the historical Mette Fischer, a rich widow ten years older than Árni Magnússon whom he married in 1709.

p. 108 Famulus in antiquitates (Latin): Servant in the study of antiquities. Antiquitas, antiquitates, antiquitatum, antiquitatibus (Latin): Study of antiquities.

p. 108 Spanish Jacket: A barrel-shaped device used for confining and humiliating prisoners.

p. 109 Mirabilia (Latin): Marvels; the miraculous.

p. 110 *De Gigantibus Islandiae* (Latin): *Concerning Iceland's Trolls.*

p. 110 *Physica Islandica* (Latin): *Icelandic Natural History.*

p. 112 The men of Hrafnista were the descendants of Ketill *hængur* ("Trout"), a famous Icelandic settler; he is described in the thirteenth-century *Landnámabók* (*Book of Settlements*) and *Egils saga.* Hálfdán *Brönufóstri* ("Brana's Foster-son"), was a Danish prince who fled from Vikings and met the troll-woman Brana, who helped him regain his kingdom (as told in *Hálfdánar saga Brönufóstra,* another of the *fornaldarsögur* mentioned above).

p. 112 *Historia Literaria* (Latin): *History of Literature.*

p. 112 Bibliothèque (French): Library.

p. 123 Grímur *kögur* ("Fringe") lived during the Age of Settlements (ninth to tenth centuries). The *Landnámabók* relates how his sons killed the chieftain Ljótur Þorgrímsson the Wise. (In the story, when Ljótur asks a man named Gestur Oddleifsson if the earth-lice, the sons of Grímur *kögur,* will cause his death, Gestur replies, "A hungry louse bites hard.")

p. 124   Gyldenløve is Ulrik Christian Gyldenløve (1678–1719), a son of Christian V of Denmark.

p. 124   Wars fought by Sweden and Denmark at the time of this novel include the Scanian War of 1675–1679 and the Great Northern War of 1700–1721. In the latter, Russia, Denmark-Norway, and Saxony-Poland were allied against Sweden in an attempt to break Swedish supremacy in the Baltic; in 1700 the Swedes landed in Sjaelland and forced Denmark out of the war until 1709.

p. 128   Boot-Katrin: A joking reference to one of the king's mistresses.

p. 129   Special-dollar (Danish *speciedaler*): Danish silver currency worth two rixdollars.

p. 133   Salvum conductum (Latin): Safe-conduct.

p. 137   Sigurður, a figure from ancient Germanic legend, is one of the heroes of *Völsunga saga* (thirteenth century) and the Völsung cycle of heroic poems in the *Poetic Edda* (see note for page 24 above). Sigurður slew the dragon Fáfnir, who guarded the Rhinegold.

p. 138   Bakki: Eyrarbakki.

p. 139   Blanda: Watered-down sour whey.

p. 140   The *Book of Seven Words:* A book of sermons, *Sjö predikanir út af þeim sjö orðum drottins vors Jesú Kristi (Seven Sermons on the Seven Last Words of Our Lord Jesus Christ),* written by Bishop Jón Vídalín and printed at Hólar, 1716.

p. 143   Grammatica (Latin): Grammar, linguistics, philology.

p. 144   Tunga: Bræðratunga.

p. 144   Skallagrímur: Skallagrímur Kveldúlfsson, the father of the famous poet and warrior Egill Skallagrímsson. Skallagrímur is described in *Egils saga* as being a great craftsman.

p. 146   Hilarius: A reference to a drinking game and the Latin names given to the shot-glasses (Hilarius being the fourth of seven) by students in Copenhagen.

p. 150   Quod felix (Latin): What luck.

p. 151 Versificaturam (Latin): poesy.

p. 151 Vigfús's grandmother inherits land to the value of a hundred duodecimal "hundreds" (100 x 120), probably five average-sized farms; an average-sized farm was worth twenty "hundreds" (2400).

p. 152 In *Völsunga saga,* Brynhildur, a valkyrie, sleeps under a spell, guarded by a wall of flame; she is freed by Sigurður.

p. 152 Tungur: Biskupstungur.

p. 156 Mary-mass: The Feast of the Annunciation, March 25.

p. 156 Cross-mass: Inventio Crucis, the feast celebrating the discovery of Christ's cross, May 3.

p. 159 Didrik of Münden was regent in Iceland in the early sixteenth century, but was killed at Skálholt in 1539.

p. 167 Salutem (Latin): Greetings.

p. 170 In nomine domini amen salutem et officia (Latin): In the name of the Lord, amen, attesting my reverence and deference.

p. 171 Item (Latin): Furthermore.

p. 177 Giant's ox (Icelandic *jötunuxi*): The Icelandic name for the rove beetle (*Creophilus maxillosus*).

p. 177 Apex perfectionis (Latin): The apex of perfection.

p. 177 Summum bonum (Latin): The highest good.

p. 178 Doctores (Latin): Authorities.

p. 178 Doctor angelicus (Latin): A reference to the philosopher and theologian Thomas Aquinas (1225–74).

p. 179 In civilibus . . . in ecclesiasticis (Latin): In civil or ecclesiastical law.

p. 179 *Merlin's Prophecies* is found in Geoffrey of Monmouth's (1100–1154) *History of the Kings of Britain; Tungdal's Vision* is thought to have been composed in the mid–twelfth century by an Irish monk, Marcus, in Regensburg. This work, which was one of the most popular works of visionary or ecstatic literature in the Middle Ages, describes the torment of condemned souls and the blessed condition of the saved. It was translated into Norse in the thirteenth century.

p. 180 In casu (Latin): In court.

p. 180   Sacramentum (Latin): Sacrament.

p. 181   Spiritus mali (Latin): Evil spirit.

p. 190   *Hretbyggja* in Icelandic can be translated approximately as "Storm-dwelling."

p. 198   Lais (Old French): Ballads or short narrative poems.

p. 203   Baccalaureus (Latin): Advanced student; one holding a university degree.

p. 203   O tempora, O mores (Latin): What times, what customs.

p. 205   Plaisanterie (French): Pleasantry.

p. 206   Commissarius (Latin): Commissary.

p. 206   Pecca fortiter (Latin): Sin bravely; sin without fear.

p. 206   Status perfectionis (Latin): State of perfection.

p. 207   Naturaliter (Latin): By nature.

p. 208   Imperfectio, imperfectiones (Latin): Imperfections.

p. 208   Praeclari et illustrissimi (Latin): My excellent and illustrious (guests).

p. 209   In temporalibus . . . in spiritualibus (Latin): In the realms of the temporal and the spiritual.

p. 210   Inexorabilia (Latin): Unable to be gotten by prayer or entreaty.

p. 210   Sebaoth: A name of God (in the Old Testament).

p. 211   This verse was written by a Danish priest H. C. Stehn (1544–1610) and translated into Icelandic by Reverend Ólafur Jónsson from Sandar (1560–1627).

p. 214   Fabulae (Latin): Fables; stories.

p. 214   America terra (Latin): America.

p. 214   Hislant terra (Latin): Iceland.

p. 215   *Liber Islandorum: The Book of Icelanders* (in Icelandic *Íslendingabók*), written by the priest Ari Þorgilsson (1067–1148) in the twelfth century, is a history of the church and the bishoprics in Iceland. Ari wrote a Latin version first and then an Icelandic one, in which he leaves out genealogical material and the biographies of Norse kings. The *Breviarium Holense* was a Latin missal written for use by priests in the diocese of Hólar. For Bishop Jón Arason, see note for page 31 above. The Þorlákur referred to here is St. Þorlákur, bishop of Skálholt (1133–1193). He was proclaimed a saint by the Alþingi in 1198, and his feast-days are July 20 and December 23 (the latter is still observed in a certain way in Iceland, even after centuries of Lutheranism).

p. 215 Schedulae (Latin): Registers.

p. 218 The stories of the Vínland voyages can be read in *Grænlendinga saga* (*The Saga of the Greenlanders*) and *Eiríks saga rauða* (*The Saga of Eirík the Red*).

p. 218 Sturla Sighvatsson (1199–1238) is a principal persona in *Sturlunga saga* (thirteenth century), a primarily historical work on the events and conflicts leading up to the acceptance of the Norwegian king's authority over Iceland in 1262. The *Völuspá* is a prophetic work contained in the *Poetic Edda;* it describes the creation of the world and the gods' activities leading up to their destruction at Ragnarök.

p. 220 Musica (Latin): Music.

p. 221 Auctor, auctores (Latin): Authorities, sources.

p. 221 Reformatores (Latin): Reformers.

p. 223 Venus hac perjuria ridet (Latin): Venus smiles at this betrayal.

p. 223 Lofn: An old Norse goddess of love.

p. 225 Coquetterie (French): Coquettishness.

p. 229 Faldur (Icelandic): A type of tall, traditional women's headgear.

p. 229 Privatim (Latin): In private, in trust.

p. 230 Opera antiquaria: Ancient works.

p. 230 Grettir Ásmundarson: A famous poet and criminal; the eponymous hero of *Grettis saga Ásmundarsonar* (*Grettir's Saga*).

p. 239 Gens paene barbara (Latin): A race of half-civilized barbarians.

p. 239 Volumina (Latin): Editions.

p. 239   Plantino: Christophe Plantin (1520–1589), a French printer. Gutenburg: Johannes Gutenburg (1399?–1468), a German craftsman and inventor, considered to be the father of the art of printing.

p. 239   Þorri and Góa are the Icelandic names for the fourth and fifth months of winter, roughly corresponding to January and February.

p. 241   Bjarni-prayers and Þórður-prayers: Prayers from the prayer books written by Reverend Bjarni Arngrímsson (1768–1821; Snæfríður's reference to this work is an obvious anachronism) and Þórður Bárðarson (d. 1690; his prayer book came out in 1693).

p. 241   Ora pro nobis . . . (Latin): Pray for us sinners now and at the hour of our death.

p. 242   Nulla viro . . . (Latin): No woman should trust a man who swears an oath.

p. 242   "Sagas of Icelanders" (in Icelandic, *Íslendingasögur*) refers to what are now generally known as "the Icelandic sagas," that is, those sagas that were written down primarily in the twelfth and thirteenth centuries and that are concerned with specific families or individuals that lived during the "Saga Age" in Iceland, the period between the settlement of Iceland (870–930) and the middle of the eleventh century (when the church began to reshape Icelandic society and culture). Sagas such as *Egils saga, Grettis saga Ásmundarsonar,* and *Njáls saga* all belong to this particular category. Due to their subject matter these sagas are also often referred to as "family sagas."

p. 244   Persons in the sagas described as being "drowsy in the evening" (in Icelandic, *kvöldsvæf*) generally turned out to engage in nocturnal activities, such as shapeshifting. Skallagrímur Kveldúlfsson, in *Egils saga,* is a famous example: some suggested he turned into a werewolf at night.

p. 246   The Great Decree (Icelandic *Stóridómur*): A court ruling made law by the Alþingi in 1564 (revoked in 1838) imposing stringent penalties for crimes against decency and chastity (the penalties of burning and hanging for men and drowning for women described in the novel are a result of this law).

p. 247   Ragnheiður: see note for page 63.

p. 248   Vulgaria (Latin): Vulgarities.

p. 250   Deo gratias (Latin): Thanks be to God (a greeting used by members of the Benedictine order).

p. 251   In cruce . . . (Latin): In the cross was hidden divinity alone but here humanity is concealed as well.

p. 253   Fac me . . . (Latin): "Let me bear the wounds of the scourge, let me be intoxicated by the Cross," from the hymn *Stabat mater dolorosa* written by the Italian Franciscan friar Jacopone da Todi (d. 1306).

p. 255   *De Operatione Daemonum* (Latin): *Concerning the Workings of Demons.*

p. 256   Mos, mores (Latin): Customs.

p. 258   Videlicet (Latin): That is to say.

p. 259   Characteres (Latin): Magical signs.

p. 259   In generali (Latin): In summary.

p. 259   Sine allegationibus . . . (Latin): Without reference to law or wisdom.

p. 266   This is a citation of a line in the *Völuspá* that refers to the apprehension felt by the gods concerning future hostilities with the giants: hostilities that lead to Ragnarök.

p. 269   Sum, ergo loquor (Latin): I am, therefore I speak.

p. 273   Hallgrímur Pétursson (1614–1674) was a priest and is one of the most renowned Icelandic religious poets. His wife was Guðríður Símonardóttir, known as Gudda of the Turks; she had been ransomed from Algerian pirates, called "Turks" in Icelandic (*Tyrkjar*) after several hundred Icelanders were kidnapped by them in 1627 (thirty-five were ransomed and twenty-seven made it back home to Iceland).

p. 275   Gálgaklettur: Gallows Cliff, at Þingvellir, where male criminals were hanged (although a precise location for Gálgaklettur is not known, some suggest that it was in the ravine called Stekkjargjá, just north of Almannagjá).

p. 276   Mensa (Latin): Table, desk.

p. 282   In praejudicio Arnæi (Latin): Against Arnas; to censure Arnas.

p. 283   Ars casuistica (Latin): The art of casuistry.

p. 283   In desperatione vitae (Latin): In despair of her life.

p. 286   Battledore: A wooden utensil (a bat or cudgel) used for beating clothes.

p. 286 Spindehus (Danish): A women's prison and workhouse in Copenhagen, established in 1662 and in use until 1928. The women labored at spinning wool and weaving clothing for the Danish army.

p. 297 Jaegersborg was the king's private deer park, located about eight kilometers north of Copenhagen. The area was fenced off by Frederik III in 1669, and the park's area was doubled by Christian V in 1670.

p. 299 Ein Land . . . (German): A land blessed by dear God.

p. 299 The Furusee is the largest lake on Sjaelland in Denmark.

p. 299 Galanterie (French): Gallantry.

p. 299 Volières (French): Aviaries.

p. 299 Ach ja . . . (German): Oh, yes, my lord, life is difficult.

p. 303 Galanthomme (French): Stately man; gallant.

p. 311 Justo dolore (Latin): Righteous affliction.

p. 311 Causa prima (Latin): Chief cause.

p. 311 Jure talionis (Latin): According to the laws on compensation.

p. 311 Studiosus antiquitatum (Latin): Student of antiquities.

p. 312 Certe (Latin): Definitely.

p. 313 *Maríusaga* is a thirteenth-century Icelandic compilation of the legends and miracles of the Virgin Mary.

p. 313 Vivat . . . (Latin): May he live, thrive, and flourish—Marteinsson.

p. 314 Rasphus (Danish): A house of corrections in Copenhagen, in use until 1850.

p. 318 Gilitrutt: This trollish name is used by Jón Marteinsson to suggest that Árni can now divorce his "troll-wife" (as opposed to Snæfriður being an "elf-wife").

p. 318 Acta, petitiones, appellationes (Latin): Arbitrament, petitioning, and appeals.

p. 318 Requiescas . . . (Latin): Rest in peace, whoever you are, amen.

p. 321 Impotentiae causa (Latin): Due to impotence.

p. 321 Omnium rerum . . . (Latin): Everything will soon change.

p. 321 The great smallpox epidemic occurred in Iceland during the years 1707–1709, and wiped out approximately one-third of the country's population.

p. 325 Das ist eine Schweinerei (German): This is a scandal.

p. 325 In classicis (Latin): In the classics.

p. 327 Non facile . . . (Latin): Men of virtue who become involved in complicated domestic affairs do not easily get out of their situations.

p. 327 Donatus was a Roman rhetorician who lived in the fourth century A.D.

p. 341 The Fenris Wolf was the offspring of the god/giant Loki and the troll-woman Angurboða, and was one of the chief enemies of the gods. The binding of the Fenris Wolf is described in Snorri Sturluson's *Edda* (see note for page 24 above).

p. 346 Bergur Sokkason was an abbot of the Munkaþverá monastery in north Iceland (late thirteenth and early fourteenth centuries). He wrote a number of sagas of saints and kings.

p. 347 Moria (Greek): Foolishness (here personified).

p. 349 Sine dubio (Latin): No doubt.

p. 349 Dignum neque justum (Latin): Neither applicable nor just. Scriba (Latin): Secretary. Famulus (Latin): Servant.

p. 351 Electus (Latin): Chosen one (here the bishop-elect).

p. 351 Bonis auguriis (Latin): Good auspices.

p. 351 Vicarius (Latin): Proxy, deputy.

p. 352 In the *Völsunga saga* there is an episode in which a man named Heimir from Hlymdalir protects Áslaug, the daughter of Sigurður and Brynhildur, by hiding her (and a great amount of gold and silver treasure and expensive clothing) in a large harp that he has constructed specially for this purpose. The saga says that when the maiden cried he played the harp to comfort her (see *Völsunga saga*, chapter 43).

p. 352 Rosa rosarum, virgo virginum (Latin): Rose of roses, maiden of maidens. Virgo ante . . . (Latin): A virgin before giving birth, while giving birth, and after giving birth.

p. 355 Suavium (Latin): Kiss of passion.

p. 356 Faeces diaboli (Latin): Devil's dregs, residue.

p. 358 Durchlaucht (German): Highness.

p. 360 Pfui deibel (French *débile*): What nonsense.

p. 361 Auctoritas (Latin): Authority. Très obéissant serviteur (French): Most devoted servant.

p. 362 Hew ick nich verstahn (Low German): This I don't understand.

p. 362 Ásgarður is the home of the gods in old Scandinavian mythology. In Snorri Sturluson's *Edda,* he euhemeristically states that Ásgarður was located in Asia Minor, and that the gods traveled from there to Scandinavia. Snæfríður's statement reflects this idea.

p. 363 Ma chère madame (French): My dear madam.

p. 363 Wat schall ick maken (Low German): What can I do? What am I to think?

p. 364 "The laws of St. Ólafur" is a reference to old traditions concerning the laws prescribed by Ólafur Haraldsson, king of Norway 1015–1028 and Norway's patron saint. *Gray Goose* (Icelandic *Grágás*) is a term given to the corpus of law existent in Iceland prior to Iceland's union with Norway in 1262.

p. 365 Ad arbitrium (Latin): At his own pleasure.

p. 365 In principio (Latin): Originally.

p. 369 Magister (Latin): Master.

p. 378 Lex Salica (Latin): A law corpus (concerning inheritances) of the inhabitants of the Rhine region in France in the fifth and sixth centuries.

p. 378 Viðey is an island in Kollafjörður, just off the north coast of Reykjavík. It was considered valuable property throughout Iceland's history. An Augustinian monastery was in existence there from 1225–1539, and in the eighteenth and nineteenth centuries the offices of various Icelandic officials were located there.

p. 378 The description of the golden game pieces lying in the grass is found in the *Völuspá* (see note for page 218 above). In the "Golden Age" described in the poem, the Æsir (the original Norse gods) spend their time peaceably, making treasures, tools, and games; their leisure is disturbed by war against the Vanir (a second class of gods) and then the Giants. The war with the Giants ends with the destruction of the world at Ragnarök, but after the destruction, when the world starts to renew itself, the game pieces of old are found lying in the grass.

p. 380 In 1262, after years of internal disturbances (tantamount to civil war), the Icelanders finally relinquished control of their country to the Norwegian king, Hákon the Old (Hákon Hákonarson, reigned from 1217–1264); a covenant was made, and a new code of laws, *Járnsíða (Ironside),* was introduced shortly afterward (in 1271; this in turn was replaced by the *Jónsbók* law code in 1281).

p. 381 Collegium, collegia (Latin): Colleges, fraternities.

p. 384 Relatio, relationes (Latin): Aspects, items, circumstances.

p. 386 Augmundus: Ögmundur Pálsson (1475?–1541), the last Catholic bishop of Skálholt. Jona Aronis is Bishop Jón Arason (see above note for page 31).

p. 391 Abi, scurra (Latin): Begone, you vagrant.

p. 401 Paa Skage (Danish): From Skagi.

p. 403 Saint Ólafur: see note for page 364.

p. 405 Beneficium paupertatis (Latin): Assistance for the poor.

For the notes, reference was made to Guðrún Ingólfsdóttir and Margrét Guðmundsdóttir, *Lykilbók að fjórum skáldsögum eftir Halldór Laxness* (Reykjavík: Vaka-Helgafell hf., 1997).

INDEPENDENT PEOPLE

Having spent eighteen years in humiliating servitude, sheep farmer Bjartur of Summerhouses is determined to raise his flocks unbeholden to any man. But Bjartur's spirited daughter wants to live unbeholden to *him*. What ensues is a battle of wills that is by turns harsh and touching, elemental in its emotional intensity and intimate in its homely detail. Vast in scope and deeply rewarding, *Independent People* is a masterpiece.

Fiction/Literature/0-679-76792-4

PARADISE RECLAIMED

An idealistic Icelandic farmer journeys in search of paradise in this captivating novel. When Steinar of Hlidar offers his children's beloved pony to the visiting King of Denmark, he sets in motion a chain of disastrous events that leaves his family in ruins and himself at the other end of the earth, optimistically building a home for them in the Promised Land of Utah. By the time the broken family is reunited, Laxness has spun his trademark blend of compassion and comically brutal satire into a moving and spellbinding enchantment.

Fiction/Literature/0-375-72758-2

WORLD LIGHT

As an unloved foster child, Olaf Karason has only one consolation: the belief that one day he will be a great poet. Over the ensuing years, Olaf comes to lead the paradigmatic poet's life of poverty, loneliness, and sexual scandal. But he will never attain greatness. As Olaf's ambition drives him onward, what might be cruel farce achieves pathos and genuine exaltation. This magnificently humane novel demonstrates how the creative spirit can survive in even the most crushing environment and even the most unpromising human vessel.

Fiction/Literature/0-375-72757-4

VINTAGE INTERNATIONAL
Available at your local bookstore, or call toll-free to order:
1-800-793-2665 (credit cards only).